D0386416

LITTLE
DID I KNOW

LITTLE
DID I
KNOW

Mitchell Maxwell

PROSPECTA PRESS

Published by
Prospecta Press
An imprint of Easton Studio Press
P.O. Box 3131
Westport, CT 06880
(203) 454-4454
www.prospectapress.com

Book and cover design by Barbara Aronica-Buck

Hardcover ISBN: 978-1935212-57-7
E-book ISBN: 978-1-935212-56-0

First edition
Printed in the United States of America

First printing: September 2011
10 9 8 7 6 5 4 3 2 1

FOR MY FATHER

MAXWELL HERBERT SHMORAK

1921 – 2006

ACKNOWLEDGMENTS

Thanks to my editor Lou Aronica for his ideas, focus, and goodwill.

Thanks to my brother, Rick, sister, Victoria, and friends Richard Bernstein and Chris Fitzgerald for reading the book as it evolved and encouraging me to continue.

Thanks to Arturo Conde for his tireless work on my early draft of the manuscript.

Thanks to everyone who worked at PBT; my story is theirs.

Thanks to my mom for . . . well, being my mom.

Thanks to Michael Maidy and Marty Pichinson, businessmen of vision and dear friends.

Thanks to Jeff Calhoun for reminding me kindness never gets old.

Thanks to David Wilk for all he has taught me and for a future together.

Thanks to Meryl Moss for knowing that acorns grow into maple trees, and to my lifelong friend Peter Cromarty for always being wise and truthful, even when the truth is difficult to hear.

Thanks to my children: Zach, a fine artist in his own right, and my daughter, Tia, who proves there is a God.

I

1976

Ilooked upon the faces of my friends and saw much passion. There was pride, fear, joy, and a great deal of angst. A palpable "what now, what next?" danced in the air. Etched on the faces of many of my peers it was clear that their next steps had yet to be choreographed. Everyone squinted under a blazing, perfect mid-May New England sun. Eyes half-closed were a metaphor for the day: there was something special down the road, though none of us could see it clearly and more importantly, none of us knew how to get there.

It was all a sea of black square caps topped with silly tassels that hid the eyes of many classmates. If offered an unencumbered view of the mirror to the soul you'd see their thoughts racing like sand flowing through an hourglass. The joyous past four years of collegiate life were ending. It was our last chance, ripe and luscious, available for the taking. The clock was ticking all too quickly. In a moment, the music would play, and those silly caps would be thrown high into the cobalt sky. When they landed, the next chapter of our lives would begin. Yesterday I was kid. A breath from now . . . well, I guess I would be a grown-up.

The black caps peppered the blue sky like thousands of little antiaircraft guns looking to take down a bomber from above. Everything slowed enough to be captured on a camera. Amid the slow motion, I looked around at the faces of my friends. Each one promised a story I wanted to know. Some tales would be filled with triumph and others with despair. Some poked a toe into unknown waters, others prepared for a headfirst dive. Yet even the bravest looked rattled by the uncertainty of everything. Their caps hit the ground without a voice, offering a mere dull thud, if that. It made me both sad and angry.

We had grown up together and changed through myriad hairstyles and heartbreaks. We loved together, we lived together, and we shared more loony nights than days. Our experiences were infused with the urgency of having to live an entire lifetime within four college years. "Don't miss out" was our mantra, and we honored it completely.

Two months before this morning's graduation, we had the cast party for the final musical we performed together. That night we had stayed up talking way past late. We had worked on numerous projects, all of which had become precious. They were equal to or, in my case, more important than our studies. We lounged on worn, faded furniture that carried the scent of old lust, stale beer, and lingering ganja that had made generations of students high, mixing into a concoction of frenzied promises. The student center was littered with empty Wild Turkey bourbon bottles and long-forgotten kegs that had been drained of their suds.

Melissa Morgan, a red-headed farm beauty from Ohio with a perfect array of freckles on her nose, drew my eyes to the denim cutoffs that hung provocatively on her perfect butt. She was bleary eyed and happy like the rest of us. She leaned over to me and planted a long, lingering kiss on my lips. I had always wondered what it would be like to kiss her. Although I had been successful with women, I never thought I had a chance with Melissa. We had admired each other from a distance, and on this particular night the wait proved to be well worth it.

She looked into my surprised eyes and said, "I'll never forget these shows, Sam. They were the most fun I ever had." Then she said good night to the group and walked slowly onto the dance floor, floating effortlessly away. It was the perfect exit for a woman who kept men awake at night with unfulfilled desire.

JB, one of my closest friends and in many ways my theatrical muse, sat across from me watching the evening fade into daylight. She had the look of a lost little girl searching for something to break away from the melancholy of the night's last curtain call, or somehow find a way to never let it go.

JB was an ugly duckling on the verge of discovering that she truly was a swan. She had made these shows happen. Tirelessly and unselfishly, she had urged us all to take up the challenge and sing out. She allowed me to find my voice—not one that sang actual notes but one that gave me the courage to lead. One I didn't know I owned. Then one day I woke up embracing what I wanted my life to be about. JB was a great and supportive friend, believing in me as I gained the confidence and desire to frolic in a playground that might lead to a career in the arts. She sat still and quiet for several minutes, her eyes practically glazed over. She took a long drag on a Lucky Strike, stared as if through me, and suddenly asked with a giggle, "How many girls did you kiss tonight?"

"Are you asking how many I kissed, or how many kissed me? I could give you the combined number if you like."

"I guess the later would suffice."

"If I tell you, you'll hate me forever."

"*Come on.* I have some perverse need to know."

"Okay," I said slowly. "Remember, though, that this is simply kissing, and we all know that tonight is like going to a kissing booth without having to pay the dollar."

"Yes, I recognize the unique nature of this evening."

I waited a beat and then confessed, "More than ten and less than five hundred."

She laughed. "You are absolutely disgusting." She paused. "You never kissed me. Even after all these years."

"I was saving the best for last."

Caught up in the moment, I leaped from my chair into her arms and kissed her like I was off to war. She lay still in my embrace as if she was being ravaged. She then rolled over, took a deep, sated breath and said, "I need a cigarette."

Only a handful of us remained now that the late hour had become early dawn. My best friend, Secunda, who had acted confidently, brilliantly in many of our shows lamented, "Now what do we do? This ride can't just end. Figure something out, Sammy."

"Yeah, we need to keep that torch burning," Secunda's younger brother James added. He had been part of the journey, building great sets, solving problems only he knew existed, and always remaining sane. He lit a killer joint and passed it around the group as if it were a peace pipe, a pact to hold on to the dreams that pulsed through our veins.

Elliot, another friend, pressed the point. "Sammy, it's the bicentennial. Add something to the party." He grinned as if he had said something profound.

"I have," I said, smiling with drunken mischievousness.

"Well?" Elliot continued, shouting as much as gobs of bourbon and fatigue would allow. "What are you gonna do? Win a theater in a poker game? Make out with some heiress? We are done here in two months!"

I held a finger to my lips and gave a long, slurred, "Shush. Believing is part of figuring it all out. It's part of the plan. If you don't sign up for the plan, there is no plan."

I gestured for the group to sit closer, and from my breast pocket took a small, folded piece of glossy paper that I had torn from *Variety*. As I opened it, my friends' eyes widened as if I were revealing the map to a treasure. In bold print was a small but arresting advertisement. Saying nothing, I let them read what it said:

FOR RENT: AMERICA'S OLDEST SUMMER STOCK THEATER.
IMMEDIATE OCCUPANCY AVAILABLE.
LOCATED FORTY MILES FROM BOSTON AND LESS
THAN ONE HUNDRED YARDS FROM THE OCEAN.
PROPERTY INCLUDES 480-SEAT BARN THEATER,
EQUIPMENT, AND RESIDENCES FOR UPWARD
OF FIFTY PERSONS. FOR TERMS AND PARTICULARS
ON THIS HISTORIC VENUE CONTACT
DR. ANDERSON BARROWS: 617-242-1200.

The party continued around us. Our cast mates danced close, flirted, and made plans to play with each other naked before dawn. Our small group was quiet, however, stunned by the small black-and-white missive I had just revealed.

Secunda, always a cynic said, "You wrote this, right?"

"No, dickhead, I did not, but I *did* find it and this, as one might say, is the plan."

Again it was quiet in the group. The music was sexy, bluesy late-night stuff, yet we were all focused.

"*This* is a good plan," James said.

"This is a plan to believe in," Secunda said, wearing a rare happy face.

"Yes indeed, this appears to be a great plan. Not that I know of plans, but if I did I would have to say this is a great plan," chimed in Elliot.

"Say it then," I said, "because to believe in the plan makes the plan."

"Who are you—Gandhi?" asked Secunda.

"*Say it*," I implored.

In hushed, sacred tones my friends all declared, "This is a great plan."

We sat back, content. We had a plan.

"I think this is a terrific plan, I really do," JB spoke up a few moments later. "But what, exactly, *is* the plan?"

The group looked at her as if she had spoken heresy, then quickly looked at me for an answer. "No need to take notes." I said. "I can repeat this anytime. I can say it backwards. First, I am going to call this guy Barrows and rent his fucking building. Before Elliot goes off to marry Madame Curie, he'll come and teach music and lead the band. Hopefully along the way he'll realize that Kat is never going to be good for him and he'll find some sincere cutie to share his bed."

"Is that really necessary?" Elliot asked.

Without hesitation, surrounded by nods of assent, James quickly replied, "Yes, unfortunately, it is. Quite."

I continued. "James, well . . . he will be James. He will make things work that are broken. He'll be our Spock, our man of logic and calm. He will roll us a joint in time of need. Secunda will act his ass off and sing his ass off and tell jokes and break a few hearts and help me find the money to pay the rent. We'll kiss every frog that will ribbet, and raise this dough."

Everyone was listening, barely breathing, not wanting to miss a moment.

I continued, "JB will tell everyone what to do. She will organize the business, hire the staff, figure out where everyone is going to live. She will listen to all the hopeless, brokenhearted beauties who believe that all boys want from them is their brains and insight into life. She will charm the press and motivate the entire town, and her acolytes will multiply."

I raced on, gathering momentum and breathing life and true belief into the plan. Then I took a beat and closed my eyes for a moment to see the future. When I opened them, I looked hard into the soul and character of my dearest friends. "And me, I am going to direct the shows. I am going to learn how to be a man. I am going to give everyone who crosses my path a memory to cherish. Then I'm moving to New York to direct and produce plays on Broadway and become famous. When I win the Tony, I am going to thank my parents and all of you." I was done.

JB said, "You really are going to make this happen? You really mean this?"

"Yes," I answered with unwavering conviction. "And the last part I mean the most."

She seemed almost frightened by my intensity, then asked, "How many girls are you going to sleep with?"

"Maybe none. I'm done being a rabbit. I'm looking to find something of substance . . ."

My friends' faces creased with expressions of disbelief. "No, really," I cried, and then added, "Besides, JB, I love you and my heart is in your hands."

A rotgut bottle of whiskey had been delivered to our group while I talked. We passed it around and the mood went from jovial to solemn. After a moment I said, "But you had all better be on board. I don't want to be in Pilgrimtown with my dick in the wind looking for backup."

"Promise," they all said in unison. That was enough for me.

Now my promises of weeks ago, the pledges made on that inebriated celebratory night, needed to happen, to take flight, to live. So as my silly tasseled hat hit the ground, it exploded in a burst of fire, color, and endless pyrotechnics of promise and winning.

Despite these burdens, or because of them, I carried no fear. This was the day my life was to begin, a time when challenges would arise and I would slay them. I yearned for all of it, good and bad. To taste, to feel, to love, to hurt. I was youth and hope; the best my generation had to offer. My time was now—today and then the next and the one after that. Remember my name, read about me in the papers, or see it all through a cloud of dust. I was about to hit a hundred miles per hour on the glorious road on which I intended to navigate my life. Little did I know that youth is not a road map, and sometimes you get lost along the way. The secret is finding your way home.

2

I headed south on Route 3, my destination Plymouth, Massachusetts. The Pilgrims had landed there in 1620 to start anew. I was arriving some three and a half centuries later. They sailed a cruel, relentless ocean to find a home. My trip was easier: forty miles of superhighway in my 1969 Mustang that still had lots of life in it. We were linked, however, by courage, tenacity, and an innate refusal to fail.

I turned off the main highway and onto the service road that offered access to America's first hometown. The midday early-summer sun gave the place an MGM shine to it. This Plymouth would have been unrecognizable to the Pilgrims. It had become a beachfront tourist center with all the trappings. There was a replica of the *Mayflower,* such a tiny vessel that I remain incredulous that it actually made the voyage. There were souvenir shops that sold saltwater taffy, postcards, and pictures of the "Rock" itself, which surprisingly was no bigger than a medium-sized watermelon.

There were lobster pots and fried clam huts, families checked into modest beachside motels, sunburns, and poison ivy. Young, pretty coeds waited tables scurrying about with fresh faces and tight, crisp ponytails. Rolling Rock beer was plentiful as were homemade ice cream, whale watches, and rental charters for deep-sea fishing. Plymouth was like so many other tourist havens across the country, ones that slept through the winter then raced at breakneck speed from Memorial Day till early September, when Labor Day would shut it all down until the next season when the cycle would begin again.

Plymouth also had the Bay, which was as blue as Paul Newman's eyes, and Cape Cod sunsets that filled the dusk with a prism of color. Robust, white, happy clouds weaved their way into a spider web that danced in pungent pastels across the sky; there were cool, icy blues, soft, languid tangerines, calming sea-foam greens, neon-yellow and wild-pink orchid. As I looked above, the question "How can I compete with that?" naturally came to mind. My answer: "Well, we all have to start somewhere."

The night sky was a soundstage with stars so bright and so close you couldn't actually believe they were real. The surf would pound against the jagged rocks on shore, either lulling you to sleep at night or invigorating you in the morning as if you had just downed a triple espresso.

Plymouth was girls in sundresses and young guys on the prowl. It was beach cottages where rent was divisible by twelve in a shack that slept six. Fun was a bargain at any price and the local taverns served perfectly cold beer in frosted mugs, keeping the whole town cool and happy during the blistering summer heat. It was also a town of hardworking, decent families who took pride in pleasing their summer visitors. When you ate a lobster or a bowl of steamers with fresh-drawn butter at a food stop in town, it was a thing of beauty so succulently delicious that you would take the memory to your grave.

Plymouth was an America where young men and women came of age under an August moon that hung in the night as if held up by invisible string. It was America in all its glory. It was the summer of 1976, and while the entire country celebrated the bicentennial, I danced through those days as if each one was the Fourth of July, complete with fireworks every night. I often thought that, as it was for the Pilgrims, Plymouth was where I would truly begin my life. Although I might not become part of history, I was certain that everyone I met that summer and beyond would always remember my name.

As I drove through town, I noticed it could just as well have been called Barrowsville. The Barrows name was ubiquitous. This was intimidating to say the least, as seeing Dr. Barrows was the first step in "the plan."

Dr. Anderson Barrows (a doctor of humanities) was the direct descendant of a Pilgrim. He was a member of the Lucky Sperm Club, which meant he was rich beyond imagination. He owned Plymouth County, and my research showed that he relished his position of powerbroker playing a Neroesque puppeteer to his minions. He'd make you ante up and then arbitrarily decide whether to deal you in. The local library was filled with tales of his mood swings. He was irascible, cruel, and snarling, a dog whose bark was matched by its bite. He must have been generous, however; his name was attached to the hospital, the nature reserve, the playgrounds, and more. Perhaps you just needed to get him on the right day.

I had attempted to set a meeting with the doctor for several weeks now. His secretary had been courteous and had penciled me in more than once. Yet it had become routine for him to cancel at the last moment or, worse, stand me up on the three occasions I had driven down from Boston at the appointed time. Frankly, it pissed me off.

The Barrows Building was set high atop Plymouth Harbor (from which on a clear day it was likely you could see England). Its architecture was stoic and ornate. The redbrick building was adorned with bright, white shutters that might have been painted that morning. Although only three stories tall, it cast a long, menacing shadow over the street and denizens of the town. Void of warmth or invitation, the structure spoke only of power and old money.

As I waited for Dr. Barrows to show, I glanced over the letters and photos adorning the walls of the lobby. It was more than a museum; it was a testament to courage and the indomitable human spirit. The history lessons here were in the faces of the early American people and the letters from home and back, telling an epic story made all the more compelling because it was tactile and personal. I felt humbled to see the hardships and triumphs of our country's true beginnings. It was an inspiration.

Finally, at 4:30 p.m., a black limo pulled up to the front of the building. A formally clad, heavyset chauffeur assisted Barrows from the backseat of the car. I had seen dozens of pictures of him in the papers, but they were posed headshots and clearly taken years ago. Nevertheless, I recognized the smug expression that Barrows wore so well. He was followed by a pair of long, shapely, tanned legs that ended only because they touched the ground. As the unlikely duo climbed the steps, my heart beat faster. I knew this might be my best shot.

Barrows and the young woman strolled across the sky-lit lobby. The late May sun was casting multiple shadows from above, creating the aura of an old forties noir movie—those that often end in *bang bang bang*. Barrows was past eighty. I'd imagined he'd look like a retired gunfighter. Instead he was soft and pasty, his comb-over in disarray. Despite expensive Brooks Brothers garb, he sported a pooch that made him look off balance, or a bit like a distorted cola bottle.

The girl with him, however, was a knockout. She was dressed to the tits in expensive crimson cotton, cinched at the waist with a black patent-leather belt. The dress must have been sewn on her, it fit so perfectly. The supple fabric highlighted her natural gifts; not just her ample cleavage but her round rear end which, although small and tight, was sensual like a Botero or a Rubens. She sported perfect white teeth and long, luscious hair.

The whole package promised something carnal. Dangerous. She prowled rather than walked. Whoever this young vixen was, you'd rather have her as a concubine than a girlfriend. She appeared loose and easy, yet she also had a store-bought sophistication about her. She was intensely attractive yet accessible—every man's dream—but she seemed quite capable of crushing you without hesitation, and with cold indifference.

As this milk-and-citrus couple strode across the lobby, I made my move. With somewhat false confidence, I raced across the marbled floor and intersected the two just a few feet from the elevator. I blocked Dr. Barrows's approach while his companion lingered back a few feet to size up this surprise intrusion.

"Dr. Barrows, sir, it is so good to see you today." He stared at me in silence, allowing me to either dig in or out of a grave. "I'm Sam August. I have been to see you three times, but your hectic schedule has prevented us from keeping our appointments. On another three occasions, our meetings were canceled at the penultimate moment."

"You had occasions to see me?" He paused briefly. "Well, of course you weren't given an appointment, for if you were, I would have honored it. I am not one to cancel or be rude."

"No, sir, of course you're not," I stammered.

"Do I know you? What is it you need or want, young man?"

My earlier assessment of his being pasty and soft dissipated as his confidence and impatience with me weakened my resolve.

"Well, sir, it is about the Priscilla Beach Theatre, and with all respect, we did in fact have set appointments. I confirmed them with your office with a Mrs. Stafford."

"Do you have an appointment for today?"

"No, sir, I don't."

"Then why should I see you?"

"Because I'm here, I made the effort and, frankly, sir, I think it is in your best interests."

"What do you know of my interests? You're just a kid."

I hesitated for a moment. "Are you a Red Sox fan, Dr. Barrows?"

"Of course I am. I have lived in New England my entire life. What does that have to do with anything?"

"Well, Fred Lynn is my age, sir, and as you know he led the Sox to the Series last year and won the MVP. He was a rookie. He had never done it before. He was a kid."

Barrows smiled—or at least his lips curled upward.

"Okay, August I'll give you an audience upstairs in my office. I need ten minutes to check in, and then we'll hear what you have to say. Lizzy here will show you up."

"Yes, sir, thank you."

He got on the elevator, pressed a button that surely read "ascend" rather than "up," and quickly disappeared into the ether of privilege. I stood across from the young woman. There was an awkward silence that hung in the air like molasses. "Have you worked for Dr. Barrows a long time?" I asked finally. "He seems a bit volatile for such a nice spring day."

"He does go up and down, that's for sure," she replied. "Sure" sounded more like "shore," as she had a hard New England accent. Her legs were great, but up close she had a certain coarseness that made her look tough and soft at the same time. All the money in the world couldn't truly disguise where she came from, and it was certainly a different part of town.

"Good job though working for such a powerful man, I suppose."

"I don't work for Anderson."

I blushed. Gratefully, I saw the elevator was on its way back down.

"Oh, are you the doctor's daughter?" I asked, as I considered it a better option than ripping my tongue from my mouth.

"No, I'm his wife."

"Oh I'm so sorry, Mrs. Barrows!" I blurted out. Certainly the tongue removal would have been a better choice.

"Why? I'm not. It has its rewards. We all play the hand we are dealt." She was steely and her gaze never left my eyes. She seemed to feel a sort of twisted joy in making me appear the fool. Mercifully, the elevator arrived and we both got in. "I like you . . . August. Pay attention, I'll teach you how to swim with the sharks."

The doors closed, my stomach flipped, and we headed into the world of old elegance and freshly minted green. The elevator quickly filled with her expensive scent of lilac; it made her seem available. The doors opened into an anteroom where she told me to have a seat. Her exit seemed staged for me to get a terrific view of her ass as it left the room oh so slowly. Whatever she had paid for that dress, it was clearly a bargain.

After a wait of more than thirty minutes, Mrs. Barrows entered and surprisingly offered me a soft, pleasant smile. "Why are you here?" she asked.

"I want to rent the Priscilla Beach Theatre this summer."

Her expression registered incredulity. "For what?"

"To put on shows, musicals. Make some people laugh, feel good. Start my life . . ."

"Putting on shows at that rundown place is the way to start a life? Andy said you went to college and I thought you were smart. "

"Going to college doesn't make you smart, being smart makes you smart."

She looked at me for a long time. "Are you flirting with me, Auggie?"

"Should I be, Mrs. Barrows?"

"Well, it don't make you smart, but it sure does make you seem like a whole lot a fun. Come on, my husband is waiting."

Barrows was seated behind a large, circular desk serving out orders to some unnamed party on the phone. Behind him were a dozen floor-to-ceiling windows overlooking the ocean. All you could see was the wisp of whitecaps dancing atop the ice-blue sea. If it was meant to inspire awe, it did so quite nicely. I stood quietly, as if waiting to be sentenced. Lizzy Barrows kindly pulled a side chair toward me and gestured that I sit and relax. Sitting was the easy part. She then exited as if by silent command.

"Okay, August, I have a file on you. When you called previously, I had my office look up your credentials, which although admirable are scant, to put it nicely."

"Remember Fred Lynn," I said.

"Unless you hold a winning hand, it is foolish to press your bet," he replied without mirth.

He picked up a yellow file folder and waved it in the air. "It says here you were an all-star athlete. What happened?"

"I got injured."

"Tough luck. How badly?"

"Enough that I am sitting here reinventing me."

"You're too young to run that place. It needs money and knowledge. Experience. You'll fall on your face before you open a show. I'd rather it stayed closed than embarrass me."

"So you don't care about my character or my plan, just my youth? What about Orson Welles, Peter the Great, Joan of Arc?"

"You sound like an idiot. Don't be so precocious. I don't like it. In fact, I'm pretty sure I don't like you."

"That doesn't really matter, Dr. Barrows. I came to see you because I thought we both wanted the same thing."

"And what is that, kiddo?"

"To see your building recapture its former glory. It has quite a history, and it would be a shame for it all to fade away. I can make it sing again, do something for your hometown, for your constituents."

"My constituents?" he asked in a huff. "So now you say you're an altruist as well?"

"With all due respect, sir, do you have a bad toothache today?"

It was clear that any effort at levity was foreign to the doctor. He replied with a terse "No."

"I came here to rent your theater. I read an advertisement that it was available and I have the resources and the desire to make it a success. Why must this be so difficult and you be so unpleasant?"

"Because I can, I have got nothing to lose and I don't like you."

"You don't even know me," I replied, thinking this was all a bit silly while realizing that money didn't equate to manners.

"I know enough. You're arrogant. You think you're entitled to what you want simply because you want it. Good looks aren't enough, son. They don't trump money. Money always wins."

"Character wins, Dr. Barrows. Character often comes up aces. It doesn't matter whether you care for me or not. What's of concern here is our mutual interest in the Priscilla Beach Theatre."

"And the girls, right, August?"

"The girls, sir?"

"Don't you meet a lot of young ladies working in the theater business?"

It was as though Barrows had thrown a big stink bomb in the middle of his office.

"Yes. I have met a lot of my good friends working on shows."

"Yes, but the ladies, August, they are resplendent, true?"

I responded with a wary nod.

"My wife could be a chorus girl. She has the looks for it, don't you think?"

I tried to avoid the land mines that littered the room. "Yes, sir, Mrs. Barrows is very attractive."

"Attractive?" he said leaning across his desk. "She is more than attractive. My wife is a knockout. Who wouldn't notice that?"

My task was to get a lease on his theater not a piece of his wife. "Dr. Barrows, I think your wife is very pretty. Trust me, sir, she could be Cleopatra and I wouldn't notice. I came . . ."

"Nonsense! Everyone has an eye for my wife. It is part of who she is. It is fun and frivolous unless you act on it. And you're her type: muscles up your ass, ambition and intellect. What you don't have is money, which makes her tick, turns her on . . ."

"Then you have nothing to worry about, doctor," I said. I waited for some more surly bullshit. None was offered, so I continued. "Can we talk about renting your building? You surely have more important things to do then fence with me, and I have work to do. Youth has its own set of impatience."

He let out a long sigh, flipped my dossier in the air, and met my gaze. The sun was beginning its rest for the night. The sky outside his window was a Monet in primary colors. I waited.

"How many runs did Lynn drive in against the Tigers last year?" he asked slowly.

"For the entire season or a single game?"

"It's all about the game."

"Ten."

"It's Friday. I'll have some paperwork to you by the end of the weekend. Let the office know where you are staying. We'll have something to discuss Monday/Tuesday. Kid, don't waste my time."

"I'll only ask the same of you, doctor."

His face was filled with some deep-down sense of being wronged. I didn't get it or care.

"You're excused," he said. "My wife will show you out. Keep your nose clean."

He ignored me when I offered my hand. Lizzy Barrows was waiting by the elevator. "You'll be hearing from me," she said.

Maybe for a cocktail later that evening, I thought. The elevator door opened and I got in. It delivered me to the lobby where mere mortals roamed and the day was no longer ruled by insecurity, vanity, or an abundance of cash.

3

I walked out of the Barrows Building into a soft evening breeze off the harbor below. I felt good about getting my foot in the door. I knew no one in town, yet the summer feel on this star-studded night tingled with promise. I got in my Mustang, started up the beast, folded down the top, and began a leisurely drive in and around my new hometown.

I needed to find an inexpensive place to stay for the next few days. Although I had a surplus of guts and a propensity for flying without a net, cash wasn't one of my strong suits. The "season" had yet to begin, so Plymouth had dozens of motels with vacancy signs blinking in neon. It was just past six, and the sky was an abstract painting you might find at MoMA: all vibrant color that if stared at long enough looked like a path leading somewhere, yet was merely a kaleidoscope, an oasis in the desert. The air was warm and carried a sweet smell of the ocean with each easy breeze off the sea.

The first time I had visited the theater I was chasing the plan. An expected brief trip to the Cape to access the situation was short-hopped due to an unexpected blast of winter and its twenty inches of snow. The storm had forced me to spend the night at an almost abandoned beachside motel, the only one whose lights were visible through the whiteout of the late-night blizzard. The following morning, as I drove for breakfast under a warm spring sun, I saw the theater compound all dressed in pristine white and glistening icicles that made the whole place look like it was draped in diamonds.

I wanted to know as much as possible about the theater to be well prepared when I reached out to Barrows. That morning I went to city hall and investigated the place, discovering a great deal about the Priscilla Beach Theatre, which was actually owned by the Barrows Foundation. It was the oldest "barn theater" in the country, staging its first performances just after the Civil War. It had many owners, managers, and famous players throughout its life. As is the norm in show business, it had seen good days and bad, long runs and seasons that never made it to the finish line.

I "let myself in" and inspected the place that very day with flashlight in hand. Immediately, I sensed the ghosts that filled the old barn. I knew at that moment that I wanted to be part of making them all reawaken, breathe again, sing a song, or tell a joke. I intended to bring the building back to life. That particular morning I had no idea how I would do so, but I knew it would all happen.

Suddenly the theater complex appeared on my left. The converted barn was more than a hundred years old. Two colonial farmhouses flanked it, and the compound was anchored by a maple tree surely old enough to have been planted by the Pilgrims. The porch that circled the structure was gray and weathered, the array of Adirondack chairs aged and in disrepair. Paint was a must for all the buildings; they were peeled like a sunburned back. The ocean was a shimmering turquoise blue less than a hundred yards away. The setting was a sepia postcard, with a history that cried out to sit up and sing.

I turned my car into the potholed parking area and sat a while with the motor off. I mused how even at my young age destiny had already altered my path. I had been a star athlete headed to college on a free ride when unexpected events rerouted my course. I was an anomaly, a varsity mainstay who chose to act in school plays rather than sports every day, all day. I was an A-list football star and a close second on the baseball diamond, yet I had angered my coaches by electing to spend hours in the theater rather than also play basketball. The theater bug had bitten me long ago, and although I could have healed and continued with sports, I had pursued this other passion—one that had earned me admittance to Tufts and accolades while there.

Growing up, except for the occasional Beatles or Sinatra song, I listened exclusively to show tunes. Broadway musicals captured my imagination. The medium transcended sports for me. The moments of exhilaration and the way it left me thinking about the talent or the message were elements I looked to explore. And here I was, poised to do so! I had passed on playing ball for a number of small colleges and universities that continued to woo me. As I sat there I felt it was meant to be: I had been injured and it forced me to change my route, and then I had discovered this place.

My reverie was interrupted by a gentleman whose look and garb were from another era. In his midsixties, his face showed he had worked outdoors. He wore overalls and a captain's sea cap. Offering me a friendly smile he asked, "Can I help you, son? What are you looking for?"

"My future," I replied.

"Don't think you'll find that here. This place is way past its heyday."

I shrugged. "What is past is prologue."

"Really? That's pretty smart talk."

"Bill Shakespeare said it."

The elderly man furrowed his brow. "Don't know the name. Does he live around here?"

"I believe so," I said. "Perhaps I can make an introduction."

I smiled, started up the Mustang, and headed out into the hovering honeysuckle-scented eve to find a place to spend my first night in Plymouth. I drove a short way down the road and stopped at the corner. If I turned left I would end up in England. I left the motor running and the car door open, walking a few yards to the shoreline. Finding four pennies in my pocket, I threw each one as far into the ocean as my arm would allow. Each shiny copper coin carried an identical wish. Then I returned to the car and drove away. I turned right, away from the Old Country, and into a new life that beckoned to me under a crisp sky dusted in burgeoning starlight.

I pulled up to the office of the Garden's Beach View Motel. I awarded it my business over the others I'd passed because its sign offered the cheapest option. The place could have been any motel on the side of any highway, filled with patrons on their way to somewhere else. Garden's might persuade you to stay longer, however, with its clear view of the glittering phosphorescent ocean. Guests had exclusive access to the beach through an old rickety staircase that led from the top of its bluff to the sandy shore a hundred feet below. What really made me feel at home, though, was the warmth and beauty of the surprisingly lovely desk clerk. Her name tag read VERONICA CHAPMAN.

Veronica was listening patiently to a disgruntled couple in their early sixties. Their complaint centered on the loss of several quarters in the vending machine.

"What do you intend to do about it, young lady?"

"Sir," she said with a friendly smile, "how many quarters did our hungry soda machine eat today?"

"At least six," the gentlemen stated with little grace.

"Perhaps eight or even ten," his wife added, equally unhappy.

"Why did you continue to feed the monster after he ate your first few quarters?" Veronica asked. "Were you just being optimistic or were you hoping to help him put all his little soda people through college?"

The wife scowled at this comment. "This is no laughing matter, miss. In fact it's theft, and we want something done immediately."

"I'll handle this, dear," interjected the husband sternly. He turned his attention to Veronica, who remained smiling and winning. "This is no laughing matter, miss. In fact it's theft, and we want something done immediately."

You had to laugh, but Veronica didn't. Instead she took charge. She opened the register and counted out twelve quarters. She walked purposefully from behind the registration desk and across the small lobby to the larcenous soda machine. She chanted some rather sweet lyrical melody, then struck the demon three times in the chest with her right hand and followed with a short kick to its oft side.

"You wanted a Fresca, ginger ale, and a Tab?" It was a more a statement then a question, for as she spoke the recalcitrant vending machine quickly delivered one of each soda. Veronica handed them to the increasingly bemused couple.

"Mr. and Mrs. Stewart, you know you're my favorite guests and I want your stay here to be the best. Please take this note to the Garden Diner and they'll give you a free dessert as a gesture of our appreciation for your business. Try the banana cream pie. It's fattening but worth every single calorie."

She opened the closet door to the right of her station and disappeared for a full count of three. Upon her return she carried two huge, luscious terry-cloth bath sheets and handed them to her now happy patrons. "Don't tell the boss—this has to be *our* secret. These towels are from the Ritz-Carlton in Boston and I want you to feel like our little beachside stop is your five-star home."

The Stewarts were grinning from ear to ear.

"You're such a dear," Mrs. Stewart said. Then to her husband, "Isn't she dear? Give the young lady something for her kindness, Henry—and be generous."

A very pleased Henry gave Veronica a crisp ten-dollar bill, and she thanked him with a lingering kiss on the cheek. He blushed and he and his wife left happy as a pair of Cape Cod clams. They had forgotten their twelve quarters and were light ten dollars, yet they were both in love with the enchanting Veronica Chapman.

I wanted to know this girl.

Her looks only threw fuel on that fire. She was more than pretty. You might describe her as ethereal: perfect skin, long, luscious blond hair, and stunning deep blue eyes that spoke to you, saying, "This was the place you had to be." She was close to six feet tall and could have been a swimsuit model had the opportunity presented itself. She wore her hair up, held by a shiny lilac pin. Her sun-kissed shoulders were toned, long, and lithe. The slightest of spaghetti straps kept her modesty in check, as her jonquil sundress offered just a hint of cleavage and the promise of more. Her lips had a shine to them that shouted, "Kiss me." The scent of fresh-picked strawberries hovered about her.

After waiting for a beat or two, I finally caught her eye. "That was amazing," I said. "It seemed eerily practiced: well rehearsed, almost frightening. By my count, you just sold three sodas for thirteen bucks plus what the machine ate. That's quite a haul."

"I know." She almost giggled. "It seems to work out that way more often than not. I don't plan on it. Just takes a life of its own, I guess."

She smiled and the birds sang sweeter and the sun beamed brighter. Our eyes met and lingered. Finally, I found my voice and asked her for a room. "Something simple and inexpensive," I requested.

"We only have cheap and cheaper. For inexpensive you have to try the place down the road." Then she offered me her cheapest room without indoor plumbing. To my delight, though, she was just flirting. She gave me a deal: five nights for $15. Then she offered her hand in welcome. I shook it as our eyes met again and I didn't want to let go. As I headed out the door, Veronica offered coyly, "I'm here from noon on if you need anything, and my shift ends at ten if you need anything else."

The girl knew how to work this boy. Rather than stand there speechless wearing an idiot grin, I opted to exit and regroup.

To my surprise, standing outside the office door was the Barrows's limo driver. He quickly smiled and offered his hand. "I don't mean to impose, but Mrs. Barrows asked you to join her for a drink this evening and I was waiting for the right moment as not to intrude."

"I'm in," I said without hesitation.

We arrived at the Full Sail within minutes. The joint was a beachfront tavern shoehorned at the intersection of Garden Road and Ocean Drive. A Crayola box of painted and faded beach cottages ran the length of the drive, all charming in a rundown sort of way. Even at this late hour, bikini-clad pretty young women cavorted on the beach under the appreciative eyes of young men looking for adventure. Clotheslines filled with towels, sheets, T-shirts, bathing suits, and more created a mosaic of vibrant colors to match the daily sunset and each morning's dawn.

Kids rode bicycles down the drive, shouting at their friends and making plans. Music filled the air, adding to nature's natural energy, playing out as life's soundtrack throughout the day. The waterfront was precious and space was at a premium. There were no cars. People arrived at the Full Sail on foot or bicycle, or in my case chauffeured limo at the request of Mrs. Barrows.

The Full Sail was at peak throttle. I thought, as I looked around, that they must only let pretty people into the place. The tavern was little more than a shack with barstools three deep in front of a simple bar made of a series of varnished two-by-fours held together by nautical hardware. There were small square tables that spilled out onto a deck where at high tide you would feel the splash of a rolling ocean.

Holding court behind the bar was the owner, named Doobie or, for short, Doob (as in "pass the doob"). Doob, who had spent three highly decorated years in and around Saigon, clearly put in hours at the local gym. His Red Sox T-shirt burst at the seams, barely holding his muscles in place. He was friendly and accomplished at the bar, popping beer bottles, mixing drinks, taking food orders, and carrying on four or five conversations with his customers without missing a beat.

There was a small kitchen just to the left of the bar that kept pumping out oceanfront delicacies at incredible speed. Sea salted spicy fries, lobster stew, grilled corn on the cob, quahogs, steamers, mussels in white wine and garlic, fish and chips, and more, all served with homemade bread and fresh churned butter. Doob's mother, aptly named "Ma," was the conductor of this culinary music.

I ordered a bottle of brew and searched for Mrs. Barrows, but found no one who resembled the explosive knockout from this morning. I decided to sit at a table outside, just a few feet from the ocean. Before I could settle in a young woman approached me. She was the essence of understated class. She wore little to no makeup; just a soft-pink lip gloss and something that made her eyelashes fetching yet unworldly. Her light-fuchsia dress stopped at the knee. Her breasts, although covered, were more than enticing. She wore her hair back, held in place by an aqua silk headband, and she had diamond studs in her pierced ears. She held a freshly lit Lucky Strike in her manicured fingers. It was quite clear that Lizzy Barrows was a chameleon.

She sat across from me, and before I could get up she made herself at home. An eager young waiter with JIMMY stenciled on his T-shirt brought an iced pink drink in a martini glass. The color of her cocktail matched the lip gloss she was wearing and her drink was garnished with a juicy orange slice suggesting a tribute to the young juicy woman about to drink it. "Jimmy" brought me a fresh beer as well and with his most sincere smile said, "Nice to see you, Mrs. Barrows. Enjoy your evening, Mr. August, sir." He ambled away like a young puppy as I thought, *There is no "Mrs." here, just this young lovely babe,* and that "Mr. August" was my father.

Lizzy leaned into the table, lifted her glass and said, "Congratulations."

"For what?"

"So many things. The sunset, the road ahead. I'm sure there's more."

"Being driven by your chauffeur to the most popular hangout in town is not worthy of congratulations. If it were this whole town would be toasting my accomplishments."

"Everyone will be, Auggie. They certainly will. By the way, people often get lost on the way to anywhere, let alone to a rendezvous that will change their life."

I noticed she was wearing perfume. I wasn't sure whether there was innuendo in her voice or just hope inside my head.

"Well, I'm happy to be here." I took a long pull on my beer. "I just followed the pheromones . . ."

"Pheromones?"

"You know, the scent we all unconsciously convey to others."

She smiled a sultry, sexy grin as she realized the nuance of the word. "So you just followed my pheromones and they led you right to me. I bet you couldn't wait."

"Mrs. Barrows, let it be noted that you asked me here tonight."

"Yes, that's true. But you picked up my pheromones." She said this gleefully, as if taking ownership of the word. "I never knew what to call it, but they've often come out in the early summer. And you picked up their scent?"

"Absolutely, Mrs. Barrows," I replied playfully.

"Then, as I said, congratulations."

She clinked her pink drink against my beer glass and drank it all the way down. Then she licked the orange for punctuation. She stared at me for a long time and winked. "How's your day been?"

I thought for a moment about the wink and the question. "Good. In fact, better than good. My day was excellent. Thank you for asking. How was your day?"

"Like all the rest. Except you showed up."

"Stranger shows up in a small town, things happen. The energy changes, as does the gestalt of the community itself."

She didn't get it, but she laughed politely, sweetly looking young and pretty. "Gestalt? What does that mean?"

"Well, the makeup of things, the configuration symbolic or actual of people or places."

"Who talks that way, Auggie? I never heard that word. No matter." As if on cue, our waiter brought a round of tequila with all the trimmings. Lizzy winked at me again. "Drink your drink."

I did. She followed suit and then sucked on her lime. It was strange how she truly was such a chameleon. Pretty, young, sweet one moment and then coarse, vulgar, and an old, sad presence in the body of a starlet.

"So what are you doing here?" she asked.

"You asked that I join you for a drink."

She giggled. "Not that, silly. I *know* that. I mean here in Plymouth."

"I told you this afternoon: I came to see your husband to rent the theater and put on shows."

She waved for yet another round. "Really? Truth: why?"

"Because it's what I want to do with my life and I think I'll be good at it."

More drinks arrived and we repeated what was quickly becoming a ritual. I was buzzed as I watched her work the lime. This time it was flirtatious, direct, and very sexy. Was it the tequila or the girl?

"Yeah, but then you have to spend time in Plymouth and talk to my husband . . ."

She stopped in midsentence and crushed out her cigarette. Then she stood up quickly, leaned over the table, and kissed me hard on the mouth. She tasted of liquor and ash. Still, her lips were soft and her hair smelled of lilac. When she was done with me, she sat back down and said with a mischievous grin, "How's your gestalt now, Auggie?"

I couldn't help but smile along with her. "My gestalt is just fine, Mrs. Barrows. Is that the tequila or the pheromones asking?"

"Pheromones? Are they related to gestalt?" She said this as though she thought she was just the cutest thing.

Before I could answer she continued, "You want to make a deal with Andy, you're gonna need my help. Andy does what I ask him to. He is one son of bitch, but he likes to make me happy. You want me to tell Andy to give you that theater, then you're gonna have to make me happy. You up for that Auggie?"

Yet another round of drinks arrived, so I didn't have to respond.

Before she had her third shot, she removed her silk headband and shook her hair free, which made her look even better than she did before. She drank and lingered yet again on the lime. Her eyes were green like a cat's-eye marble, and I was lit, and young, and stupid.

"You come by my house tomorrow noon and we'll work something out," she said. "I'll get Andy to give you financing as well. I mean, we all need money, right? It'll be fun. Bring your pheromones."

Then she walked out of the Full Sail to her waiting limo. I wasn't the only one in the bar to watch her ass sway as it left the place.

Sarah Vaughan sang "Mood Indigo" on the jukebox. I took in a deep breath of crisp, salty air that cleared my head just a bit. The ocean was aglow under a black, starry night. I looked at the moon, which seemed to race across the sky as if chasing something important. Sometimes the unexpected little things say a lot. As do the lips of a stranger.

4

I lingered for a while, then began the long walk back to Garden's Beach View Motel. It was just shy of ten o'clock on this late spring night, yet it felt much later. The sky remained crystal clear, and blazing stars and a robust orange moon lit the road. There was no one around. The streets had rolled up early; other than the warm, heavy breeze off the bay, there was a disconcerting calm.

Still, my thoughts were racing. I wanted to produce some shows. Sow my oats. Seek my bliss. It all seemed there for the taking, like the brass ring on a carousel; yet one that doesn't come around as often, perhaps only once. I should have been elated that Mrs. Barrows had suggested that by noon tomorrow I might be on my way to making some magic. Instead I felt confusion and angst. What the hell was going on? Was I going to fuck this up, blow this chance for lack of knowing what to do? *Man, I'm still a New York neurotic, even after four years in Boston.*

I told myself to relax, but I felt overmatched. What was expected of me at noon tomorrow? I thought about my father and where he was at my age. Six thousand miles from home in a bunker somewhere in Europe. He had real problems, true stakes. Freezing his ass off and eating K rations. There was no pink-lip-glossed beauty offering herself to him. It made me feel guilty and spineless.

I had a buzz from the alcohol, or her kiss, or her perfume, and a seemingly endless walk in front of me. I found a beachside pay phone and asked the operator for the local taxi company. She gave me the number for Garden Cab, I dropped a dime and ten minutes later a beat-up Chevy Impala drove up to meet me.

My driver was a heavyset man in his midfifties sporting a long ponytail, tattoos, and a belly that made you wonder when the baby was due. His cab smelled of stale cigarettes and beer. It was a short ride home; I managed with the windows down.

I retrieved my key from the front office. Surprisingly, Veronica was still manning the fort, and she greeted me with a big friendly smile. Noticing that I was drunk, she came around from behind the desk and steadied my walk with her arm firmly placed behind the small of my back.

"Quite a night, handsome," she said. "There's a whole summer ahead. Pace yourself. You can't live it all at once."

I said something dumb and obvious about her being "really hot," as if she had never heard that before. She helped me climb the steps to my room, opened the door, and navigated me to the side of the bed. Veronica pulled off my shoes, arranged the pillows under my head, and headed out.

Before leaving the room, I stopped her with a question. "Why is someone as pretty as you working at this crummy hotel?"

"Why are *you* staying here?"

"Because I have no money and *you* are the desk clerk."

"That's sweet. So if I wasn't attractive it would be all right to work here?"

"Yup. I mean *nope*, don't I? It's just that people like you seem to have it easy. And you're really pretty."

"People like me? What does that mean exactly?"

"You are extremely attractive." I slurred this.

"Did you just say I looked like a tractor?"

"No, you're pretty. If you *were* a tractor, you'd be a pretty one."

She paused for a long time. "I'm working here because I need the money for school. I work at the front desk so I might get the chance to meet someone like you." She said this with her tongue firmly planted in her lovely cheek.

"If I had any money, I would give it to you," I said.

"Why would you give me money?"

"Well . . . because . . ."

"I'm pretty?"

"Yup."

"Then you're a dope."

"Yup," I said proudly. "Hey, where are you going to college?"

She sat at the very end of the bed. "I'm going to Boston University to become a shrink. I just finished two years at community college and worked here and at odd jobs to save as much money as I could. I like to watch people and their behavior. I think this'll make me a good shrink. I can tell things about people just by looking at them."

"Like a fortune teller?"

"If you'd like to look at it that way."

"My fortune says you want to kiss me, right?"

"See, I knew that about you: that you were an unabashed flirt."

"What else?"

"You're ambitious and on a mission. You're a person who chooses life rather than allowing it to choose you."

This inebriated silly exchange had taken on new depth. "We are both too young to think those things, to figure it all out so quickly."

"You'd be surprised. Our lives are there for us to make something of. To do less is a disappointment."

"Have you read *The Fountainhead*?"

"No, do you think I should?"

"Yes, I most definitely do."

She looked hard into my eyes, as if trying to figure something out.

"So will you kiss me?" I asked.

"No," she replied very quickly and with absolute certainty.

"But everybody kisses me. It's like a ritual, maybe even a tradition. Why won't *you* kiss me?"

"Because everybody kisses you."

"That's a real shame because you're such a pretty tractor." I began to wonder if the room rate was going to go up if I didn't stop talking.

"And although there is a certain charm about a drunken flirty lug, it's fleeting and I'm better than that."

"That is *so* wise," I said, sadly knowing she wasn't going to change her mind.

"No more trouble for you tonight, big boy. Lights out till morning."

She got up from the bed and left immediately. I lay there, unable to let the day or thoughts of her end. After a while I noticed there was a phone on the bedside table. I picked it up and was immediately connected to Veronica at the front desk.

"You're supposed to be asleep, Mr. August," she said kindly.

"Just one thing and then I'll be good," I replied. "Could you connect me to long distance?"

I waited a brief moment, then gave her the number of my dad.

5

My father picked up on the third ring. "Dad, it's me. Sorry, I know it's late."

"Sammy, we've been waiting all day to hear from you. You okay?"

"I'm good. Tired, but good."

I brought him up to speed, but I didn't want to sound too self-indulgent. My father had been struggling in his work over the past years, yet he remained strong and good humored. He always assured my family that the worst had already happened, and better things were coming. His optimism always got us through, and it rubbed off on me. I had always been fearless, but the encounter with Mrs. Barrows made me feel cheap and vulnerable; I needed to reach out to my dad for advice.

I could see him smiling through the phone. "You have your whole life ahead of you. Don't use up all your adventures in one day."

"You've been talking with the blonde?" I asked. "She just told me the same thing before I called you."

"But for different reasons, my son. Her agenda is much different."

"What's her agenda?"

"The answer is the joy of being you. Youth allows you to find out."

"So what do I do tomorrow?"

"Don't rush into things. Just wait and see where everything goes."

From where I was standing, though, there were only two choices: either I slept with the wife of a powerful man who could launch my theater career or I drove out of Plymouth without any other prospects. Even if I did sleep with her, it didn't guarantee I would have complete control of the theater. She could always use our affair as leverage to get other things from me, or her husband could drive me out of town if he found out.

"Dad, we both know what's going to happen."

"No, we don't. Perhaps we think we do, but in truth we don't."

"I don't want to be some asshole who doesn't think of consequences until I've already screwed up or hurt someone. I want to do what's right."

"You have to play the entire game and make your decisions as you move ahead. Take charge of the situation and don't let anyone force you to do anything that makes you uncomfortable. I know you—you don't make bad choices. Trust your instincts and you'll know what to do."

"Okay, Dad. I'll keep you posted."

I hung up the phone, turned on the TV and watched highlights of the Red Sox beating up on the Indians earlier in the day. I dozed off before I heard the final score.

6

The next morning I headed toward the beach and quickly found my stride. My legs felt strong, and as I ran along the beachfront my feet made a rhythmic, percussive sound on the damp sand that drowned out any of last night's doubts. I thought of all the women I'd slept with in college, and how none of them offered the allure, adventure, or adrenaline of Lizzy Barrows. She was the unknown, charged with fire, chaos, and bliss—a dangerous but enticing cocktail.

When I returned to the hotel the morning clerk handed me an envelope from Mrs. Barrows. "Thanks. Do you think it might be a letter bomb?" I asked.

She laughed. "I make no promises, but if so, rest assured I'll let your parents know what happened to you and why you won't be home for dinner."

"Much appreciated. Good to know."

The envelope contained a brief letter from the Barrows Foundation stating its willingness to lease the Priscilla Beach Theatre to me and to fund the theater program with fifty thousand dollars. It was signed by the president of the foundation, which according to the expensive letterhead, was Lizzy Barrows. I reread the letter to make sure I hadn't misinterpreted it. I didn't find any of the stipulations for the lease or the money objectionable. Just then the last clouds outside my motel window disappeared, and my room flooded with a bright, beckoning light. "*Okay,* I thought, *if that's not a sign . . .*"

I got in my Mustang at just after ten-thirty. I thought I'd grab a quick breakfast to steady my nerves and calm my stomach. I pulled into the Garden Diner up the road, taking a seat alone at a booth near the window. A friendly waitress took my order of orange juice, fried eggs, corned beef hash, and dry English muffin. The food arrived quickly, but my mind was elsewhere and I didn't taste a thing. I perused the newspaper someone had left at an adjacent table. The Yankees had won yesterday with Munson hitting a grand slam, while Catfish had won his seventh.

I paid the bill, left a reasonable tip, and returned to my car. I headed over to the Barrows's mansion with time to spare. The sun had burned off the morning rain, leaving the grounds as green as a fairway. The air smelled of fresh-cut grass, rich topsoil, and honeysuckle. There was a wisp of a breeze that offered just a scent of the ocean down below. There was one car in the driveway, a bright-red two-seat Mercedes that must have just left the showroom. To my surprise the door was ajar, with a small note on scented paper taped prominently over the doorbell:

Auggie, I am on the back deck. Let yourself in and meet me there. Don't worry, I won't accuse you of breaking and entering it's safe in that regard.
L.

I entered the quiet house and made my way to the back deck. I was amazed by the enormous size of the home. The vaulted ceilings made me appear small and insignificant. I found the deck and watched Lizzy quietly. She was wearing a two-piece bathing suit with a revealing halter top that dramatized the unforgettable line of cleavage that had fired up my imagination the previous afternoon. A thin sarong wrapped around her hips, gradually revealing the muscular outline of her long tanned legs. She let her hair cascade sensually over her smooth bronze shoulders, making her body even more desirable. I could barely keep a clear head. I tapped on the glass door and was enthusiastically received.

"Prompt as usual," she said as she greeted me with a smile and a chaste kiss.

"I like being on time. It shows respect. In the theater it's often said that if you are five minutes late you must multiply the minutes by the number of people waiting for you. That adds up quickly. I'd rather be early, in fact. For all you know, I could have been loitering for some time on the grounds."

"Security would have picked you up, but I slept with the judge a few years back and you'd be out on bail in no time."

"Fortunate for me."

She offered me a seat on a redwood chaise with a blue canvas cushion. Then she pulled a bottle of chilled Krug from the ice bucket nearby, filled a glass for me and topped off her own. She wore no makeup and was absolutely ravishing. I wondered if God was on the Barrows's staff as a lighting designer. Mrs. Barrows would have been a sight in a blackout, but here in the noonday sun under a cloudless sky, it was hard not to stare. Or run away.

She raised her glass. "To you, Auggie. To our summer together. To your wants. Whatever you're looking for, I'll help you find it."

We clinked glasses and drank.

I looked away and saw several sailboats on the horizon. I decided to say something before the silence became uncomfortable. "I wanted to thank you for last night. Also, thanks for the papers this morning. I've gone over them a few times and spoken to my dad. I'm ready to sign."

She took the envelope from me and removed the papers. She perused them quickly, not reading a word. Then, using the railing as a writing surface, she signed her name and turned to me. "Now you." She offered me the pen and watched me intently as I signed.

"Congratulations, Auggie. Now the pressure is on you to deliver. Your ship has come in—and in Plymouth that means a bunch. Let's celebrate." She emptied the bottle of champagne in our respective glasses and drank. I watched her arch her neck as she drained the last drop of alcohol in her crystal flute. She poured me another glass, and I began to feel warm and flushed. "I have your check upstairs in my bedroom, why don't you come with me . . ."

"If it's all right with you, Mrs. Barrows, I'd prefer to wait down here. I'm feeling a bit lightheaded and I might not make it safely up the steps."

"Suit yourself," she said as if I had a third eye. "While I'm gone, pop another bottle."

She walked off the deck slowly but deliberately. I watched her narrow ankles disappear up the stairs. I sat there thinking how I didn't even like champagne, and how one bottle of this stuff cost more than my car. I was a bit reticent to see where a second bottle might lead, but I was beginning to lose control of my head. I needed to pace myself so I could play the entire game. For the moment I wasn't winning, but I certainly wasn't losing either. I wrestled with the cork, which exploded out of the upright bottle sounding as if I'd pulled the trigger on a snub-nosed 38.

Lizzy returned. "What you shooting at?" she asked coyly.

"Doubt and insecurity."

She was now wearing a red silk robe, partially open, with a matching sash. The swimsuit was gone, and if the robe slid any further she would be wearing nothing but a smile. She took a long drag from her cigarette and blew perfect smoke rings into the air.

"Doubt and insecurity?" she said. "What the fuck? Here's your check—now don't screw things up." She finished her cigarette and flicked the butt into the ocean a hundred feet below. Classy.

I took the check and held it away from me to admire the five numbers to the right of the dollar sign. All those zeros. My dream was starting to come true.

She filled the flutes again and asked me to sit next to her. Then she opened her robe and placed my left hand softly on her breast. She pressed her lips on mine and moved my hand down toward her navel. I was quickly aroused and began to lose control of my thoughts.

She kissed me again, this time practically demanding a primal response. *Remember*, I told myself, *play the whole game.*

I jumped off the chaise. My boner was pressing uncomfortably against my jeans. The scene was comical, but as real as one could imagine; I felt like Jerry Lewis. I was afraid to move too quickly as I might stumble, fall on my boner and break it

"What is this all about?" I said to her. "Do you believe in my project or do you just want to fuck me?"

Lizzy cornered me against the deck railing. She moved in confidently for the kill, then stopped about a foot away from me and let her robe drop onto the floor. "Breathe, lover. Grab the champagne and meet me upstairs. You need to thank me properly."

I said nothing as she climbed the grand staircase to her bedroom.

I thought of the talk with my dad. The alcohol made me feel brazen. I wasn't afraid of this woman. I picked up her robe; it smelled of lilac and smoke. I collected my thoughts, found the envelope in which I had brought the contracts, and took a moment to write Mrs. Barrows a note:

Partner,

> *Thanks for the dough. I was advised not to live my entire summer's adventures in a single day. Maybe dinner and a long talk will help my reticence disappear, but for the moment we have work to do. You may think I am an idiot but for now, see you, doll. Good luck to us both.*

> *PS: Put some clothes on. I wouldn't want you to catch cold.*

I left with the check folded in my breast pocket. I drove to the Plymouth Savings Bank to open an account and make a $50K bet on my dream. Mrs. Barrows would have to wait at least until the check cleared before we could resume our cat-and-mouse game. Next time, I might even let myself get caught.

7

The Plymouth Savings Bank, established in 1806, was built of stone. It reflected the no-nonsense Puritan values of hard work and innate strength. It sat high above the knoll as if keeping an eye on the denizens of the village and their money. The leaded-glass windows, placed in an orderly fashion across the facade of the building, had tinted panes that cast a prism effect on the steps leading into the offices.

I went to the bullpen, where Mrs. Saunders greeted me. She was a gray-haired woman approaching fifty. Her navy-blue suit made her look attractive and slender. It came adorned with a name tag above her left breast pocket. Her lapel had the bank initials PSB embroidered next to the emblem of a pilgrim. She quickly extended her hospitality and offered me the chair next to her desk. Her eyes widened when I told her I wanted to deposit $50,000. I quickly signed a multitude of forms for setting up the account, then handed Mrs. Saunders the check. I saw her wide, happy eyes narrow in disappointment.

"The Barrows Foundation," she mused. Then in an offhand fashion she warned me to stand back from the check, because it might bounce up and hit me in the eye. "Is this a standard banker's joke?" I asked, surprised and without a hint of mirth. "How long before these funds are available?"

"Well, if there are no problems, considering that it's a local check being deposited on a Saturday, you can have the money as early as Tuesday afternoon."

"Do you foresee any problem?"

"No, no, nooooo. It's just that I've been working here since the Pilgrims landed and I'm always cautious. Small banking has its surprises. If I'm not overstepping my bounds, you might want to talk with Marty Stanhope who runs the White Cliffs Resort a few miles up the road on Route 3. He's . . . Well, you might want to chat with him. But please don't tell the Barrows."

"Rest assured," I replied. The woman was more than hinting at something, so I thanked her with a smile and walked out into the afternoon sun.

8

The banker's reaction had thrown me a bit. Perhaps Marty Stanhope could enlighten me. I soon arrived at the motel and found Veronica behind the front desk. Each day she looked more attractive. I couldn't take my eyes off her near-see-through flower-patterned dress. Her firm, round breasts were held in place by two delicate shoulder straps. I wondered how they were able to support that magnificent chest. Putting lust aside, I dove straight in and asked if I could keep my room for two days at a discounted rate while I was away in Boston.

She smiled and told me she would make an exception as long as we both kept it a secret. "I won't tell if you don't. In fact, there are a lot of things I won't tell if you ask me not to."

To me, her body language suggested something carnal and her eyes reinforced the same. It was if she were saying, "Take me in the back office and bend me over the file cabinet." I began to wonder why I didn't. So far I had been extremely lucky in this town. A gorgeous woman was ready to strip me down and have her way with me. Now I was reading signs from Veronica. Yet I hadn't done anything about either. I blamed it on the musicals. That overwhelming desire to produce a play was eroding my libido. I swore I would reaffirm my manhood as soon as I took care of some theater business in Boston.

"Hold my room for two days and I'll take you out for drinks on Tuesday night when I return. We'll keep that between us as well."

She shook her hair back and smiled a dazzling smile; she looked like a cat purring with contentment. "No secrets to be kept, Sam. I'm flattered you would like to take me out, but I regretfully pass."

"Why pass?" I implored. "And with regret!"

"Because the regret in saying no is finite rather than the long-lasting kind I fear would occur if I gave you the opportunity to work your charms on me." She said this with a slight giggle, then her face flushed.

"I promise I won't be charming. I'll be the opposite. I'll be the anticharm, the antidote to charm, the abolishment of charm. I will have charm removed from the dictionary. Really, trust me."

She tilted her head. "That's charming. You just can't help yourself. You're like lighting a match in a room filled with gasoline. So . . . no."

"Okay then, Ms. Chapman. I won't be showering for the rest of my stay. I'll make you dislike me enough to go out with me."

"Now, that's a novel approach. Have a good night, Mr. August."

Veronica leaned across the front desk and gave me a sisterly peck on the cheek. She smelled like strawberries and looked good enough to eat.

I was speechless. I hovered for a moment thinking of something clever to say, but she went back to work, clearly not interested. I thanked her sincerely for the deal on the room and left.

I paused a moment in the parking lot. I realized that within a few days I would never see Veronica again. I could live with that. There were other fish in the sea. I mean Plymouth *was* a seafood town.

Why did that ring hollow?

I took the stairs to my room two and three steps at a time, then opened the door. I grabbed my old football canvas duffle bag with the words *South High 1972 Unbeaten Division One Champions* stenciled in cursive on the side. I threw in some clothes, my toiletries, and the novel I had been reading for the fifth or sixth time: *The Fountainhead*. If Salinger's *Catcher in the Rye*, with its rebellious overtones, was the book for junior high school, then *The Fountainhead* was my book for college; it identified my road to individualism, integrity, and the pursuit of brilliant, pristine artistry. The lead character in the novel, architect Howard Roark, was an inspiration. Roark lived his life with grit and conviction. He believed that

men have been taught that it is a virtue to agree with others. But the creator is the man who disagrees. Men have been taught that it is a virtue to swim with the current. But the creator is the man who goes against the current. Men have been taught that it is a virtue to stand together. But the creator is the man who stands alone. The artist is life. Those who live off his ideas and his toil are second-handers living a second-hand life, not their own.

When his work was betrayed, Roark did more than simply complain. He destroyed his building, as it no longer reflected his vision or integrity. An artist's work must be accepted on his own terms. He had the great courage not to care if others embraced him. Each time I read the book I wanted to howl at the moon and say, "Let me be Howard Roark for a single day and I will be closer to being a true artist."

I called the front desk. "The answer remains the same, Mr. August," Veronica said in what surely sounded to me like a smoky, throaty, just-been-fucked voice.

"Do you sound that way with everyone?" I was forced to ask.

"What do you evea mean?" she replied. Mellifluous to be sure. My libido was clearly not broken; it had been reignited by the charms and rejections of Veronica Chapman, the blond goddess shrink-to-be. Maybe she'd continue to drive me crazy and I could make an appointment with her.

"Please connect me long distance to Boston," I said, and then I gave her the number for Secunda.

The phone rang twice and Secunda picked up with a gruff hello.

9

I had met Secunda, also known as Josh to our friends, during my second year at Tufts. He was a senior finishing up his sixth year while assuring his wealthy parents that he would graduate before the seven-year itch sent him out to pasture. Secunda was many things, one of which was a bit of an asshole. To say that he was unique was to suggest Willie Mays could hit a little and Monet had somewhat of an affinity for lilies.

Josh's real name was Albert Feldman, a moniker he grew up hating as it was devoid of poetry and lilt, particularly for a short, stocky Jewish kid. So he changed it to Secunda. Other than being vertically challenged at just shy of five feet eight inches, Josh had grown up quite handsomely. He looked like a young Anthony Quinn in *The Guns of Navarone* and managed to pull off the kind of goatee worthy of Errol Flynn in *The Adventures of Robin Hood*.

Secunda always wore suits. These usually reflected his dark mood—navy blue, black, brown—in a fabric to match the season: linen for the summer months, light wool for the spring and fall, and heavy cashmere in the winter. He wore expensive shirts buttoned to the collar and finished off each outfit with boots that added nearly three inches to his height. He spent hours in the weight room and boxed semipro every weekend at a thirties gym in South Boston. He had the anger and menace of an Irish cop with a right cross to match. Secunda was spoiled and he let everyone know it. He drove a red Alfa Romeo convertible and ate at Boston's best restaurants, flashing his gold Amex card like a magic wand.

His extravagance was complemented by his talent. He played the trumpet like Armstrong, sang like Paul Robeson, and could interpret a character on stage with the instinct and charisma that only God could bestow. With women Secunda was always in demand. He regularly showed up with yummy eye candy on his arm. He was the envy of many. His relationships were monogamous, intense, and all too brief for the women he dated. He was often off wooing the next heart while the one left behind was still breaking. He was also indispensable to my project.

"The eagle has landed," I said thinking myself rather clever.

"What?" asked Secunda.

"The eagle has landed!"

"Okay."

"Neil Armstrong said that when he walked on the moon."

"So?" He was clearly baiting me.

"*So?* That was a good thing, and what's happened here in the last twenty-four hours is that the plan is working."

"Why didn't you just say that instead of all this moon stuff?"

"Secunda! The plan is going to happen!"

"Good for you, Sammy."

"That's it? Good for me? I've been here a day and it's already coming together."

"That's the curse of being a superstar, Sammy. No one expects any less. I'll be there tomorrow. Where are you staying?"

"Garden's Beach View Motel. It's at the intersection of 3A and Rocky Hill Road."

"It must be cheap. I don't lodge cheap."

"It's cheap, not diseased."

"Be nice and I'll buy you a lobster tomorrow night."

"Deal."

"I'll be there by noon. I'm going to bring JB and James. If the 'plan' is going to happen we have to keep them in the loop. Know anybody who can find me a date? I can't just break bread with the three of you. I imagine some attractive woman there wants a lobster."

"Noon at my motel. I'll work on the date. Have James bring his tool kit. And stop on the way down and pick up some high-beam flashlights. I'm going to eat a five-pound lobster, by the way. Do you know why?"

"Because *the eagle has landed!!!*" we both screamed through the phone with unbridled joy.

"Noon tomorrow, Sammy." And then he was gone.

A moment later I picked up the phone to speak to Veronica. "Yes, Mr. August. May I help you?" Why did she always sound as if she was flirting?

"Veronica, I know this is short notice, but I've had a change of plans. Would you please reconsider and let me take you out?"

"You know, Sam, I'm not the only fish in the sea. You're in Plymouth and it *is* a seafood town."

Now that was weird, I thought.

"Sam, drive into town. You'll find a date in a heartbeat. You're adorable, but I'm just not in the market for what you are selling." She said this so sweetly. I liked her. I really did.

"Okay," I said with resignation. "Where do you suggest I start?"

"Stay away from Lizzy Barrows."

I thought she was going to say more, but she remained silent.

Then just before I hung up she added, "Try the White Cliffs. It's always full of surprises. Ask for Sidney. I'll call him and tell him to buy you a drink. Go have fun. You're over twenty-one and there are girls everywhere. You won't be lonely for long."

The phone clicked and I had no time for rebuttal.

My day had been a roller-coaster ride of emotions and events. A shower refreshed me and gave me a second wind. I dressed in my one pair of blue jeans, well-worn sneakers, and red alligator shirt. I grabbed a white hooded sweatshirt that said TUFTS across the front. I realized as I checked my hair in the mirror that I looked a bit like the American flag. *Oh well, it's Plymouth.*

I was clean shaven, my hair as always was somewhat unkempt, dark, with a soft curl that prevented me from looking too coifed. I smiled, thinking I looked better than good. Plymouth was waiting and I had baited the hook.

I put the top down on the Mustang and headed easily down Route 3A toward Plymouth Bay and the postcard village that surrounded it. I drove past the high school and the playground that bore the name Barrows. I slowed as I passed the tourist places like the Plymouth Plantation, which replicated the original settlement of more than three hundred years ago. The houses were so tiny. Where would someone my size sleep?

It was still early and the wharf was quiet. Neon signs flashed happily and painted the harbor in a prism of color. The restaurants prepared for the on-slaught of hungry families soon to arrive, and the bars waited for tonight's party to begin. I was eager for action, so I headed north looking for distraction and company.

The sky, which had earlier been clear and bright, was now gray and cold. Big puffy clouds were blocking the moon and obfuscating the stars. They looked like huge cotton balls tarnished and covered with soot. Rain was definitely on the way.

I pulled into a local watering hole called the Moondog, basically a dou-blewide trailer home selling whiskey and beer. I parked in the crowded lot, put the top up in anticipation of rain, and headed inside. I ordered bourbon neat and watched the crowd as if doing research on the human condition.

The Moondog was a relaxed place to see friends and coworkers, but at the same time one could imagine that on summer nights when the hour got late it was an environment that brewed trouble and contempt followed by cheap, petty bar fights. I imagined it peopled by wealthy tourists or the college crowd from Boston or Providence who would arrive in season and go slum-ming. All pleased and privileged they'd come looking for one-night stands with the local working class. The guys who worked with their hands and backs were fit and strong, willing and desperate. This was also the place to meet the girls that someone like Veronica Chapman went to high school with, who would get naked fast for a guy who a drove a Porsche or flashed the promise of easy money.

I finished my drink quickly. There was nothing here for me, at least not tonight. I decided to try to find Marty Stanhope and query him on the Barrows. I took a deep breath outside the smoke-filled bar, started up my car, and got onto Route 3A heading south in the ebony, rain-filled night.

I drove for the next ten minutes or so, thinking about all the possibilities rattling inside my head. Bonnie Raitt sang softly on the radio; bluesy, sexy, practically promising an imminent tryst and making that sort of thing seem strangely so very important.

I slowed down and turned left in front of a brightly lit sign that read:

THE WHITE CLIFFS
PLYMOUTH'S LUXURY BEACHFRONT HOMES
FINE DINING, LIVE MUSIC
DANCING UNDER THE STARS

I wasn't going to be doing much fine dining on the cash in my pocket. Still, I proceeded up a long, winding gravel road. Deep, dense woods bracketed each side. The night was black and the only light visible inside my car came from the dashboard.

Then suddenly I arrived at the end of the road and light was everywhere. An enormous glass building seeming to radiate with white heat was perched on the edge of the cliffs overlooking the Atlantic. The place looked like a spaceship about to take off. I pulled up to the valet, got out and tossed the keys to a guy whose name tag read WILLIE. I headed inside.

I O

The White Cliffs was Vegas with an ocean as its backyard. The continuous aural din was that of crashing waves rather than slots, yet the crowd and lounge music were a perfect match. The restaurant seats were upholstered in red leather, with black wood and polished chrome trimmings. The half-circle bar was elevated three steps above the dance floor, from where you could see a galaxy of sky; tonight it pelted windswept, angry raindrops against the windows. The drinks were served in big, heavy goblets, and you could nurse one for hours while you looked for a mermaid to wash ashore. Behind the red-vested barmen hung a floor-to-ceiling gilded mirror that doubled the view of the room. There were dozens of booths and myriad tables all dressed with white, starched tablecloths, each adorned with lit candles that reflected like fireflies against the plate-glass windows soaring twenty feet above, abutting the domed top hat of the roof.

Left of the bar was a shiny, black baby grand. A tuxedoed musician whose tip jar held perhaps fifteen singles and at least one fin played it with great earnestness yet modest talent. He was in the middle of a medley of Carpenters tunes, and on the dance floor dozens of fortyish couples made their way randomly about. The room was in full flight, with more than three hundred people in a space built to handle two hundred and fifty.

To my delighted surprise, seated at the bar was Veronica. She was talking animatedly with a girlfriend who, if not for Veronica's presence, would have been the most beautiful girl in the room. I approached the bar and ordered a bottle of beer, feigning indifference to her presence. We were just inches away from each other but neither made an effort to close the gap. I picked out a choice barstool, asked for a guy named Sidney, and waited to see what would happen.

Veronica was wearing blue eye shadow with a hint of glitter that magnified the natural color of her eyes. Her cheeks had a touch of blush, and she wore her thick, blond hair down and tasseled so the overall affect was one of "do me," or "how do I look having just been done?" Her long, tan legs were bare, satin smooth, and perfect. She wore a faded denim miniskirt and a white tank top that dramatized the curves of her waist and breasts. She was braless, and her nipples poked through like the erasers on a Ticonderoga number 2 pencil. She carried a classic western denim jacket over her right arm and a big canvas bag on her left shoulder. Black ostrich cowboy boots went to her midcalf and must have added two inches to her long, lithe frame. Again she smelled of strawberries, and her lips were glossed with a tint of red. I found it difficult not to look at her nipples.

I took a moment to collect myself then, because I couldn't stand the suspense, said in a voice that didn't sound like mine, "Veronica at the White Cliffs. Funny how I found my way here only to find you. It does seem strange that you passed on my invite but ended up in the same place as if you had agreed to join me."

"Coincidences do happen, you know. This is a small town and there aren't a great many options to occupy a rainy night."

I took a long pull on my beer and reveled in the irony.

"This is my friend Kellie," she said. "We go out together often to keep each other out of trouble."

Kellie wore a pink halter top and low-hung, tight, new blue jeans. Her red hair was the color of an Irish setter's, and it framed her face perfectly. She had soft, slightly freckled porcelain skin and bright-green cat's eyes. She wore a touch of lipstick and no jewelry other than a charm bracelet on her right wrist.

She offered her hand and said, "So this is Sam August, Veronica's newest topic of constant conversation. Six foot four's worth of temptation, trouble in extra large." Then she added coyly, "It is so nice to meet you. I wish we had more time to get acquainted, but it's almost eight and I suddenly remember that I have an early appointment in the morning. A girl has to get her beauty rest." She stood up from her bar perch and patted the seat, making sure I would sit down.

I stared at Veronica for a long time. Inside I was smiling all the way to my toes. Maybe the "charm riff" had opened the door. She stared right back as though we were in a contest to see who might blink first.

"So, Ms. Chapman," I began, "other than being—how can I say this nicely?—a mindfucker, what else would you be willing to share now that we're here by 'coincidence?'"

Veronica tapped the bar top and in a whispered shout to the bartender said, "Sidney, two tequilas, and back 'em with a beer." Then she added with a flourish and a beaming, happy grin, "Make it snappy, my good man!"

Sidney bowed slightly, offered a knowing grin, and set about preparing our drinks.

"Isn't this place fabulous?" she said turning to me. "Don't you feel like you're in a fairy tale and you must get home by midnight before the coach turns into a pumpkin?"

Sidney brought the drinks and kissed Veronica on the cheek. Introductions were made. He was sixty, if not older, with a pleasant, round face and bushy gray hair that circled his bald pate. He had obviously spent years in the sun and his spotted, deeply creased face showed the damage of the elements.

Tall and fit, he carried himself like a former athlete. He had an easy smile and a firm handshake. We sized each other up and then Sidney said, "Good to meet you, kid. College boy, huh? You be nice to my girl here or there'll be hell to pay."

He took Veronica's hand in his and looked at her with great fatherly affection. "If you need anything else, honey, just let me know." Then he pointed at me with intensity in his eyes and returned to his business.

Veronica picked up her shot glass and suggested we toast. *Clink.*

"Who's driving us home?" I asked.

She paused while raising her glass and said, "As of yet there *is* no 'us,' and this one drink is where it ends between you and me. Sidney can call you a taxi if need be. She tilted her head slightly and gave me a breathless look that melted my heart. "Are you going to drink with me or not, big boy?"

With the question hanging in the air, we began to drink very slowly, our eyes never leaving one another's. I was glad I had not bedded Lizzy Barrows that morning in what now seemed a long, long time ago.

I paused, then lifted my beer glass to toast Veronica. We clinked again and drank. I could feel the heat rising from my feet all the way up to my soul.

I I

And so the evening had begun. We sat at the crowded bar amid a sea of humanity noticing nothing but each other. It was as if there was a spotlight shining, one that muted the cacophony surrounding two individuals who were quickly becoming an "us."

Veronica had been born and raised in Plymouth, the youngest of three children and the only girl. Her dad was a fisherman, as was her grandfather. One of Veronica's brothers worked with her father and the other was serving time in the state pen for a bar fight that had gone horribly wrong. Veronica's mother was a supervisor for a cleaning service that worked the hotels and estates throughout the area. No one in her family had gone to college nor had ever lived more than ten miles from where they were born. She described herself as a people watcher, having observed tourists come and go her entire life. Once she got her degree, she intended to hang up her psychiatrist's shingle in some urban haven like Boston, New York, or San Francisco. She had been working part-time jobs since she was eleven, and she'd saved wisely.

She didn't loathe Plymouth; she just knew too many friends who had grown angry and frustrated by their flatlined service jobs, leading them nowhere but the bottle, divorce, and one wasted life after another. She described the town as akin to a nightclub, all glitter and gold in the evening, but depressing and sordid in the morning with nothing but stale smoke, sweat, and rancid beer.

Patrons paraded across the dance floor as the piano man played dozens of tunes. The only lyric I heard was "I only have eyes for you." It could have been minutes or hours or an entire day that had passed when she leaned in close and whispered in my ear, "You know, you are really sweet. Who taught you that to listen is to get lucky?"

"You don't learn much about people from hearing yourself talk," I replied.

"That was amazing," she said, pulling back a bit. "It seemed eerily practiced, well rehearsed, almost frightening."

"No, Veronica, it is all as real as rain."

We were silent for a beat. Then another. It felt as though there was nothing we could say to match the moment. The piano man was on a break. The place had become quiet, and the wind had picked up, as had the rain. The drops were percussive against the windows, and I could see their distorted reflection in the mirror behind the bar. I had come to talk with Marty Stanhope, for discovery. Yet I had found a different kind in the deep-blue sensual eyes of this special girl.

Sidney walked over and placed a platter of shrimp in front of us. They were huge, the size of softballs, garnished with lemon wedges, horseradish, Tabasco, and little red plastic toothpicks with the initials WC emblazoned in white. He stared at me, then without looking at Veronica asked with a wink, "So, sweetheart, ya like this guy? Ya havin' fun?"

She measured me with her eyes, took a long pause and said, "He'll do for now. I'll let you know if anything changes."

Sidney's gaze stayed on me. "So what are you doing here in Plymouth?"

"Working. Research," I replied.

"What are you researching?"

"I'm trying to rent the Priscilla Beach Theatre and put on some shows this summer."

His brow furrowed. "You talking with Barrows?"

"Yes, sir."

"Be careful. The old man is a fuckin' bastard and the woman is a black widow." I nodded warily.

Sidney continued. "What kind a shows do you want to put on? Musicals?" I nodded.

"You a queer?"

"Not the last I checked."

Veronica jumped in. "No, Sidney, he's not. I can assure you he most definitely is not."

"How you so sure, sweetheart?" he asked.

"Woman's intuition. Nothing more."

Sidney fixed me with his gaze again. "You got any references? Anyone vouch for ya?"

"My mother would say nice things. I dated a lot in college, broke a few hearts. Does that count?"

"Remember what I told ya, kid. Be nice to my girl or there'll be hell to pay."

"Not to worry, Sid. Being nice to Veronica is a privilege. I'm just fortunate she has the time for me."

His severe look turned to mirth and then a belly laugh. "I'm just fuckin with yous kid, that's all. Veronica told me she was coming in tonight and I got permission to treat you right if I liked you. And I do. So does my girl here." He placed a wine bucket on the bar with two crystal flutes and poured us each a glass from a bottle that read *Dom Pérignon Vintage 1968*.

"A millionaire's milkshake," he said. "Have fun, kids." Then he walked the length of the bar and drew a pint for one of the other customers.

Veronica and I giggled and drank, and I realized that for a guy who didn't like champagne I was getting pretty darned used to it. The piano man began to play "The Way You Look Tonight," and Veronica took my hand and led me to the parquet floor where we danced cheek to cheek. The piano man picked up the tempo and we were soon moving to a faster beat. I thought it apropos that we could both rock and roll all over the dance floor but also, more important, dance close without stepping on each other's toes. The music slowed down again. I whispered in Veronica's ear, "Who the hell is Sidney?"

Our slow dancing soon deteriorated into nothing more than grinding up against each another. I was aroused and desired Veronica more than ever, but I was afraid that Sidney might jump the bar to wallop me. Considering the size of my boner, no one would have blamed him. I took my sweatshirt off and tied it around my waist.

"Clever," Veronica said. "Let's eat. Our table's ready."

We were seated at a table next to the window. The shrimp crunched a bit when you took a first bite. After this came huge cherrystone clams covered in stinging horseradish and dabs of Tabasco sauce, and lobster meat pulled from the shell and bathed in butter. Dessert was cherry pie with a cream cheese crust topped with gobs of whipped cream. Delicious foreplay.

The rain came harder now, drumming angrily against the pane. The night was still black as ink, and all one could see were the phosphorescent whitecaps dancing above the swirling invisible sea.

Veronica poured us both a glass of Napa Valley white, the Dom Pérignon long gone. I realized the piano man had gone home and Sidney was offering last call to the remaining stragglers, who had already had enough. I reached for her hand and she allowed me to take it. Without words, we both knew it was time to go.

I 2

Outside, it was pouring. There was a strong, cold wind off the ocean that turned the stinging raindrops horizontal. "Willie" was nowhere to be found; he had left my car alone in the empty lot with the windows wide open. It was flooded, clearly going nowhere for a while, and despite the cold, brisk wind I was in no position to drive. I didn't trust that Veronica was capable either.

"My car is fucked," I said as I rolled up the windows, "and you're tipsy. I think we should go inside and call a cab."

"I don't think so," she shouted. Then she sprinted toward the woods, her boots splashing through the shiny puddles and her clothes drenched and clinging within seconds. "Come on, you chicken. Get wet." I watched Veronica for all of a heartbeat and then raced to catch up with her. My gut told me there were still some surprises ahead as Monday night had turned to Tuesday morning.

Veronica had disappeared into the woods. I was hoping she'd left a trail like Hansel and Gretel, but unfortunately there was nothing. She was just gone. Was that her surprise—leaving me freezing and stranded in the pelting rain with a disappointed libido? I began to inch my way into the harrowing forest. The wind whistled and the trees seemed to come alive with palpable menace. I squinted in the dark and saw a sliver of light coming from the open door of a barely visible house. I moved ahead faster until I could see that the house was ablaze with light. I ran to the door and found Veronica's soaked denim jacket on the floor. I picked it up and warily pushed myself quietly inside.

The house was decorated to replicate a yacht. The floors were buffed white and shimmered. The sofa and accompanying love seats were casually dressed in rich blue canvas trimmed in white. A floor-to-ceiling window mirrored nothing but the sea. A cream-colored chenille throw was draped over the couch and a lush carpet sat in front. The walls were wheat yellow and pristine. All the glassware was crystal. Just to the left of the window sat a fireplace with crackling, crisp, hissing logs. A galley kitchen stood to one side, well appointed with a wet bar and all you needed to prepare a feast. It spoke of money and it spoke to me.

Staged photos hung orderly on the wall. Smiling models in happy family hugs and smiles, and the requisite puppy. Although posed, these pictures were warm and appealing. For fun I imagined Veronica's face and mine on the gleeful mom and dad.

She called from one of the rooms off the hall. "Sam, close the door. It's freezing in here. Take off your wet clothes and give them to me." She reached out from the doorway all bare shoulders and long, naked legs. Her wet hair was plastered to her face, her makeup all but gone. I gave her my shirt, sweatshirt, socks, and my only pair of jeans.

"*All* your clothes! I'm throwing everything in the dryer."

I complied and gave her my underwear. In return she handed me a thick terry-cloth robe. Then she instructed me to check the fire and relax on the couch. I found my way to the sofa and looked out the window, seeing nothing but darkness.

After a moment, Veronica entered from the hallway. She was wearing an identical robe and hugged herself as if she were cold. Her hair and been swept off her face and she had reapplied her lip gloss. She was a vision in simplicity and promise. She walked to the wet bar and asked me what I wanted to drink.

"What are my choices?" I asked.

"Let's see here," she said as she sorted through the bottles. "We have brandy, brandy, and . . . brandy. What do you think?"

"I'll have a brandy."

"Good choice."

She generously filled two large crystal snifters. Then taking long, lithe steps, she walked over and plopped herself down on the couch next to me. "This should warm you up," she said, handing me a glass. She leaned in close and wiped the rain from my brow with the sleeve of her robe. I put my brandy down and took her glass, placing it carefully on the floor. Then I moved as close to her as one could without joining at the hip. I looked into her eyes, stroked her hair for a brief moment, and then leaned in to kiss her.

She jumped from the couch and quickly moved away. She retied the sash on her robe, putting all body parts off limits, and reached down for our brandies. She handed mine to me, then took a long drink, motioning for me to do the same. She smiled like she had a secret, or many secrets. Ones that I really wanted to know.

13

I stood up to gather my thoughts and allow my heartbeat to return to normal. I remained aroused, my boner poked through my robe like Pinocchio's nose after telling a pack of lies. I realized how difficult it was to have an intimate conversation when one could use your penis as a hat rack. I paced and thought about Willie Mays in an effort to get smaller. I sat back down a few inches from Veronica, who remained tantalizing and naked under white, fluffy terry cloth.

"Okay, doll, where are we?"

"This is the model home for the sales office," she answered as if my query was so simple it didn't merit a response. "The company my mother works for has the cleaning contract on the entire complex. I borrowed the key."

"Got it. Who's Sidney?"

"Sidney is a distant cousin of my father's. Although not actually an uncle, he has played that role in the family for years. Sid had a successful charter boat long before I was born. During the off-season he'd work with my dad." She paused. "About two years ago he got in some serious trouble and Barrows only made the situation worse."

The wind continued to howl outside our window. One of the logs in the fireplace popped, sounding like a gunshot. I jumped a couple of inches off the sofa. Veronica clearly noticed and I felt a tad foolish.

"What kind of trouble?" I asked.

"Sidney lost his wife and started doing crazy things. He got in fights in town, chased young women, drank too much, and made a lot of bad bets with the wrong people. He owed a lot of money and these people were threatening him. He went to Barrows's local bank to take out a loan on his boat. He wanted to fix his mistakes and thought that would be the end of it. Barrows agreed, the bank agreed, and then at the eleventh hour reneged on the deal and Sidney was fucked. The guys he owed the money to beat him up really bad. They forced him to sell the boat to stop any further trouble."

"You mean there's a mob in Plymouth? I thought there were only clam shacks? This sucks."

"Sam, don't be so naive. We're forty miles from Boston. Small towns have bad people just like the big city does. My brother is in prison for Christ's sake. Shit happens."

I stared at Veronica. She had dealt with some real shit. The stuff that I only read about or had seen in movies. I had underestimated her in all the ways women hate. I'd typed her as a vixen. I was a shallow idiot.

"Why does everyone hate Lizzy Barrows?" I asked.

Veronica's face flushed with anger. "Because she's a whore. She sticks her big tits in everyone's face and thinks that will get her what she wants. She's like twelve years old and she married that old man for his money. She helps send my brother to prison and she gets a new Mercedes. She spreads her legs as easy as warm butter on hot toast. She has no discretion and . . ." She stopped to breathe. "Enough. I have a question, Mr. August."

"Shoot."

"Would you like to take a shower and go to bed?"

"Let me think about that for a moment . . . *Yes!*" I shouted, too loud and too eager.

Her hips swayed past me and I watched with great attention as she made her way to the shower. Halfway down the hall she dropped her robe; I watched her walk naked into the bathroom until she closed the door. After a beat she stuck her head out again and said, "It's late and cold. We can drive home in the morning. There's a shower in the guest room, and towels and a toothbrush in the closet. There are sweat pants in the dresser that you can wear to bed. Don't get the wrong idea. You and I will not be getting naked together tonight nor any night. I think you are simply wonderful, but fate needs timing, and for us the clock is all askew." Then she blew me a kiss and slowly closed the door.

I stood there for a moment and watched the last log in the fireplace turn from ember to ash. I looked down the hall to where Veronica's spectacular butt had disappeared and shouted with false indignation. "Naked! I wouldn't want to see you naked if you were the last woman on earth. I am not interested in seeing a woman like you naked. The idea of seeing you naked makes me want to stick pins in my eyes!"

I waited for any response but all I heard was the water running and Veronica singing "I'm Just a Girl Who Can't Say No." I walked to the guest shower and turned the water on nuclear hot. I disappeared into a haze of steam, any thoughts of carnal delights with Veronica going down the drain with the scalding water. I got out after only a couple of minutes. I figured the sooner I got to sleep the less confused I would be about her behavior and the events of the past twenty-four hours.

14

Veronica drove Route 3A at close to seventy miles an hour. The speed limit was thirty, checked by radar. I was following in my waterlogged Mustang. It was just minutes past eleven-thirty in the morning and her shift began at noon. The rain continued angry and cold, accompanied by a vicious wind off the sea. The sky was black as night. Miraculously, we arrived without incident at the Beach View, at which point I drew a breath for the first time that morning.

Veronica parked in front of the motel office, ran through the rain and sat next to me in my car. She kissed me chastely on the cheek and said, "Gotta get ready for work. See you tonight at eight. Souza's by the wharf. I'll get Kellie to be Secunda's date. He'll love her. She's cute and loose. Some might even call her slutty." Then she took my face in both her hands and said sweetly, "Thanks for last night, Sam. I had a wonderful, wonderful time." Then she kissed me on the mouth so softly that if I hadn't been paying such close attention I would have missed it. "You really are a gentlemen. Why couldn't we have met earlier when life was simpler, or ten years from now when we might turn into something magical?"

She danced away through the heavy raindrops to begin her day. I thought it *was* magical. And if we had met much earlier in life, we both would have been just learning to read.

I began the trudge back to my room to wait for Secunda and friends. As I reached the stairs I spotted his red Alpha followed by a woody Jeep Wagoneer. Both cars arrived at breakneck speed, leaving a wide wake behind them. James and JB remained in the Jeep. Secunda quickly exited his convertible. He was wearing his trademark outfit, protected from the elements by a western duster that stopped just short of the pavement. He came up to me and offered a wide, welcoming grin and a firm handshake. "Nice day," he said. "Did you order it special for me? Just to be safe, *I'll* order dinner." He looked around. "You're actually staying here?"

"Yup."

"Do I have to?"

"Rooms are already booked and guaranteed on your credit card. Also, we got you a date for dinner. I met her. She's extremely cute and, according to local legend, extremely loose."

As the words came out of my mouth, I realized how incredibly stupid guys were and felt some shame over being one of the pack. I sloshed over to James and JB and tapped on the window, which JB cracked an inch or two. The car smelled of weed and cigarettes. James smoked pot and JB was never without a Lucky Strike. Together they smelled like an ashtray.

"You have the stuff?" I inquired. JB nodded and James offered a thumbs-up.

"Follow me," I said. I waded across the gravel and got into Secunda's car.

I became extremely anxious the moment we left the parking lot. I felt as if my judgment or my vision was suddenly on the line. I had talked up this opportunity for weeks now. I had waxed eloquent with Secunda and friends about how perfect the place was and now I was about to stand naked before my peers. I wished the weather were better. I was certain the place would look more inviting under a blue sky and blazing yellow sun.

Secunda was taking the old, winding highway slowly. The Priscilla Beach Theatre was three miles ahead on the ocean side of Rocky Hill Road. Old porch-front homes, small beach cottages, an occasional home trailer, and big, modern sun palaces reaching toward the sky lined both sides of the road, all standing unwelcoming under the endless gray, pelting rain. There was not a single person in sight. Secunda drove silently, taking it all in, his expression stoic and unchanging. On our left the ocean swirled restlessly some three hundred feet below. I was feeling tense and wondered if I'd oversold things.

We took the last S-curve and got to the theater. My worries instantly disappeared. The place was my Oz and Rocky Hill Road was built out of bright yellow bricks. My spirits soared. The old marquee, though in need of gallons of fresh paint, had great character and radiated gravitas. The drive-in movie lettering hung randomly from the signage spelling out gibberish, yet all I saw was CURTAIN AT 8. BOX OFFICE NOW OPEN!

The large, circular driveway was in gritty disrepair. The rain had left the potholes overflowing with muddy water. A truckload of white gravel, some sunshine, and a summer ocean breeze would fix that within the blink of an eye. The two large farmhouses that flanked the entire north side of the property stood strong, protective, and inviting. They too could use a coat of fresh paint but at the moment that was of little consequence. An enormous maple towered above the houses and canopied the redwood picnic table that rested nearby. A converted icehouse that functioned as a small, somewhat funky office complemented the compound. A large parking area off to the left sat opposite the houses. The lot resembled a manicured fairway and the deep, lush green grass added a wash of color to the grounds.

Straight on about two hundred yards from the road was the theater. It was dark red and weathered, but despite its worn exterior it stood nobly against the drenching rain. It was magnificent. The theater was surrounded by a railed, planked deck with benches and plantings spaced every few feet or so. Near the entrance to the building was a horizontal hatch that when pulled open would reveal a concession stand large enough to serve everything from snacks to cocktails. The magic words BOX OFFICE were lettered over a small window just to the right of the front-of-house doorway, and a breathtaking sign hanging below the ticket window read THIS PERFORMANCE SOLD OUT. About forty feet from the front entrance stood three stunning dogwoods all in full spring bloom, a blizzard of white and pink petals that only Mother Nature could have manufactured. *Amazing*, I thought. *This is simply amazing.*

We all sat for a few minutes. I knew Secunda was in the fold. He nodded his head slightly, as if bopping to some percussive beat. His stoic expression had turned into one of measurable mirth. A Chinese fire drill ensued. The car doors opened and we formed a small circle under the hundred-year-old maple. The rain bled through its leaves and landed on us intermittently.

JB wore a yellow hooded slicker. The rain popped against the plastic sounding like dozens of centipedes tap dancing. JB was short for Joan Bach. "Bach" was given to her father at Ellis Island because the officials considered his German name unpronounceable. Stanley Bach had survived Buchenwald and come to America to forget a horrid past and begin a new life. He had begun by earning chump change in a bakeshop and now owned a chain of bakeries in and around Manhattan. JB never spoke of her parents, and we never asked her why. She was a quintessential New York stereotype: fast talking, chain smoking, loud in her speech and shrieking laugh, boorish, pushy, and manic. JB slept little, pined over men who never gave her a passing thought, and dressed her rather frumpy, short frame with considerable charm. She had been by my side these past years whispering support on each show.

James, who was Secunda's younger brother, had kept his birth name of Feldman. Unlike Secunda he was tall and soft, with skinny arms and a potbelly that hung over his belt. He had hair that could have doubled as a dark helmet. He wore nondescript jeans, Timberlands, and a different band T-shirt every day. He slouched, and his hands were always stuffed deep into his pants pockets.

James was a genius. He had graduated Tufts in just two years, and in the fall would be attending Harvard Medical School. His deliberate speech cadence complemented his subtle wit and reminded us all of Spock. He could fix anything, and approached every chore without emotion but rather with guile and logic. He always had incredible pot, which when smoked put you into a short-term coma and then had you racing to the nearest doughnut shop to inhale two or three dozen varieties of fried dough.

JB lit a cigarette, avoiding the raindrops to do so. James did an awkward soft shoe while staring down at his feet. Secunda stood tall and straight, arms folded against his barrel chest. My gaze moved from one face to another, looking for clues to their respective thoughts. My heart was pounding. Not a word was spoken but everyone's eyes were sharp, alert, and smiling.

James spoke first. "If we're going to do this, then let's do this!" He grabbed his toolbox and a crowbar from the Land Rover. JB shrieked a laugh and followed with four huge flashlights while Secunda removed another two from the trunk of his Alpha.

"Let's start in the barn," James said, "and see what we have there."

JB suggested we move the cars. We were about to break in, which was obviously a crime, and she thought it best not to attract attention. She even suggested we call Barrows and get actual permission.

"Not happening," I said. "It will take too long and I want to do this before we're all too old to care."

"Fuck it," Secunda said. "The only one out on a day like today is Noah, and he can't get a warrant."

The rain came down harder.

James approached the front door of the old barn and surveyed his options for entry with a quick sweep of one of the flashlights. The three of us watched intently while he took something small from his toolbox and poked around for a few moments. The door popped open. James gathered up the remaining three lights and entered the building.

"Wait there," he barked. We huddled against the rain. Minutes passed.

"Okay, come on in," James instructed at last.

The inside of the theater was lit up like a movie premiere. James had taken a small generator from his toolbox and somehow connected it to the house lights, which now lit the entire building with an amber wash. *Wow! Pow* and *boom!*

We walked quietly through the building. I checked my emotions to try to keep things in perspective. JB shrieked a laugh and lit her next cigarette before the last went cold. Secunda climbed the steps to the stage and clapped his hands to check the acoustics. I thought that stupid but said nothing. He paced the stage, walked center and put his arms up with dual peace signs, hunched over like Nixon, and said, "I am not a crook."

James had wandered backstage and reported with enthusiasm on the fly space and the specifics of the system, telling us that it was more than we would ever need. JB shrieked from behind the back wall that the dressing rooms were really nice and then shouted that the scene shop off left was "far out."

I stayed near the back of the house and listened as my friends reported their discoveries. Secunda walked from the stage to an alcove house right and said with great conviction, "We can put the orchestra over here." James had begun a quick inventory of equipment and read off a yellow pad. "We have at least two hundred fifty lights, and I see three spots up in the balcony." JB reported with dismay that the restrooms were disgusting.

I sat in the third row center and motioned for my friends to join me. The seats were from an old movie palace, purple velour with ornate armrests and high wooden backs. There was no center aisle but rather one on each side of the house with plush purple runners that matched the seats. Everything was a bit worn, but nothing bordered on seedy. There was a "crystal" chandelier that hovered over the house; it was incongruous in an old barn, yet it added a certain elegance to the rustic room.

"Okay, what do you all think?" I asked.

"It's a fucking disaster!" Secunda said.

"Yes, that's true," JB replied, "but it could be *our* disaster."

"James, what about you?"

"It's perfect. It has just enough charm and just enough decay to make it attractive. It's a deluge out there and there is not a hint of water in here. The stage is solid. I also checked out the basement. There are enough props and furniture to do shows in an amphitheater. Big brother, you are an asshole."

"Whoa and whoa. I said it was a disaster but that's not necessarily a bad thing. I'm in full bore. Sammy, what do we need? Where do we stand?"

The side door of the building suddenly burst open. At first I thought it was the wind. Unfortunately I was wrong. Two police officers entered. They wore long, black slickers, highway patrol hats, carried drawn nightsticks, and led with deep angry scowls.

"What the hell is going on here?" asked the short, stocky one.

"Back up against the wall and let me see some ID!" demanded the other. His hand was perched on his pistol.

We did as they said. James was mellow, although I couldn't understand how. If they searched his car they'd find enough weed to send him up the river. Surely he'd miss medical school. Secunda was surly but obeyed. JB was insanely flirtatious, and to my surprise it was with the short, stocky cop rather than the taller one with blue eyes. I was polite and handed my driver's license to JB's newly intended. Eying his name tag I said, "Officer Donahue, sir, I have been working with Dr. Barrows this past week to reopen the theater this summer . . ."

"Barrows know you're here?"

"Well, not exactly, but I had a meeting with Mrs. Barrows Sunday evening to discuss the transaction and met with her yesterday to sign a letter of intent. In fact, the Barrows foundation is funding the whole project."

The tall, blue-eyed officer jumped in. "Listen, fella, the whole town knows about your meeting with Barrows's wife, and from what I heard it didn't seem like you was talking business. Now, you either have a right to access or you don't."

JB approached her beau, examining his name tag. "Officer Thomas Donahue, may I call you Tommy?" The cop nodded and slowly put away his nightstick. The blue-eyed cop had removed his hand from his gun. "You can call me JB if you like, or Joan if you'd prefer. Perhaps we should have gotten permission for access, but we haven't done anything except inspect the premises, and if you would give us a moment I'm sure Sam could get Mrs. Barrows on the phone." Her eyes batted at Tommy and he was now more than relaxed.

Blue-eyes remained a pit bull. "I'm certain Mrs. Barrows would be accommodating." He used the word to suggest something more. "She always is. Always. But as of now I have you for breaking and entering and I'm bringing you down to the station."

Even Tommy seemed taken aback by this news. Secunda jumped in. "Are you kidding me?" he said, his voice draped in sarcasm. "You have nothing better to do today than harass us because we're checking out an opportunity here in this town. Why don't you call Barrows before you book us? Better yet, drive over to his place and speak to him and his wife. You may find that you're looking pretty stupid after a wee bit of investigation. Maybe on the way over you can cuff some old lady for walking too slowly across the street."

"Shut up, Secunda!" I pleaded.

JB moseyed over to the man she was going to marry and said, "Officer Tommy, can't we settle this down a bit? We're not looking for any trouble. Just the opposite, we plan to be here all summer. You guys can come by anytime. Bring you wives and we'll leave you free tickets."

"I'm not married," Donahue said. "Neither is Officer Cutler."

"How terrific is that?" JB said, beaming. "Cute, single guys coming to the theater! What's your favorite show?"

"Officers," James said, "may I suggest something?" No one objected. "We are all staying at the Garden's Beach View down the road. In fact, Mr. August has been there for several days. If you have the station call perhaps that would prove we're well intentioned. We won't run way while you check into our story."

Cutler stared at me with surprise. "You know Veronica?" His question was imbued with distrust and a touch of "you lucky bastard."

"Yes, sir, I do. I think if you speak to her, she might even have some good things to say about me."

He shook his head as if to shake away any ill will. He was smiling now without reservation. "So you know Veronica Chapman and Lizzy Barrows. You poor, hopeless bastard. You'd be better off if I arrested you."

He chuckled, rechecked my ID, and offered me a bemused release. "Okay, Sam, I'm letting you go. But if I find out you're BS-ing me, I'll be by the motel quick as day. Now get your friends out of here. Tom and I will close up."

"Welcome to Plymouth," Secunda muttered under his breath.

James packed up the lights and other equipment. Secunda helped with contempt creased across his face. They walked to the cars.

"Officer Donahue," JB said, "my friend Josh is taking us all out to dinner tonight at eight o'clock at a place called Souza's. Is it nice?"

"Yeah, Souza's is great, ain't it, Walter?"

JB flashed him a smile. "Wonderful. Perhaps you'll join us tonight at eight. It would nice to see other friendly faces. Also, perhaps you could show me how to crack my lobster." She said this last line with a wink.

Officer Donahue nodded, his tongue practically hanging out. JB sauntered out, and I marveled how someone lacking in the A-list physical tools of flirtation could be so expert at it. I lingered a moment. "Thank you, officers," I said, and then with a slight bow I headed back out into the rain.

Cutler shouted after me, "Hey, August, Lizzy Barrows and Veronica Chapman—make sure you see them one at time and never in the same place. Safer yet, in different states! You poor, stupid son of a bitch."

The rain came down harder.

15

Secunda and I occupied a table at the Full Sail. We sat next to a window overlooking the ocean, which was finally inching toward calm. The rain continued but it was more of a mist now, and the gray sky that had blanketed the day showed specks of blue. The bar was practically empty. Just after four in the afternoon was not peak time at the local watering hole.

Doobie was behind the bar readying his station for the onset of the happy-hour rush. At the moment he had but a single customer. He sliced oranges, lemons, and limes, filled the cooler with myriad bottled beers, and opened endless jug wines all with the practiced hand of a master.

JB and James had headed out for reconnaissance. We had agreed to meet at Souza's in downtown Plymouth a few minutes before eight. In expectation of a luscious lobster dinner, we just drank beer. Secunda nursed his second brew while my first one was left untouched, both warm and flat.

After the officers Donahue and Cutler had freed us, Secunda suggested we do some research. We wanted to find out more about Barrows, see what all the tumult was about. What did Cutler mean when he said Lizzy and Veronica would be better off in different states? What did we need to know to make sure we got the building? We drove to the town hall and then to the local library.

As we drove to our respective destinations I brought Secunda up to date on the events of the past few days. I told him everything, including the tales of Lizzy Barrows's naked and Veronica's erratic behavior. He listened intently as we drove. "Women. You can't live with them and you can't shoot 'em," he said, making it sound both wise and original.

We discovered a great deal that afternoon. Barrows seemed to be in the papers quite often, and most of the depictions were unflattering. His wedding to the fabulous Lizzy was a gossip writer's dream. The stories about their May-December romance were plentiful and practically all unkind. The Barrows family had been an icon in Plymouth, credited with hundreds of good deeds over the years. But over the last few years the pendulum had begun to swing.

The trial of Eddie Chapman, Veronica's brother, was covered, in all its gory details. Lizzy Barrows had been a hostile witness. Sidney Sutter was credited with championing the young Chapman and financing his legal defense. Chapman was given a reduced sentence and with some good fortune could see the light of day pretty soon.

The most compelling discoveries were about the Priscilla Beach Theatre. The last two management teams that had rented from the Barrows Foundation had arrived with little fanfare and begun their seasons with good notices. Yet they had been forced to close before the calendar turned from August to September, without explanation. The only comments we could find were terse quotes from Barrows that spoke to his "disappointment and dismay" over "the dire financial mess" left in both situations.

Dusk had settled in. The bar had filled up and the conversations were animated and friendly. As we packed up our things for our rendezvous at Souza's, Doobie walked over to our table. He was a hulk; he had smoker's teeth and heavy skin. His voice was much higher than his bulk would suggest, making him sound a bit like Felix the Cat. After we made the appropriate introductions Doobie said, "Guys, I am here every night till after two. I know everything that goes on in this town. You talk to a lot of loose lips when you tend bar. You need something, you reach out. Anything, anytime."

He offered his hand and we shook. His grip was strong; I felt some of the small bones just below my wrist shatter and go numb.

"Don't be strangers. The drinks are on me, and don't leave a tip. I own the place."

16

Souza's was located in the heart of downtown Plymouth. The wharf was a concrete waterfront where blacktop abutted once-blue water marred by carelessly discarded trash. Although no longer pristine and shrouded in tourist tackiness, the wharf still had its appeal; its energy, history, and promise of excitement overcame the lack of picture-postcard perfect. Myriad visitors walked in couples, foursomes, or larger random groups that were liquored up, a moment away from some sort of scene. By eight o'clock the families had come and gone, and as the evening turned late the wharf became more Pottersville and less Bedford Falls. The crowd encompassed a full spectrum of patrons. There were young, pretty people. Girls with bouncing hair, fetching sun-kissed cleavage, and smiles that radiated joy. The young men who accompanied them were fit and buffed, with biceps that burst from their short-sleeve T-shirts. They were stylish with hair combed and sneakers that spoke of the day's trends. As they held hands or walked arm-in-arm with their girlfriends, an unconscious musical nod of their heads said, "I got it! Life is sweet."

Yet there were just as many overweight, middle-aged couples and groups of friends whose bellies were round and full, stretching their shirts to the point of distortion. The women who walked alone had gone to seed as well, strolling with big, expanded bottoms, waddling toward their next stop with no concern about how they'd look in a swimsuit when the summer heat arrived.

The wharf had the vibe of a seaside state fair, churning out a medley of scents: fried fish and crustaceans, beer, and funnel cakes fresh and sweet covered in powered sugar. It was a place that stayed open late and grew more festive and raucous with each passing hour.

Souza's was the size of a football field. It could have been an army mess hall or summer camp cafeteria. Dozens of family-style tables lined the utilitarian dining room. Ceiling fans whirled above and the sliding-glass doors opened to what had evolved into a perfect early-summer evening.

The family-owned restaurant boasted the finest lobsters on the Cape.

What it lacked in style it made up for in cleanliness and service. When you entered the place there was an enormous tank filled with hundreds of black lobsters, some so large they looked like they belonged on the set of a sci-fi movie. Souza's menu was limited, focusing on its specialties. They steamed, stuffed, and broiled lobsters, serving them with steamed clams, corn on the cob, and Indian pudding à la mode for desert, topped off with iced pitchers of beer that kept the patrons jocular and happy.

Secunda and I parked the car in the public lot about a quarter of a mile from the restaurant. From there it took us fifteen hard-fought minutes to work through the evening crowd. We arrived at our destination at eight sharp. There were fewer than ten empty tables; the other two hundred were all active and buzzing.

We quickly spotted James and JB. James was drinking beer and JB was smoking, her eyes looking furtively for the arrival of Officer Tom. I chatted with Secunda, who insisted on waiting up front to greet his date. I reminded him that he didn't know what she looked like, and he reminded me that he was an expert at sighting slutty girls.

I saw JB waving enthusiastically to Officer Donahue. He looked quite handsome in a pale-yellow cotton button-down, which he wore over faded Wranglers and finished off with white basketball high-tops. I imagined her having visions of what to wear on the day he was promoted to detective or on their wedding day as she patted the seat next to hers, inviting him to sit close by.

"Been here long?" I asked as I took a seat next to James.

"About a pitcher's worth," he said. He poured me a tall glass. "Catch up."

I drank thirstily, while thinking about what Veronica would be wearing tonight.

The events of the evening slowed. James and I nursed our beers and talked quietly. Secunda had approached a couple of women mistakenly thinking they might be Kellie. One rejected him with disturbing ferocity. I found myself thinking that we all had different opinions of what slutty might look like, as both the young women he approached appeared more chaste than wild to me.

At our table, JB and Officer Tom were engrossed in deep conversation, and the beer pitchers had been refilled. All the while Veronica remained MIA. It was now twenty minutes after eight.

Secunda walked over with our waitress in tow. Margie was in her early thirties and pleasant looking if just a tad Rubenesque. She had a big, easy smile and wore several studs in both ears. Her hair was piled on top of her head and held in place with a rhinestone-covered clip. Secunda had already won her affection with a $100 tip.

He sat next to me in a mild huff. "The last girl I talked to is entering a convent next month. The first one I approached was four months pregnant and looking for a husband."

He clapped his hands twice and asked for the attention of those at the table. After acknowledging Officer Tom he got up and walked over to him. With a touch of melodrama he embraced our afternoon nemesis, kissed him on both cheeks, and with eyes locked welcomed him to the festivities. JB shrieked with laughter. Tom, although nonplussed, laughed along and offered his thanks.

Secunda returned to his chair. He looked over to Margie and asked, "What is the house specialty?"

"Um, lobster," she replied with smiling sarcasm.

He was enjoying himself. "Okay then. Eight three-pounders and something larger for my friend over here." He pointed to me. "Start us off with some steamers and bring corn with the dinner. Eight shots of Patron, please, with lime and salt, and replenish the beer when you get a chance." Then he tipped her another C-note.

When Kellie arrived looking cuter than last night, she asked who Josh was. Secunda stood up gallantly and offered his hand.

"I'm Kellie, Veronica's friend. Sorry I'm late."

"Well worth the wait," Secunda said, offering her a seat next to his and introducing her to the table.

Margie brought the tequila and the appropriate accoutrements. She brought new frosted mugs and fresh pitchers of crisp, wheat-colored lager. Then smiling at Secunda, she returned to work.

Veronica arrived a few minutes later and waved an envelope in my face. "I'm late because this arrived just as I was leaving. It's scented. Here, smell it." She pushed the package closer to my face. "It appears to be from Mrs. Barrows. Maybe she dipped it in her whore-scented, cheap cologne to give you something to remember her by other than her being an easy, uninspired lay." She turned to Kellie. "What's the name of the perfume she wears, Bitch in Heat?"

She dropped the envelope onto the chair next to me and downed a shot of Patron. She sucked on a lime, pursed her lips, shook her mane of blond hair, and came up with a smile. "Hi, everyone." She acknowledged Officer Donahue with a familial "Tommy" and blew him a kiss across the table. She greeted Kellie with a hug and complimented her outfit. She stood and offered her hand to JB, James, and Secunda, adding a sincere "nice to meet you." She repeated the tequila routine again and suddenly her cheeks were rosy and all hint of dismay had vanished. I folded Lizzy Barrows's letter quickly to avoid any further complications and put it in my jeans pocket.

Secunda lifted his glass of Patron and toasted the table: "To new friends, to new adventures. May our get-together be the beginning of something special, something we can share with our children and their children as well." He took special note of Kellie on that last line and finished with, "L'chaim." We all drank.

Kellie was a sweet, virginal vision. Sexy, true, but if you told me she had never been kissed, I wouldn't have been surprised. I wondered what a slutty girl was supposed to look like. Then I again realized how stupid guys could be. If the stupid-guy club needed a leader I would be elected president in a landslide. I drank my beer and waited to see what would happen next.

Secunda was a terrific host. He got acquainted with Veronica and talked up JB to Officer Tom. He made sure everyone was enjoying the first part of the meal and kept the glasses topped off. Margie buzzed about attending to our needs. Veronica was friendly to everyone—except me. The Barrows note burned in my pocket, but I was afraid to open it before dinner.

Kellie, who had excused herself just minutes ago for reasons unknown, returned all smiles and yummy. As she sauntered back to the table I noticed how her top pushed her breasts up into what was the perfect position. Perhaps it was the tequila, but I thought if I ever developed man boobs I'd ask her where she bought that particular garment.

At her side was a very slender brunette with long, straight hair that reached her coccyx bone. She was pale and wore dark eye shadow and heavy eyeliner.

She had a long, lean figure that was extremely attractive if a bit bony for my tastes. She was early twenties, had dark, dark eyes and an easy grin. She wore cutoff denim that made the word "short" insufficient. A black T-shirt that read CAPE COD WHALERS was tied above her waist, showing her bare, taut midriff. On her feet she wore white high-tops and no socks.

Her smile suggested she'd had a couple of cocktails. She was open and friendly as Kellie made the social overtures. When it came time for James to be introduced, Kellie announced that Maggie, the brunette, was here as his date. Kellie couldn't imagine the evening "which was so much fun" continuing without James having someone on his arm. Maggie agreed and began chatting up James. I thought it sweet, yet wondered as I sized up Maggie whether she was really slutty. Then I decided my head would explode if I focused on the issue much more this evening.

Eventually, the table was littered with the remains of eight lobsters whose lives had ended. They died to please us, to sate our appetites, and to act as an aphrodisiac to four young couples. They had fought a good battle and lost. Perhaps they would be honored in lobster heaven. As for us, the evening was just starting.

After dinner I watched everyone at the table. JB was in an intermittent lip lock with our soon to be Boston detective. She was so enamored that she even allowed him to put out her last two cigarettes in the leftover desserts without protest. James and Maggie seemed connected in some cerebral way as they spoke in hushed tones. Kellie was affectionate with Secunda, all within the boundaries of decorum. I still wondered how to get past being just pals with Veronica, which at the moment remained the lost challenge of the evening.

As my gaze moved about the table and I watched the interface between our disparate groups, I was filled with pride. There was no division of class or background or cash reserve. We were all in, new friends high on the adrenaline of serendipitous, unexpected relationships. Then I walked to the end of the table, sat next to Veronica and put her hand in mine. I squeezed it gently and then stroked her hair. She held my hand tightly and rested her head on my shoulder.

Officer Tom refused to allow any of us to drive, so Secunda ordered a fleet of Garden cabs and we made our way down Rocky Hill Road. Our destination was the old barn theater that in essence had brought us all together.

17

The compound looked different under starlight and a clear sky. The dogwood petals were more vibrant, the lush green grass of the parking lot seemed ready to putt for a birdie, the big barn conjured images of theatergoers milling about on the deck discussing the evening's performance with great enthusiasm.

The cabs pulled into the driveway and came to a quick stop. We jumped out and stood in a circle coupled up and happy. James asked Tommy if he would mind if we broke in. Tommy paused to consider his answer. "Yes I will, but I'm going to be kissing JB over here and that might take a while. Check in with me again in a few days."

JB shrieked in approval. James grabbed his toolbox and Maggie's hand and headed toward the theater to "let us in." This time, if you blinked, you missed his sleight of hand. He turned the lights on and the amber wash in the house radiated romance; all we needed was some music to complete the mood. Secunda and Kellie pushed the piano onto the stage and she sat at the dusty out-of-tune upright and played the ivories. She was good.

While she played a bluesy bit of free-style jazz, we all stopped to take in the magic of the moment. Josh ran to his car and returned with his trumpet in hand. He played a short riff to capture our attention then began a sultry version of Ellington's "I Got It Bad and That Ain't Good." When Veronica asked me to dance, we found our way hand in hand to center stage and began a slow foxtrot that I hoped would never end. Maggie leaned into James's chest, and with arms wrapped around each other, they moved so slightly it was almost imperceptible. JB sat "fifth row center" next to Officer Tom; they held hands and beamed at the unscripted set of events playing out before them.

Ellington turned into Gershwin's "Embraceable You," and then, without a change of mood, Porter's "Love for Sale." Kellie played the melodies and Secunda jammed a loose yet perfect set of harmony and counterpoint. If you weren't in the room you wouldn't believe this was all happening. I held Veronica close and realized I had completely forgotten that the note from Lizzy Barrows remained unopened in my back pocket.

We left the theater and walked the hundred yards to the ocean. Large boulders were visible with each crashing wave, phosphorescent and glowing intermittently in the night. In the distance, the sea was so calm you could understand the old belief that the world was flat.

It was past two and an orange moon sat within reach just above the water. We had all been quiet for some time when Tommy suggested a late drink. We reclaimed our cab fleet and headed to the only bar open after hours. Within minutes we pulled up to the Moondog and I wondered if the magic of the evening would end inside this watering hole.

Veronica and I lingered as the group went in. She held me at arm's length and said, "I'm sorry about earlier tonight, and yesterday, and tomorrow. You aren't to blame for my being so flighty. I realize I'm acting like a tease and that's not right. I like you, so much really—in fact from the moment you walked in to the office I've thought about you constantly. And then last night we had so much fun, and again tonight.

"I see what goes on in your life. You make things go, people vie for your attention, you make them believe that anything is possible. I don't know anyone like you. Your friends adore you, and you can't fake that. Secunda would take a bullet for you. But even though I've known you for all of five minutes, I've made up all these bad roads we'll take if we get together.

"I've waited for what seems like forever to get out of Plymouth and start a new life. What's in it for us to fall for one another? A few weeks of summer fun and then a sad September goodbye? I want my new life to start with a clean slate with nothing holding me back. That makes me afraid of you. You'll break my heart and I'll pine for you when you do. I can't do that to myself. I have simply been through too much. My life is not here. It is down a new road and not with a boy who is just passing through."

I looked at her intently and thought how my parents got married two days after they met. A few days ago I had never heard of Veronica Chapman. Tonight I simply wanted to hold her hand and know her better, and she was closing the door on feelings that would linger long after she had gone. *Give it a breath, give it a chance*, I thought. *Don't say goodbye to something before you've finished saying hello.*

I ceased my inner monologue and spoke quietly to her. "You know, Veronica, when I was in school some of my friends and I would get together at the start of each semester to look at the incoming directory of freshman girls. We called it the 'pig book' because it had pictures of the frosh girls and their hometowns and such, and we would discuss who was a 'pig' and who was worth calling. Then we'd set out to get dates with anyone who well . . . measured up. We all thought it was pretty funny and clever on our part.

"But now after some of the life lessons you've unexpectedly and regrettably taught me, I realize that the pig in that whole equation was me. I've grown up as such a narcissist, and why? What have I done to merit that sort of self-indulgence? I said to my dad the other night that I want to learn to do the right thing in my life, but here I am a few days into being a grown-up and I feel like I'm on the verge of becoming an asshole and chasing you when you clearly don't want to be caught."

"I like that you called your dad for advice," she said quietly. "Being caught by you would be a blessing for any girl."

"Just two nights ago you told me that our lives were there for the taking and anything else would be a disappointment. Aren't you guilty of just that?"

"I'm guilty of a great deal more," she said sadly.

The night felt very still. I needed to take a deep breath, but there seemed to be no air in which to do so. "You know it's not about doing something, it's about doing the *right* something. I want to read Lizzy Barrows's letter to you."

I retrieved Lizzy's missive from my back pocket. From inside the bar we could hear Linda Ronstadt on the jukebox singing "When Will I Be Loved?" The breeze rustled the trees gently, and laughter from the bar found its way outside. The neon bar light blinked on and off, lighting Veronica's face intermittently in blue.

I opened the expensive, scented envelope. It smelled like Lizzy Barrows's silk robe, but I thought it best not to mention that. Inside was letterhead that read THE BARROWS FOUNDATION, DEDICATED TO THE ARTS AND HUMANITIES OF PLYMOUTH, MASSACHUSETTS, ESTABLISHED 1947. Neatly typed below that was the following:

Dear Mr. August:

The Barrows Foundation regrets to inform you that we have ordered a stop on the check issued to you on Saturday, May 14, 1976, in the amount of $50,000.

This action in no way should be construed as unwillingness on the Foundation's part to participate in your renting and operating the Priscilla Beach Theatre this summer. It is simply that the Board of Trustees has some additional concerns as to your funding, experience, and references. If you would be kind enough to attend a meeting with the trustees at 5:00 p.m. tomorrow, May 15, at my home, it is my sincere hope that we may resolve these issues.

Please call to confirm your attendance.

Thank you.
Mrs. Anderson Barrows, President
The Barrows Foundation

Attached to the letter was a small note card with the initials EJB embossed on top. In the cursive hand of the doctor's wife it read: *"Sam, don't fret about this. It will all work out. Come tomorrow and we will fix things. Then we can truly go and celebrate together. XOXOXO, Lizzy."*

"This is fucked up," I said. I returned the letter to its envelope and placed it in my jeans pocket. I gave the handwritten note to Veronica and asked her to keep it in a safe place, just in case.

"In case of what?" she asked.

"Just in case we need to find that fragrance. Bitch in Heat."

"I wish I could let you kiss me," she lamented.

"Well, there's something we agree upon."

She took my hand and said, "Let's go meet our friends."

I followed her into the Moondog.

18

The place was a cloud of smoke. The lighting was terrific if you had leprosy, a harelip, or your picture on the post office wall. There were no windows, so you could smell the sweat, alcohol, and heavy perfume. The bar had originally worn a Formica top with trimmed oxide chrome. There was a chalkboard menu on the wall listing the day's specials and a jukebox opposite the bar where Jagger was singing about his lack of satisfaction. The kitchen was tucked away on the left, the size of a small elevator cab. The cook was black and large and looked like he could probably double as the bouncer. There was a pool table on the right, which cost only a quarter to play. Quarters were lined up tableside indicating there were dibs on the next game.

One came to the Moondog for the diversity. There was a group of young women who could have been friends of Kellie or Maggie, and a bunch of muscular yet overweight fellas in their midforties. Several older women sat by the bar using their looks to persuade several buff guys into plying them with drinks. Someone was getting laid before morning.

We pulled two tables together and waited for a round of drinks that Tommy said were his treat. Jagger had stopped screeching and Sinatra was singing "Witchcraft." No one danced, but there was some toe tapping and some fingers snapped. I figured we could all have this last drink then call it a night. If I were a betting man I would have bet that no one would be sleeping alone when it was time for lights-out, except me and Veronica.

The door opened and a man, late twenties, tall and fit, walked in. On his arm was a striking woman with dark hair, a short skirt, and fuck-me pumps. She draped him like a mink stole, for she was indeed expensive and the real deal. They had clearly been drinking. It took all of a nanosecond to realize the woman was Lizzy Barrows.

Our table went silent. I knew her, as did Tommy, Kellie and Maggie knew of her and James and Secunda caught on quickly. Veronica not only knew who she was but was well acquainted with her history and effect on this small town.

Tommy leaned in and said, "Veronica, leave it alone. No need to start something." Secunda whispered that I might just want to say hello to Lizzie, "You know, for professional reasons."

I put my arm around Veronica. "What do you want to do?"

Lizzy and her date had caught sight of our group and were simply staring us all down, their eyes filled with unexplained contempt. John Sebastian sang "Daydream" on the juke. The irony was as heavy as the smoke that filled the room.

A few seconds passed yet it seemed like a very long time. I didn't breathe. Veronica's rage flashed across her face.

Mrs. Barrows's date shouted, "Veronica Chapman! Hey, how's your brother Eddie. Is he getting any sun these days? What's he up to? Oh, that's right, he's studying license-plate making at the community college." Then he laughed. John Sebastian had finished his song and no new tune had started up. The place began to get quiet.

Tommy stood up and said, "Gary, pipe down. This ain't happening tonight."

"Just being friendly, that's all!" Gary responded. His words were a bit slurred.

"Focus on your date, buddy, and leave us be."

"You saying that as a cop, or are you looking to stop me from asking a personal question of Veronica Chapman?"

"Shut up, Gary, or I'll lay you out because you deserve it for being an asshole, and then I'll cuff you because I can."

Lizzy Barrows pushed Gary away a few steps and turned him toward the bar. Tommy sat back down and the crowd began to collectively breathe again. But then she skewered me with her eyes and shouted, "So, Sam August, come down from Boston to pick up some local girls. Slumming are you? You seem to be good at it!" Then she turned back to the bar as if I wasn't in the room.

LITTLE DID I KNOW

Veronica stood up slowly. Secunda and I did as well. She walked over to Lizzy Barrows with a shot of Jack Daniels in her hand and stood directly behind her, so close that Barrows must have felt Veronica breathing on the back of her neck. After an eternity, Lizzy turned around. When she did, Veronica slapped her hard across her cheek. Then she threw the whiskey in her face and started back to our table.

Gary reached out harshly to grab Veronica and I stepped in his way. He hit me with a right-hand that just missed my eye and glanced off my ear.

"Son of a bitch," I exclaimed in pain.

Secunda stepped in the guy's face and shouted, "Enough!" Gary tried to hit Secunda with a right. Secunda easily ducked the punch and responded with two quick left jabs that landed perfectly, as did the right cross that followed. Gary crumpled to the floor as if shot.

Secunda picked up Gary's drink, downed it, and calmly said, "Good night, Mrs. Barrows. It was a pleasure meeting you."

He threw a C-note on the bar. "Thanks for the cocktails." Then he turned to all of us and said, "Let's go, guys."

19

We all found our way outside quickly. The neon bar sign blinked blue and washed us in an eerie, distorted light. We lingered outside, looking for comfort from one another. No one spoke for a while; I think we were all trying to take in everything that had just happened.

Then JB started to laugh quietly and within an instant we all started cackling. "Well, that certainly killed the buzz," she said, gasping for air. She went on to make fun of my feeble efforts to protect my companion while Veronica defended my lame gallantry.

Fatigue quickly settled in after a long night and Secunda suggested that he would put everyone up at the motel. Tommy said he had a shift in the

73

morning but would "tuck JB in" before he headed home. Maggie and Kellie had their hands intertwined with their dates, and Veronica held me tightly around the waist as though she was never going to see me again. *Wow*, I thought, *what a night. If they continue like this, I'll be old before I finish my youth.*

We piled into another fleet of waiting Garden cabs and headed back home to the motel. Veronica did spend the night with me. We said little and washed up. She put on a T-shirt of mine and I wore boxers to bed. I didn't sleep, but rather stared at the ceiling wondering what damage had been done to the young woman lying next to me and why it caused her to shut her heart on something with the potential for good. Wasn't fleeting joy better than none at all? As the sun rose I had yet to find an answer.

I stirred early. Veronica was in deep sleep. I grabbed the phone and sat on the deck just outside my room. I took out a list of questions I had compiled since my first meeting with Barrows on Saturday. Then I called the front desk and asked to be connected to a number in Manhattan.

Harold Feldman, Secunda's father, was in his office every morning by 6 a.m. making gobs of money as one of New York's most powerful litigators. His easy demeanor belied his reputation in court, where he was feared and respected; he seldom lost a case. He liked me and had given me an open invitation to free legal counsel.

Harold picked up his direct line almost before it rang and sounded genuinely pleased to hear from me. I immediately brought him up to speed, including the fight, the stopped $50,000 check, the charges against Eddie Chapman, and more. I mentioned Lizzy Barrows's aborted naked seduction, but left it G-rated. In response he offered quiet, measured, quality advice. He pointed out that I should put aside anything that distracted me from my goals until I accomplished my agenda. He also told me that I should avoid getting involved with the underbelly of a small town. I was to spend the summer there, nothing more.

He outlined all possible scenarios for the 5 p.m. appointment Mrs. Barrows had suggested. He stressed that I needed to separate the leasing of the property from the foundation's funding of the venture. Last, he offered to send an affiliate from his satellite office in Boston to attend the meeting. I took notes, thanked him, and hung up. I decided I'd let Secunda sleep in for as long as it took me to shower, at which point I was going to need him to join the fray.

Davey Molson was a third-year associate at Harold Feldman's Boston firm but looked like a poster boy for the FBI: tall and lean, wearing a power suit with a crisp white shirt and red silk tie. Clear skin, bright hazel eyes, and a clipped, confident cadence to his speech. He had a Clark Kent chin and the posture of a marine at attention.

Davey had attended Amherst where he was small-college All-American tailback, then gone on to Harvard Law School. From his demeanor, I got the impression that he intended to become the governor of Massachusetts by the end of the month and president of the United States shortly thereafter. However, on this Wednesday afternoon in May he was sharing a pizza with Secunda and me at the Kingston Sub Pizzeria, eight miles north of Plymouth on the east side of Route 3A.

Harold had briefed Davey that morning on everything. His plan was both specific and precise. We rehearsed it as if it were a scene from a courtroom drama. We ran it several times with Molson coaching us on probable questions. He drilled us continuously about projecting the proper attitude and respect and assured us we had the necessary documentation and credentials to force an arrangement for leasing the theater from the foundation. All the drama and intrigue of the past few days was of no import to our needs.

"Leave it alone," he urged. Then we ran it all again from the beginning.

20

The Barrows's driveway was littered with a Cadillac, a Lincoln Continental, and a new Mercedes sedan that suggested the importance and affluence of the Barrows trustees who waited for us inside. We arrived in Molson's red GTO convertible and Josh's Alpha. The Barrows Foundation may have had age and money on its side, but we had a cool muscle car and an Italian babe-mobile. Secunda wore a jet-black poplin suit and contrasting midnight-blue linen shirt buttoned to the neck. Along with these he had on black lizard cowboy boots and a scowl. I had sprung for a new, white button-down, which I wore with my jeans and a navy Paul Stuart sport coat that my dad bought me the weekend I left for college. I felt we exuded confidence as we rang the bell on the large, ornate door.

Inside, Dr. Barrows was wearing what I came to learn was his signature outfit: blue blazer, crisp white shirt, red ascot, and Gucci loafers. He offered his hand and ushered us into the living room. Lizzy sat on the sofa wearing a pale-blue business suit and white starched blouse. She stood up and greeted us as if last night had never happened. Her hair was pulled back in a French ponytail, and even though she wore flats her legs still rocked. We were introduced to the trustees. Mr. Vander and Mr. Jordon were cut from the same cloth. One had a thin mustache and the other . . . well I don't really remember. They were mid-to-late sixties and looked like their underwear was too tight. I felt the need to check my digits after we shook hands.

The third trustee was more interesting. Miss Susan Golden was a striking woman in her early forties. She wore black bolero pants and a gold linen blouse that screamed money. The outfit was designed to show her considerable assets without being overt, and it all worked beautifully. She wore her glossy auburn hair to her shoulders, her makeup was precise, and in her right hand she carried a tumbler of bourbon on ice. She was all attentive, alert, and flirtatious but somehow managed to come off as nonchalant at the same time. Her interest seemed to be in the sport of things and the presence of three handsome young men. Miss Golden would certainly vote for Mr. Molson when he ran for president.

We all stood in silence. The antique grandfather clock moved time forward slowly, each tick seemingly louder than the last. Lizzy was clearly practiced at the art of role-playing. Last night she was a drunken bar slut, this afternoon the elegant young bride of the town's most important citizen.

The clocked ticked yet again. It was precisely 5 p.m. Barrows invited us all to sit. Then he began. "Mr. August, thank you for coming this evening, and thank you for bringing your associates to clear up the misunderstanding that seems to have developed."

"What misunderstanding is that, doctor?" I asked.

He hesitated, then smiled at his wife. "It seems that although both Mrs. Barrows and I were most impressed with you when we met on Friday, it was quite clear that no formal arrangements were made and no term for the lease of the theater was consummated. Our enthusiasm for you and your budding organization remains high, but we do have certain responsibilities to appropriate due diligence."

My gaze had moved from the doctor to his young wife, who licked her glossed lips slowly with the verve of a predator.

The doctor continued. "Even if we can come to an agreement this evening as to a lease arrangement, there are issues as to your ability to provide the necessary fiscal requirements in order conclude the transaction."

"Dr. Barrows, sir, I meet all requirements to lease your building. You and Mrs. Barrows, the president of the foundation, encouraged me to believe the same—so much, in fact, that she signed the lease and issued me a check for fifty thousand dollars. She then stopped that check for no apparent reason, which is clearly a gesture of bad faith. As to my assuming the lease was acceptable, I took my lead from you and Mrs. Barrows. As you must know, I received a call from Mrs. Barrows following our initial meeting inviting me to join her that evening to discuss the theater. I paused for effect just like Davey and instructed. "Mrs. Barrows was extremely enthusiastic." I let that hang in the air and then continued. "In fact, I think the word 'enthusiastic' could not be more appropriate."

I had pronounced "enthusiastic" as if it had fourteen syllables, and the air was thick with subtext. Jordon and Vander looked grave, nodding ever so slightly. Their calm was not reassuring; it was all too practiced to be genuine. Secunda had not moved since he sat down, and Molson took what seemed like important notes and shuffled his files. Susan Golden had gotten up and topped off her glass of bourbon while probably wondering what Davey looked like with his shirt off.

"Dr. Barrows, sir, your wife explained to me that she was the president of the foundation and had full authority to enter into agreements on its behalf. Our reading of your by-laws reinforces her claim. Additionally, when I met with her she gave me a check drawn on the foundation's account, which I understand further enforces the commitment to my organization as the lessee."

All the while, Lizzy Barrows kept her cool exterior as if my remarks had no affect on her. The room fell silent. Were we done?

"Young man, enthusiasm is not enough to lease you one of America's most historic properties. You may think you have the ability and know-how to run a business of this size, but there are other groups vying for the use of the building. With all due respect, you are a callow youngster who can't move ahead without my foundation's financial support."

Lizzy moved to the doors in front of the deck, positioning herself as a distant observer. Even in business attire, she had the uncanny ability to subtlety promise deviant sex as a reward for her bidding.

"Dr. Barrows, I'm afraid I don't understand this sudden change of heart." My words were measured and respectful, but it was clear the exchange was no longer friendly.

Miss Golden chimed in. "Yes, Andy, tell Mr. August about the board's change of heart. I'm a trustee, my heart hasn't changed a bit. It has, however, began to beat a bit faster since these young men arrived." She offered a small, almost imperceptible bow toward Davey and went to refill her tumbler yet again.

Molson looked up from his papers, caught my gaze and nodded as if to say, "Now, Sam, throw a punch."

"Dr. Barrows, I am renting your building this summer." I let the statement sink in so it was clear that I was prepared to fight this out until I was declared the winner. "I have researched the requirements necessary to do so under your by-laws and I have brought counsel here to reinforce my position. We are delighted that Miss Golden is here, as she is listed in your charter as both a trustee and of counsel."

Susan Golden interjected. "I am counsel for the foundation. Until today, it was never interesting. I can't wait till Mr. Molson puts his cards on table, or whatever else he chooses to do, or put, on the table." Her voice was heavy with bourbon and it was clear she thought herself adorable.

Davey looked at her with decorum, although her body language lacked any, and conveyed simply , "Are we playing cards? I thought we were here to conclude a deal. Once that's finished we can play whatever you'd like, Miss Golden."

For the first time since I entered the house I heard the ocean below and the trees rustling in the evening breeze. I stepped back into the conversation.

"Dr. Barrows, sir, Mrs. Barrows, ma'am, Mr. Vander, Mr. Jordon, counselor—Joshua and I are only interested in delivering a wonderful product to your community this summer. With our talent and connections, the theater will be lit with excitement, help tourism, and provide jobs and revenue for your city. We will refurbish the place and bring it back to its former glory.

"As to references, I have three letters of the highest recommendation: one each from two of my senior professors at Tufts and one from the dean himself. As to character, I have brought more than a dozen letters from universities across the country inviting me to attend their schools—not only for my athletic ability but also for my possessing the highest character. Their words, not mine. Lastly, I have a stack of notices saying that my work as a director is more than good and deserves and merits a venue for those talents to mature."

Davey presented documentation of all of this. Barrows was more than annoyed. "That is all very fine young man, but you have no money and I have no intention of giving you any. Any tenant must show unencumbered funds in the amount of fifty thousand dollars, as well as sufficient security for any lease to be valid. Therefore, and with pleasure, I must vigorously rebuff your intent. You will have to find some other place to spend your summer vacation."

I put up a hand. "Okay, Dr. Barrows. Indulge me for one last moment. Your foundation is reneging on your president's commitment to me of fifty thousand dollars?"

"Yes."

"Other than my fiscal shortcomings, you and your trustees think I am a worthy tenant and would agree to me as the lessee if I could make rent and provide security by end of business tomorrow?"

He looked about the room. His cronies Vander and Jordon looked pleased, as if they were bank examiners in a Capra film. Lizzy stood unscathed, while Susan Golden acted as if the music had stopped in a game of musical chairs and she had no place left to sit. I said nothing and stared at my faded sneakers.

"I have money, sir," Secunda said. "According to your by-laws, if someone provides ten percent of the needed cash obligations then they will have seventy-two hours in which to meet the final obligations. I am, as they say in the theater Mr. August's angel. Davey here has a copy of my bank statement showing a balance well in excess of twenty thousand dollars, as well as an affidavit prepared by Mr. Molson that I will hypothecate these monies to any business entity that executes a lease on the property. The balance will be provided as per the by-law demands. Additionally, I have a cashier's check made out to the foundation for twenty-five thousand dollars, which will be held in my attorney's escrow as security to cover initial working capital, any unpaid bills, or any damages that may occur. This amount exceeds those requested in your own by-laws."

Barrows was stunned. I wondered if his next question might be, "Who stole the strawberries?"

I continued at breakneck speed. "I must remind you all that the president of your board solicited me, enthusiastically, and urged me to execute your lease. She then presented me with a check, which was stopped for no apparent reason, although I would be more than happy to sort out Mrs. Barrows's intent."

It didn't appear that anyone wanted to engage in such a dialogue. Davey smiled behind his eyes and without actually saying it, conveyed "you are on a roll, boy."

"It is not my intent to cause conflict or embarrassment to the Barrows Foundation. Rather it is to honor *my* purpose, the one that set all this in enthusiastic motion. I wish simply to make the theater soar and to recapture its past glory. In my opinion, you'll be lucky to have me as a tenant and member of your community."

I looked around the room. Mr. Vander and Mr. Jordon looked as if they were in the early stages of coma. Perhaps drooling was next. Miss Golden looked flushed and titillated. The good doctor was clearly upset, but restrainedly so.

Within moments his agitation increased. He spoke slowly and quietly, but then his words rushed out of control. "Yes, I understand. Everyone here has the best of intentions. But I am an older man. I have lived a life that you all should envy and I am not used to being challenged! Remember you are dealing with the Barrows Foundation! I am not to be played or pushed into a position that I don't embrace. I will not tolerate being played. I run this town!

"You young people, including my wife, have a sense of entitlement that makes me wonder where our youth is headed. What have any of you done or accomplished? Who are you? The young! You all want to go to heaven, but none of you wants to die. No sacrifices. No getting down in the trenches and seeing something through. You have embarrassed me in my own home. You have suggested improprieties that are infused with disrespect and condescension. You . . ."

Then he stopped, breathed deeply, pulled the pocket square from his coat and slowly wiped his mouth. After this, he folded the square precisely and returned it to its place.

There was stunned silence. *What the fuck?* I thought. *And they say that show business people are crazy?*

Finally I spoke. "I mean you no disrespect, sir. Respect is earned. It is not showered upon you because of seniority. Trust me, I respect and admire what you have accomplished in your life. True respect begins with the strength of one's character, not with the number of years one stays in the game. Age and experience do earn one certain privilege. Those privileges do not include judging me without merit.

"You don't know me or where I came from or what makes me get up in the morning or what is in my heart or if I am a man of courage or substance. You can make those judgments after you have observed me and grown to know me. Then I will honor your opinion. Our respective ages have no relevance in this regard. You'll have the balance of your funds within the given time frame."

After a moment, Susan stood and walked slowly across the room and put her hand on Barrows's shoulder. Whether it was to gain her balance or show compassion, I wasn't sure. "Andy, stop this. Pull yourself together. They are not responsible for your situation nor for the world turning. Give these boys what they want and let it go. Don't impose your issues where they don't belong." She refilled her glass yet again and took a seat next to Davey.

Secunda got out of his chair and walked to a large chess set that sat near the alcove window overlooking the sea. It was one of those sets with two different teams instead of lookalike black-and-white pieces. This one, painted in brilliant detail, was of sailors from different ships, truly a work of art. Secunda picked up one of the kings, the captain of the blue sailors. He eyed it for a moment and dropped it on its side, disturbing the placement of the other pieces. Then with more than a touch of irony he looked directly at Barrows. "Checkmate."

Barrows sat motionless, as if he had to okay pulling life support from a family member. He raised his head slightly and said, "Okay, boys. You deliver in seventy-two hours and I will 'welcome' you to Plymouth." Then in a child-like whisper he added, "But don't look to me for help as I won't answer such a call."

There was little else to say.

Lizzy Barrows hugged herself and looked out the glass doors and away from the room. Davey packed up. We attempted respectful goodbyes to all and left. To my surprise, Barrows caught up with me just as I was getting in the red Alpha.

"Sam, what happened between you and my wife?" he demanded. His eyes were penetrating and full of rage. "You stay away from her. You stay away from my girls. No more, do you hear me?"

"If you want to know anything, doctor, I suggest you ask your wife or 'your girls,' whoever they may be," I said as I pulled my arm away. Then I offered to shake his hand, which he declined.

I hopped into the waiting car. Davey pulled the GTO out of the driveway, heading south; Secunda followed. Seventy-two hours seemed like a short breath in a fast race. In less than a minute I realized the Mercedes sedan that had been in Barrows's driveway was dogging us. Behind the wheel was Susan Golden, counselor at law.

2 1

I was surprised and vexed by what had just happened. Then I remembered something my father had always told me: "Once you have made a choice in life, that choice begins to make you." Of course I was happy. My friends and I had gotten exactly what we wanted, at least for three days. Yet at what cost? I had been in Plymouth for a week and the body count of adversaries was already quite high. I had heeded Harold's advice, focused on our objectives, and achieved them. But I wondered about personal responsibility. I had unexpectedly become aware of some strange doings in America's hometown: a cognizance of an underbelly of corruption, perhaps intimidation—at the very least something "off." To ignore it seemed a continuation of some deep-rooted narcissism, which was not the person I wanted to be.

My dad had assured me that "I would do the right thing" and perhaps I had, but perhaps not. He had also said I had to "play the whole game." As of the moment I felt I was winning. I played football for many years and in turn I knew there were still many plays left in their playbook. So I suggested quietly that we head back to the motel and reconnoiter. We had no other choice but to win the game.

Secunda had just put up $45,000 on my behalf without even telling me that was his intention. I don't think I'd ever had more than $1,000 to my name; I'd worked my ass off during the past four years to pay for my education—at $6,000 per year, a daunting task. Yet another of my father's mottos was, "If you plan to play in a big casino, make sure you can cover your bet." Was Josh's $45,000 the ante? Were we all in for the next $30,000, which we didn't have?

Secunda looked over at me. "Hey, smiley, who died? Someone crap in your hat?"

"Blow me," I countered. Then I turned to him with a big fake ear-to-ear grin. "Man, you just put up 45K for me. Big-time risk. You know you didn't have to do that."

"It's not about having to do anything. Sometimes the difference between having and needing is blurred. Not this time, Sammy. We all need purpose in our life. Hell, I've been in college for six fucking years. If I hadn't jumped on your dream, the chances of me finding my own would be decreasing exponentially by the day."

Secunda pulled the car onto the shoulder of the road and turned off the engine. "Sammy, enjoy the moment, at least for a while. You'll have plenty of time to worry and a fuckload of burdens to bear. If you want, we can stop and buy you a big globe, and you can carry it on your back all day every day. But for now, smile, you bastard, and grab the brass ring you're always talking about. Otherwise, I'm taking you down."

He started the car again and pulled back onto the highway. The sun was resplendent as ever. Man, God was consistent when it came to painting pictures. Josh turned on the tape player and pushed play; the cast of *Annie Get Your Gun* belted "There's No Business Like Show Business." I knew there were accidents in life, but this song at this moment was not one of them. Secunda knew how to play a scene.

No business like show business, huh? Well, I was about to find out. Then I remembered that Irving Berlin wrote that song in fifteen minutes. I had three whole days. *Piece of cake,* I thought. At that point I asked Secunda to pull over again. I opened the passenger door and threw up.

2 2

It was Monday, 6 p.m. You give someone seventy-two hours and they will use all of that time, to the very last minute, to get the job done. Not me. Not with so much at stake.

I locked myself in the pay phone at the motel with enough change to anchor an ocean liner and pulled out a clean, yellow legal pad. I wrote down whatever names came to mind: family, friends, roommates' parents, guys I played ball with, and guys whose names I didn't even know how to spell. By the time I was finished there were 137 names on my list. There had to be $30,000 in gold there.

I leaned back and took a deep breath. It would take guts to call some of these people. In some cases it had been years since we spoke. Some carried broken hearts or animus. But it mattered not. I picked up the phone and dialed my first lead. Then my second, third, fourteenth, and more. Within four hours I had finished more than half the names on the yellow pad. I had raised some money; more than I might have imagined.

My first calls were fruitless. Old "friends" who thought my idea was folly but did offer to buy tickets if they were in the area. My first success was an associate of my father's who had become a family friend, Marty Miller. He had been a ranger during the war, one of those insane soldiers who would scale mountains, kill the enemy, then grab a smoke before the next raid. He still spoke with a clipped cadence as if ready to begin his next suicide mission before finishing his cigarette.

"Marty, I believe in this. It's what I am meant to do. Will you support me with an investment?"

"I'll send you five hundred dollars," he said without hesitation. "Now give me the address, send me some paperwork, and make me proud." He hung up before I could say thank you.

I now tardily realized that taking in this money would require some documentation; $30,000 was a boatload of dough. I called Harold Feldman. As always, he was friendly and supportive. He explained that the funds would have to be in the form of a loan, as there would be securities violations otherwise. I was silent for a long time. "Does that mean I have to pay the money back?" I asked, afraid of the answer.

"Do you believe in this venture?"

"Yes, Mr. Feldman, I do."

"I'll prepare a simple agreement and mail it tomorrow. It will also include a check for $1,500 dollars."

"Thank you, sir." I hung up feeling quite blessed.

I called Jack Kennedy whose sons both played football with me. Jack was connected to the disappearance of Jimmy Hoffa, and the call and request made me nervous.

"You don't want to borrow money from *me*," he said. "Missed paybacks are tough in my world."

"I know, sir. I thought about that before calling, but you have always been so kind to me."

"You played ball with my boys, son. That's different than borrowing money from the teamsters."

"Nevertheless, sir, I need the help."

"How much?"

"I need a total of about 25K."

"You have guts, August. I'll send off a check for 5K. No paperwork, just your word." He hung up. My heart beat faster than a jack rabbit running from danger.

That brought up the tally—and obligations up my ass. It was past nine, really too late to call anyone else until morning, but as I was on a roll. I found one more number I thought offered promise. Hank Watertower was my college roommate's dad, and he always wore a smile and carried loads of cash. He'd come up every six weeks or so and take six or seven guys to dinner at the famous Anthony's Pier Four. We'd eat lobsters and tell stories of university life, talk of girls, and imagine the futures we all had planned. Mr. Watertower had made a small fortune by inventing a home yogurt maker and thought his success was all rather serendipitous and silly.

Hank picked up on the first ring and seemed agitated. When I asked if it was a bad time he gave me a terse "no" and an unfriendly, "What is it, Sam?"

I gave him the spiel and he was silent throughout.

"I like you. You were a good friend to my son in school, but this is not an investment. This is a loan I'll never see. I'm not happy you called me on this, and don't do it again unless it's something real."

"We all have to start somewhere, sir." I said. "Obviously I caught you at a bad time. I'm sorry, sir."

"Character wins, son, and you have that," he said with a tinge of a smile in his voice. "I'll send you five hundred dollars, but don't fuck up."

"I won't, sir. I assure you I won't."

"Goodbye then, Sam, and good luck."

I was spent. I headed over to the Full Sail and ordered a shot of Jim Beam, which calmed my nerves. Then I had another shot. As I headed off to bed, I decided to throw the heavy line tomorrow and reel in a whale. I had no idea who that whale was or what my bait would be.

23

By seven-thirty the next morning, I was back in my phone booth office sipping a coffee laced with heavy cream and seven sugars. It was the only thing sweet about the morning. The sky was gray and promised a cold rain within the hour. Although I had made progress the night before, I felt to some degree that I had a pair of twos and was still throwing markers into the pot.

I began the day with some safe calls—cousins, aunts and uncles, parental friends—asking for amounts that would be hard to reject. This was fruitful and empowered me to reach for another big prize.

One of the finest men I met while at school was a Mr. Tucker Holly. He lived in Boston where he ran a fourth-generation family banking business. His daughter Mary attended Tufts and appeared gracefully in some of our shows. She was elegant like her dad: tall, lean, and attractive. I called Holly and was put directly through to his office. He was in an early meeting, but his secretary told me he could see me in an hour and a half; he had a small window so I shouldn't be late.

I ran to take a quick shower and put on khaki slacks, a clean, white T-shirt, and my blue blazer. I pulled the Mustang onto to the highway moments later and drove as if chased by enemy agents. I arrived at Holly's State Street office with just minutes to spare.

His assistant, Samantha, offered me coffee and showed me into a conference room large enough to kick a field goal. Moments later Holly arrived, looking presidential in an expensive blue suit, red power tie, and buffed, black wingtips. His well-cropped gray hair was parted neatly on the side.

I told him of my predicament and he was clearly amused by my chutzpah. He asked in a strictly business manner if I understood that whatever money he chose to give me was an obligation of mine to repay and that it was a gentlemen's arrangement he would never call to collect. However, if I failed him I should never come calling again.

I looked him in the eye and answered with a firm and confident, "Yes, sir."

He excused himself for a minute and returned promptly. "I don't mean to be rude, Sam but I have a meeting on Federal Street." He handed me an envelope and added, "This is the best I can do, son. Good luck."

I sat in the regal conference room for some time, afraid to open the envelope. Samantha brought me more coffee and I finally steeled myself to look. Inside was a check for $10,000! They were the prettiest four zeros I had ever seen.

Despite my good fortune, the weather that Tuesday night failed to reflect my mood. A persistent, chilled precipitation hadn't let up all day, and my phone booth office was an inch deep in water. Veronica made friendly visits offering encouragement and coffee. Each time she came by I wanted to talk to her, to try to edge closer. However, I had a mission to accomplish, so I left those thoughts for another day. I had $19,000 in commitments and twenty-four hours until checkmate.

I was tired. Even good news and good people like Mr. Holly cause fatigue. The calls I made now lacked a certain zip, and the results matched. By nine o'clock I had raised $300, but it had been a hard go and I'd become dispirited. I was ready to pack it in and head for the bottom of a shot glass when a name came to mind that wasn't on the list.

I dropped a nickel in the slot, asked for directory assistance in Los Angeles, and requested the number for an Irving Podrake. Irving was a distant relative. He had left the shtetl and the pogroms before he was a teenager. He had found his way to Southern California and a series of menial jobs that come without an education or family. Irving moved on to real estate management, then ownership, and then great wealth. I had been sent to visit him when I was about thirteen and had spent a week in his astounding Beverly Hills home.

Irving was tan, tall, and dapper. He drove a Bentley and had a beautiful, younger third wife. Still, for the week I was with him I sensed intense loneliness, and he treated me like a surrogate son while I was there. We went to a Dodger game and Disneyland on a VIP pass, and he took me shopping. When it was time for me to head back east, he offered me a big check to pay for college, but I refused, thinking the size of the gift inappropriate.

Christina, Mrs. Podrake, answered my call. She was friendly and even curious about how I had been and what I was doing "now that I was truly a young man." She mentioned that Irving had always liked me and he remembered the time I had spent with them fondly. That's when she informed me that Irving had died more than two years ago. I offered far-too-tardy condolences and she asked me why I had called. Though I felt awkward doing so, I explained. She told me Irving would have wanted to help; she would send me $3,000. I found the entire experience humbling.

At 6 a.m. on Wednesday, I sat in the Garden Diner and assessed my situation while drinking my usual concoction of coffee, cream, and heart-disease quantities of sugar. I read the sports page. There had been a triple play in the Angel-Indian game, which I took as a good omen. Unusual events on the diamond tended to lead to good things in life. Still, with only eleven names left on my list, it was difficult to see how I wasn't going to come up way short.

I drank a fourth cup of java and flirted with Eleanor, a married waitress in her thirties who was a lifer at the Garden Diner. I had a desire for ice cream, so I ordered some. Despite the early hour, Eleanor brought me a double scoop of vanilla, and as I ate an idea took shape in my crowded brain.

Garden's Ice Cream Shoppe was just down the road and I was there in minutes. The place was a mere shack established in 1912, but it was as much a part of Plymouth as the *Mayflower* and the Rock. Other than the Barrows, the Garden family was the most powerful in town.

I sat in the Mustang with my yellow pad and started to run some numbers. If we sold every seat in the Priscilla Beach Theatre this summer, it would result in forty thousand drives by the ice cream stand. To be more conservative, I assumed only 50 percent capacity and that half those people would have bought ice cream even if they weren't going to a show. I felt it reasonable to project that the theater would generate about seven thousand cones or, even better, more expensive shakes and sundaes. Additionally, the fifty staff members PBT employed would find their way to the old Shoppe throughout the summer, as well as their families when they came to visit. Therefore, if Garden gave me the remaining money I needed, he would be ahead of the game. I thought this was so creative and brilliant, I couldn't imagine it not working. I spent some time writing it all up with charts and calculations. At three I met with Papa Garden.

He held court in a small office behind a cluttered desk. He was huge, with ragged hair, snaggled teeth, and a tough, raspy voice. But he appeared friendly and he shook my hand while looking me directly in the eye. He offered me a seat and asked why I had come to see him. I told him the whole story, from Tufts to Barrows to my emergency search for funds. I showed him my charts and he responded with a grin that grew quickly into a belly laugh.

I sat bewildered, wondering if he thought I a fool or a visionary.

"You make that shit up, kiddo? Do you actually believe it?"

"Yes, I think it's viable. You'll sell more ice cream if you take my deal."

He nodded slowly. "You want coffee? A shake? Burger?"

"No thank you, Mr. Garden."

"Call me Papa."

"Still no thank you, Papa."

"Anything?"

"I want you to lend me seven thousand dollars and take my deal."

Again he grinned and it turned to laughter.

"You are quite a kid, kiddo."

"Yes, sir. I am that, sir."

He reached into his desk drawer and pulled out a checkbook. My heart was racing.

"How much?" he asked.

"Seven thousand three hundred and forty-one dollars."

He wrote the check and handed it to me. "Do me four things, kid."

"Anything, sir."

"Don't tell anyone I did this, put on some good shows, pay me back, and on the way out try the orange pineapple. It's new."

"Consider it done, sir."

I shook his huge mitt and walked out into the midday sun, which I was sure was shinning just for me.

Wednesday night around seven, I met the group back at the hotel. We were giddy with excitement as we tallied our booty. The checks had all arrived overnight through a new service called Federal Express that actually delivered packages overnight—what a crazy idea, huh?

I had raised $31,700. We were in business. However, within seconds our unbridled elation was shot dead by something Secunda pointed out: the checks would take days to clear and our deal with the Barrows Foundation was for certified funds or cash. The whole episode had been a charade. We were done.

I looked at a room full of long faces. "We will reconnoiter here tomorrow at ten a.m.," I said. "We'll figure something out."

Then everyone left to go shoot themselves.

At 9:45 the next morning there was a loud knock on my door. It was Sidney, Veronica's uncle from the White Cliffs.

"How big are your balls?" he asked, entering the room without invitation.

"My balls?"

"Yeah, your testicles, your balls. *Guts,* my boy."

"I'm proud to say my testicles are very large."

"Good, then follow me. We still have time to find your rabbit."

I followed Sidney's old Buick as it weaved down a dirt road heading east toward the ocean. He was tearing it out at full throttle and the dust was overwhelming. Minutes later we pulled up to a stone house that verged on being a mansion. Sitting in front was a late-sixties, black Cadillac convertible, a late-model red Corvette, and a wagon of some sort with tinted windows that prevented you from seeing inside. We got out of our cars and were greeted by a guy named Chance. I figured he was serving as a bodyguard here but that his regular job was the offensive line for the Boston Patriots.

Chance spoke briefly with Sidney and then he told us to wait. Within moments, a fortyish tough guy came out and asked what we wanted.

"The kid has almost thirty-two thousand dollars in checks. What's the vig on giving him 30K cash on what he's got?"

The tough guy ran numbers in his head. "These checks are good?"

"Yeah. You got me if they turn rubber."

"Okay, then thirty-two thousand five hundred."

My heart sank, a feeling that was becoming tiresome.

"Deal," Sidney responded quickly. He took my $31,700 in checks then reached into his pocket and counted out eight crisp hundred-dollar bills. Chance went inside with my checks and Sidney's cash. Ten minutes later, he returned carrying a beat-up duffle.

"There's 30K in cash in there," the tough guy said. "I don't care what you use it for. Your checks bounce, I come after you, which I don't want to have to do. Let's just be friends, it's better that way. The name is Colon, Johnny Colon." Incongruously, he offered me a handshake and a smile. "Nice doing business with you, kid. Good luck."

As we drove away toward Barrows to deliver the gelt, it hit me hard and true: I was officially in the theater business.

24

I moved into the red house at the theater compound the following morning. Davey had arranged for Susan Golden to deliver all the keys and appropriate paperwork on our lease. Most importantly, she promised the power would be on so we could find our light, which was very important to stage work. We had paid up with time to spare, so from now through September 15, PBT was our new home.

Susan said she'd meet everyone there at 9 a.m. As I pulled into the driveway fifteen minutes early, she was already holding court with my posse. They were all sitting around the redwood picnic table enjoying the breakfast goodies she had brought, seemingly as a gesture of goodwill. There were fresh muffins, warm croissants, fresh OJ, and enough pastries to give a diabetic a seizure. She was also pouring expensive champagne in honor of the occasion.

Susan wore her auburn hair in a straight ponytail with a trace of makeup. She had on a backless sundress that fit her body beautifully, but was more appropriate for a much younger woman. Nevertheless, her bones were clearly worth jumping, and perhaps Davey had had the privilege last night.

We toasted, and she wished us all well. "Anything you guys need, don't hesitate to call." Then she bade farewell with quick hugs, kisses on the cheeks, and an occasional formal handshake. Not one of us missed that she lingered a while when saying goodbye to Davey and that her hand spent a great deal of familial time on his butt.

When she left, James lit a joint and passed it around, as if we all weren't high enough. "This is to set the mood," he said. "Listen up."

James had rigged two enormous speakers and mounted them on the ice-house office. He moved dramatically to an extension cord that ran from inside the office to the compound, and with a flourish married the speakers to the outlet. Music filled the morning air. The decibel level made the buildings shake, and chased flocks of birds out of the tall grass and from under the eaves of the two large houses that skirted the compound. It was the overture from *Man of La Mancha*. This was lyrical, powerful music, filled with hope and promise. It was quintessential show music, and as we passed around James's pot we all got goose bumps. He pumped the volume even higher, and the orchestra finished with a rousing version of "The Impossible Dream." We giggled, laughed, and sang along with outsized enthusiasm. Several of us were off key, but it all sounded just perfect to me.

JB then got us to work. She pulled out several yellow legal pads that listed everyone's assignments and started barking out orders.

There was so much to do. The houses were a disaster. They needed cleaning and a boatload of paint. The plumbing and heating seemed fine, but there were roaches and dead rodents; JB said she'd prefer to pee in her pants than use any of the toilets. We needed beds, dressers, and kitchen fixtures. The ovens worked, but they emitted an odor that reeked of death. She said that while inspecting the red house she'd found it difficult to breathe. She was not alarmed, but thought the walls were either filled with angry ghosts or animals, perhaps skunks or a large community of raccoons.

JB had a list of vendors, starting with the gas company for the hot water heaters and cleaning supplies. She was calling in troops from Boston tomorrow to assist with the cleanup, including actresses who'd be with us for the summer, production staff, and friends who simply wanted to help the cause. She told Secunda and me to go to Boston and assemble our tech staff with Bryan Duncan. He was going to design sets and lights, and Mike Kasen was going to act as the resident technical director making sure things were built on time and that everything worked properly. Mary Holly was going do the costumes, which was a double win for us. Mary was an occasional girlfriend of Secunda, which kept things interesting, but most important to me was that she could really sing; she would play all the ingenue roles throughout the season. JB had arranged for audition announcements to be distributed at every college and university within a hundred miles of Boston and set up free audition space with Tufts.

My musical director, the fabulous Dr. Rosenstein, my choreographer, the leggy Ellie Foster, and the best stage manager on the planet, Jojo Backman, were all eager to begin. Knowing they were my foundation would allow me to sleep at night. It was like having an outfield of Mickey, Willie, and the Duke.

JB informed us that James was here to do his thing, which included pirating UHF stations (so all the Trekkies could watch endless adventures of the *Starship Enterprise*), setting up music throughout the compound, overseeing our phone systems, and relighting the marquee. With extra glee in her voice she told me she had a plan to get the perfect press agent. The guy worked in New York, and she and I were headed there on Sunday night. Josh was going with us to meet a guy in the Bronx by the name of Louis Rosenberg who played a mean trombone and was all set to contract our pit players for the right price.

JB was going to work with Doobie at the Full Sail and Tommy to find us a crew to do some of the work, and since we needed a cook to feed everyone, she thought she would check in with Ma.

When JB finished at last, we all sat for a moment thinking of the scope of what we were about to do. James passed around another joint then blasted Ethel Merman through the sound system singing "Everything's Coming Up Roses" from *Gypsy*. We listened and believed her. Even Secunda got up and danced.

25

Tufts University was founded in 1852 by Charles Tufts. Women were invited to attend beginning in 1892, when Jackson College for girls opened and became part of the university family. Mr. Tufts donated the land, a parcel known as Walnut Hill, as the site for the original campus. The hill was the highest point in Medford, Massachusetts; from the school one had an unobstructed view of Boston a scant five miles away. Charles Tufts nicknamed the college "the hill of light" and scripted its motto "Peace and Light."

P. T. Barnum, the circus showman, was a great benefactor of the university, and his name fronts many important buildings there. In fact, the school mascot is Jumbo the elephant, which of course was the face of his world-renowned three-ring extravaganza. Unfortunately, in 1888 a campus fire burned the Barnum museum to the ground, destroying all the memorabilia he had gifted the school. Even the famous stuffed Jumbo was lost in the blaze. Nevertheless, Barnum's legacy remains; Jumbo was recreated by a hardworking taxidermist, and Tufts continues on as one of the most prestigious institutions of higher learning in the land. More important for me and many of my classmates, Tufts had the best looking coeds in the nation.

I was admitted to Tufts on a fluke. Through happenstance and serendipity, I received an audience with the dean of admissions and literally talked my way into acceptance. One moment I was a former high school athlete in limbo, the next a "Jumbo." I convinced Dean Palmer that I would make a difference if he admitted me, and I am proud to say I did. Now, four years after my audience with the dean, I was back at school, this time in the bowels of Cohen Auditorium, auditioning what seemed to be the complete student bodies of the major universities and professional schools that gave character to the great city of Boston.

JB had arranged for the use of several studios in the basement of the antiquated building. The hallways were backed up with dancers in tight leotards who stretched endlessly, catlike and alluring, as they prepared for their sixteen bars. When I took short breaks to get some fresh air, I'd walk through the sea of long legs and cleavage and think how much I loved show business. There were also singers waiting their turn. They sang scales to ready their voices or snippets of the show tunes they were going to audition with. Meanwhile, young actors were speaking passionately and with the greatest of animation to imagined persons. It was all a bit unnerving.

I always loved auditions. The room was filled with hope and the belief that the next person to try out would be terrific, life changing, or electric. I felt a bit like Tom Greenwade, the scout who discovered a sixteen-year-old Mickey Mantle streaking effortlessly across an Oklahoma ball field. However, not all precious stones dazzle upon first look; it was our job to find coal and transform it into diamond.

I also enjoyed the attention. I liked commanding the room, making acting suggestions or adjustments to the readings, flirting with the pretty dancers, or asking what seemed to be innocuous questions to get a sense of someone's personality or sense of humor. I marveled at the talent of some and wondered how so many people thought they had any talent at all. *Find something else to do*, I often thought. Then I considered the comment made about Fred Astaire's first screen test: "Balding, weak voice, dances a little." *Shut up and give everyone in the room the benefit of the doubt.* So each time the door opened and a fresh face walked in, I offered a welcoming smile and asked, "Hello, Mr. Mantle, what are you going to sing for us today?"

In the studio with me were the best of Boston's graduating artists. At the piano was our musical director, Dr. Elliot Rosenstein. Elliot was not yet an MD but he was on his way. If it weren't for medicine, he would have been working on Broadway as a conductor of all the great musicals. When he was six years old, his parents took him to see *The Music Man* on Broadway; when they returned home Elliot sat at the family piano and played the entire score.

The "doctor" was the most beloved student at Tufts. He was quite handsome, looking a bit like Omar Sharif without the pretense. He had deep olive skin, piercing dark eyes, a slight but fit physique, and a thick mustache that made him seem as though he were wearing a perpetual frown. Elliot's fatal flaw and personal heartbreak was that he was in love with Katherine Fitzgerald, a woman who used him without remorse. Katherine was a blue-collar Medford girl on a free ride at Tufts because her mom worked in the infirmary as a nurse. She drank way too much Jamison's, fucked the frat boys when drunk, and smoked three packs of Marlboros a day. Dr. Rosenstein was a bit broken up by her vices; smoking being the one he minded most. One day in front of dozens of friends he announced that he was going to eat a pack of cigarettes to get Kat to stop her nasty habit. He ended up in the hospital for over a week with stomach trauma. I often wondered if Elliot was willing to do an entire frat house so that she would stop that as well, but the situation never came up.

One thing Katherine had going for her was a stunning voice that at top range, in full glory, would bring on an onset of chills. She was pretty, but a bit worn from the smoke, the booze, and the indiscriminate fucking; therefore she had the ability to play older.

Auditioning the dancers was our choreographer, Ellie Foster. The daughter of a top Dupont executive, she'd grown up in affluent Westchester and was headed for her MBA at Wharton in the fall. She was coming to PBT because dancing was her true calling, yet the pressure imposed by her corporate dad would not allow her to seek her bliss. Tall and lithe, Ellie had been dancing her whole life. She was also very sweet and so desperate for attention it broke your heart. Whether because the door on her love for dance had been shut or because she was acting out toward her domineering father, Ellie dated anyone and everyone, ending most evenings on her back. I was thrilled that the next four months would give her so much to remember and cherish.

In the studio and running the auditions like Patton's assistant was Jojo Backman. Jojo was stocky yet pretty; femininity was not her strong suit. She was the captain of the girl's field hockey team and looked the part. She was a big hugger and an easy cry. She smiled often and was the shoulder on which all girlfriends cried when stupid boys did them wrong. Jojo was planning a career in show business and she had the discipline, the moxie, the drive, and the trust fund to make that happen.

It was our first day of auditions. We had been in session for almost ten hours. Faces, songs sung, long legs, and scenes read all began to blur. Everyone had notes or headshots to remind them who they had seen. I rarely used such tools. I usually knew in an instant who I wanted, who worked for me, who was worth watching. True, it was helpful to remember someone's height or coloring to know whether they matched up properly (no six-foot-three leading men if your leading lady barely topped five feet).

It was also important to flesh out the chorus so they could play all the small roles that gave a show texture, color, humor, and something continually new and fresh in order to catch your audience's eye. The singers' voices had to blend so they had a specific sound and didn't just hit the notes. The dancers' figures needed to be varied—some petite, some tall and buxom—to satisfy every taste.

I also looked for character and commitment in the individuals themselves. Over the next hundred days all these young men and women, with hormones raging, identities forming, and insecurities growing or fading were going to be living in confined quarters, working hard and playing harder, falling in and out of love, drinking too much, and partaking in illegal substances. They would find themselves naked and regretful in the morning, yet they would also soar to unmitigated triumphs on stage.

Everyone who came to Plymouth for that special summer would be part of a small city, an enclave, and a truly unique community. They had to be willing to take endless risks, fly without a net, and sing as if they didn't need the money. They had to do press events and charm strangers. They had to work late and wake early. They had to perform when tired or recently blown off by their latest love. They had to reach deep and find out if they indeed had real talent, or mystery, or desired IT. They had to figure things out on their own, long after rehearsals had ended, and bring their creative energies and stamina to midnight rehearsals that began just a short while after an eight o'clock show had ended.

Perhaps most of all, they had to want to work for and with me, because I was going to be demanding and relentless. I wanted young artists dedicated to an orgy of ideas, emotions, passions, and the unbridled desire for greatness. I told everyone I considered hiring that if I didn't see a comet of affirmation flash across their face or burn in their eyes I would thank them and wish them well.

Jojo finally called the day to an end. She would meet us at nine in the morning with a file of those we were ready to hire, those still under consideration, and those we thought should find another career path. No one should be late.

I walked from Cohen Auditorium, which was located at the base of Walnut Hill, and climbed the endless stone steps that led to the apex of Tufts University and its magnificent view of Boston and beyond. I had just spent more than ten hours in a basement, seeing nervous young performers whose scent was pungent with anxiety. It was truly beautiful atop the hill. The sun was almost gone and the sky was turning from azure to midnight blue. The stars complemented a fading moon, and the distant skyline of Boston looked like Oz. The quad that abutted the new library was awash in spring foliage, while the huge, ancient trees Charles Tufts had given the college more than a hundred years ago rustled and danced, with the cool spring breeze their accomplished partner.

I climbed the last steps to the library. I entered the modern edifice, all white stone and shimmering glass, and found my way to the microfilm machines. I had an early morning for sure, but I was not going to sleep that night until I'd done some research on a woman from Plymouth, Massachusetts—Susan Golden, attorney and board member of the Barrows Foundation. I was no PI, true, but my instincts told me that surprises were on the way. And that Ms. Golden's background would head the list.

26

I was asked to leave the library as Friday night turned into Saturday morning. A heavyset clerk with lots of wild hair and rimless glasses told me that the stalls closed at midnight; she had a date and needed to leave. I lingered, but was ushered out by a friendly yet firm security guard.

The temperature had dropped precipitously while I was researching Golden. It gnawed at me that she had been so accommodating even while on the side of an adversary. It made no sense. As I walked briskly down Walnut

Hill to retrieve my car, I had to remind myself of Mr. Feldman's admonition that I was "not a private investigator." Nevertheless, I had just discovered that Susan Golden was not the budding acolyte she pretended to be. She had a rather famous father: a certain Dr. Anderson Barrows. And he had a grandson with a glass jaw who was a Plymouth badass with a history of unfriendly encounters that usually ended in a police report. True, I was a nice Jewish boy with more of an affinity for show tunes and chorines than for sleuthing, yet the info I had just uncovered made me want to continue the pursuit. I wanted to flesh it all out and make headlines. Admittedly, I was wired after a full day of auditions and now my evening's role-playing as detective Nero Wolfe, but sleep was not on my immediate agenda.

The campus was quiet. Classes had ended two weeks earlier, and summer school was yet to begin. A few lights dotted the facade of the larger dorms and threw off harsh shadows that suggested Kafka had been involved in the design. A pizza delivery guy was bringing a hot pie to Stratton Hall, and Kenny Loggins could be heard on the stereo from somewhere deep inside the girls' dorm. A beautiful coed with large, unencumbered breasts that stretched out the word JUMBOS on her thin T-shirt called down from her window to let the pizza guy know he should "just come on up." I had spent a great many nights in Stratton Hall endeavoring to seduce Kathy Blaine. It never happened, and I eventually moved on to other more accommodating Jackson Girls. As I walked by I thought that pizza would be nice and then slowed my stride in a failed attempt to be invited up for a slice.

I retrieved my car from the near-empty lot next to Cohen Auditorium and drove to the pay phone on the corner. I called Veronica, not knowing what I'd say even if I did catch her before she shut down the motel office for the night. I let the phone ring more than ten times before giving up. Disappointed, I repocketed my dime. I put the top down on the Mustang and looked up at the star-studded New England sky. The air held a distinct chill, so I turned on the car's heater while I considered my next move. I decided to drive to Secunda's Back Bay digs and drag his sorry ass out of bed. We'd grab a beer in Kendall Square, where I'd tell him of the incredible day he had just missed while we'd watch a collection of nubile Boston University coeds shoot some pool.

Secunda and I sat in Jimmy's, a dive bar off of Kendall Square about two narrow blocks from Fenway Park. The place was a hybrid of college hangout and holding cell for hundreds of rabid Red Sox fans. If the Sox won, the joint was happy. If not, the beer poured more freely. Whatever the outcome, whatever the season, I always found the pool table occupied with the lovely "Terriers" from Boston University who came to the bar in tight jeans or short skirts to meet boys. I always left Jimmy's happy.

It was inching toward 2 a.m. and we were on our third or fourth brew. Even at this late hour, Secunda wore a light gray suit with midnight blue stripes and an electric blue shirt with some sort of dots all over it. I wore my jeans and a cutoff faded chambray shirt. Secunda's beard was neatly trimmed and his boots spit-polished.

"Sammy, you have to focus on the task at hand here. I don't give a fuck who is fucking who in Plymouth. I don't need to like Barrows or his illegitimate daughter who poses as a legal eagle and then spends the night playing with Molson's testicles." He paused to let the word "testicles" hang in the air for effect. Then he continued. "Now you tell me, for at least the fourth time in the last hour that you can't believe that Barrows's wife is fucking that douchebag I punched out the other night. Well, why not? I would do her, and so would you. Oops, you didn't." He chuckled. "So the mom, also known as the hot lawyer, is chasing Davey boy, the wife is doing the grandson, and soon they'll have a bunch of kids with no teeth and all move to Louisiana."

"Secunda, you can't pretend that this stuff is normal. Something is going on and we should get to the bottom of it."

"Why?"

"Why?"

He ordered another round from a waiter who looked like a chorus boy past his prime. We both took a moment to notice the glee of the girl pack nearby. One of them, a short Rubenesque redhead with big boobs had holed out the table, and her girlfriends cheered her on as if she were Carlton Fisk. Josh motioned for our chorus boy and ordered the girls a round to honor Red's success.

"Because it's fucked up!" I said. "Nobody is telling us the truth about what's going on. Veronica's brother is in prison because of that asshole . . ."

"You don't know that do you, Kojak?"

"Who said they have to tell you anything, let alone the truth? Just hope they stay out your way so you can be Hal Prince instead of some Jewish Shaft. Do you want to play cops and robbers, or do you want to make some money so I don't lose my trust fund and you can pay back all those crazy people who love you so much they gave you money?"

"You know that when good men do nothing bad things happen."

"Who said so?"

"Me."

Secunda laughed long and hard. He pulled out two expensive cigars and offered me one. I declined. He bit the end of his stogie and then took his time lighting up. The smoke billowed up to the old tin ceiling. After a moment, the air cleared a bit, and I found Secunda staring at me through the lingering smoke.

"This stuff is important," I said. "You should take things with a tad more consternation."

"A tad more consternation? Who says that sort of thing? Who are you, George Hamilton?"

He got up from the table and approached the girl pack surrounding the pool table. Their conversation was animated and friendly. They all looked my way while a nerdy-looking brunette with a rockin' bod caught my eye and smiled. I nodded acknowledgment and quickly drained the remainder of my beer.

In a moment, Secunda sauntered back my way smoking like the Jersey refineries on Route 95 and sat back down. He waved our chorus boy over and ordered an assortment of drinks: new beers for us and a bottle of tequila for the table. "The girls are joining us in ten minutes," he said. "What else do you have to tell me?"

"Okay, listen up. We were at it today for more than ten hours. We need twenty-four kids to cover all the roles and doubles. Some of the company you already know. We saw this girl today from Amherst. Unbelievable voice. The room shook. When she sings 'Another Hundred People,' watch out."

"How were her legs?"

"Why would you ask me that?"

"Just fuckin' with you."

"Be serious for a minute. You know Christina Stewart?"

"I remember you dated her. Can she sing?"

"Well enough, but she's funny. Who knew? She's like Imogene Coca! She's hot and funny. She'd even make *you* laugh, you fuckin' churl."

"Good." He puffed the stogie and his eyes scanned the room.

"This girl came all the way from Yale. This girl had the best tits I have ever seen."

"Better than Janet Kessler?"

"Yeah, better."

"You've had enough to drink."

Secunda held up one finger and gestured to the girl pack to give him one minute. With his other hand, he held the waiter at bay for a moment. He smoked his cigar and drained his beer. He looked at me with a mixture of contempt and affection. Then he stood and took my face in his hands, pulling me from my chair. I felt like Fredo before Michael gives him the kiss of death in *Godfather II.*

"I know this matters. I'm going to show up every day down there, and I'm going to act my ass off. I'm going to listen to what you say and make sure others do as well. But I'm going to have fun as well. And so should you. I put up money for your dream because I love you and think you're good at this. It's not my bliss or greatness that got me on board. It's yours. Ten years from now, of the fifty people you plan to bring to theater camp, maybe two or three will earn a living doing the stuff they are going to love doing with you for the next four months. You're going to break more hearts this summer then you ever could imagine. Just fuckin' relax and act your age. Be a kid a bit longer, for Christ's sake. Because when that's over, it's over. This may be your game, but it's my football. What do you have at stake? Some borrowed money which we would have to really fuck up not to pay back. If you get in my face, though, then I pass. I take my money and go home."

He still held my face in his hands, but backed away so there was some distance between us. "Now these girls are coming over to join us and have some fun. I'm telling you to have some fun. Flirt, dance, and if you're lucky, make out. Take someone home. The tall geek with the glasses likes you." Then he looked into my eyes with a combination of fury and deep fondness and gave me the kiss of death.

I sat back in my chair dazed by alcohol and reprimand.

"Fuck you, Secunda! I have plenty at stake. There is more to me than chasing pussy and drinking. If we're not good this summer, then why bother? "

"I work tomorrow. Tonight, I continue to play. Caring too much is just as bad as not caring at all, Sammy!"

The girl pack joined us, and the chorus boy brought the drinks. Secunda poured everyone a shot of Patron, and with glass held high he said, "To my friend Sammy. May he gain some perspective before exuberance is lost and life becomes a boring burden. Drink up, everybody." They did.

"You too, Sammy."

"Asshole," I muttered and put the shot glass down.

After a moment and a deep breath, the jukebox came back into focus. I heard Eric Carmen singing "All By Myself" loud and specifically for me. The nerdy-looking brunette walked over and sat on my lap. She had let her hair down, removed her glasses; she looked pretty damn good to me.

"Hey, Sammy," she said. "My name's Lucy. Dance with me."

I sat still, thinking about my exchange with Secunda.

I fuck up and I go home, I thought. *Yeah, like that's a win for me. Pick up shit forever while everyone else moves on to the next gig and I have one foot in the purgatory of failure.* I sulked some more. Then I noticed that Lucy's eyes were playful and full of late-night longing. Even through the bar smoke, I smelled a hint of perfume. Her tank top clung tightly to her body, and her firm breasts were at eye level.

"Come on, Sammy. It's four o'clock. What do you have on your agenda that's more fun than dancing with me?"

"I've got to work in the morning."

"It *is* morning. It's just up to you to know what to do with it."

With that, Lucy walked me to the middle of the bar, put my hands on the cheeks of her ass and placed her head on my chest. I smiled weakly. The jukebox played "If You Leave Me Now." Lucy rubbed up against me.

I had plenty of stakes in this game, more than anyone had yet to realize. Yet Lucy was right: the stakes would be there later this morning. For now, fun was beckoning. I pulled her closer, lifted her chin ever so slightly and kissed her. The music seemed to swell, I thought about Veronica, which was unfair to both girls, and was grateful that nine o'clock was no longer just a heartbeat away.

27

I pulled into the Cohen Auditorium lot just short of 8:30 a.m. It was a perfect late-spring morning. The air filled with a sweet combination of crisp clean grass and honeysuckle. A tall, gangly runner was doing sprints on the track while a couple of coeds ran leisurely side by side in serious conversation. There were less than a half-dozen cars about, and the early-morning sun was warming the day nicely. I hadn't been to bed, but I felt alert and eager for the day to begin. I had stopped at the local convenience store to wash up and brush my teeth in their men's room. I needed a shave, but so did many recently graduated college kids who were up early in Beantown under a budding May sun. Before heading over to the auditions, I stopped at the local diner and picked up a twenty-ounce coffee that I mixed with lots of heavy cream and seven sugars. I was ready to greet the day yet had nearly thirty minutes to spare. I sat on the steps outside the auditorium, opened the *Globe* to the sports section, and began to drink my coffee.

Secunda walked up from behind me and sat down. He carried a box of doughnuts and a large container of java. "I brought you some breakfast," he said sheepishly.

"Thanks, but I already picked up some coffee."

"Then have a doughnut. They're fun. Can never have too much fun, you know. You have fun last night?"

"Yes, yes I did."

"Too much?"

I thought for a beat and smiled. "No, just the right amount."

"Have a fuckin doughnut. We have to start work soon or Jojo will have our ass."

He held out the box, and I took a moment to choose one. I opted for a glazed. It was still warm. I took a bite. "That's a damn good doughnut."

"Made it myself," Secunda said. "I looked something up for you this morning. It's about Mickey Mantle. You heard of him?"

"Yes, Josh, I have heard of Mickey Mantle."

"Did you know that he played eighteen years in the big leagues? He got up to bat more than ten thousand times. He struck out more than eighteen hundred times and walked more than seventeen hundred times. So do you know what he had to say about that fact?"

"No, but I'm sure you're going to tell me."

"Yes, I am. The Mick said that the average player gets up to bat five hundred times per year. Therefore, he spent seven years of his time in the big leagues never hitting the ball."

"I can't imagine Mickey Mantle ever saying 'therefore.' What's your point?"

Secunda continued. "Do you also know that Mickey Mantle struck out more times than anybody who ever played?"

"Yeah, but he also hit more home runs than anybody but Aaron, Ruth, Mays, and Killebrew."

"That's right. Now let's not be late." He stood up, holding the remaining doughnuts. "You're Mickey Mantle. You're going to strike out some, but you're gonna hit a lot of home runs this summer, many of which will head deep into the night and never come down. That's what happens when you swing for the fences. Every time Mantle came to bat, he had stakes in the game. Just like you."

Then he headed toward the front door of Cohen Auditorium. I followed. Just before we went inside, a strikingly handsome young man charged in front of us. Breathlessly he asked, "Do you guys know where the auditions for the Priscilla Beach Theatre are being held?"

"Downstairs in the basement," Secunda told him.

"Thanks," he said, and dashed off.

We went inside.

28

We began seeing people at nine sharp and worked without a break with the goal of concluding by five. We saw dozens of kids in all shapes and sizes. Some with talent and some that deserved a bus ticket home. We saw some people who wanted the gig so bad that we felt an institution would be a safer place for them to spend the summer. We saw others who were cavalier and seemed simply to be passing through on their way to someplace else. Best of all, we saw some terrific people. Dancers with long legs, flat tummies, and tight tushes who could hit the beat and then hit it again and again and again. We had singers who gave us goose bumps, who were quick learners and pitch perfect, and we had actors who could read the phone book and make it sound funny.

One of the first guys we saw was a kid from the Boston Conservatory of Music. To call him handsome was to say Linda Carter might turn a few heads doing that run in her Wonder Woman costume. He was also cocky. His name was Zach Rush. Zach was more than six feet, trim and fit. He had perfect auburn hair that he combed straight back, yet it fell a bit with a perfect wave. With his neatly trimmed goatee, he could ride in on a horse singing "Camelot." He was wearing a light, white cotton turtleneck and black slacks. His resume listed dozens of great roles played at good schools, and his resume picture was even better than the real thing.

"Would you like to sing first or read?" I asked.

"Sing, if that's all right."

"What did you bring?" said the good Dr. Elliot from his seat at the piano.

Zach pulled a book from his knapsack some one hundred pages thick. "How about 'Maria' from *West Side Story*?" I found myself not liking this guy. He was too good looking, too full of himself, and he told us that "Maria" was from *West Side Story* as if we didn't know. What an ass.

He began. *"The most beautiful sound I ever heard . . ."*

The entire room went WOW. No one breathed until he was finished singing—in perfect pitch with perfect timbre. Ellie's face was flushed when he was done, and I guessed that her underwear was damp from multiple orgasms. I hated the guy. Not because he wasn't great but because he was so good I simply wanted to punch him.

"So you can sing," I said without emotion, and the room mocked me for my lack of enthusiasm.

"Yes, a little bit," Rush replied with his big, stupid, perfect teeth smiling just right.

"Would you like to read?" I asked, almost hoping he would stutter.

"Sure." What was he so happy about? Didn't he know it was early in the morning and show business was a bitch? "Side C?" he asked.

"Jojo will read with you," I said. "Any questions?" I hoped he'd ask if he could leave now and forget we ever met. Instead, he took a seat across from Jojo and began the scene.

One must note that in the musical *Company*, this particular scene is the denouement of the entire show. It is between two friends, one a midthirties, uncommitted bachelor and the other a three-time bride in her early forties, rich, bitchy, sexy, and on the prowl. The scene needs confidence and nuance. It needs understated sex and a sense of danger. When the married woman comes on to the hero, we have to wonder if she means it or is just attempting to jolt him so he might join the game of life. It's a tough scene to pull off even after hours of rehearsing with an actress, not just a stage manger reading lines.

They began. Jojo read professionally, offering very little but keeping the cues coming. Zach Rush—Zach Fucking Rush—was electric. He was sexy and flirtatious, vulnerable yet tough. He had humor and a certain edge that made the whole thing textured, dramatic, and thrilling. The guy was great.

I looked at his resume to see if he had played this role before and come in with a replica of a previous performance. The role of Robert did not appear.

I looked around the room. Everyone was dumbstruck.

Elliot stepped in. "Zach, would you mind singing something from *Company?*"

Zach couldn't have been happier. He took center stage in the studio and then, with Elliot playing gracefully, Zach Rush sang "Being Alive," my favorite show tune in the world, better than one could ever imagine.

"Well, Zach, that was all fantastic. Really great. Thank you," I said. The others in the room tried to speak, making a series of indistinguishable grunts that sort of sounded like a herd of cows grazing.

"Thank you," Rush said. "Thank you so much."

"Zach, why do you want to come and work for us?" Elliot asked sincerely.

"Well, great parts. I have heard a great deal about you guys, and I saw your production of *Follies*, which was terrific. My folks live on the Cape, and my girlfriend lives here in Boston. Most important, I truly want to do something quality this summer and then kick off my career in New York."

"Zach," I asked, "and please don't take this the wrong way—are you a dick?"

"What?" he said, the question carrying much more weight than you might imagine from a word with a single syllable.

"I'm sorry. I know it seems rude, but you are so good and we would want you with us so badly, unless you're an asshole, you know, difficult, a diva."

He laughed. "Wow, this is flattering, I guess. No, I am not an asshole. I work hard and I love doing theater, and I would like to be with you this summer. It would be a huge break for me. I have only one request."

Here it comes, I thought. "What is that, Zach?"

"If possible I'd like my own room. I'll take less money if I have to, but a private room would be important to me."

"That's it?"

"Yes, sir," Rush replied with his big, stupid, perfect teeth.

"That's just fine, Zach. We can make that happen. Jojo will call you tonight. Welcome aboard."

Rush left the room knowing he'd be spending his summer on the Cape.

Jojo Backman got up from her chair and walked over to me. "'Don't mean to be rude, Zach, but are you a dick?' Well, I don't mean to be rude, Mr. Director, but you're an idiot. Do you want bad people to work with us, or do you only want them to be good if they have big tits and long legs?"

"It's not that," I said, trying to hold on to a shred of dignity.

"Really."

"They guy was just *so* good. I mean, he's sensational. He's gonna be a diva and I'm the one who will have to deal with it . . ."

The room erupted with a collective moan.

"It will be *our* problem," Jojo said, her voice void of any warmth, "not solely yours. Let the guy show up before you dislike him. And grow up, you moron. You can't cast all the parts with cute girls. Focus."

I was humbled. I asked that we bring in the next person, before a trap door opened and I ended somewhere subterranean.

Next was a redhead. Frizzy hair. Big voice.

Leggy wonder from Harvard. Pass. She should go to medical school.

Beefy character actor. Huge voice.

The one girl I was ever truly in love with came in and sang "Adelaide's Lament" from *Guys and Dolls*. I listened to her sing and turned to goo. She'd never noticed me when we were in school and she offered complete indifference today, but she had shown up. I was going to cast her.

Handsome guy. Pretty boy. Dark features. Hired.

Big heavyset girl. Good voice. Funny. Wants to dance with the other chorines. No way. Her ass needed its own zip code.

Janet Kessler. Enough said. Hired.

A kid all the way in from Philly. Looked like a rock star. Tenor. Amazing.

Really cute dancer from BU. Great voice. Really bad skin. Sorry.

Alan S. Kopit—ASK—from Tufts was a great friend of mine through my four college years. This morning, Kopit was wearing a canary-yellow golf shirt, navy Bermuda shorts, and moccasins with white socks. If he were carrying binoculars you'd think he was out bird watching. Atop his thick head of hair he wore a Cleveland Indians cap that he must have owned since he was six. It was faded and worn and gave him an aura of gravitas. Kopit was short with a big, easy smile of Chicklet-white teeth. He looked like a cross between Howdy Doody and Peter Noone of Herman's Hermits. He had been in several shows we had done over the years and loved the musical theater. Yet he was a less than an adequate singer, moved awkwardly, and had the comic timing of a broken watch. But through it all his enthusiasm shone through, and the fact that he was having such a good time on stage projected across the footlights and made the audience share his joy.

He sang. He read. We all needed to discuss the boundaries of friendship when we made our final choices a bit later in the day.

New gal. Eat a salad.

New guy. Take a shower.

New gal. Marry me.

Next. I'm quitting the business. Going to law school.

Next. Kill me.

Next. Wash your hair.

Next. Is that hair?

Kill me. Marry me. Is it five yet?

What was I thinking?

She's awesome. He's great.

Our good humor was waning. We had seen so many good people I knew we would have more options than we could have ever hoped to find. Jojo told us we had ten more minutes and then we were going to take a short break and come back and cast our shows.

Then a mom walked in. She might have been a grad student or on the GI Bill, but I was certain she was a mom.

"Hi," Jojo said with a welcoming and curious smile. "Can we help you?"

"Yes, I hope so," she answered. "My name is Elaine Feston. My son Ronny is outside in the hall. We drove up this morning from Long Island. Ronny is finishing his junior year in high school and wants very much to audition for you. I wasn't sure if you'd see him because of his age. So I came with him to let you know that if you choose him, well, I would be one hundred percent behind him and you."

Wow, I thought. *Even if he's any good, would he fit in? Would it be legal? What about the pot heads?*

"We'd be delighted," Jojo said.

Ronny Feston looked like a high school kid who'd never seen the sun. He was slight, yet stood straight, and if he was nervous you could never tell. He wore crisp, pressed blue jeans, brand new unblemished Keds, a pink, cotton button-down with a polo pony on the breast, and a black tie with comedy and tragedy masks embroidered in silver. He had a mop top of curly locks. Without a word, he brought his book over to Elliot at the piano. He went through music, gesticulating for effect, telling when to punch it or slow down. He could have been Dean Martin talking with his musical director.

Feston walked to the center of the room, gestured for his mother to take a seat, scanned us all, and said, "I am Ronny Feston. Thank you for seeing me today. I am thrilled to be here. I'm going to sing 'Trouble' from *The Music Man*."

He nodded to Elliot at the keyboard, and Elliot played the intro to one of the great songs in the canon of American musicals. Then Ronny Feston sang. He had grace and confidence, nuance and humor. He had the body of a dancer and moved on all the right beats. He held galvanizing eye contact and made you hear the story of the song like it was the first time. Ronny Feston was a star. A bright, shining star that makes the sky sparkle, the theater a place to visit, a nugget of gold one might find in the rolling rivers of Northern California.

He finished. I turned to his mother and said, "Mrs. Feston, does Ronny have a curfew that you'd like us to enforce this summer? Because he's officially on our dance card."

29

I drove south on Route 3 toward Plymouth. It was yet another perfect New England evening, more midsummer than late spring. I was headed to the theater compound, knowing it would be my home for the next hundred days. The past week had been an all-out sprint, and I thought about how my life had changed in just seven days. I would be sleeping at PBT tonight for the first time. It would be a sign that this was real, authentic, and tangible, no matter how wildly insane, no matter how circuitous the path to its front door had been. As I drove through downtown Plymouth, I felt as if I were part of the community. I held a certain fellowship with all these other vendors who were now my neighbors.

It was May 20. The company would be arriving in two weeks and the first rehearsal was a few days thereafter. On Monday, I was heading to New York City to "steal" a press rep. Secunda would travel with me and we'd secure the band.

Veronica had agreed to meet me for a casual dinner. I had promised to proffer no expectation; tonight we'd be just an old couple visiting and catching up on the events of the day, sharing a burger and a bottle of red. As I parked my car down by the wharf, I saw her waiting for me on a bench overlooking the bay. I realized that, although I had only been away for two days, I felt as if it had been a long, long time since I had seen her smile.

Veronica didn't appear as pleased to see me as I had hoped. She was awkward and her eyes looked everywhere but at me. She gave me a quick hello and darted to the railing that overlooked the bay, doing anything, it seemed, to avoid connection.

It was early evening and the sun was setting behind the dozens of boats that danced gently in the bay. The wind off the sea was refreshing and pungent. They say that sometimes feelings lie, but often so does the weather.

Atop the knoll sat the stoic Barrows Building, which watched over the bay with disdain. I found it telling that whenever the sun disappeared and the air chilled, it was because it was blocked by the Barrows fortress rather than by a cloud moving within a sweet summer breeze. I sat on a bench and waited to see when Veronica would finally turn and address me. Sensing bad news, I was anxious, but in no rush to see how this would play out.

The harbor bell clanged long and strong. It was seven o'clock. She turned, but stayed by the railing. She leaned against it as if needing support. I would have moved to her, but her energy was that of a force field keeping me at a distance. Her face was drawn and she looked tired and deeply sad.

"Hi," she said in a whisper.

"Hello. It's nice to see you."

"I've been thinking about you a lot," she offered, still barely audible and still not moving.

"Okay then. And what were you thinking?" I asked, more afraid than curious.

"That I will miss you and . . ." Her words hung in the air like poison.

Breathing was hard. "That I will miss you, and that I am so sorry and sad, because I think you are so special and I want to know you, to . . . but I can't."

"Can't *what* Veronica?"

"I can't see you, Sam. I'm not brave enough. I said you'd break my heart, but that's not what I'm afraid of. It's that I will disappoint you, and that would stay with me forever."

She had turned back toward the sea and away from me. I could no longer read her eyes. The ambient happy sounds of the village mocked me. "Veronica, what are you talking about? What happened? Are you fucking Sybil, for Christ's sake?"

She turned to me, and with contempt overtaking any kindness she said, "While you were gone, I thought about it all again. Us." Her voice cracked with emotion. "I spoke with some people . . . some friends . . . and they told me to stay away . . . that I should stay away, that I had better stay away." Her last words were caught in the wind and stolen before I could be sure she had actually spoken them.

Frustration got the best of me. "Okay, Veronica," I shouted across the distance, "play the part of some freak in a bad melodrama. Bravery and courage go hand and hand and you have neither. Disappoint me? You already have."

She looked at me as if for the last time, wiping away tears that covered her cheeks.

"You are so stupid, Sam! Pay attention. You think I work at that shithouse motel because it's the best I can do? Someone like me?"

She didn't wait for an answer. Instead she shouted, "Goodbye!" and ran down the shore.

The sun disappeared behind the Barrows Building, and the warm, late-spring evening suddenly turned cold. I remained still for a long time. I had nowhere to go and no inclination to seek company or solace.

What had happened, really? A girl I had known for a week had dumped me without explanation or reason. I was momentarily stunned. It would pass. I hadn't come to Plymouth to meet Veronica Chapman. I had come here to work, to find my way. If I let this girl distract me from that task, I was a fraud. I would have convinced my friends and my investors to participate in a charade. I would have lied to those who believed in me and, worse yet, deceived myself.

Yet I did meet her and that reality held on long after the sun was gone and the midnight blue waters of Plymouth Harbor reflected the glow from shore. Finally, at way past nine, I stood and examined my surroundings. I walked slowly to the large granite mausoleum that housed the famous rock. I walked aboard the *Mayflower* and looked out toward England. I looked up at the sky to find a star to wish upon, but the options were far too many and I could not choose one that promised hope. Then I wondered what I was actually hoping for.

I wasn't ready to return to PBT. I thought I'd sit and think some more, try to put the thoughts of lost possibilities behind me. I saw that the bench was occupied by an elderly gentleman wearing a Red Sox cap and an oversized Sox sweatshirt. He seemed relaxed, at peace and happy. He was enjoying an ice cream cone, savoring each lick as if it would be his last. On second look, I realized that I knew this man. After a moment's hesitation, I elected to sit down next to Dr. Anderson Barrows.

30

"So, Young August. A stranger shows up in a small town and things happen. The energy changes as does the gestalt of the community itself. Oh, and I know what the word means. How's your gestalt today, Auggie?"

He took a slow lick of his ice cream, relishing his clever repartee while revealing that discretion had left the Barrows lexicon long ago.

"I have had better days, sir, but I'm doing fine. Youth comes with many second chances."

"Sort of like a cat with nine lives?"

"I don't think a single bad day uses up a life, sir."

"How many bad days then, before you are down to eight, or seven, or even two"?

"I've never thought about it. I don't fear that I am in jeopardy of running low, of that I can assure you."

"The arrogance of youth," he said, spitting the last word.

"I'm an optimist. I believe in good."

"The *folly* of youth."

The wharf was at full throttle by this point. Myriad musical genres filled the crisp night air. You could choose one to match your mood or circumstances, but my choice was elusive, so I let them cascade over me, wondering if one might find a home.

"You know, August, when my father built the Barrows Building he chose the site at the top of the hill behind us for a reason."

"And what was the reason, sir?"

"So that he could look down upon the citizens of his town and decide whether he approved of how they lived their lives."

"Your family may own the buildings in Plymouth, but not the people. Your minions are not puppets, and you don't pull the strings or make them dance."

"Really?" He grinned. "How are things going for you with that beauty Veronica Chapman? From my window up above, it looked as if you were encountering some rough seas." He stood before I could respond and looked at me with a perverse angry gleam in his old sad eyes. "Oh, and Auggie, would you like to finish this ice cream? Better yet, why don't I have enough sent over to last the summer. That way you'll never run out. It's my favorite: Rocky Road."

With that, he began a slow walk up the steps to his loony bin at the top of the knoll. In the distance, I heard a cuckoo clock count out ten hours, each call louder and more resonant than the last, and all proffering a bit of dread.

3 1

Monday morning could not have arrived quickly enough. Secunda had decided to sleep in; he was going to take a late-morning flight to meet

JB and me in Manhattan. We each had specific tasks, and completion was set for late afternoon with our return to Plymouth that evening regardless of the hour. JB and I had picked up coffee and doughnuts before we hit the road. I drove and JB talked and smoked.

Another day dressed in the glamour of show business.

Between the drive to New York and the journey home that night, JB and I had plenty of time to talk shop. Instead, we spoke about our lives, how we got to this place, and where we hoped the next four months might lead us. Sure, we wanted all good things. Who doesn't? Love and money and family. To do something meaningful and to make a difference. To dance with pink elephants on lazy afternoons. To have people repeat and vest in the things we had to say and to offer. To live with courage and appetite. To stare down fear. To be better than ordinary. To stretch our limits and to get right back up when disappointment or loss or ill will knocked us down. To avoid repeating the errors of our parents. To be both reckless and wise. To be kind. To find time to breathe and listen. To lose our way because of passion and not from a lack of thought or purpose. To be judged by those who called us friends and by those who loved us. We wondered how long the names on that list of friends would remain or why they would be deleted and who, if anyone, would replace them.

JB and I had known each other for three years now and in the life of a young person that is a fair percentage of one's time on this planet. Yet, as we drove south on Route 95, I realized we had never really talked about things like this before.

"JB, I really don't know anything about you."

She laughed. "You know more about me than I do. I mean when you talk, I listen. When I talk to myself, I don't hear a thing."

"I'm not talking about broken hearts or foolish pursuits or the times you got me home or convinced me not to be stupid . . ."

"Which were many."

I grinned at her. "What are you looking for?"

"To please people," she said simply.

"Why? To make them happy, or to make you happy?"

"To be liked, I guess."

"And has that worked for you?"

She answered by not answering.

"Don't you want people to like you?" she said eventually.

"Not really. I mean, they will or they won't because of who I am. If I work for their acceptance, I turn out not being me, so then they're liking an impostor."

"How about if they have something to offer that makes you better?"

"I am open for business."

"Well, I like you. Just in case you care."

"That makes me very happy."

We parked the Mustang uptown and took the subway to the theater district in Times Square. JB had arranged a brief meeting at the press office of Broadway's most powerful and honored producer, Hal Prince. She had begged for and won a brief audience with a young intern by the name of Bobby Stevens. We arrived on time for our fifteen minutes at twelve sharp. Bobby had agreed to show us photos of the original Broadway productions of some of the shows we were to present over the coming weeks at PBT.

Bobby was a few years older than me. He must have bought his clothes at Brooks Brothers, because he was crisp and starched in a white, cotton, short-sleeve dork shirt decorated with a plain blue tie. He had a new haircut perfect-pasted with Brylcreem. He wore tortoiseshell glasses and offered a pleasant yet distant smile. Although he was tall and thin, my guess was that the chances of him doing a single pushup were slim and none.

The office was New York hustle-and-bustle, nondescript in decor. The place employed ten people, all of whom talked animatedly and with a distinct range of emotions. Dozens of show posters adorned the walls. There were celebrity photos and copies of interviews and large newspaper ads in abundance. For all the energy that filled the room, I noticed a void of anything personal at anyone's workstation. No pictures of kids or wives appeared anywhere. Despite my exhilaration at being in a real Broadway office, I found that fact more than a touch disturbing.

Bobby showed us into a small, cluttered room off the side of the main office. He pushed aside several files and offered us a seat. He gave us a stack of some two hundred or so photos and said, "Okay, guys, enjoy. I'll be back to check on you in a while. Please be careful. Some of the pictures are originals and, you know, actually I shouldn't being doing this so . . . anyway, I'll see you in a bit." He then left us alone.

JB pulled out a satchel from her big Mary Poppins bag and unfolded it on the table. We quickly went through the pictures and selected forty of what we thought were the best. JB put them in the canvas satchel, all the while eyeing the door to make sure we were not disturbed. She zipped up the bag and placed it on the floor. Then, for reasons unknown to both of us, we pretended to look at the remaining photos as if that would distract someone from our heist. We sat for the longest two or three minutes of my life and then got up to leave.

I led the way with JB on my heels. We walked directly to the front door and stepped into the hallway, practically running to press the down button on the elevator. Instantly, we heard a loud rattled call from behind us and footsteps gaining ground. We decided the elevator would not arrive in time and slammed through the exit door and raced down the stairs.

A piercing alarm went off and I screamed, "What the fuck?" JB raced ahead, taking three or four stairs at a time, giggling all the way. We heard Bobby Stevens shouting after us and his tone was far from cordial. We descended all eight flights without caution for our limbs or physical well-being and burst out into the lobby of the building.

Stevens was right on our heels, screaming with increasing urgency. I looked over my shoulder to check his whereabouts and slammed into two young women waiting for the elevator. They fell to the ground, pissed off, and had little receptivity for my sincere but hurried apologies. JB was on the street now, and I dashed to the curb to meet her. Stevens was a step behind me as JB hailed a taxi and we both got in before the cab came to a full stop.

"Drive!" JB screamed. "That guy's crazy. He must be an out of work actor!"

The taxi fishtailed and moved off the curb at tremendous speed. Stevens chased us and pounded on the rear of the car to stop. We didn't. We looked back at our pursuer who was shouting raging obscenities and offering us his middle finger.

JB thanked the driver for saving our lives. She lit a cigarette and exhaled. I felt as though I needed to find a restroom. We looked at each other and laughed. I shouted, "What the hell are we doing, JB?" Then we laughed some more until we had to stop or pass out for want for air.

"Now that's the way to get someone's attention," JB shrieked. I had no doubt we'd hear from Mr. Stevens before we had our morning coffee. And when I did I'd make my pitch.

3 2

Our trip to the Bronx didn't go as well.

We met Secunda and the music contractor Louis Rosenberg at his studio. It was a surprisingly short and hostile meet-and-greet. Rosenberg asked for more money than we had agreed to on the phone. I rejected this renegotiation, but Secunda undermined me and caved in. I lit into him and stormed out.

Now on our way back to Plymouth, JB was none too pleased with Secunda either. The exhilaration of our narrow escape from an enraged press intern was replaced by our mutual frustration with Secunda's disappointing efforts. No one had spoken a word in hours. We passed the time with the radio on, not paying much attention to it. As we rolled over each concrete block of the seamed highway, the tires made a rhythmic flip-flop sound; its hypnotic cadence could have easily lulled me to sleep. The top was down, and the smoke from JB's ubiquitous cigarettes cast a fleeting shadow on her expressionless face. There was no fun in this journey.

For some reason, JB looked prettier than I had ever seen her. Her dark eyes glistened in the night. Her hair was full and lush. She had no idea I was studying her and so her face was open, hiding nothing. She resonated intelligence and, in a strange way, peace.

"Hey, Joanie," I asked. "When did you start smoking? I mean, how old were you?"

She thought briefly. "Eleven."

"Wow."

She took a long pull on the Marlboro.

"Why?"

"I don't really remember. To get attention, I think."

"From who?"

"My father. Boys. Anyone."

The words held their place in the air. The speed of the car could not disperse them. They were heavy and made me sad. "Did it work?"

"To some degree, yes. More with boys than with my father. Nothing works with him."

"You guys don't get along?"

"We don't *get*. We just are. He's mad at the world for what he went through. He's embarrassed by his past and his accent, and he thinks I'm ashamed of him."

"Why?"

"My father spent four years in a camp. I will never know what he endured because he will never tell me. So I will never truly know him. I love him. I let him know that as best I am able."

I turned the radio off; it had just become noise. We sat in an awkward silence.

"I'm not, you know, embarrassed by him," she said. "I think he's amazing. What he has done with his life. What he's given me and my sister."

"Do you tell him *that*?"

She smiled weakly but without regret. "I've tried, but he's never heard me. I'll start again when he's ready to listen."

I considered this for several beats and then said, "Joanie, why are you working with me? Giving so much for so little?"

"You're like my dad, Sam. I'll tell you when you're ready to listen."

"I am."

"No, you're not. Trust me. But I love you, so I'll let you know when it's time." She lit a cigarette off the fading ember of her last. She turned on the radio and Nat King Cole came on.

"Unforgettable, that's what you are. Unforgettable, in every way."

We drove north about an hour from home, arriving before midnight.

33

We made a quick stop at Garden's Liquor Shop on our way into Plymouth. It was minutes before they closed, so we raced through, buying jug wine and a case of cheap local beer. The clock struck midnight as we turned down Rocky Hill Road and saw PBT on the left.

James had worked his magic. The old marquee was painted. Just days ago, the letters had hung randomly on the sign spelling nothing but gibberish. Now they were all in perfect alignment:

NEW SEASON OPENS JUNE 24TH

FOR INFORMATION AND TICKETS CALL 617-242-1200.

I felt like crying. JB shrieked. I stopped the car. We jumped out, did a little dance, and hugged each other. Then we returned to the car giggling, hugged each other yet again, and proceeded to the parking lot.

There was an impromptu gathering around the redwood picnic table. James sat stoned, refilling his bong. Diana Cohen and Debbie Racer, who had arrived that morning from Boston, were seated across the way from Doobie, the bartender from the Full Sail. He was drinking Jack Daniel's from the bottle. The drinking and smoking had clearly been going on for a while.

A few hundred feet from the front door of the red house and halfway to the party lay four huge dead raccoons with frozen, angry faces. *Maybe the Bronx wasn't so bad*, I thought.

"What's on the agenda for tonight?" I asked. "Are we getting arrested for smoking pot, public intoxication, or animal cruelty?"

Doobie drained at least a third of the Jack, wiped his mouth with his sleeve, and said quietly, "I shot 'em. Had to be done. They were after the girls here. Mean sons of bitches."

James, Debbie, and Diana nodded without a word. James took a toke from his homemade bong and the water bubbled inside the jug.

"This sucks," I said.

"Worse for them raccoons," Doobie offered.

"What did you shoot them with?" JB asked, sounding a little frightened.

Doobie held up a huge shotgun. "This."

I looked at the dead animals. They were extremely dead. "Doobie, are there any shells left in that gun?"

He thought a minute, and drained some more Jack. James's bong bubbled. Debbie and Diana joined in with James. More bubbles. "Don't think so," Doobie replied.

"Hey, Doob. You're a little more than lit. I think you should let me take a look at the gun and put it somewhere safe," I suggested.

He sighed. "Suits me. Done enough shooting for the night."

More bubbles from James and the girls. I took the gun and carried it carefully into the office, placing it under the desk. Then I walked back to find out what had happened.

Diana and Debbie got up slowly, each taking one of my hands. They walked me toward the far end of the red house. James and JB followed. Doobie remained seated. We got to the side door, old and covered with years of cracked paint, which opened directly into their bedroom. Debbie nudged it open then ran three–four steps away from the entrance. James pushed it open all the way, inching his way inside. I followed. The room looked ransacked. The girls' suitcases lay open on top of the two old sleigh beds that hugged the walls. Clothes peeked from the partially open drawers of the dresser nearby. The ceiling had caved in, and there was dust and plasterboard everywhere. In the middle of the room were three more dead raccoons. The two large armchairs that overlooked the massacre were covered with a nasty mixture of wine and dust that had met unexpectedly during the raccoon fracas.

"What a fucking disaster." I said.

The smell was more than putrid. James looked both high and nauseous. I decided to take my leave. He followed, closing the door behind him. I walked with the girls back to the table, grabbed the bong, and made some bubbles. Then I opened the wine JB and I had purchased, poured a full glass, and chugged it. Then I drank a beer. Finally, I sat down with the group.

Things were quiet and still. And very weird.

Diana and Debbie were Jackson girls who had wanted to join the team. From their expressions and the bombsite that was their bedroom, they would surely reconsider and return for a fifth year at Tufts.

Debbie had volunteered to work as the house photographer. She had grown up outside of Kansas City and had been taking pictures of the vast endless sky that blanketed her father's farm since she could remember. Debbie was a big-boned, tall, and awkward girl with large breasts and a shy but pretty smile. I don't think she had ever kissed a boy. In addition to working with her camera, she would also help out on tech crews. Diana was a Park Avenue prep school princess here to work as our marketing director. She had porcelain skin, light eyes, and a short bob haircut with a sexy wave that dropped over her forehead. She was thin, with boobs smaller than Secunda's. She loved Dr. Rosenstein, and we all believed she was saving herself for him.

Right now, both looked ghost white. I drank another sixteen ounces of jug wine.

James spoke at last. "I was helping the girls set up their room. We had all done a cleanup this morning. Painted the place and washed down the floors. I set up their music and had the bong going all day."

The girls nodded in silent acquiescence. Numbed, they moved very little.

James continued. "Around six o'clock we all seemed to have an urge to eat. Admittedly, it was dinner time, but to be honest I think the bong exacerbated everyone's hunger."

Debbie croaked out, "I was starving," then continued to stare ahead.

"When we got back, we started to unpack," Diana said. "The music was loud and fun so it took a while."

"Took a while for what?" I asked.

"For us to hear the scratching."

"It just got louder and louder," James added.

No one spoke. With eyes still closed, Doobie reached out and found the open bottle of JD and drank as if he were a thirsty man stranded in the desert.

"The scratching got louder and louder, almost manic," Diana said. It sounded like there was a ghost or a demon in the room . . ."

Debbie picked up in midsentence. "Then this huge raccoon fell out of the ceiling and landed on my head. The dust and dirt were like an avalanche and the raccoon held on to my head."

She was sort of laughing. Or was she crying?

"She looked like Davy Crockett with a big coonskin hat," Diana said with a hybrid of tears and laughter. "Then three more raccoons fell out of the ceiling and onto our heads and then onto the floor. They were waving their paws and they were pissed off. It was really scary. We screamed and ran from the room."

No one was laughing now. "The four raccoons had me trapped," said James, "and I shouted to the girls to call Doobie before they called the cops."

The girls hugged and James bubbled. JB smoked. Doobie's head rested facedown on the table. I took another shot of Jack.

"This really does suck," I said to no one. A dead raccoon stared from under the dozens of fireflies blinking light.

James continued. "I'm playing lion tamer with the four raccoons, using the end table to keep them at bay. The girls are screaming outside, the raccoons are definitely stoned by osmosis, and they are eating everything in sight. I figured I was next and imagined the headline in the local paper: 'Future Surgeon Coon-killed in Beachside Love Nest.'"

Doobie lifted his head from the table. "I got there as soon as I could. I shot three of the bastards right away, but the fourth one got away." His face returned to the table. "Then James ran outside and closed the door."

Suddenly everyone started to relax, then smile, then we all broke up. Crazy loon laughter filled the night.

34

Soon the laughter died. It was just short of 3 a.m. and we had no place to sleep. My room was in disarray, and who knew what furry creatures might visit later that night. The girls refused to risk another attack of the black-eyed monsters. James had set up shop in the attic of the white house, but even if we all crashed there the compound had no hot water yet.

I decided to call Veronica at home. Fuck Barrows and his innuendo. Last I checked, there were no puppet strings on me. Despite the hour maybe she would take my call, perhaps arrange a room at a low rate, or at least allow us all to crash for one night at the group rate of six shit-faced fools at a dollar a head.

I walked somewhat shakily into the office and dialed her number. I hoped she would pick up and not some angry father or protective older brother. Good fortune was with me.

"Who is this?" she said after answering on the fourth ring.

"It's me," I replied, holding my breath.

"Sam, are you all right?"

I exhaled. "Veronica, we had a shootout here at the Plymouth Corral and we need a place to stay."

"Shootout!" she screamed in a loud whisper so not to wake her family.

"No people were shot, but we are in a bit of a conundrum."

"I'll be there in fifteen minutes."

She hung up before I had a chance to respond.

Veronica pulled into the lot in less than ten minutes. She wore a hard expression that was only mitigated by her PJ bottoms and a tight tank top that revealed more than necessary unless you wanted the navy to follow you around. She walked purposefully to the middle of the compound and saw the coon massacre, then continued toward the red house and peeked inside. The ruins did nothing to lighten her mood.

"Where is the gun?" she asked, addressing no one in particular.

I told her I'd put it in the office.

"Who brought the gun?" she said.

"Doob."

She walked over to Doobie and lifted his head off the table by his long hair. She looked him dead in the eye. "Do you own a license for that gun, Doobie, or is everyone here going to jail?"

"License," Doobie uttered. Then she just dropped his head and it splatted on the table.

She looked at us, her eyes burning. "This is what is going to happen, and it is going to happen fast. Ladies, get the trash barrels and throw all the liquor into them. If anyone wants any more, then drink it within the next thirty seconds or you can all go to hell."

Everyone suddenly found their sea legs and the booze; all of it was gone before time ran out.

"James, take your weed machine upstairs and out of the way. Sam, put the gun somewhere in the theater where no one will find it unless they are really looking."

She walked over to Doobie and picked his head up by the hair again. "Doobie!" she shouted in his face. "Get to your car and go to sleep. Now!" She let go of his head, and it again slammed on the table. She put her face next to his and shouted, "Now!" He perked up a bit, gathered his wits, and headed slowly toward his open Jeep Wrangler.

"Sam, find some branches and cover the animals. The ones inside as well. Then you and the girls park the cars so they hide this mess as best as you can. Now get going and meet me right here in five minutes, or you're on your own."

Everyone obeyed. I watched her walk into the office and make a quick phone call. Whoever she called was either awake or she didn't care one way or another. When she returned to the redwood table, all of us were finishing our appointed rounds, awaiting further instructions.

Man was she adorable.

We were a tattered and sorry lot. She looked at us with disdain tinged with affection. "We are going to go to the motel. We'll go in my car and Sam's Mustang. If you girls need something to sleep in, grab it real quick."

We stood with our backs to the red house and listened like a platoon of good soldiers. Then we heard a chilling crash, and Veronica's eyes became the size of saucers. She hesitated for a moment, tried to speak, but nothing made it past her lips. Finally, as she turned away from the house and began to sprint past us to the cars, she shouted a plaintive, "Run!"

It was like a horror movie. We obeyed, yet all of us took a look behind to see an army of fifteen or twenty rabid raccoons dashing toward us to kill us and then eat us. Sobriety returned in a flash, and we raced toward the cars. It was a long hundred yards to run in the dark. The fireflies flickered and the coons growled. No, actually they roared. I got to the Mustang, turning my key in the ignition. No one was laughing now.

As I drove off, I looked in the rearview mirror and saw the army of wild animals. They appeared to be shouting at us. "We'll get you next time, you motherfuckers," they seemed to be saying. Then I saw them lick their paws with anticipation and relish.

3 5

It was well past 4 a.m. Veronica had found a room for JB, Debbie, and Diana: a double with a folding cot. The girls were grateful for clean sheets and the respite from Raccoon Nation. James was ensconced in an oversized linen closet.

Veronica didn't ask anyone for a penny. She had made my friends hers and, even amid this poor behavior and these unattractive circumstances, was showing her generosity and spirit. She put me up in the VIP room, but explained I shouldn't get too excited since there were rarely any VIPs in Plymouth. Most of the time it was used for storage files or cleaning supplies. Nevertheless, it was warm and clean and boasted a huge king-sized bed with fresh sheets and free HBO. I was tired, but sleep was not about to happen.

Veronica paraded about the room in her clinging tank top and PJ bottoms. She was tall and lithe as always. In the week since we had first met, we had danced the flirt-trot often. Stood on the precipice of magic, kissed sweetly, and contained simmering passion. When I was away from her, she was often front and center in my thoughts. I understood her reluctance to complicate her summer with a boy who was just passing through, yet Barrows and his Machiavellian puppet diatribe needed explanation, if not so she and I might be together, then simply for sanity alone.

Suddenly, without a word she left the room, and I sat quietly wondering whether she'd be back. I lay with my head against the pillow and closed my eyes. I had no answers. I had been up since six in the morning and if I went to sleep, life would still be there when I woke.

Just then Veronica walked in carrying a bottle of milk and a box of Oreos. She poured the milk into the motel water glasses and handed me one. "Do you think milk might taste better if it were served in crystal glasses?" she asked.

"Don't know," I said. "Until this week, I never drank anything from crystal other than on Thanksgiving at my Aunt Rene's. I like milk, though, even from the carton."

"Drink," she insisted. I did, and the milk was cold and delicious.

We were quiet for a moment.

"So?" she asked.

"So," I replied.

"For a guy who never stops talking, you have very little to say."

"You think I talk too much?"

"No."

Nothing was audible outside other than the pulse of the ocean. I popped an Oreo in my mouth and followed with a long swig of milk.

"You have anything to say?" I asked.

"Too much for tonight. Even for a summer and beyond," she replied sadly but mixed with a mischievous grin.

"What does Barrows have?" I started, trying to take this conversation forward.

"Money, bitterness, and a trunkful of trouble. He is a bad man, impervious to the consequences of his actions. I hate him." Her face was flushed. She no longer looked sad. Now she looked angry, her eyes furtive and darting.

"He wants to break you like you break a wild stallion. He wants to own you like he owns so many others. But he can't—and he knows it—and it is driving him insane."

"That's a kind characterization."

"As I said the other night, it's a small town and shit happens. As I cried my way through yesterday, I had another thought: maybe my last summer in Plymouth should include a boy who is just passing through and I should not be afraid or make his decisions for him. I decided I want to get on the roller coaster with you and scream and shout at the wind till we are breathless. And if we go off track . . . well, at least we had a ride."

She paused. Slowly her furrowed brow disappeared and her face lit up with a big warm sloppy smile. "And I think riding with you would be a nice thing to do."

Veronica Chapman had invited me to enter her orbit.

"Do I need to buy a ticket or do I just get on?" I asked.

"You *are* the ticket, big boy."

"That's very show biz."

"I'm a quick study."

She sat down on the bed and pulled me toward her and kissed me. It was a cocktail of kindness and lust and longing.

She got up and walked to the dresser to get more cookies. I wanted to throw her on the bed and ravage her until she moaned and screamed but it didn't seem appropriate. Instead, I watched her put more treats on the plate and sit back down on the edge of the bed.

"Do you want to sleep with me, handsome?" she asked.

"Yes, I do. It is quite late."

"*Sleeping* is a euphemism. How about some lust, sweat, and orgasms?"

"With you?"

She slapped me on the side of the head. A few moments later, she began to remove her tank top. I took her hand and stopped her, pulling her next to me. She didn't say a word, just nestled as closely into me as she could.

Despite all the thoughts racing in my head, not one distracted me from the moment. "Veronica, I can't have sex with you tonight."

"Why not?" she asked, making it clear that she really wanted to know why.

I spent some time thinking about my answer. "Veronica, sweetheart, I'd have to be dead not to want to have sex with you. Even then I'm sure I'd make every effort to do so."

"So? Do you think I'm loose, that I fuck anybody?"

"No. Well, actually, I did when we first went out. I mean, you always look so available. You make no effort to hide how great you look . . ."

Her faced flushed with anger. "I'm pretty. Is that a bad thing? Should I dress like a fucking nun? Would you prefer if I dressed like I just escaped the convent? You think you would have cared two shits about me if I didn't look and dress the way I do?"

"No, I probably would not have paid you much attention."

"So, you won't fuck me because you think I'll be with anybody. Is that it?"

"I didn't say anything of the sort. In fact, I won't fuck you because I have been with *anybody* and now I want to be with *somebody*."

Veronica got off the bed and walked over to the chair where she had thrown her sweatshirt. She put it on and began running the zipper up and down in an awkward sort of way. She went over to the dresser and picked up the bottle of milk. "You want a refill?"

"Sure."

She sat back on the bed and poured the remaining milk into my glass. There was barely enough left to coat the bottom. She threw the carton casually across the room, then sat drawing circles with her finger on the sheet. She avoided my eyes.

"What else can I get you?" she asked at last.

"*You* are the somebody, Veronica. I think you're the somebody."

She looked up at me with tears welling in her electric blue eyes. "Somebody. Somebody is good. Other than the burden of being pretty with a fantastic body that makes mere mortals turn to stone . . . somebody is good."

Then she kissed me on the cheek for a very long time.

Veronica climbed under the covers and pulled the blanket as high up to our chins as possible. From under the covers, she removed her sweatshirt and discarded it with a flourish. Then came her tank top. Her panties followed. She rubbed up against me.

With her head resting on my chest, and smiling as if she had one big special secret, she said, "Get some sleep. You're going to need it. Big day tomorrow and it starts early. That shit with those raccoons could get you in a whole lot of trouble. Oh, by the way, big boy, I am totally naked." I felt her breasts press up against me and she wrapped her long legs around mine. "Sorry you can't do anything about it. You see, I'm not just anybody. I am somebody."

I stroked her soft hair and moved her so she rested in the crook of my arm.

Plymouth was now a kingdom of magic. It promised more. Yet as I lay in Veronica's arms, I thought, *If this is it, then there is indeed a God, and he is kind and rich and offered a bit of giddyup.*

Veronica sighed and pressed even closer. If you could make a musical out of all of this, it would run forever. I closed my eyes. If it took months for them to open, well, that would be all too soon.

36

Veronica was true to her word. The morning began early. She had roused me from a deep sleep by 7 a.m. and given me fifteen minutes to meet her outside. When I did, she was standing next to her car holding two steaming cups of coffee. Her hair was in a long ponytail, and she wore a white form-fitting T-shirt and blue jeans that hugged her butt as if painted on by a grand master. How did anyone, especially me, ever rebuff her overtures?

She handed me my coffee and suggested I follow her. We sped down Rocky Hill Road. The morning was chilly, but the sun was already making things right. Veronica turned into the lot at PBT. The marquee remained lit, shouting out the news of our new season, and again the sight of it gave me a thrill.

In the driveway were two pickup trucks with business names on their doors. One was a tarnished navy-blue fifties Chevy whose sign read IRON'S PEST CONTROL, the other a shiny red El Camino, sporting WHITE CLIFFS OF PLYMOUTH.

Seated at the picnic table in casual but crisp outfits of denim and khaki were two guys; one I knew a little and the other was a stranger. They were eating a box of doughnuts and drinking coffee. As I approached the group they stood up to greet me.

"Hi, Sidney," I said as I shook his hand and offered a friendly grin.

The guy I didn't know said, "Morning, Sam. Johnny Iron. Good to meet you." He presented a firm handshake.

The dead raccoons from last evening lay a few feet from us; they now had visitors in the form of ants, flies, and other vermin.

"Sam, I brought Johnny by because yous got a serious problem with these animals here," Sidney stated. "They're dead, you know?"

I looked at the carcasses of the fallen raccoon family and remembered how close their relatives had gotten to extracting revenge. "Yes, Sidney, they're dead."

"You shoot them?"

"Nope."

"Who did?" asked Johnny Iron.

"Is that important?" I asked. "If this is a problem, then let's talk about fixing that, and then we can move on to the recriminations."

Sidney looked peeved. "Veronica, honey, comes over here so I can understand what your college boy is saying."

She sashayed over from the table, licking the powdered sugar off a doughnut.

"Sam, these animals are dead," said Johnny Iron. "They pose a health issue. You know, disease and all. And they are going to fuck up the smell around here pretty darn quick."

"You think these suckers are dead?" I deadpanned.

Johnny Iron took another look to make sure, looked back at me, and said, "Yeah, they are, Sam. They're dead."

"Quit fuckin 'round here, college boy," Sidney said sharply. "This ain't funny. You got animals here that were shot. Somebody goes to jail for that shit in Plymouth County. Even if yous got a license for the gun, there's no license that allows you to shoot coons. You got to make this go away. Veronica called me, so I dragged my old ass out of bed to help yous. So now what's it going to be?"

"I'm sorry, Sid. I am certain you came to help and I am very appreciative. But can I ask you this? You can't shoot 'em even if they're about to make you their dinner?"

"Funny," he said red faced, voice rising. "You think jail is funny?"

I realized this wasn't amusing anymore. "Okay, guys, what do I do?"

Johnny jumped in. "I can get this all cleaned up and stashed away. Hose down the grounds and disinfect that room there. I can even come back and check the house and the grounds for colonies . . ."

As I was mulling this, a shiny black king-cab Ford raced into our circular driveway and the driver jumped out. He was muscular, wearing a tight white T-shirt, with a Red Sox cap pulled down over his face and shades.

"Pay me three hundred in cash," Johnny continued. "Less than an hour, this all never happened."

"Three hundred bucks!" I said. "This is bullshit. I have nothing to do with these raccoons . . . I'm going to speak to the landlord and . . ."

The guy from the black truck had been lurking just outside the circle of our conversation. He now took off his cap and sunglasses. He took a few steps closer to me, and with his arms folded against his chest, nodded in my direction.

"Gary Golden," he said. "We met the other night at the Moondog. I know the landlord, and he won't give a shit."

"Yeah, I understand that you and Barrows are asshole buddies," I said. I made sure to put special emphasis on the word "asshole."

Gary ignored my quip and continued. "As your friend, I should tell you three hundred bucks is cheap to stay out of trouble in this town. So is a grand, three to Johnny here and the other seven hundred to me to keep it all under the radar. Trust me, money well spent, especially for the new kid on the block"

I pointed to his left cheek. "Quite a bruise. Did you have an accident?"

"No," he answered, arms still crossed and with no glint of humor behind his dark eyes. "But it's a small town. Accidents happen all the time."

Suddenly, Veronica tripped over something, and as she stumbled, her coffee found its way all over Gary Golden's crisp clean white tee. "Sorry, friend," she said.

"I guess you're right, Gary," I added. "Accidents *do* happen."

37

It was midafternoon and the day had settled in better than its promise of early morning. Dead animals, bribes, and coffee spills do not an omelet make.

Johnny Iron erased any remnant of Raccoon Nation and the girls had moved into their bedroom, which was now rodent free and freshly painted. Work on the business of our business was actually getting done.

Earlier in the day, wearing a liter of hot coffee, Gary Golden had looked a lot less tough. I thought that with much of his menace denuded it was a good time for him and me to have a chat. "Hey, Mr. Golden," I said, "if I actually had a spare seven hundred dollars and if I was crazy enough to agree to give it to you, the only way I would do that would be to shove it up your ass."

He didn't seem to appreciate my attitude.

"Additionally," I added, "you might want to know that my friend Davey Molson has a pair of panties with one of those summer camp name tags sewn on the band that reads 'Golden.' I don't think the panties are yours, Gary—too small, I imagine—but I'm pretty certain they would fit your mom." He wasn't wild about that comment either.

"Oh and, Gary, get the fuck out of my face." As he left I called after him, "Don't you want your mom's panties?"

I felt pretty cool about all of this until Sidney put an arm around my shoulder and said, "College boy, you're a moron."

Maybe the morning was indeed a portent of the rest of my day.

38

It was early dusk. The sunset was on its best behavior. The breeze off the ocean was scented and cool. The compound was ablaze in pinks, violets, eggnogs, jonquils, and aquamarines, all dazzling in their splendiferous spring grandeur. It was all a delicious buffet of nature. JB, James, Debbie, Diana, Elliot, Jojo, Secunda, and I sat comfortably under the big dogwood tree that stood in front of the theater.

I felt as if we needed an oversized calendar to check off the day's goals and accomplishments. We'd had so many over the past few days. Unfortunately, we also had some enormous distractions and unforeseen obstacles. I thought of the many films I loved growing up, all of those great Hitchcock movies about ordinary men placed in extraordinary circumstances. I looked at my friends. We were extraordinary dreamers, yet had enough character to elevate the next four months from the benign to the sublime. We just had to stay the course.

JB laid out the agenda for her crew, which included chores for Debbie, Diana, James, and herself. Jojo updated us on the status of actors' design issues and scheduling. Secunda had actually met with the licensing libraries and secured the rights to the shows we wanted to do. I don't know if he overpaid for those rights or offered to send someone's kid through college, but we were clear.

Doobie, looking very green, had been by earlier in the day and, along with Veronica's brother Tommy, put together a maintenance crew that would make the place ready for inspection within days. I considered the possibility that we had all read a few too many Winston Churchill speeches in our day, but I liked Winnie, and the allies did win the war.

I felt it important that we figure out Plymouth. Secunda was right: it didn't matter who was fucking who in this town, or who was corrupt or a saint. Who paid their taxes, hit on underage girls, or tipped less than 10 percent. I knew that at some point our sense of righteousness would get us in trouble. Yet, if I were to be any good at directing this summer, I had to have a clear head to do so. So did my cohorts. We were puppies and we had elected to run with the big dogs.

As we continued our meeting, a Garden cab pulled into the driveway and stopped at the office. A young clean-cut young man wearing jeans, white sneakers, and a powder blue poplin button-down shirt got out and paid the driver. As he surveyed the property, I noticed his body language change from tough to mellow. A smile creased his face and he looked happy. Bobby Stevens appeared pleased to be in Plymouth.

39

Bobby noticed me across the compound. He was no longer mellow. He walked briskly in my direction and I met him halfway with an extended welcoming hand. "You found us!" I offered, sounding a bit jollier than I intended.

He avoided my proffered hand and said, "You stole my photos. I did a nice thing and then you ripped me off. You're an asshole."

"I'm sorry, Bobby, but I didn't steal your pictures. I had every intention of returning them."

"When? Before or after I got fired?"

"Neither," I said, speaking evenly. "Bobby, you made the trip up here. It's a beautiful evening. Sit for a few minutes and have a beer with me and my friends. If after I explain you still want to punch my face in, I'll offer you my chin."

"I came here to keep my job. Maybe have you arrested."

"Bobby, please have a beer with me."

He looked as if he had just kissed a lemon. He looked around the grounds and reluctantly agreed to sit. I grabbed a beer and sat across from him at the redwood picnic table. I raised the bottle and gestured for us to clink. We did.

The compound was postcard perfect. The ocean could be heard down the road less than three hundred feet away. Bobby drank a long pull on his beer and ran his hand through his hair. I could sense he didn't want to remain angry.

"Thank you," I said. "For sitting with me. Making the trip up here. And letting us steal the pictures."

"I knew I shouldn't have left you alone," he grumbled.

"You know, the beach is just down the road. If you stand on the bench, you can see it."

"I don't do that well in the sun. Fair skin."

"It's nice at night as well. You should see it. The rocks are phosphorescent. They light up the sea. It's a little bit sci-fi."

"Why did you steal my pictures?" He asked this without anger, just really wanting to know. "I could have called the cops."

"I needed you to come up here and I thought it was the best way to make that happen."

His brows knit. "Why did you need me to come up here?"

"Because I need to sell thirty thousand tickets this summer and I need to get the newspapers all over the Cape to write about us and I need the *Boston Globe* to say we're the second coming. You can do that."

I thought I might have him. A moment passed.

"I have a job. So thanks for the beer. Now give me back my pictures."

"You don't have a job like this one. It's only four months. I would think your internship will be waiting for you after Labor Day. Guys with your skills and vision can find intern gigs every day, but here it's all yours to make sing. To make our noise. To make a legend."

JB, Secunda, and the rest of the PBT elite wandered over and surrounded the table. If Stevens was planning to bolt, he'd have to run through them. They introduced themselves and expressed how excited they were that he was thinking of working with us. James replaced his empty beer with a fresh cold one.

We all explained why we were there for the summer. We showed Bobby the theater, the backstage, and the scene and costume shops. We walked to the beach and chatted as we all sat watching the waves and the phosphorescent rocks reflecting against the early night sky.

By nine o'clock we were figuring out how he could ask for a leave of absence and still keep his job. Secunda offered to buy him a lobster, show him the wharf, and welcome him big time. Bobby agreed, but asked to speak with me for a minute in private. The girls suggested they pick up Veronica and head downtown. Bobby and I could follow and talk on the way. We'd all meet at Souza's.

As Bobby and I drove, I rehashed much of what we had discussed over the past few hours. "One of my professors did his graduate work at Colgate University then took his first teaching job at Tufts. You know him. He was at Colgate during your senior year. Gerry Collins. When I told Gerry what I was doing this summer, he insisted that I had to get you to play. After all, you put the Colgate 13 on the map. You made it matter. When I found out you sang with the group, I knew I could win you over. I mean, your own press office, on the beach, free reign, and you can be in the shows. All I needed to do was get you up here."

"You sure are a confident guy," Bobby said. "It's more than obnoxious, you know."

"Yes, to the latter. It's all a front, to the former. But, Bobby, I know this: if you work with us, everyone will know our names. We will leap to the front of the pack, and I guarantee it will be one terrific ride."

"I believe you," he said. "But the audacity of stealing my pictures works once. You better do for me what you promise, because I need the tools to win."

"I promise. To keep my promise."

In that moment, the bar got higher. We had a true professional on board, and he was giving up something of value to play in our sandbox. The risk was shared, and winning the game now offered even greater potential for reward.

"How big are the lobsters at this place?" he asked.

"As big as they need to be for you, Bobby. I promise."

We stayed in town till the place closed. Anything with a shell on it we ate. Sweet crisp lobsters, succulent pink shrimp, clams and oysters bathed in fresh horseradish and Tabasco. We all wore bibs that captured the drawn butter as it ran down our appreciative, happy chins.

When I played football, I learned that "chemistry" was when your team won. Chemistry in the theater was fallacy. Sure, it was good to get along, but it was always art before community. If the work was good then the community thrived. Despite the best of intentions, loyalties in the theater are found in the length of applause, and when that fades, so does the rest.

Bobby's complete focus was on achievement. His goal was to sell seats and put our troop on the map. Yet as the evening grew late, it was evident that behind his eyes were intentions far greater and far more ambitious than I had ever seen in anyone. He had a look of raw ambition, as if he were saying, "This gets me to where I want to be. This offers a path to who I want to become." To see that in a stranger's eyes was scary.

We all toasted Bobby Stevens with one last iced brew at Souza's. I caught his expression as the glasses clinked. It was calculating, where I expected warmth. Looking at him, I felt older, as if I had lost something held dear. Innocence.

40

Secunda, James, and I each did our daily chores from dawn to dusk. We were like Paul Muni in *I Am a Fugitive from a Chain Gang*. Tough, backbreaking labor all day that left us broken and spent by evening. True, JB and the "women" were strained to the limit as well, but their tasks were more cerebral. Kasen, Duncan, Holly, and their crews had jobs to do to make the shows happen on time. All that tomorrow offered to us, the three schmucks with aching backs, was more of the same. It was fun, though, and we had our share of laughs.

One early, damp morning, with sunrise at least an hour away, we tackled some of the shrubbery, clipping back rose bushes whose thorns painted pictures in red upon our faces. That afternoon, hundreds of pounds of fertilizer arrived for us to spread. The three of us looked at one another and I said, "What, and give up show business?"

Secunda lost it. He ripped open each bag of cow shit and hurled the manure at the flowerbeds, all the while grunting and screaming expletives at the plants. James and I watched in awe at the enormity of his efforts and misplaced passion. Piano music from rehearsals accompanied this meltdown, making the whole thing look like an old silent movie. When Secunda was finished, the manure had indeed been spread, except for the considerable amount he was wearing himself. He lay on the ground, covered in cow doody.

There was simply too much to do: houses to paint, a kitchen to repair, the signage to bring into this century . . . and then there were tickets to sell, actors to welcome, and, oh yes, shows to put on.

There was only one way to respond to this. "Beer, gentlemen?" I suggested. Quickly, we were off to the Full Sail for brews. On the way, I realized one very important thing: horse manure, bullshit, and its relatives can always wait until tomorrow.

The next days flew by and jobs were accomplished. At night, we'd toss off responsibility and become young again. We looked for love or drank at the local bars, walked the beaches or danced with abandon at area clubs. We returned home buzzed, alone or with a soon-to-be lover on our arm.

Doobie and Veronica brought in their crews, and within days the place was transformed. The two old faded farmhouses were restored to their original colors, one in crimson red and the other in the clean white of a long-lingering January snowfall. Show tunes played throughout the compound on James's makeshift speakers, and the crews danced from task to task. During breaks, groups of ten and twelve would walk to Garden's. Papa would smile.

We finished the trimming of the tired landscape, planting armies of azaleas, zinnias, and robust rows of purple, white, blue, and red tulips. The compound was a sea of color and the scent of spring. A new city was built, orchestrated by desire and accompanied by the music of our genre. I felt like I was presiding over the resurrection of a small city.

Doobie's mom came on board, bringing dozens of grungy local workers to scrub the kitchen clean. Shining chrome replaced rusted stovetops, linoleum floors were waxed and countertops made to glisten like a showcase for Sears.

Bobby completely redesigned the marquee; now it looked like it had been brought in directly from Times Square. He created a brand and logo for the theater. He removed the old signage letters and replaced them with colorful backlit plastics that beckoned everyone who passed our way with the titles of each show.

JB, Diana, James, and Debbie had opened the box office, and inside the small cubicle were almost thirty-five thousand tickets waiting to find eager buyers. The stacks of color, each assigned to a specific day of the week, offered a rainbow of promise. Sell these suckers, and the world would be a shiny beacon to the entrepreneurial spirit.

Delivery trucks came and went, bringing food and supplies for the house, lumber, paint, and hardware for the scenery, and fabric for costumes. The police department came by every few hours to check in on us. Tommy visited most often, and it seemed that whenever he did, JB disappeared for a bit only to return with a flushed face and a wink in her grin.

Early one morning before the sun was even on the radar, there was a loud pounding on my door. I rolled out of bed half asleep to find Johnny Iron, who had been so helpful with "raccoon night." He stood drinking a big cup of steaming coffee, wearing overalls without a shirt. Over his shoulder there was a virtual mountain of white gravel. It was meant to fill the potholes throughout the compound, not to replicate a pyramid.

"Hey, Johnny, the pharaoh send you?" I asked.

"The pharaoh? I don't know anyone named Pharaoh. JB ordered this last week."

"How am I going to move all these stones? I'll need a bulldozer. Why didn't you spread them around the compound?"

"That's not what you ordered, and it's more money"

"I'll need fifteen, twenty guys to get this done."

Johnny considered that for a second. "I can get you some guys."

"How much?" I asked, perking up.

"More than the bulldozer."

"So get me the bulldozer."

"Can't. It's booked."

I was beginning to think he was enjoying himself.

"Why didn't you hold it for me?"

"You didn't ask."

And the carousel of idiocy continued. I walked over to Johnny and put my arm around his shoulder.

"Can we get you some more coffee? Breakfast? Moses?"

"I don't know a Moses, but I will take the coffee."

"Okay then. We'll figure something out later."

I looked at the gravel Matterhorn and asked myself, *How?*

"Sam, you're not happy with this delivery. I can tell, because I know of people."

"Is intuition part of the purchase order?"

He didn't know an Intuition either.

"I will put the stones back on the truck and dump it where you want."

"Who'll put the rocks back on your truck?"

"My guys," he answered quickly.

"Who pays them?"

"I do. I do what it takes to make my customers happy."

The coffee and bacon smelled extra appealing. I put my arm around his shoulder and said, "You're a good man, Johnny Iron. What would you like for breakfast?"

41

Everywhere you went at the compound, you always heard music. Lots of it. Our days played out to the beat of a soundtrack.

Secunda had worked out a deal with our orchestra leader, Louis Rosenberg, and days before rehearsal, ten of his players arrived with their instruments roped to the top of their straining station wagon. Louis's ten guys were an eclectic group, ear ringed, tattooed, big grins, and facial hair. Some were tall and gregarious like Louis, others sullen and intense, but they all seemed to perk up and embrace the ocean air and were quick to notice the bevy of chorines that increased with each new day's arrivals. These New York City boys knew they were in the right place.

I have always marveled at the artists' ability to create something from a blank page. Whether they built or composed something, or simply wrote it, you could see their ideas becoming part of a greater reality. Mary Holly was one of these talented artists. She worked long hours in the costume shop hunched over a sewing machine, surrounded by satins, feathers, and sketches haphazardly taped to the walls. She wove our ideas into short, skimpy outfits or elegant, cascading dresses that complemented Duncan's and Kasen's work in the scene shop. Together, their work melded into a world that would miraculously change from show to show.

After twelve-hour days, we would have dinner at dusk. We'd barbecue burgers and dogs, and mingle in the compound. Then for breakfast Doobie's mom would serve stacks of pancakes, endless bacon and sausages. The scent of hot coffee mingled with the sunrise. Ma had kids in at 5 a.m. squeezing fresh juices. Everyone carried a script or a music book. The musicians practiced their brand of jazz, adding more hues to the colors of the day.

In addition to all the work, we formed cliques and smoked pot and drank too much and had sex on the beach or in our rooms. Stage-door Johnnies wooed our chorus girls, and we were sent good-luck gifts from all sorts of members of the community. It was one long joy ride and we felt bulletproof.

One afternoon, Lizzy Barrows drove up in her red Mercedes and walked purposefully to the box office. Diana greeted her, and after they chatted back and forth, Mrs. Barrows came looking for me. She carried two large stacks of tickets and wore a smile on her face. Under the afternoon Cape sun and wearing a simple outfit of jeans and alligator polo shirt, she looked like a young, sweet coed.

"I just bought eight hundred tickets to your shows," she called.

"Thank you, Mrs. Barrows. Are you going to stop the check or let it clear this time?"

"Come on, Auggie, be nice."

"You're right, I'm sorry. I'm sure you'll enjoy the show. Have a good afternoon." I started to leave.

"Come over to the house," she said suggestively. "I'll teach you how to swim . . . and you won't even need to bring a bathing suit."

"Your overtures are indecorous to say the least," I said, my voice oozing with condescension.

"Ooh, one of your fancy words! 'Indecorous.' Does that mean you'll be by to see me?"

"No fancy words, Lizzy. It's simply one you don't like to hear: no."

"How about, *'You're fucked, you smart-assed prick?'* You like to hear that?" she shouted.

The compound fell silent. She walked right at me, leading with her chin. "You think you can come into our town—Andy's town—and play by your rules?" she barked in a heated whisper. "Think again, shitpot. *You think you're better than me because you use fancy words and think you're some kind of kike prince?*"

I almost slapped her, but then she would have won.

"No, Lizzy, I don't think I'm better than you because I use fancy words. I think I'm better than you because I *am*. Then again, you don't set the bar very high. Now, unless you want to buy some more tickets—for cash—get off the compound."

I walked away, still stupidly thinking that harlot or not, she was one great-looking girl.

42

Within days of settling into our quarters at PBT, James began making friends with the "weed people" in town. Hence, each evening many of us would congregate in the loft he had built for himself in the attic of the white house and partake of their offerings. The festivities commenced at 7 p.m. sharp.

The crowd varied from night to night, but the reason for getting together was to watch reruns of *Star Trek* that James had pirated from local TV affiliates in Providence and Boston. Many of us loved Captain Kirk and the crew; as we reviewed episodes we knew all too well, we smoked the bong, drank beers, discussed the day's events, and planned for tomorrow. Dates were made for late "rendezvous" on the beach that meant "I'll meet you there naked."

One night, Doobie showed up at the *Star Trek* fest with some new weed from a friend. It was pungent, unlike any other pot we'd smoked. Nevertheless, we already had a good buzz and I led the way with two long drags. Others followed, but more temperately.

It was a cold New England spring night; there was a damp breeze off the water and an unexpected chill in the air. The wind kicked up and an occasional gust made the entire house creak, while the trees outside whipped with an ominous tone.

I felt very uncomfortable after my tokes on the new weed. I was uneasy— or somewhat unhinged, to say the least. When I stood up my balance was shaky. I remained somewhat dazed until I found the blue TV screen and locked on to it like a pit bull with a bone. I was frightened by what I saw. Something had happened to Spock. He was injured. His brain had fallen out of his head and no one, either on the *Enterprise* or in James Feldman's room, seemed to notice or care. I became more agitated as I saw Spock's brain leave the TV set and roll across the attic loft and down the steps onto the compound. I shrieked, *"Spock!"* and ran in pursuit.

Most of those in the group thought I was being goofy. But Secunda, JB, Bobby, and Veronica followed me out. By the time they reached the compound, I was racing toward the ocean in irrational hysteria shouting, "I'll save you, Spock!" As I ran I shed my clothes.

What I heard later was that Veronica suggested she call the police and Bobby Stevens laid her out. "Call the police!" he shouted at her. "Get him arrested and this place shut down?"

"He's fucked up on something, Bobby. What would you have me do? Drop to my knees and pray that he won't fucking drown?"

"No, I would get on the phone to everyone you know and get them down here and stop this before he ruins his life."

With tears running down her face, Veronica ran to the office and reached for the phone. Simultaneously, she picked up the compound's PA mic and shouted, "Everybody up, report to the office now." There was no need to say it was an emergency; you could hear it in her tone.

Our friends who had been in the attic with James raced into the fray. They had heard my howling as it cut through the stillness and chill of the rainswept night. Secunda, Elliot, and Duncan chased after me. James ordered Debbie to run to the theater to get flashlights, rope, and first-aid materials and bring them to the shore.

I had a big head start on everyone, so when Secunda reached the beach, I was at least two hundred yards into the face of a frigid Atlantic. My voice had become muted in the distance, but I was still shouting for Spock's salvation. Debbie arrived with the flashlights; several of the others had driven down to the shore and pointed their car headlights into the night sea. James, Duncan, and Kasen showed up on hot-wired jet skis from local beachside cottages and hit the water with engines screaming.

I remember swimming away from the shore, and although I could hear voices behind me and see streaks of car lights, I continued to swim straight ahead, just within reach of Spock's brain. I felt no fatigue and no chill—just the single purpose to save the Vulcan. There were beams of light everywhere. One moment I was visible and the next I had disappeared. I began to swallow water and realized that I needed to rest a moment, or neither Spock nor I would make it home alive.

Whatever had sent me more than a half-mile out to sea had begun to wear off. I was taking in increasing amounts of water and I was now shivering, my lips blue, my limbs numb. I wanted to shout, but I was breathless and no words were audible. I treaded water, but my legs cramped. I still heard shouts that sounded like "hold on," "stay strong," and "we got you," but with each passing second the words faded, becoming indecipherable. All sounds were muted now and everything moved in slow motion.

I was ice. Exhausted, I went under, cold and limp. Light flickered above me with no direction or purpose. I was under for a while. As I pushed myself up with all my might to catch some air, I came away with more water than I could handle. I choked, my lungs filling with water as black as tea. Then I saw nothing, felt nothing but a deep, bone-chilling cold . . . In a final instant I was no longer conscious.

43

I lay in my room directly off the compound on the first floor of the red house. I was wrapped in so many blankets that I felt mummified. My head was throbbing and my bones were still ice. Most of the witnesses from yesterday's near-catastrophic event had left shortly after I was safe on land. The difference between tragedy and anecdote is faint. They had almost seen my death play out and wanted to build a Chinese wall around my impetuous behavior.

Bobby Stevens was the first to visit me. He was terse and made me feel the fool. He acknowledged that it could have been he who had partaken of the PCP-laced pot, he who might have acted outside the boundaries of safety. However, I was the one who had gathered everyone here in Plymouth, and my responsibility to be a grown up transcended the others'. He told me he hadn't joined up to promote or condone tragedy. He was grateful I was all right, yet this was a business arrangement. His loyalty was to the opportunity and not to foolishness, no matter how benign it appeared before taking a turn into darkness.

"Are you staying on?" I asked.

"Yes," he replied. "Even fools overcome their mistakes. I still have faith in you, but don't fuck up again."

"I promise," I said. Then he left without a smile.

It was close to midnight. Since everyone was gone, the compound was silent, yet the wind whipped the trees, and the rain spanked the buildings and pelted the windows as if threatening to break and enter.

After a while, Secunda came in without knocking. He wore a heavy expression and his energy was low. He stood for a long time, his arms resting across his chest, staring intently at me. It was uncomfortable, and he made no effort to soften the mood. At last he pulled up the only chair in the room and sat very close to the side of my bed.

"You're okay, that's good. This was reckless. I've known you a long time and seen you do some crazy things. You never should have been so careless.

Put yourself in danger, all of this in danger. My brother has already heard it from me. I asked him to find out where that pot came from. Then we're going to deal with it and it will all be over. Over."

He looked tired and sad. His shoulders sagged, his strength was drained. He looked old and lacked his usual aura of force and menace. "I don't care what happens next as long as it is what you want and you are safe. We close tomorrow and send everyone home. No sweat. We lose some money, but not our way. You matter more than this dream."

I bristled. "You know, if you throw an interception on the first set of downs, it doesn't mean you shouldn't play the game."

"I'm playing. But not to lose. If you put us in a position to lose, then I think we should all go home." He leaned over me and kissed my forehead like a father putting a young son to bed. He walked out of the room without further comment.

I lay there searching my soul. This was my gig. And I needed to hold myself to a higher standard. When Sidney called me a moron a few weeks ago, he was right. No chasing windmills or fighting battles that even if won were not worth the pain or the bloodshed. Drink in moderation, chase the girls, and maintain perspective. Tonight could have been a tragedy. Instead, it was a wakeup call.

The door to my room opened slightly and without sound. No one appeared, and I thought perhaps it was the wind. After a moment, Veronica entered without a word. She looked wan and tense with an air of vulnerability. She greeted me with a nod and whispered a barely audible, "Hi." Then she sat in the chair next to the bed with her hands folded in her lap. Her eyes met my gaze but there was nothing to say.

Less than an hour ago I thought I was done. Veronica had waited for Neptune's verdict while helpless and wounded on shore. Whatever had happened with us these past electric days was over, yet now as we sat there inches apart, it was being given a second chance.

I sat up and reached for her, and she was in my arms in less than a heartbeat. Our mouths met and we kissed as if it were the last time we would ever see one another. I stripped off her clothes amid a cacophony of verbal intimacies. There was anger and release in our actions; no softness or foreplay, just a ravishing of one another with the hope that the fear and remorse and regret of the night might be vanquished. She was as perfect as I had imagined. Her skin was like satin, her body warm and open and available. We consummated our love-making with an explosiveness I had never imagined. I actually felt fireworks. I caught my breath and thought that almost dying was not such a bad thing if it led to something this good.

We lay naked and spent in each other's arms for a long time. Then Veronica spoke.

"You know, Sam, I've lived through nights like tonight too many times. It's one of the reasons I decided long ago to leave Plymouth. Drunk driving, stupid violence, reckless drugs, petty squabbles about forgotten issues that put people in jail or into the ground. I drink, I smoke weed, and I've spent time with boys or foolish men who don't know why they're looking to fight, other than that it's in their blood."

"None of it is any good. It's like betting your life, and if you win you get a free beer. Big fuckin' deal. My brother didn't do anything wrong, no different from the kind of mistake you made tonight, and he is in prison. You never know what consequences will come from what seems to be an innocent circumstance. I miss Eddie. Until just now, I was already mourning you."

I said nothing. It was one of those times when a man should simply listen and not try to resolve anything.

"When you arrived in Plymouth, I sensed you were different and I wanted to know you. I thought you were the kind of guy I was leaving Plymouth to meet. So I put aside my fears and worked hard to insinuate myself into your life. Even short term. Even for just the summer. I see the way you go about things, the way you take over a room, and the way your friends listen to every word you say. It's inspiring to me and I want you more and more. To be with you. To have that aura transferred to me so I can have some ownership of it once the summer's gone and you move on to the next task, the next dream, the next windmill."

Veronica's speech had become halting, as if emotion had overtaken her thoughts. Her eyes filled with tears, and they slowly found their way down her cheeks. I lay there waiting to hear what came next.

"You said I was somebody. Not just anybody. And I believed you. For two reasons. One, it's true. More important, you're the only man I ever met who was smart enough to see it."

She wiped her nose, gathered her remaining thoughts, then presented them clearly, without tears or hesitation, as if they were fact.

"I want to be here with you this summer. I want to work at your side and I want to make love to you and keep you safe and champion everything you do. I want to remember this summer as the time I came of age with a real man as my partner, and I want it all to be fun. Tonight, I was scared, and, no, I am not asking for assurances. But if there is danger, I don't want foolishness to open the door for its arrival. You're too smart and too terrific to give that up because you allow the stupid boy in you to detour the great man you'll become."

She didn't look any less tired or wrung out, but she sure did look great.

"Your rehearsals start the day after tomorrow. It's a jump off a hundred-foot cliff and we all can't wait to brace ourselves as we hit the water. I just want to be there and want you to be pleased that I feel that way."

She got up, dressed, and just as Secunda had, kissed me on my forehead, long and sweetly, like a mother putting her kid to bed. She turned and opened the door. The bracing wind whooshed into the room with the rain close behind in a subtle mist.

"You know where Doobie got that pot he gave James for you and your friends to smoke?" she asked.

I nodded. "Gary Golden."

"How did you know?"

"It's all very theatrical. By the way, there's nothing you've done since I met you that hasn't pleased me."

"I'm easy on the eyes."

Then she turned out the light and closed the door behind her. The sound of her footsteps diminished as she walked away, across the newly laid gravel. With each step I heard her moving closer to me rather than farther away.

44

The entire PBT company had arrived by Sunday noon. Tomorrow, May 31, would be Memorial Day. Rehearsals would begin on Tuesday at 10 a.m., and our first show would open on June 21, just three weeks away.

To commemorate our first day together, Secunda had invited everyone to a clambake on the beach that evening at seven-thirty. Since the first day of work wasn't until Tuesday morning, no one was concerned about staying out or partying late. Secunda's clambake was out of a beach blanket movie. A show tune from *Carousel* was apropos as well: "It Was a Real Nice Clambake." Indeed it was, and more.

Secunda had arranged for fresh crustaceans of every size and shape. Skewers carrying shrimp, lobster, clams, scallops, and fresh corn hovered over a bonfire the size and scope of the *Hindenburg* in full demise. Huge vats of guacamole and various dips were available. Iced coolers housed bottles of beer from numerous breweries, and we had wine from high-end California vineyards. He provided Caribbean music by finding a group who played steel drums with an island beat while tushies swayed, and strangers danced close and got quickly acquainted.

Actors being actors, there was a great deal of sleuthing as each performer eyed who might threaten them for accolades or attention, or the heart of some boy or girl they had already set their sights upon. People were animated and open, wide eyed and eager to be part of this initiation.

I had never expected to have a girlfriend this summer, but as people arrived throughout the day, it seemed that Veronica and I were welcoming them together. She didn't tell anyone we were a couple; she just presented herself as the company manager. Still, we held hands a lot and kissed frequently.

I imagine that in life dozens of people rarely gather to perform a task in which everyone truly wants to be there. We were all on the Cape because it had been a dream, perhaps one vested long ago, or in some cases a new one not yet fully formed. I wanted this moment to be recorded in my memory for a long time. It was a pivotal event in my life. I knew that some of this would crumble and the perfect picture I saw tonight would fade. Nevertheless, if we accomplished nothing else over the next four months, I was bursting with pride for having gotten this far.

I found Veronica in a crowd of joyous, animated strangers who would become our friends. I held her hand and enjoyed Secunda's party. Tonight was a night to cherish. We would deal with tomorrow when it came.

45

Veronica and I decided to sleep late on Memorial Day and then head into Provincetown for an Italian feast. She got dressed in a cute sundress with a flower pattern that was short but modest on top, and piled her hair into a Sox cap. Her face was sans makeup but for a hint of lip gloss that made her very kissable. I had washed my jeans and complemented them with a new lime-green cotton, collarless shirt with the sleeves rolled up.

Once we were ready, Veronica rushed me out into the compound. At least half the company had gathered around a shiny, new, powder-blue Chrysler van with a big red ribbon tied to the front grill. Some of the people from the company held a large sign that read HAPPY BIRTHDAY, BOSS. Secunda stepped forward with an amazingly large grin.

"My birthday is not for three weeks," I said.

"We know that, but with everything that's in store for you, none of us are sure whether you'll make it another three weeks. So here you are, you bastard. Enjoy. This is from me to you. JB wouldn't let me put in the budget."

Then he gave me the keys. I hugged him, and for once in my life had nothing to say. Not because I didn't want to—I didn't know how. I walked around the truck and saw that PRISCILLA BEACH THEATRE had been painted on each side. Everyone applauded and cheered.

I grabbed Veronica's hand and helped her climb into the passenger seat, then walked around to the other side and opened the door. I looked at Secunda and gave him a most sincere thank you. I got behind the wheel, started the engine, and drove out of the compound while honking the horn and waving like I was in a presidential parade.

As we turned onto Rocky Hill Road I looked at Veronica and said, "Wow."

"You want to know the real surprise of the day?" she asked. "We're having dinner with my parents."

I thought of the old expression about mixed emotions. You know the one: mixed emotions are when you drive your new car off a cliff to avoid dinner with your girlfriend's parents. I pulled the van onto the shoulder and put the car in park. I then put the emergency brake in place thinking it was a metaphor for the conversation I was about to embark on.

"Why," I asked "did you make plans with your folks and not tell me? We're just getting started. A week ago, I was just some boy passing through and now I'm a guest at Mom and Dad's?"

"You're not just a boy passing through. I never thought such a thing. Now we're together and I'm so proud of us, of me for trusting you. And look how happy we are. I can't stop smiling, and it's been a long time since my parents have seen me this way."

"It's too soon, Veronica. It's too much."

She looked sad and confused. Not upset or angry, more as if she had taken a wrong turn and was lost late on a dark, moonless road. "No it's not," she said quietly, "It's part of our journey. We have less than a hundred days together and we have to live it *all* before the sand runs through the hourglass."

"When you're our age, Veronica, a hundred days can be a lifetime. And who put a limit on us anyway?"

"You. Your ambition, your focus, ferocity of purpose, your goals and need to prove yourself, never taking a breath. You'll move on, you can't help yourself. You'll be opening the next door before you close the one behind you."

"And where is the trust in that?"

"It's real, I'm holding on. But I want us to live each day with an abundance of color, so when the sand is all gone it will take a long time for those colors to fade."

"And meeting Mom and Dad makes those colors bright? It's just that simple?"

"Nothing is simple, Sam. You know there are no absolutes."

She moved closer, laid her head in my lap and looked up at me with those eyes that made a sapphire sky seem gray.

"You know what I've been thinking, doll?" I said. "That I want to meet your folks."

Veronica put her hand gently upon the back of my neck, sat up, and kissed me long and lingering. I thought, *This would be a nice way to spend a hundred days or a lifetime, whichever turns out to be longer.*

I started up the van and drove back onto the highway. I wondered how much wine would be served with our meal. Then I looked over at Veronica and saw that she was indeed happy, almost as much as I was.

She turned on the radio. "The Things We Do for Love" was in full lyric.

46

We stopped for wine, and I was faced with my first meeting-the-parents decision. Should I spend more than I could afford or buy something that filled a jug and was really manufactured to get a buzz on, fast and cheap. I choose the former, mostly because the label was attractive and the vineyard was in Napa. Once we arrived, I was glad I went for upscale.

The Chapman home was small, tucked away in a cul-de-sac abutting an inlet off Plymouth Harbor. It was shaded by ancient pines, and the sunlight filtered through the trees like magic hour on a movie set. The home although small was pristine. Fresh paint, buffed floors, and a gallery of family pictures chronicling a good simple life. This afternoon it was filled with the breath of spring flowers and yummy scents finding their way in from the kitchen.

Veronica's parents were truly excited to meet me, and their warmth and easy energy made me feel special. Her oldest brother, Tommy Jr., was the perfect host, pouring me a huge glass of wine without waiting for my request.

The backyard was no more than a slip that housed Tom Sr.'s boat. A small table that nestled in between the sea and the deck was covered with a few dozen beautifully prepared tea sandwiches and a cold summer soup that was the origin of those delicious culinary aromas; it complemented the Napa chardonnay that was disappearing all too quickly.

Veronica introduced her mom as Julia, and if the adage that young girls become their mothers was true, then Veronica had many years of beauty ahead of her. Julia was an older version of her daughter, but in the right light they might have been sisters.

We sat around the small table under the ancient pines; the inlet sea lapped sweetly against the docked fishing boat, and the air smelled of Christmas trees and a natural sea-scented cologne. It was rich man's weather, and I thought of Barrows alone and unhappy in his magnificent soulless mansion. I was glad I had come, and not only because it made Veronica happy.

We ate and talked about unimportant things. Yet their simplicity made them profound. Our eyes met and we listened to one another and connected. Mr.Chapman asked if I would like to see the boat, then took me on a quick tour. We stood atop the bridge and looked out at the blue water reflecting against a cloudless sky. The breeze off the inlet was brisk. It ruffled the vessel's colors and made my shirt cling against my skin.

Tom Chapman asked me to sit, and pulled up a deck chair and sat close so we might speak to one another in private. As he gathered his thoughts, I realized I'd been invited to spend time with the family because Veronica's dad had something to share.

"This boat was my father's," he started. "I'll give it to the boys when the time is right. Fishing is a good honest profession. Veronica's other brother worked the boat with me and Tom, but he's been away now four almost four years. Did Veronica tell you?"

"Yes, sir, but only in passing, and I didn't feel it my place to ask for more than she offered."

"When Eddie went away, Veronica cried every day for two years. Every day. I mean real tears; not just sadness, but grief. She dropped out and left us for a while. She didn't leave town or run away, it was just that she became a shell of the girl she was growing up."

"I can't imagine, sir, what kind of pain the loss of a son or a brother causes," I responded, not truly knowing what to say to this man I had known for mere moments.

"Eddie's coming home," he said. "He is not lost, just 'missing in action.' Did you fight in Nam?"

"No, sir, I did not."

"College kept you home?"

"That and a terrific lottery number."

"I fought in Korea, my dad in World War Two. We were both in the navy, and Tommy Jr. spent two years in Asia and came home in one piece. You never know where danger finds you. Barrows. You watch out . . . you just be careful. Would you have fought if they called you up?"

"I wasn't forced to make that decision, sir. God was smiling on me, I guess, and he kept me safe."

"You believe in God, son?"

"Yes."

"That's fine."

I could hear the happy voices of Veronica and her mother finding their way up to the bridge from the table below, giggles and laughter being swept away into an endless horizon. No clouds, an early crescent moon revealing itself in a sky of cobalt blue, time unrushed and of no consequence.

Tom Sr. went below and returned with two beers. He handed me one, took a long pull on his, and sat close by again on the deck chair.

"You Jewish?" he asked.

"Are you, sir?"

"No, of course not." He laughed as if I had asked if he was green.

"I like your daughter, Mr. Chapman. She wanted me to meet you and your wife and so here I am. Nothing more."

"There is a lot more, son. Ten days ago, Veronica came home smiling for the first time since Eddie was arrested. She talked all night about this boy she had met at work. Her face was bright and animated. She was a girl again. *My little girl.*"

"My mother always said, 'What doesn't kill you makes you stronger.' We somehow find a way, don't we, sir? A way to get through all the stuff that comes along."

He regarded me for a moment. "You be nice to Veronica, son."

"Yes, sir," I replied, and offered my hand to seal the deal. He took it, held it firm and strong, then looked deep into my eyes.

"What are you looking for?" I asked.

"Kindness."

"And what do you see?"

"Just what I was looking for, son, and a great deal more. Now let's go see my daughter smile. Then you two can be on your way."

47

When I was in college, I was never a very good student. I took courses that began after noon, and would never consider a Friday-morning lecture. I crammed for midterms and final exams. I read only the books I wanted to read. I used Cliff's Notes to get through the rest. I loved college, but the structure and the preparation required didn't much work for me.

Except when it came to any course that dealt with the theater. Anytime a playwright was assigned, I didn't just read the play, I read everything the playwright ever wrote. I did it for me and not for the grade. I also acted in many school shows. I was competent. Like a .280 hitter who bats sixth with a bushel of doubles. I paid attention and I saw what worked, what captured the audience. I watched the directors.

I came to believe two things. The first was that you never truly have all the answers; if you did, the theater would be a science and not an art. More important, a director must never lie to an actor, for if he does, the whole production is doomed to become a lie. Tell the actor the truth, help make him be better to find his way. Clarify his actions, advise him how to use his body, how to measure the beat. But never lie—as it stunts growth and kills creativity. The actor's reward is in a fine delivery, not bogus rhetoric from some pontificating student director or false praise from someone with a PhD.

On Tuesday morning, we had our first rehearsal. JoJo and her management

LITTLE DID I KNOW

crew had dressed the stage with some fifty chairs in one big circle. The entire PBT company was in attendance. They had arrived early, wide awake, with their eyes and bodies suggesting they were ready to get up and dance. It was like a first date. Everyone wanted to look good and be liked, so they pretended to be who they perhaps were not. All too cooperative and oh so lovely. They laughed at all the casual jokes and listened with intense sincerity.

Usually at a first rehearsal there is a "table read" where the actors sit around and read the play. It breaks the ice and allows for discussion about the characters' motivations and backstory. What did the playwright mean when he said that? Why that song lyric or orchestration? It is also good for the designers to hear the piece out loud. It is also fun.

However, PBT was summer stock. Five fully produced musicals in ten weeks. Eight shows a week dictated how much time was left for rehearsals, and it didn't allow for a great deal of analysis of character or motive or backstory. Additionally, we were presenting famous musicals with dialogue, music and lyrics set in stone. *Cabaret, Funny Girl, Anything Goes, Company,* and *The Fantasticks* were part of musical theater lore. The gold standards. The songs and scenes had been played thousands of times. These shows were like the great classics authored by Hemingway, Fitzgerald, Faulkner, and Rand. Each time they were revisited by the reader, or in our case the performer, something of the reader was brought to the written word.

There was no table read. We didn't have time. I had said that I had told everyone what I expected from them at their auditions or at the beach or through Jojo. I let Elliot speak regarding the music and Ellie regarding the dance. They reminded everyone that rehearsals set the steps or the notes, but perfecting their work had to be done their own time. Whether they were jogging or working out, eating dinner, shaving, or showering, they had to find ways to turn the sketch into a picture. They were allowed an occasional respite for making out or a ballgame or a brief letter home. But that was it.

I told them that Joe DiMaggio played every inning as if it were his last because, as he explained, "There was someone in the stands who came to see Joe DiMaggio play for the first and only time, and that fan deserved to see the real deal and not some faded copy of Joe DiMaggio who might be tired or bored, or upset about something that day."

"We are all Joe DiMaggio," I explained. "Whoever comes to see us deserves the best that we have to offer. If one of the greatest athletes of all time could give that to his public, we should be ashamed to offer any less."

I looked at everyone seated in a circle in that old barn that had been putting on shows since the slaves were freed, and offered a final thought. "Everyone here has to want to be here. In some shows you will be the star, and in others you'll play backup and give the star a foundation from which to shine. Whatever role you play, you must commit with all your strength and all your heart. Otherwise, you will be cheating yourselves, your friends, your audience, and me. If you don't feel comfortable with that, then get up and go home."

There was quiet in the theater. No one got up to leave, which I thought was a good sign. "Okay then," I said. "Let's go to work."

48

When I was a sophomore in high school, I was the only one in my class selected to be a starting player on the varsity football team. It was sort of one of those good news–bad news talks with my coach. Mr. Serpe told me I was a first-team player. That of course was the good part. Then he informed me that I would be up against the best middle linebacker in the state on Saturday morning when we scrimmaged with Roosevelt High. My stomach turned and I wondered if I really wanted to play varsity football.

As the days approached, my showdown with Rock Mental on Saturday morning, his legend grew. Yes, his name was truly "Rock Mental." He had been all-state the past four years and was already guaranteed a free ride to Ohio State. Roosevelt had been undefeated since he'd joined the team. He weighed 250 on Monday and 280 on Wednesday, and by Friday night he tipped the scales at over 300 pounds. He was as fast as Jim Thorpe and as violent as Jim Brown. He never missed a play; those who went against him rarely finished the game. He was a Viking. He was a Hun. He was Paul Bunyan, Ulysses, and Goliath. And I was dead.

I didn't sleep well leading up to Saturday. I was anxious at the thought of being beaten to death by this thyroid freak, yet determined to show up and do the best I could. I studied my playbook and film on the guy. I figured he was vulnerable to certain trap blocks and that in playing him, the second and third blocks were as important as the first if I intended on making it home. I practiced extra hard with the line coach, ate well, and took all my vitamins. Friday night, I rested and prayed. When Saturday morning arrived, I got on the team bus and headed east to face a most certain and unceremonious ending for an all too brief high school athletic career.

We arrived at Roosevelt high and began our warm-ups. All of my team-mates were on the lookout for Rock Mental. They were more nervous than I was about facing this human Loch Ness monster, and their sympathy for me could be inferred from their stoic expressions. But no one sighted him. If he were that enormous, you'd think he would stand out in a crowd, but no one on my side could locate this brooding giant.

Just before kickoff, Coach Serpe approached me with a wide grin. He said, "Sammy, you're going tear it up out here. I got faith in you." Then he slapped my butt and moved away. I felt no better about my fate and continued to search the field for Rock Mental.

Unexpectedly, Coach Serpe returned to my side, laughing. "Sammy, Rock Mental graduated last year. He's starting at middle linebacker for Ohio State this afternoon. Now go make some hay."

I did make some hay that day. In fact, I played a terrific game. We won the scrimmage by more than thirty points, and the bus ride home was raucous and happy. We had kicked some ass that morning.

Amid all the chaos, I sat alone a while and thought that sometimes when the worst actually happens it's never as bad as you think it will be. More important, the things in life you most tend to worry about often take you away from the things in life that really need your attention.

I was brooding over these thoughts as I sat on the deck at the Full Sail and sipped tequila a week after our first show had opened. The bar inside was packed, but out on the deck it was quiet and the ocean was almost as smooth as glass. A chilly mist descended from above, casting little shadows on the mirrored seatop. The deck was empty except for two women in their late twenties who were obviously looking for company. As they eyed me, I was tempted to tell them they should take their business inside.

Bobby Stevens pulled up a chair and sat next to me. He had been right about his fair skin; the Cape Cod sun had not been kind to him. His face was bright red. He was in good spirits nevertheless. He told me he thought the show was terrific and I shouldn't worry about what had been small attendance to this point. It took time for word of mouth to build. He mentioned that the season didn't really begin till after the Fourth of July, and assured me the crowds would pick up then. He reminded me about all the press we had received and the big article that was to appear in the *Globe* early next week. He added that the goal was to sell thirty thousand tickets over the entire summer and not in the first week and a half, and that he had every confidence we would do so.

I nodded silently and sipped my tequila. I noticed the two ladies had gone inside for better pickings. Maybe Bobby was right, but I didn't think so. I believed that when you opened, whether on Broadway or in a small town, you should generate some sense of urgency in people to get to the box office and buy a ticket. It was true we were selling more each day, but our increases were nothing for anyone to get particularly excited about.

Then I told him my Rock Mental story. He laughed but didn't see the connection. I explained that while we were all so concerned about the quality of our product, we had neglected or at least so far failed to let the world know it existed. We were so concerned about being beaten to death by Rock that we overlooked the essential fact that he was now a "Buckeye."

The company had been so professional. Our first shows were excellent: crisp, clear, precise, and imbued with a joy that flooded over the floodlights, even though the story itself was about dark things. The crowds were enthusiastic, staying afterward to compliment the young actors. Morale and dedication remained high, but playing in front of less than a hundred people a night—our best was a hundred and seven—had to take its toll. Christ, we only had fifty-three people at our opening!

I walked back into the bar and ordered two shots of Cuervo gold with two beer backs and returned to Bobby. We clinked our glasses and threw back José's poison; wincing, we chased it with a swig of cold beer. We sat for a while. There was no show tomorrow, since it was July 4, and the company was scheduled for minimum rehearsals. We could stay out late and misbehave if we wanted; there was no homework to do.

"We have to finish these drinks and head back to the theater," Bobby said with a certain sense of urgency. "We have to round everyone up, even the local kids. Hell, I'll even call Gary Golden if it will help."

I went to the bar and came back with two more shots of Mr. Cuervo. I thought if I couldn't sell tickets sober I might as well try it drunk.

"We have to make a splash." Bobby continued. "We have to do something they have never seen here in Plymouth. We have to pull off a stunt and make everyone, whether they are locals or just passing through, remember our names."

"Okay, I'm in, " I said. "Where do I sign?"

"I signed us up to be a float in the parade tomorrow. I located a big flatbed trailer that will be at the theater in about fifteen minutes—"

I cut him off. "Bobby, this is stupid! Nobody goes to parades anymore."

"They might in Plymouth on the Fourth of July. It's the bicentennial, for Christ sake. Even if there aren't lots of people on the parade route, we will win first prize with our float and that will get us on TV. We need to do this. Otherwise, we are going to play to a lot more empty seats. Trust me on that. I should have realized this sooner, but people aren't coming because we don't feel like a winner. The experience we are offering is like kissing your sister or going out with a girl who is your best friend. Everybody knows we are here, but they don't believe they have to call tonight or they'll get shut out."

"Bobby, no one goes to parades. What does the float look like that you're so sure we'll win, anyway?"

"The float will be everything we want the public to know about us. Our shows will be represented on the float as miniature versions of our sets, and the van itself will carry a replica of the barn. It will be filled with our chorus girls in skimpy outfits, and who won't notice that? The entire orchestra will play everything from show tunes, to Sinatra, to the blues, to patriotic melodies.

We'll serve drinks in the heat and sing. Everyone will join in and they'll hear us in Boston, and they will remember us and talk about us. Those who hear of our day on America's birthday will buy tickets and tell their friends."

Man he was good.

"How skimpy will the girl's clothes be?" I asked.

"Naked. They will be practically naked."

"That should sell tickets. Naked is good."

I went to the bar for one last refill, then returned to Bobby.

"I am calling your marker," he said. "You promised to back me and I'm not letting you say no."

"I did promise, that's true."

I raised my glass and he his. We clinked, winced, and followed with a swig of beer.

"It's after midnight," I said. "When does this parade begin?"

"Nine o'clock this morning."

"Well then, what are we waiting for? There are naked girls waiting to ride this float!"

49

As luck would have it, we were able to round up nearly everybody in the company. Bobby and I recruited JB and Tommy, James, Feston, Debbie, and Ellie. We quickly explained our emergency and they scattered off to the beach, to knock on doors, and to the local watering holes we all seemed to frequent. Within thirty minutes, everyone stood in the parking lot waiting for instructions or at least an explanation.

In the center of our circle was the powder-blue birthday present lit to the tits by a dozen cars whose headlights all pointed directly at the van. It had heated up over the past few hours, and everyone was dressed down in shorts and T-shirts, eager for news about what the fuck was going on. James had put a loop on the sound system, and due to the late hour, it was the soft smooth sounds of Johnny Hartman. The place looked like Area 51; all we needed to complete the picture were a few aliens. Yet I took comfort in the fact that it was early, and who knew what might happen next?

Bobby and I stood by the van. I held a large piece of white poster board rolled up in my hand. Bobby held a clipboard and had a whistle around his neck. If it were another time or place, this would look like the beginning of a track meet. Doobie's Full Sail truck pulled up. He removed three large kegs of beer and placed them on the picnic table, then began to fill plastic cups with the crisp amber brew and pass them around.

"You all know Mr. Bobby Stevens here," I said. "Tonight he will lead us on an important adventure." I held up the poster board and turned it a few times to make sure everyone got a good look, then handed it to Bobby and said to the group, "This is Bobby's marker, and he's calling it. So whatever Bobby says, we do." I turned to Bobby. "What do we do?"

Bobby unrolled a huge sheet of paper on which the PBT float had been rendered just as he had described it to me less than an hour ago, although the girls weren't naked in this version.

Kasen laid out a giant paint-by-numbers set which, when painted in the appropriate colors, would be hoisted together to replicate the big barn theater. Once complete, it was to be worn by the van like a form-fitting jacket and topped with the roof of the building and the high-flying sign that Bobby had designed earlier that week.

Enormous, it would be seen from miles away as it snaked down the parade route. Kasen had hooked it up to a flatbed trailer that must have been the length of half a football field; on this platform were built little replicas of our coming season's shows. They sprouted up like little cities, a twenties neighborhood that housed *Funny Girl*, an opulent ocean liner where the characters of *Anything Goes* romped, and the modern steel and coldness of seventies Manhattan that acted as the backdrop for *Company*. Germany in the 1930s for *Cabaret* and a minimalist stage set for *The Fantasticks*. Attached to each mini–show city was a pennant flag intended to wave on what promised to be one of the hottest Fourth of July ever.

The entire orchestra had been set on the flatbed and secured in place. The generator Bobby had procured was plugged into the cigarette lighter, which was going to keep that sucker going until Christmas. The float took shape around the band, who were playing a medley of songs and styles. It was like turning the knob on a car radio and you'd catch snippets of different artists and genres. Bebop, swing, raucous jazz, show tunes, and sweet melodies floated up toward the sky and accompanied the stars as they found partners and danced.

Additionally, Kasen and Duncan had strung a series of red, white, and blue Christmas lights to the top of the flatbed, around the replica of the barn, and attached them to the instruments. When the band played hot, the colors were rich and vibrant, dancing on their own like a chorus wearing tap shoes. When the music was soft, the mood and the lights became subtle, just kissing the sky for effect, dancing cheek to cheek, flushed and ready for the next step.

Time flew by, and it was nearing six in the morning. The temperature was already hovering at 80 degrees. By noon it was expected to break the long-standing record of a hundred and six. We gathered around Bobby to receive our final instructions.

"We have to drive like Arnold Palmer, talk like Winston Churchill, fight like George Patton, and ask for forgiveness like Tricky Dicky. Now, let's go make a new tradition in this town! Girls, be sexy, as if anything else were possible, and, guys, stay out of their way."

The company roared with approval. Bobby could have run for office.

Bobby had arranged for our float to be the last in the parade, just like Santa's sleigh is the last attraction of the Thanksgiving Day event. He insisted that no one in town had ever seen what we were about to show them. All the girls were decked out in skimpy, sexy showgirl outfits featuring short-short dance pants, teddies, and thigh-highs from the upcoming show. Mary, the costume designer, had made simple, age-appropriate complementary outfits for everyone else to wear.

Veronica, Diana, Debbie, and JB were suddenly transformed into alluring chorus girls, and playing the part came naturally to them. The guys and the band were dressed in nautical wear to reference *Anything Goes*, and even the dozen young kids who'd been up all night working with us wore little sailor suits with white cropped hats. The band could be heard in Boston and was ready to play a panoply of musical genres and patriotic ditties. Last, Ma and Doobie had fixed up gallons upon gallons of iced lemonade with just a slight spike in it ("for the heat" as Ma explained). We set off to the parade route.

I was appointed driver of the float. To avoid any problems, I had to run the van with the heat on full blast so the fan would cool the engine. I was a man about it, and intended to drink lots of water and an occasional iced beer. I made Veronica promise she would wipe me down before the day was over. Oh boy, how I loved show business.

It was a quick drive to Plymouth Mount, where the festivities began, and then a nine-mile slow descent down Plymouth Hill into the heart of the town, at Plymouth Knoll. The knoll had a viewing stand that held nearly a thousand spectators, and nearly five thousand more populated the grassy hill down to the water. The entire parade route was four, five, six deep in people all along the way. This was Americana at its greatest, and when I mentioned to Bobby that all he had forgotten was a twenty-one gun salute at the end, he smiled and gave me a sweaty hug, saying, "I didn't forget a thing. Not a single thing."

Then, as the floats ahead of us left Plymouth Mount to the cries and cheers of the crowd, we waited our turn with glee. Our band sounded stupendous, our skimpily clad girls were like delicious lemon drops. The minisets of our other shows were eclectic and eye catching, and the float itself, this big theater barn on wheels covered with patriotic colors, was breathtaking. We had over fifty actors, actresses, and musicians on the flatbed. It was awash in America. The best of family and youth and innovation. A fantastic gift for Uncle Sam. Two hundred candles on the cake that awaited us down by the knoll.

Before I got behind the wheel, I found Bobby and kissed him on both bright-red cheeks. I needed to shout to be heard. I screamed right in his face, "There are those decisions that change a mood or a day or even a week, but this one, Bobby, changes a destiny. You are *fucking fantastic!*" I released the brake on the powder blue van.

If I were ever elected president and a motorcade took me to my inauguration, it could not be any better than these few hours in Plymouth. The crowds moved along with the van as we crept forward. We had fifteen to twenty people on each side of the bus as we headed into town. The music from our orchestra became the music not just for the entire parade, forgive me, but for all the people of Plymouth. You could hear the tunes from miles away, and there was a selection for every generation.

Under Louis's direction, the guys played swing and jazz and Sinatra. "Fly Me to the Moon," "The Summer Wind," and of course "My Way." They played Basie with trombones low and strong and trumpets soaring. Ellington's "I'm Beginning to See the Light" and "Take the A Train." They played show tunes and people sang along with "Seventy-Six Trombones" and the Beatles! Everyone sang along with "Let It Be."

The crowd following us grew bigger and bigger. Despite the heat, the cast was roaming the parade route with offerings of Ma's spiked lemonade. We handed out flyers championing our shows and the season. Cameras flashed everywhere, and some PBT chorine or actor could be found in uncountable photos, smiling with families, becoming part of their keepsake for the summer of '76.

Occasionally, local reporters hopped in alongside me to conduct brief staccato interviews. What could I say? A picture said it all and this was some snapshot. This was Woodstock without the mud or the LSD: a lovefest, an unscripted happening still gaining momentum.

The Pied Piper float continued to make its way toward Plymouth Knoll and the five thousand attendees waiting its arrival. The viewing stand was packed as if anyone who was anyone or hoped to be anyone was there hoping for a photo op. The crowd that followed us became larger and more festive; the band cranked up the volume and kept the minions dancing all the way. The heat was a blessing; it exaggerated the day, made it memorable simply for how hot it was, ensuring embellishment of the legend of PBT throughout the years.

As we took the last turn from Plymouth Mount and made our way to the knoll, I was certain I would shortly die of heat prostration. It must have been 150 degrees inside the van, but as of the moment I cared not. This was one big, fucking joy ride and I was not getting off until the amusement park had shut down for the night.

As we descended the last hill, all the young kids who had worked with us through the early morning ran through the crowd handing out placards with lyrics on them. The cast and others carried glasses of Ma's "lemonade," which in this heat packed a punch. We were now in full view of the thousands of people who blanketed Plymouth Knoll. Louis Rosenberg shouted, "Hit it," which was followed by a drum solo orchestrated to let the greatest of celebrations begin.

The crowd started to applaud loudly and joined in with whoops and hollers. Then before the noise had found its apex, Danny Davis, our man with a horn, blew his trumpet like he was the angel Gabriel. The notes were true and clear and electric. The riff was complex and joyous, and cut the summer heat with a sound so cool the weather disappeared. It was a precursor to "When the Saints Go Marching In," and after a moment the whole orchestra was playing and those "saints" were marching and the crowd was on its feet cheering as if it were game six of the World Series last year when Fisk hit his home run into the October night.

Our cast was everywhere, serving lemon punch and dancing with kids and grandmas. And if anyone wasn't tapping their feet, well, that lasted for as long as not at all. Everyone held up the placards with the lyrics to "When the Saints Go Marching In," and quickly the crowd was singing in counterpoint and the number was more powerful, more electric, and more full of hope and optimism than was humanly possible.

Flashbulbs clicked by the hundreds as the float moved slowly toward the end of the route. Every person as far as one could see was singing and cheering and dancing their ass off. Husbands kissed their wives and little kids climbed onto the shoulders of their moms and dads so they could take the moment in. The float stopped at the bottom of the knoll and the applause and laughter and whooping and hollering cascaded over us like a tsunami. The crowd roared as twenty-one young men standing at attention in militia uniforms lined the shoreline.

The band stopped and the disparity between the volume a moment ago and the silence now was chilling. A sergeant's voice shouted, "Take arms!" and each solider shot his rifle into the sky. Twenty-one times. On the last shot the orchestra and company launched into "God Bless America" with all its history, meaning, and pathos. The crowd joined in immediately.

Thousands of voices singing all the way from their soul. Hats found their way over hearts. Daddies picked up their little boys and girls to hug them, and tears ran down the faces of oh so many. Then just when you thought it had all reached the highest crescendo possible, the song ended on the lyric *"my home sweet home,"* and fireworks were unleashed above the bay.

Plymouth, Massachusetts, would never forget that day, and neither would anyone who had the good fortune to wake that morning and through some serendipity, or the grace of God, be part of the experience of it all.

50

It was almost 6 p.m. The horizon was mixture of deep purples and blacks. The heat of the day was waning. A slight breeze had found its way through the cauldron, and a few pastel cottonball clouds moved lazily across the eggplant sky. By midnight, the air would be cool and clear with a shine so vibrant you'd feel you could actually reach out and touch the stars. The weather was like life in so many ways. Perfect, yet ever quixotic and endlessly surprising. A moment of safe harbor, comfort, peace, yet vulnerable to the counterpunch of a ghastly storm, some dark clouds. And then, well, you find yourself navigating out of the swells of an unexpected, angry, biting sea.

51

Not every day brings joy and triumph, at least at the level we had all experienced earlier today. Bobby rode the high throughout the night. He had arranged for live features on the news from six major affiliates. Practically everyone was interviewed, and more pictures were taken that summer afternoon than at a Kennedy wedding. I was interviewed so many times that I could predict the questions before they were asked. Our chorus girls were given the key to the city and the mayor was quoted as saying, "This has been the most important day for Plymouth since the Pilgrims first set foot upon the land over three hundred years ago." Adding, "There was no way our ancestors were as attractive as you young ladies." Despite the inappropriateness of a sixty-year-old mayor leering at our girls, everyone cheered. He told us the city wanted to host us at the White Cliffs that evening. Again the crowd roared.

When asked to speak I said very little, but what I did say made Bobby proud.

"My friends and I are so very grateful to be spending our summer in Plymouth. Your graciousness and generosity tonight will remain with us forever. I ask you to bring the same ferocity with which you have praised us today to our box office and buy tickets. Call your friends to do the same. Drop all other plans you may have and make the experience of theater here on the Cape a top priority. Let us celebrate the summer of America's two-hundredth birthday by sharing music and laughter and dance before Labor Day too quickly arrives."

The crowd cheered. And seemingly within minutes the phones began to ring. They rang as if it were Christmas eve. They rang like the Hunchback was working overtime with abandon, grace, and power. Maybe it was time to start relaxing and have some fun.

52

The party at the White Cliffs was a hoot. The company danced with anyone who asked. The food was a royal banquet of the best of the fresh seafood that appeared in Plymouth on any festive occasion. An ice sculpture of our float served as centerpiece, and everything was served by happy-faced waitpersons in starched white coats and goofy chef hats.

Dr. Rosenstein was asked to sub for the tuxedoed piano man. Rich and

Secunda sang, and as did Feston and Fitzgerald. They sang upbeat songs like "A Lot of Living to Do," "Witchcraft," and "Let's Face the Music and Dance," which turned into a group number. Trudy Phillips, our long-legged blonde from Amherst sang a sizzling rendition of "My Heart Belongs to Daddy." The young men lined up to propose while some of the wives filed for divorce.

The tuxedoed piano man returned and played "What a Wonderful World," to which the good doctor and Diana Cohen danced for a long time, in their own space, their ardor for each other abundantly clear.

Fitzgerald joined Veronica and me at the bar where Sidney was plying us with all types of libations. Aware of Fitzgerald's woes, Sidney ordered her a Jamison, straight up. He lifted her chin a bit and looked deep into her Irish green eyes.

"Sweetheart," he said, "yous a beautiful young girl, yous sing like a bird, yous got legs long enough for two, and blue, my darling, is a color that fades, either in the wash, over the night sky, or when it invades your heart. That mustache kid, trust me, he wants to be where he is. You had him and you let him off the line. Happens every day and more than wit boys. Drink this Jamison, and within an eyelash you'll be dancing. Trust me." He kissed her on the nose.

Fitzgerald drank the Jamison and let it settle, warm and soothing. She then took Sidney by the chin and kissed him for a little too long, but maybe not. She looked him in the eyes and said, "I do believe you, Sidney. Without a hint of reservation, I believe you." Then, rather loudly, "Who do you have to fuck to a get another drink around here?"

Sidney shouted over his shoulder, "Axel, here, now," and Axel was standing there handsome and tall and so very pleased to be so.

"You can really sing," he said to Fitzgerald. Sidney brought the next Jamison, and Axel offered it to Kat. She looked him up and down, liked what she saw, and asked, "You ever been in a fraternity?"

"No," he replied.

"Good" she said, and kissed him on the mouth, lingering just long enough to be noticed. "Now dance with me."

And they did. But the doctor and Ms. Cohen failed to notice.

My friend ASK walked over with Janet Kessler on his arm. He was so

LITTLE DID I KNOW

pleased with life that his big red Howdy Dowdy face was about to explode. Janet too was in heaven, and what a couple they made. What did this drop-dead beauty see in this Cheshire Cat–faced powerbroker to be? But who cared? If you could bottle what they had between them there would be world peace.

Alan asked if the others could excuse us a moment and took me two steps from the bar. With eyes filled with intensity and love, he hugged me and said, "You did all this, you fucker. And you let me come along for the ride. I love you like my brother . . ."

I pushed him away a foot or so and got his attention. "No, Alan you, *all of us*, did this. You taught me that if I believed in everyone, *we* could get it done. I'll vote for you whenever you are ready, but not if you let Janet slip away. If that happens, I'll kill you." I hugged him a tearful guy hug, and he reclaimed his rightful place beside the well-endowed Janet Kessler.

Veronica and I ignored the rest of the evening's intrusions. I wanted to dance close to my blond Helena. I wanted to cherish the smell of strawberries that cloaked her hair. I relished in the fact that even though I was part of a generation of people who had sex before they even finished saying hello, I had somehow stumbled onto something deeper with Veronica. Other than the reckless moment we had shared after the Spock episode, we were loving and affectionate, but not indiscriminate or screwing like rabbits. What was happening between us was too rich, too glorious. This was not a fleeting fancy to be tarnished by the pleasure of a moment, no matter how impassioned or wild or intense. I was surprised I wanted more, something that would linger long after. Being twenty and bulletproof was not enough. I wanted something to build on, something or someone to hold on to. If that made me a child from another generation, then I say that youth comes with an eraser.

Filled with liquor and the high of the day I rambled on to anyone who entered my orbit.

"I am unique. Not one of many," I said with all my might. "If I break or shatter on my ascent, or stumble in my pursuit, if I smash to the pavement on the way down, I would hit the concrete with a smile, for I had a cause, a mission. It does not matter how small, in the scheme of the world, it may be. Just look around the room. Every great cause started with one 'yes.' The difference between a fool and an optimist is just one yes. Because with the strength of one yes we can move the earth. Odets said it! Yeses for the hundreds of thousands of people who have to believe in something. The simplest journey is the most profound."

I was talking to no one yet I was talking to everyone. Alcohol has a way. I said all this not in answer to a question, but because I was looking at Veronica's lovely face and she just let me go on and on, agreeing with a gesture of her eyes as I continued from my barstool.

"It's what we are all saying, what we are all longing for, what the little have-nots need to make them breathe and grow and soar. When we wake each morning, we should teach our kids that tomorrow is better than today. We'll make the most of it. *We* make the most. A good day is when you open your eyes. We will work hard, endlessly in pursuit of our passions. When we say hello on gray Sunday mornings or when times are tough, we will still manage to smile and say 'how are you?' We are the best of the best of the best. Kings. We are the future. Be just, for if not, then when your world hangs in the balance, well then, who will be there to take your hand and lead you from the heart of darkness?"

Sidney walked over to our end of the bar. "Can I get you something, baby?" he asked Veronica. "A muzzle for your orator here?"

"You could call my honey here a taxi. I'm afraid he thinks he's a prophet. A good one perhaps, but he's a little all over the place. Maybe it was the heat of the day"

"Or the seven tequilas," Sid replied. "Cab on the way, sweetheart."

I had run out of batteries. Veronica poured me into a cab and put me to bed.

When I woke, there was a heavy rain cleansing the morning air. Veronica and I were entwined like vines in a jungle. As I had railed last night, I promised that today was gonna be a good one, because we'd opened our eyes. For that matter, my day was already excellent; I had woken up next to Veronica Chapman.

53

Walt Frazier had swagger, as did Earl "the Pearl" Monroe. The '72 Dolphins had it as well, and so did Cassius Clay as he stood over Sonny Liston. Swagger is not a given right but something earned, which makes it that much more special.

The parade gave us all swagger. It felt better than sex. Our feet didn't touch the ground. The jokes that had gotten mere titters in the last performance would slay them tonight. Our reviews, which we'd thought good, were sensational now after a second reading. We were Yaz in '67 and Jean-Claude Killy in '68. We were the US Navy at Midway, and Churchill when he read the phone book. We were Seaver in '69 and Willie Mays in '54. We were unhittable. Unbreakable. Bigger than life. That allowed us to relax and get close to being as good as we were told we were.

Today, Saturday, we would close our first show, *Cabaret*. Our second production, *Anything Goes*, would premiere on Monday. The compound felt different. We went about our rehearsals with a desire to make each performance that much better. Yet the level of intensity had changed. It was no longer the regular season but the opening game of the World Series, where ordinary moments became extraordinary, and every one of us was Joe DiMaggio. The parking lot was backed up with cars and the stacks of tickets diminished like the pounds off a crash dieter. We had become the "It" event and wore that mantle with a sense of pride. Now we needed to sustain it.

Curtain time was at 8:30 p.m. We had never sold more than 107 seats for a performance since we had opened. Yet here it was closing in on 5 p.m. and we had a waiting list that exceeded a hundred people.

The early morning drizzle had given way to pure sunshine, and by eight o'clock Van Gogh might have painted the landscape. Our car boys were waving their flashlights like magic batons so that our patrons felt safe, and they tipped accordingly. Programs sold at the concession stand like memorabilia from the Tony awards. As the director, I knew that final performances always had a special something about them, like the first kiss of a relationship or the last day of summer. I sat at the red picnic table taking it all in, feeling quite the cock of the walk. It was ten minutes to showtime, and people lingered, hoping for a cancellation or even a standing room spot or partial-view seat.

It was 8:22 p.m. Suddenly everything went black.

The compound, the streetlamps, the lights that offered a path from the parking lot to the theater were dark. The office, the houses, the box office, the exit lights, the houses surrounding the compound were ink. Black night. A sea squall had covered the sun, the sea swells were eight feet high, and we were sunk. We of course had emergency lights to guard against any real jeopardy, but within an instant festivity had been replaced by doom and concern.

"Fuck," I said several times with escalating levels of discontent.

I ran to the office and called the electric company. A young perky voice answered on the first ring. "Hello, this is Emily. May I help you?"

"Light, Emily, we need light. I'm Mr. August and—"

"What a great parade," she interjected. "I'm planning to come to see a show next weekend with my boyfriend and my mom and dad. Roy, my boyfriend, has never seen a musical."

"That's so great," I said. "I'll look for you when you arrive. Emily, what's up with the lights?" I asked this as if my leg were on fire.

"Oh, sir," she answered so calmly that I wanted to smash her face against a cement wall, "it's a downed wire. A driver hit a pole on Rocky Hill Road." She giggled. "But we will have it fixed in a jiff."

I held my breath. I looked across at the deck packed with a sell-out crowd. My fate rested on the definition of "jiff." Hesitantly, and with an anvil resting on my chest, I asked Emily, "How long is a 'jiff'?"

She mused for a moment then said two words that stabbed me in the heart and twisted it with glee. "An hour."

I ran across the compound and told Jojo what was up. "We have an hour to kill until the lights come back on. Keep the company ready and on their toes."

"An hour?" she exclaimed. "No one will wait an hour."

"No choice," I said. "I'm going to lie and then lie again. I'm not letting four hundred-plus people leave here tonight pissed off that all they got was a warm Coke."

I ran to the balcony where Duncan and Kasen ran the two spotlights and told them to put them on auxiliary power so we could get some light in the building. Kasen reminded me that "the emergency spotlights were working but the spots made everyone look like a cadaver."

"Do what I say," I commanded, then raced toward the orchestra pit and Dr. Rosenstein.

He listened, and Louis Rosenberg, his first chair, said at least twenty times, "Cool, my brother." I guess that was good.

I raced to the front of the theater and asked for the audience's attention. The house quieted instantly. "Hello, everyone. I am Sam August and I want to thank you—"

Rousing applause, some whistles, and audible comments all filled with goodwill and a spirit of unbridled joy cut off my introduction. This too was good.

"Thank you so very much. Thank you for being here tonight. In the spirit of the theater, the show will go on!"

Then I explained how a car had hit a pole and cut off the electricity, but that the electric company said the power would be back on in fifteen minutes. It was a beautiful night. We opened the concession stand for free drinks, and the band played. I encouraged the audience to get up and dance under the stars.

I watched the clock. Every minute was a lifetime, and the crowd could turn ugly if someone had a babysitter waiting or if they were looking to get laid and their schedule was tight. It was now close to 9:10 and long past the promise of "fixed in a jiff." Smiles began to turn into impatience and people inquired about refunds. I thought briefly about torching the entire place.

At 9:15 I stood in front of the crowd with the hope of defusing the growing discontent. "Ladies and gentlemen, I understand that General Washington's lights went out during his post-holiday dinner and that the Continental Congress had problems with their air conditioning right after they signed the Declaration of Independence."

None of that was close to funny, but I did get a few chuckles and realized there was some goodwill left in the tank.

"I have just spoken to the electric company and they have informed me that the lights will be back on in *less* than five minutes." My nose grew and my sphincter tightened, but the crowd responded with a round of hearty applause. "I thank you for your patience tonight. Everyone here this evening can take his or her stub down to the Full Sail after the show and Doobie will buy you all a cocktail."

I clapped my hands a few times and asked if everyone was comfortable, and nobody threw anything at me. I took that as a good sign. I ventured forth. "I thought it would be fun if we offered you something special tonight, something that only live theater can offer. As you know, you are here tonight to see the closing performance *Cabaret*. It's not your classic musical comedy, but it's a great show that I'm sure you will enjoy immensely. Our next show, which opens Monday night—don't ask when we sleep—will feature the music and lyrics of Cole Porter."

The spotlights were in my eyes and I couldn't see anything. But I could hear the crowd rustling, and it appeared to be interested in what I was saying. I looked stage left, and Bobby was giving me the hand signal for "hurry it up or we give you the hook and then beat you to death." I quickly moved on. "So we thought it would be a nice gesture, to thank you for your patience, to give you a preview of *Anything Goes*, then go right into *Cabaret*." The response was spirited and sincere.

I thought of Emily at the electric company; it was now more than an hour since we had spoken. I made a mental note that when she came to see the show next week I'd make sure she sat behind a pole.

"Great," I said. "Now remember you are seeing a number from *Anything Goes*, which is rousing and fun. The lead character is played by Katherine Fitzgerald. Kat, take a bow." Katherine stepped forward in her Nazi prostitute outfit and took a bow. "Katherine's character is imploring Gabriel in heaven to shine down goodwill on the characters of *Anything Goes*, none of whom are Nazis."

Oh boy.

"So with Dr. Rosenstein conducting the orchestra and the PBT company in their thirties Berlin garb, we offer you a rather unusual sneak peak of *Anything Goes*. Please note that, until the lights go on, this number will be performed with the auxiliary spots that offer no color or theatricality. We need your imagination right now. If this bombs, my mother's going to make me go to medical school!"

The theater filled with chuckles. "Ladies and gentlemen, PBT presents *Anything Goes* via Berlin, 1932. Let your imagination take flight. Enjoy, and thanks."

The curtain rose. The company took their positions in white-hot cadaver light. They looked surreal wearing Berlin outfits when the song they were about to perform was meant to be sung from the deck of an expensive frivolous ocean liner. I walked stage right and Veronica gave me a shot of JD and a huge kiss. The cast was ready for the downbeat. And the rest of us were ready to run.

Dr. Rosenstein shouted, "One, two, three, four," and waved his baton.

Berlin vanished. Everyone began to sing about Gabriel and his horn, and how he played it with a vengeance. The dancers danced and the chorus sang their asses off. Danny Davis hit each trumpet riff. Fitzgerald sang "Blow Gabriel" like a star, followed by the chorus, followed by Danny blowing Gabriel's horn, and then again and again, and the audience was clapping and cheering and they were glad they had stayed.

At the apex of the number, when all twenty-four cast members and twelve in the band were singing their tits off for Gabriel to blow that fucking horn . . . *the lights went on!* The blacks and grays and shadows that had cloaked the stage suddenly became Oz, and the stage was alive in a rainbow of color. The cast took it a notch higher and the band blew the roof off the building; the audience leapt from their seats as if propelled. It was unlike anything you could ever have imagined, because you couldn't make this stuff up.

Bobby Stevens cried in the wings. First the parade, and now this. Applause cascaded over the stage in wave after wave, and with each bow the company took the crescendo grew louder. Finally, after six bows Jojo kept the curtain down and announced that *Cabaret* would start in ten minutes and asked that everyone remain seated. Of course, at that point no one was seated.

Light had come upon us, and with the release of tension and the curtain down for a ten-minute break, the cast went into some crazy dance, a hybrid of an American Indian ritual, a twenties Charleston, a sixties twist, V-J and V-E Days, and Times Square on every New Year's Eve since Adam kissed Eve.

They hugged and leapt into one another's arms and did handsprings and released enough energy to light the nation. The last couple in a lip-lock was the good doctor and Diana Cohen. He had left his station at the pit to share this crazy moment with someone who had waited for a long time to turn his frown-mustache upside down.

"All good things come to those who wait, Diana." I mused.

Now they all had a show to do. Oh, the magic of live theater.

54

My father was born in 1921. His father, Samuel Shmorak, was a WWI hero of Russian descent who wore his many medals for bravery stoically across his chest. He married my grandmother Anne after meeting her on leave in London during a three-day pass. She married him on her fifteenth birthday and less than six months later was living in the blue-collar town of Lynn, Massachusetts, twenty miles outside the city of Boston.

Samuel was a blacksmith with arms like Popeye. He never read a book, and used to give my brother and me hate lessons: wops can't be trusted; mick bastards are thieves; kikes (his own kind) will steal from you if you look the other way; and darkies . . . you don't want to know. These life insights were dispensed whenever he drove down to see the family in New York, which was about four times a year. Other than to come in the house to use the bathroom or sleep, he would sit in his car for the entire visit for no other reason other than to be obstreperous.

The Depression had hit when my dad was just under ten, so he worked jobs his entire childhood like so many others of his generation. He enlisted in the army after Pearl Harbor and spent three years overseas. He was D-Day minus six. He was on a troop carrier headed to the South Pacific when Harry Truman essentially ended the war by dropping the atomic bomb on Japan. Harry probably saved my dad's life.

He met my mom (who was born in a taxi on the way to the hospital) in 1946, on a blind date; he'd been coerced into attending the rodeo by his best friend, Norman Schletsky whose girlfriend's girlfriend refused be the third wheel. The rodeo was on a Friday night, and my parents were married that Sunday afternoon in a very expensive service at the Mayflower Hotel in Manhattan. My mother, an affluent college girl, had been betrothed in a pre-arranged marriage to a rich Mexican Jew by the name of Miguel she had yet to meet. She had my dad write a Dear John letter to her fiancé on Saturday night; by the time he received it, my mom was Mrs. Shmorak. After living with that lovely new married name for less than a week, she informed my father that he either had to change it or they would have to get divorced. My father, who at the time was August Herbert Shmorak, became Herbert August. The American dream played on into the fifties.

When not dodging enemy fire in the army, my dad had produced and written many shows. His new father-in-law convinced him to give up his budding career in radio to provide a better life for his new family. He went to work for my maternal grandfather in the garment business. Lots of Jews, lots of gonefs and hondling, and all too much disappointment. He was a talented music producer in postwar radio and a frustrated, if more affluent, garment salesmen after making that unfortunate life choice. My dad always told me, "Follow your passion and money will follow." He didn't and it didn't.

Nobody knows what couples are like when they're alone. Nor does anyone really know whether their family is functioning well. Because until you leave the nest it's the only family you know. You think it's the way all other families relate and behave. Your home is normal, and the word "dysfunctional" never comes into play. Sammy Davis Jr. said he loved the neighborhood he grew up in, until he left it and realized it was a terrible ghetto.

When I was a kid I loved sports. They were important to my dad as well. We shared something, and it allowed him to win, because in athletics I seldom came in second. I was good at all of them: bigger, faster, and stronger than my peers. I was always the first one picked, and my identity in my early years was based on my ability to hit the ball out of sight and run over a multitude of would-be tacklers.

My father came to every ballgame I ever played. Right through high school, in any weather on any day at any appointed time. He was always there, standing alone, watching with true intent. He brought a friend once to a football game during my junior year, but I was injured in the first quarter and played sparingly throughout the remainder of the contest. That was the last time he ever brought anyone to one of my games. To my great confusion and dismay, my mother never saw me play a single game of any kind. Ever.

As a young athlete, I was vested in the ethic and philosophy of the great football coach Vince Lombardi. My coach Mr. Serpe, also Italian and also a graduate of Fordham University, threw Lombardi platitudes around as if he himself had led the Packers to victories in the first two Super Bowls. Of course I listened and made them my own.

As I grew up, I began to realize that most quotes from famous people, which initially sound so profound, begin to ring hollow when placed within the context of the life that swirls around them. Not everybody wins, even if "you leave it all on the field," nor is a man's character measured by "whether in his heart he found a way to win." Sometimes the other team is luckier, has a better day, or are simply better.

I came home from college one semester to visit for a week in late February. My dad had a beautiful office on Madison Avenue that he had secured through some barter arrangement. He looked enormously prosperous in those digs, while in reality he was struggling financially and trying to figure out a way. He didn't have less character or skill or smarts or desire than other men who traveled to the city each morning on the 8:11 to Penn Station. Throughout that week in late winter I went with him each morning to his office and watched him make dozens if not hundreds of calls to make something happen, find some light, score some points, or just get up off the mat. Yet for whatever reasons, nobody was taking his calls; his messages were never returned during the week I was there. I thought more highly of my father during those five days than ever before. He never lost his sense of humor. His eyes were alert and focused, and he listened to my daily issues as if he didn't have a care in the world. I watched him and learned that it is easy to have character when you are winning; the true heart of a man is tested when he is flailing.

Vince Lombardi said many things that were quoted in practice, and I heard them all. I remember two:

They may not love me now, but when flushed with winning, they will love me later.

It's not whether you get knocked down, it's whether you get back up.

And so it goes. It was about halfway through my hundred days at PBT and I had learned so many lessons. Two I will never forget. The first was that Vince Lombardi's words offered sage advice. Although somewhat worn, they still held power and truth. The other, and more important, was that I realized my father was a good man. Flawed or mistaken at times, but good, and that is sometimes enough to win.

Not every script is a winner, but you still have to play it like it's Shakespeare.

5 5

We opened *Anything Goes* less than forty-eight hours after Emily from the electric company made good on her promise to give us light. With all the parade hoopla, the light event, and the general buzz, we were sold out that night. This was terrific, but there was no joy for me that evening. The show in my opinion, not shared by the actors or audience, was shaky at best. I chalked it up to the whirlwind ride of the past few days, or fatigue, the lack of tech time on the changeover to a new show, or just a natural predictable slump. Even Ted Williams took an 0–4 on occasion. I gave specific notes after the performance and thought tomorrow would return to normal.

It didn't.

I found it interesting and somewhat disturbing that even at our young ages, and with little to no professional experience, the actors started to behave like many of the great stars whose bios I had read across the years. They retained their zeal, but now it carried a hint of rebellion. In small, subtle ways they were saying, "I'm good. Don't bother me with being Joe DiMaggio." The girls were divas and the guys were . . . well, what is the equivalent of a diva? Assholes!

None of us had written the songs or lived the birth of the original Broadway material. True, I wanted commitment from everyone and I was getting it, but the focus was distorted, becoming about "me." This was summer stock and it was supposed to be fun. Yet the notes of the previous evening went unheeded, and rehearsals that day brought unnecessary tensions, at times taking us to the precipice of verbal fisticuffs. I had little patience for it all.

On the heels of our instant celebrity, the *Patriot Ledger*, the paper covering the four corners of the Cape, assigned a big-time reporter to spend the day at the theater, to attend rehearsals and become acquainted with the company. The reporter, Marc Seconds, had seen the closing of *Cabaret* and the opening of *Anything Goes,* so he was up to speed on recent events. He was a nice-looking, midthirties professorial type wearing fashionably beaten-up jeans and a faded-pink poplin shirt. He wore his hair in a buzz cut and had thin wire-rimmed glasses. Seconds was pleasant and complimented everything he had seen so far. He also was clearly smitten with Carol Duteau, a young lady with the fabulous breasts we had cast out of Yale. It turned out Seconds was an "Eli" himself.

It is always dangerous for someone outside the rehearsal process to sit in as a guest. An actor's instinct is to please the audience, and when a stranger is present actors often "perform" rather than use the rehearsal to prepare. They press. Jokes become forced and fail to land, pacing becomes disjointed, and beats linger long enough for a truck to drive through. Confidence diminishes. Insecurities mount, and dental surgery up your ass becomes a more attractive option then continuing.

We weren't putting on Chekhov or Strindberg or even Arthur Miller. We were presenting a thirties fluff musical with a sensational score and a storyline as deep as a wading pool. Nevertheless, if an actor mugged for a false laugh or didn't invest in the character's dilemma, then it was all a sham. The audience tunes out, and what is supposed to be froth and fun becomes, well, stupid and boring.

There were three things on the punch list that morning. If we could fix them quickly we could exponentially improve on our next performance and get to work on our next show instead of reviewing the one now in performance.

Near the end of act 1 was a series of four entrances and exits that piggy-backed on each other. The laughs were in the visual, a sequence of rapid-fire exits and entrances that forced the eye to follow the joke. Unless they were timed correctly, they lay like a pancake with each subsequent joke working hard to cover the failure of its predecessor.

I explained the concept, which was not difficult and had worked quite well in rehearsal. But when the sequence played in front of an audience, each entrance and exit was extended for no other reason than to get an additional titter. Now the whole thing didn't work. It was selfish, and after thirty minutes of running the bit to no benefit, I asked harshly what the fuck was going on. No one had an answer because to give one was to admit their lack of commitment to the show and the pettiness of their actions. I told them in no uncertain terms that it sucked, and then moved on. Tension was palpable and the reporter from the *Patriot Ledger* was at the ready with a quill dipped in venom-laced ink.

The next bit of business involved our sixteen-year-old mop-headed young star, Ronny Feston. Six weeks ago he would have blown the Boston Patriots for this gig, and now he was Marlon Brando. He had a small scene in which he played a stowaway conning the show's comedic lead in a game of craps. It was screamingly funny. Feston was adorable, and his cadence and use of his body were impeccable. He played the scene with Secunda, who amped it up. It was our version of Laurel and Hardy.

But when a gag works to perfection, less is more. Feston, though, milked it, stretching it out to the point where it was vulgar and mean-spirited and all about him. He left Secunda to pick up his shit and stopped the momentum of the escalating laughter, all but bringing it to a halt. Ronny was a kid, and perhaps he didn't understand, so we discussed it. He still resisted. Vociferously. He wanted his laugh.

I explained that Jerry Lewis had written that "comedy is a man in trouble." Once a character's jeopardy is gone, the dilemma is no longer funny. Feston remained adamant. Rather than have a confrontation, I called a ten-minute break.

I was livid and called Jojo over for a talk. "What is this bullshit? You're the fucking stage manager and this stuff has been rehearsed and set. We don't have time or energy to play fucking Stanislavsky this afternoon. All of a sudden they get some laughs and some kudos and they think they're fucking Charlie Chaplin. You end it now. You tell that little imp that if this continues, he can call his mom to pick him up and take him home yesterday."

I said all of this in front of Marc Seconds; he was taking notes so fast his pen seemed propelled by nuclear power. I pulled Jojo out of his earshot and added, "You want this shit in the paper? Fix this, damn it!"

It was clear that Jojo wasn't too pleased with me. "Five minutes," she shouted. "Company on stage in five minutes." Then she pulled Feston off to the left wing and ripped him a new face.

The last thing I wanted to fix was a scene with Zach Rush and Mary Holly, who played the young lovers in the show. They sang a beautiful Porter ballad in act 2, and they had been terrific around the piano and in rehearsal. Yet the greed for a laugh had gotten to them as well; they'd sung it on opening night without any sense of stakes, as if their love affair mattered not at all. They'd mugged for the cheap laugh, and no one cared because their characters didn't.

I gave the note. Elliot ran the song. They played it correctly, and all was good. Reason had returned.

"Notes after lunch," Jojo announced. "We'll meet on the deck in forty-five minutes. Kasen has tech notes to fix and needs the stage. After notes we start rehearsing *Funny Girl.*"

For the moment we were done.

56

I studiously avoided Marc Seconds during break. I knew when we let him into our inner sanctum he'd get to see it all," both the good and the bad. This morning he had seen a bit of both. Now I wondered what spin he'd put on what he had learned. Was he a decent guy or a prick?

Distraction would be a good remedy, so I hoped he'd find his way to a seat next to Carol Duteau and we'd all have a better face on for his article after some fresh air and sandwiches. Marc was smart and smooth; within minutes he was talking up Carol who seemed a bit flustered by all the attention. They weren't talking sports.

I raced to my room and changed into a swimsuit. It was a dry summer day, nearly 90 degrees. The sun lit the brilliant sky, which reflected off the ocean creating an enormous canvas of perfect endless sapphire. Practically sprinting toward the sea, I dove in and swam. I pulled through the water for minutes before taking a breath. The moment was bracing and cleansing. I was eager to get back to work and push beyond the mounting misery of the early morning.

As I headed back to the compound, Veronica was waiting with a lush terry-cloth towel and asked that I sit with her and take a breath. We sat close on the sand. She wore a lilac sundress and her hair was pulled back in a tight ponytail. She wore no makeup. Her eyes matched the sea, and her skin was smooth and silky like rich Egyptian cotton.

"You okay, baby?" she asked. "Tough day so far. Silly, really."

I stared into the horizon and ran my fingers against her thigh, an elixir for anxiety. "That guy from the paper seems decent." I said.

"What are you going to do?"

"I'm going to do my job and give my notes and make our show better."

"And?"

"And what?"

"What if the stuff from this morning doesn't go away?"

"Since when did Iago join the company? Sometimes I think we just have to play the game by instinct. I'm going to kiss you because I like to and then I'll see where the day leads."

After we kissed, Veronica told me that I had five phone messages from this morning.

"The building inspector is coming by at nine a.m. Sidney is coming by for *support*. The fabulous Golden family is also stopping by tomorrow for a chat. A Mr. Colon called. And best of all, the police called."

"Any of that sound good to you?"

"Not one bit," she answered with a smile.

I was compelled to kiss her again.

"Sidney could be good." I said.

"Sidney is always good. It's just what accompanies his visits that sort of feels like someone is peeing in the punchbowl."

"Can't argue with that. What did the police have to say?"

"Ellie Foster was involved in a situation at the Moondog last night and Police Chief Warren wants you to drop by to discuss it before the end of the day."

I stood up, took her hand and pulled her to my side. We walked back to the theater with our arms around each other's waists, and she asked, "You hungry? Do you want me to make you something to eat?"

"No thanks. Too distracted. Preoccupied."

"You wanna eat me?"

"If the offer holds till after rehearsal, I'm in."

"Deal."

Just as we left the beach, a seagull swooshed down and picked up a sand crab and swallowed it whole before it even began its ascent. I wondered who was having a worse morning; the crab or me.

57

The cast and crew wandered onto the deck on time but lacking any urgency or verve. Some were still finishing their lunches and others who had been to Garden's were nursing the last of an ice cream treat. I had told Veronica that we'd have to see what developed, but I was already formulating an approach.

Jojo called the rehearsal to order. I sat at the top of the steps that led to the balcony and spoke down to the company who sat randomly on the stairs and cross-legged on the deck. I enjoyed giving notes. I liked the back and forth of an idea and the commitment to making something work or setting it so it could mature. I complimented actors or dancers on little things, so they were rewarded for working on subtlety and acknowledged for their efforts. And if I was not sure why something was missing, I engaged the actors and my creative team to find a solution. Very rarely, if ever, was there an underlying tone of uncertainty, so of course I was unsettled that it existed today.

We were in uncharted territory, with no history of having worked through such vicissitudes in the past. The press was present, and members of the company—again for reasons unknown to me—wore chips on their shoulders. Clearly the next ten minutes would shine a light on or crush this brewing discontent. I spoke for several minutes. I tweaked certain beats, refreshed and rethought some small blocking, and ran line sequences in different tempos and cadences.

"Secunda, the stateroom scene. Every entrance has to be exactly the same, physically and in delivery. It's funnier in threes."

He nodded his assent.

"Mary, on 'All Through the Night,' don't sing it to Billy, sing out to the house. It's confusing if you sing to him. I mean, he's in jail and you're not."

She scribbled the note into a little journal.

"Kat, you're starting 'Kick' too blue. You're playing a chanteuse, not Billie Holliday. Lighten up the beginning and it will make the finish stronger."

"Got it, boss," she said spiritedly.

"ASK, you are killing the laugh on the 'hot pants' line. Let the laugh happen and *then* do the take."

"Shit, I thought I had that right," he replied.

I gave dozens more notes, and the energy was good. I asked Elliot to give music notes and had Ellie give hers to the dancers. I discussed a quick change with Jojo that had been bungled, and we worked out a different approach so we wouldn't have to go to black. I was feeling that we were back on track.

Feelings lie.

I returned to the two scenes we had rehearsed earlier in the day. The problematic one with Feston, and the keystone cop visual that had played so poorly.

It all went up in an instant. Feston was aggressive and said, "What I'm doing is funny and it should stay. I have to be comfortable, and you're asking me to do something that doesn't feel right. It's your job as the director to make us feel good about what we are doing and be at ease." With the other scene I also got attitude and similar bullshit from the ensemble members about their comfort zone and their belief in that what they had chosen to play.

I sat and listened. My heart beat faster, but I didn't reveal what I was thinking; I let the whole thing settle. I gave all in attendance the chance to add a final thought or retract the foolishness that had just been proffered. I looked to Secunda, Elliot, Ellie, and Jojo, and gave them time to chime in with anything useful. I was stunned and I was furious.

We could all hear the chatter from inside the house where Kasen was working with the crew on fixing some tech problems. The box office phone at least once a minute, and we could hear orders being taken, although the words were garbled and we didn't know what nights or the number of tickets ordered. Louis and the band were rehearsing outside on the deck behind the red house, their music clear and cheerful. Marc Seconds looked only at his yellow pad, making eye contact with no one.

After another few moments of the unsaid hanging in the air, I began to speak. I was measured at first, but soon found myself snowballing and throwing a few haymakers. First to Feston. "It's not my job to make you comfortable. You want that, then go to a resort and have them spritz you in the face when it's hot and bring you an iced cocktail to put you at ease. What you're doing is not funny. It's bad, and that is no longer up for discussion. You know what some people think is funny?"

He offered no rely.

"How about dropping your pants and showing your ass? You think that might get a laugh? How about a big fucking loud fart? That might get a titter or make you look like a gross lowlife. You have two choices right now and I'm giving you *one fucking second* to tell me what you want to do. You choose to do what I tell you to do, and you do it with grace and manners, or you get the fuck out of here, and out of kindness I'll give you the bus fare home.

"Now as to the rest of you who seem to want to reinvent the food chain of how notes get incorporated or directors are respected, I give you the same choice, but with less tolerance because you're older than Ronnie and should be less stupid. Know that I respect all of you. I hired all of you and until this morning when someone put something in your coffee, I had only pleasure in working with you.

"You're tired. So am I. You feel unappreciated. Tough shit. Go home. I'll have fifty people from Boston in before you get packed to leave. You want to give the orders, then produce your own fucking show. You don't like my notes or my direction, then go direct you own fucking show. You don't like me, well read *The Fountainhead*. The marquee says 'Sam August Presents' over the title and then it names me as the director. I have the right to expect my name to represent my work, and what I think is good. Feston, you're sixteen years old. Maybe that's too young to do this. Maybe you should go write a book on how much more you know than me."

I was humming now and surprised at the intensity of my vitriol. I was throwing body punches, not thinking of consequences.

"You know why you're all here? Because Josh Secunda believed in this idea and put some skin in the game and I made a thousand phone calls. I found this place and with many of you, put it all into play, *and because you are all good, but you're not good enough unless you actually show up and get your heads out of your asses*. All of a sudden you want to challenge my authority and me. Then go home right now. Those of you who stay, take the notes we worked on and put them in the show or I'll send you home. No more discussion. We begin rehearsals for *Funny Girl* in ten minutes."

I turned to Elliot. "Please begin with music and work with Ellie on the opening. I'll be back in an hour, as I have an audience with the chief of police. Anyone want to give me notes on how to play that hand?"

There wasn't a sound from the company. There were looks of incredulousness, disappointment, anger, and hurt, but not a sound. I wasn't sure who knocked who down, but we'd see very shortly who had the character to get back up. As I walked to the car, I remembered that Lombardi had said they came back to loving you when you won. Was it really true? Time would quickly tell.

58

Chief Warren was a round, affable fellow. He had a trimmed gray beard and was fifteen pounds too heavy. If his uniform were red, you might mistake him for a young Santa. Upon arrival, I was ushered into his conference room without delay. His staff was eager to please. There were sandwiches of either old meat or new cheese and soft drinks. The whole feel of the meeting was that of a social, so I breathed deeply and took a seat. I grabbed a Coke and downed it, and then a Sprite and did the same. Variety in your refreshment is always a good thing.

The chief asked an Officer Richardson to sit in with us as he had information about the situation. "Situation" is indeed an all-purpose word. Richardson was a looker. Straight out of central casting. His thick, jet-black hair was perfectly in place. He had bronze skin, light-blue eyes, and a perfect smile that was both warm and legit. His uniform fit like a tailored suit, and his demeanor was friendly and open, almost suggesting that we should all have a beer. He was also a fan of our two shows, praised the excitement of the parade, and was appreciative of the attention the theater in Plymouth had received since our arrival.

Warren, Richardson, and I sat with a court reporter who was unofficially taking notes.

The air conditioning was antiquated and the room was hot. Not Africa hot, but more than uncomfortable. There was a slight breeze from the open ocean-view windows and some air movement from a slowly turning ceiling fan. The AC simply made a grinding noise. I was glad I wasn't a cop.

"Mr. August," the chief began.

"Please call me Sam," I said.

"Sam, we have a problem with one of the young women who work for you." He checked his notes. "Ellie Foster," he said matter-of-factly.

Before I could respond, there was knock on the conference room door. The court reporter excused herself and opened it to reveal an unexpected attendee. Veronica Chapman stood there, as businesslike as one could imagine. She had on a blue suit and white blouse. Her hair was in her classic ponytail and she wore navy-blue flats that matched the color of her outfit. She looked asexual, if that was possible for Veronica.

Introducing herself immediately she said, "I am here to take notes for Mr. August. Sorry I'm a bit late." Not waiting for a response, she took a seat next to me at the table, threw a yellow pad in front of her, and was ready to go.

"What's the problem with Ms. Foster?" I asked. "Has she done anything wrong?"

There was a long silence, and then Officer Richardson spoke. He removed his glasses, put them on the table, looked me in the eye, and spoke from the heart. "Sam, my name is Scott Richardson. I have worked here in Plymouth for the past four years, and I have an impeccable record."

Chief Warren chimed in, "That is a hundred percent true. Scott is one of our finest officers." He was looking at me and I nodded. Veronica took copious notes.

Scott continued. "I met Ellie when your group first arrived about two months ago. We met at the Full Sail just before Memorial Day, and I began to see her . . . "

"Has she done anything wrong?" I interrupted.

Silence.

"Has she done anything wrong?" I repeated.

"No," said the chief. "Please allow the officer to proceed."

"Sam," Scott said, "I met Ellie a few times in the evening. Also for lunch and even an early breakfast. Then, whenever I could, I pressed my schedule to make time. I liked her. I still like her, very much in fact."

"Has she done anything wrong?" I asked again.

"I think Ellie is in trouble, or if she is not yet she will be. I needed to bring that to your attention." Officer Richardson stared at the scarred wooden conference table, waiting for some sign to continue. The sounds from the street played out like a discordant series of notes, everything in a minor key.

I was grateful for Veronica. She didn't have to act out this charade as my support team. She was prescient. She knew something was amiss and that I might need more than guile.

"Scott," I said, "I know Ellie. She's a fantastic girl. I also know she has issues. If her indiscriminate behavior has widened outside the boundaries of safety, then I can't allow that on my watch. Please, you're someone who cares about her, so tell me, what's going on? Off the record. No judgments. Ellie is my friend . . ."

Scott was silent. He wanted to tell me what was troubling him, but I think he had expected this to be more confrontational.

"Look," Scott said, "Ellie is a very needy girl. When I first met her, it was really fun. It was all new to me, I mean about what she did and where she came from and where she was going. The first night I met her, I took her home and she stayed till morning. She is sexy, and sweet, and eager to please. It was fantastic. And still is. Except that it is all getting a little creepy."

"Creepy?" I asked. "How?"

Chief Warren looked constipated. The court reporter's eyes were wide, as if she couldn't wait to share this steamy story after work. Veronica was still, yet she held my hand with strength under the pockmarked table.

"Because I can't keep up with her," he said sadly. "I have to work and I can't see her every night or when she has an hour free from rehearsal. I either satisfy her sexually or she gets abusive. If she doesn't take her clothes off for someone every night, she simply won't go home until she finds a willing partner. I care about her. But this sort of behavior is not normal. Needing to fuck somebody every night! Last night, she didn't even check in with me. Later on, I heard she left late with an untrustworthy fucker." He was quite emotional as he concluded. "Ellie is a sweet girl. She's lost, but she is a sweet, kind person. I think she's compromising her safety."

This was very disturbing and way beyond my job description. "Chief Warren," I asked, "is Ellie breaking any laws?"

"No, Sam," he replied, "but she is going to break some hearts, starting with her own, and then all to soon trouble will follow. Something has to be done."

"Are you suggesting Ellie Foster is acting like a whore?" Veronica asked.

The chief looked at her and then at Richardson. No one was pleased to be in the room.

"Ms. Chapman, if Ellie Foster was a prostitute, we would not be having this meeting. Ms. Foster is a young woman in trouble. She has made it known by her actions that she is available sexually to anyone—literally anyone in this county—and I need all the help I can garner to keep her safe."

"The fact that Ms. Foster chooses to have sex with numerous people in the county does not brand her as a bad person, sir," Veronica snapped. "If it did, we'd have a whole lot of bad people in Plymouth County."

"Young lady, there *are* a lot of bad people in this county, and that's why we are having this get-together."

"Gentlemen," I said, "may I ask you to meet me at my place tomorrow at six? I need time to think and to take action." They agreed.

I left ahead of Veronica; she followed me out of the parking lot as if we were two strangers. About a half-mile down the road, I pulled over and she joined me in the front seat of my car. We sat for a few quiet moments and then I put my arms around her and said, "I am so lucky to have met you, Veronica. I can't imagine my future without you."

After a moment she replied, "Good. Because if you did it could get mighty awkward around here. I'm the lucky one, handsome, but you have rehearsal in ten minutes." She climbed out of the car. "Don't be late. It's one of your pet peeves." Then, with that coy look in her eyes, "Is that offer to eat me still up for consideration?"

Before I could respond she got in her car and drove off.

59

As I parked at the compound, JB came running to greet me. "You have three more messages from a guy named Johnny Colon. He said he's called four times today. He demands you call him, or he'll stop by unannounced."

"Just call the bastard back and let him know I will ring him a soon as I can. If he's not happy then tell him to come see the show soon and I'll grab a quick drink with him afterward."

"All good," JB said. "Your rehearsal is on stage in three minutes. It's with Feston, Fitzgerald, Elliot, Christina, and Ellie. The rest of the company is on the red deck setting the opening for you to look at. Jojo is running that."

"It's showtime," I said. Then I opened the door to the theater and entered the building. Light swept through the house and disappeared as the door swung shut behind me. I took a seat on the second-row aisle and watched the rehearsal. All the tension from the morning was gone. Feston looked like the kid who auditioned, both confident and giving. Ellie, the girl I just learned was fucking all of New England, was running the rehearsal with grace, charm, and verve. Elliot worked on the delivery of the song during every minibreak. Fitzgerald was a pro, precise and focused. Christina, who was a sexpot off stage, was playing her character with an ease and simplicity that made you forget her looks and believe in what she was saying. She was playing the mother of the prissy Englishmen in *Anything Goes*, and she caught laughs as easily as one catches fireflies darting in the night.

The stress and tension of the other elements of the day vanished. I liked watching good work and the innate joy it created. The energy was so positive that I started wondering if I had overreacted this morning. They ran the number again, and it was better than the previous go-round. Although not a major piece of the show, it was a showcase for the comic talents of Feston and Christina, and comedy needs to be crisp. Secunda wandered in and sat next to me. Ellie looked out to the house and asked, "Should we run it again?"

"Just a moment, Ellie," I replied.

Secunda put his arm around my shoulder and whispered in my ear. "Don't you say a fucking word, nothing nice. You shut up. They deserved your tirade this morning and that's why they are working this way. Stop trying to be Capra and think Machiavelli. Say it with me."

Slowly we said together, "It is better to be feared than loved because you can always make someone fear you."

Then I added for our amusement, "Love is another matter all together. . . . Ellie, just run it again and set it. It's—" Secunda grabbed my arm.

"Just run it again. Then take five and meet back on the stage. I'll have JB bring the rest of the company around and we'll go over a few things. Hit it."

They did the number and it was really good. *They* were really good.

"Two steps forward and two steps forward," Secunda said. "Keep your testicles. You'll need them later this summer, I promise. I'm proud of you, Sammy boy."

I sat alone in the empty theater, thinking of what I was going to say. As I heard the company wander into the building, my mind was still blank. *Someone throw me a cue*, I thought, *preferably one that will piss me off.*

Everyone took seats within the first three rows. I noticed that Marc Seconds no longer sat aside from the group, but was now attached to Carol Duteau's hip. In addition to the cast, the rows filled with most of the orchestra, Diana, Debbie, Ronny, James, and Bobby who was back from Boston. Sort of like standing room only.

I sat on the front of the stage and Jojo stood a few steps behind me with clipboard in hand. I ran my gaze over the faces in the first rows of the theater. "There is a difference between playing hurt and having an injury," I said. "When you play hurt you have to work harder to sustain your usual level of performance. That is difficult to do, but it is part of maturation. Playing hurt is something we all must learn to do. Injured is a different thing altogether. The burden of injury means that you are damaged and have to get healthy so you can excel."

I offered no warmth or mirth in my delivery, just the facts and my very specific message. "I believe—and what I believe is what matters tonight—that this morning's fractious behavior was the result of playing hurt. We are not injured, just hurt, and therefore we have to work harder to sustain our usual level of performance."

An audience of stoics began to loosen ever so slightly.

"Tonight you will run the show as rehearsed and set. You will play it with joy and energy and relentless pacing. You will play it like the first time and remember that you all want this job. No one has put a gun to your head. If you do that, and I know you will, the show will be markedly better than last night's and even better tomorrow. You will regain whatever confidence was dinged, and you will make us all proud. We have a busy day tomorrow, so notes on tonight's show will be given by Jojo, Elliot, and Ellie on note cards. If you have questions on anything, we will be available at nine forty-five in the morning.

"I found today's events very difficult. There is no guarantee that we won't have more of the same down the road, but I can assure you they will exacerbate tensions and create less productivity each time they occur. Let's do our best to make sure we don't have to deal with this sort of BS anymore."

Everyone was listening. Marc Seconds was managing to look at Carol Duteau's tits and take notes at the same time.

"The three best things about today *are*?" I didn't wait for an answer.

"One: you get to do a show tonight. Two: I get to watch it. Oh, and three: we're sold out."

Everyone began to applaud and it intensified the way football players escalate their antics in a pregame huddle.

"Break. Now let's play ball!"

60

The show was terrific. I took very few notes from my seat in the balcony, which I gave to Jojo, who distributed them to the company as they got out of costume and readied for the remainder of their night. Sitting on the deck nursing a beer I watched some of the audience members, a spectrum of types ranging from dashing to dowdy, waiting at the stage door and asking for autographs or photos. I saw friends of the company offering congratulations, and I heard ambient bits and pieces of conversation about how great this was or how much they enjoyed coming and so forth.

The night sky was a solid, dark blue with glittering stars that looked like handfuls of neon rice had been thrown into the sky at some wedding. I continued to watch the postcurtain travails unfold. By the time I had finished my brew and sought another, I realized for the first time that no one from my company had asked me to join them for a drink, a late pizza, or a drive into town. I sat a few minutes longer before I concluded that it was not an anomaly, but a statement. *Okay*, I assured myself, *they will return when flush with winning*.

Then Veronica walked up and sat next to me. She was quiet but looked on the verge of a giggle. "Hey, big boy," she said. "I'm calling that chit you offered earlier today and it's getting late, so unless you're a man who lacks integrity, I suggest we get started."

"Do we need any condiments?"

"Noooo . . ." she said with an outsized shake of the head. Then she took my hand, and I followed her into the bedroom on the first floor of the old red farmhouse.

6 1

Thursday promised to be eventful. I had slept intermittently after 5 a.m. and had been staring at the ceiling for nearly an hour. I had appointments with a motley bunch today, and was haunted by the specter of unannounced visitors I had yet to meet. I had no intention of seeing anyone unless I knew their agenda, and at the very least I intended to be clear headed and alert. I felt like Will Kane hours before High Noon.

I disengaged from my luscious girlfriend and crawled out of bed carefully, threw on some shorts, a sleeveless T-shirt, and running shoes. I whispered in Veronica's ear that I'd be back in thirty minutes. "If anyone calls or shows up while I'm gone, they can wait," I told her. "And if they become hostile or difficult, tell them to eat shit and die."

"I will," she said, "but only if you kiss me first." So I did. Then I left through the back door and ran toward the ocean.

During my run I had a lovely encounter with Janet Kessler and ASK. They walked back to the compound holding each other closely with a blanket wrapped around their shoulders. It was clear they had spent the night together, with a multitude of stars as their comfortable. They made no effort to avoid me. In fact, they seemed happy and proud that I had discovered them together. ASK was one of my best college friends and had just realized a long-pursued dream. Whatever good fortune awaited him, he had perhaps found his life's springboard.

The ocean has a certain aura at dawn. Quiet and soothing, it makes everything seem possible. It also helps you put your problems in perspective when you compare them to the size and scope of the unending horizon. Some were arriving at shore with the expectation of magic and some lingering after a miracle night.

I worked my body hard, my mind and heart filled with optimism and a positive attitude for the day that awaited me. Attitude is one of the rare aspects of your life you are able to control, and I was choosing to be upbeat. I sprinted the last three hundred yards down the shoreline and then jogged back to the compound ready to get back into the game.

The driveway was crowded with cars. The redwood table at the center of the compound was surrounded by people who looked like they were waiting for a free buffet. I slowed my jog to a fast walk so I could take in the scene. It was well before seven, but the place was teeming with people and drama.

Gary and Susan Golden, Officer Richardson and Chief Warren were seated at the front of the table. Secunda, despite the muggy July morning sat among our guests wearing his trademark Hickey Freeman blue-linen pinstripe suit and smoking his usual Cohiba stogie. Dr. Rosenstein looked a bit wan, as usual, as if he needed a good night's sleep. On the other side were seated a municipal official and the *Patriot Ledger*'s reporter Marc Seconds. The official wore a prominent shoulder patch that identified him as a Plymouth building inspector. JB, Officer Tommy, Veronica, ASK, Janet, and Sidney rounded out the rest of the table.

"Good morning, all," I said with forced cheer. "You're all early, but we'll figure that out together. Sorry about the weather. Give me a few minutes to clean up and I'll be right out to greet you properly." I walked quickly back to my room to change, feeling the eyes of some of our guests shooting bullets into my back.

I returned within ten minutes, freshly scrubbed. No one had moved from the table, and the mood was still heavy. The rain continued pungent and sweet. But before I could join them, Sidney intercepted me and put a firm right arm around my shoulder, walking me away from the action. He smelled good, as if he were wearing a high-end cologne, and he carried an energy that suggested he had been up for hours.

"Hey, college boy, you being good to Veronica? Shes talks about yous all the time. Shes happy."

"Good," I said. "I'm glad she's happy. She makes me feel the same way."

"Nice. Now, Sammy, yous got a lot of shit at that table. Yous can play them or you can get played. If theys play you, then it's a bad morning, 'cause they win and losing sucks."

"I agree, Sid. Winning is always better. What's up? Who's on my side?"

"I am, Veronica is, and I bet a bunch of your college pals are wit ya. And the cop, that Dudley Do-Right. That's enough. Just play it close, no yelling, no punches, all good." Then he turned me so I was facing my guests.

I noticed a difference from the usual demeanor and dress of the Golden family. I was surprised by how attractive Susan looked. She was dressed down in form-fitting jeans and a crisp, Brooks Brothers daisy button-down. Her hair was combed without any trace of sex. Her makeup and outfit were age appropriate. She was a lovely midforties woman.

More interesting was Gary. He looked more preppy than tough, wearing navy work pants and a white golf shirt tucked in to reveal his sculpted body. He had replaced his work boots with penny loafers resplendent with shinny copper coins. He didn't seem menacing, and he even brought a hint of a smile. It was a nice change; I wanted to run out and buy doughnut as a gesture of my appreciation. Then the Plymouth official walked purposefully toward me.

"Mr. August, my name is Martin Duggan. I am the senior building inspector here in Plymouth County."

"Nice to meet you, sir. *Why* am I meeting you, sir?"

"Unfortunately, I have a list of violations that unless repaired and inspected by this afternoon will force me to close your building immediately."

I noticed two of the cast, company members Karen Ross and Julie Watkins, leave their rooms and head toward breakfast. The door swung closed behind them, slamming hard against the doorstop. A phone rang several times in the office, then stopped. Rain washed over the compound, giving the moment some production value.

"May I see this list, Mr. Duggan?"

"Yes, sir." He sorted through his briefcase.

Secunda got up and moved a bit closer to me. ASK stepped a couple of strides away from Janet and began to listen more intently. There was a sense of ill feeling in the air, and the compound became inordinately quiet, like the OK Corral before the first shot was fired. Gary Golden got up from the redwood table.

Mr. Duggan handed me a typed formal-looking sheet of paper with no official city heading. Scratched across the top of the page was PLYMOUTH COUNTY BUILDING DEPARTMENT. Anyone could have written it, and I was sure that someone with deceitful intent had. I looked at the document for some time. There were inspections listed, but with no dates. In addition, the inspectors' signatures were illegible.

I returned the paper to Duggan. "So that's it? This log with no dates or names or actual specific violations entitles you to come here and threaten to close my business?"

"I assure you, Mr. August, there is no threat here. As the watchdog for the safety of this county, I am prepared to shut your doors."

"'Watchdog,' Mr. Duggan, is an interesting choice of term. May I see that list again?"

The building inspector obliged. While I studied it, Duggan offered a solution. "Due to the timing of the situation and the tremendous losses you might incur as well as the poor press you might receive, may I suggest another alternative, Mr. August?"

"You are the watchdog, sir. You can suggest and do anything you'd like, except shit on my grounds, because I'd insist you clean it up or eat it, depending on what your suggestion is."

That cast a pall on further conversation. I looked at the paper again, but only saw red.

"There is no reason to be rude, Mr. August. I am only doing my job."

"Right. And again, what is that job?"

"I am the head of the Building Department here in Plymouth County and I am assigned to keep places of assembly safe."

"Okay, you're right, I should not be rude, at least until I hear your suggestion."

"Thank you. If you pay a violations fine of six thousand dollars, we can consider the matter closed."

Who would believe this guy? Don't we have rehearsal in a few moments? Maybe I can get Ellie to fuck him in lieu of the six grand. What are all these spectators going to do when this plays out? Does Julie Watkins ever wear a bra to breakfast, and why haven't I noticed before what big breasts she has?

I looked at Duggan through narrowed eyes. "Do you have a boss?"

"Yes, sir. I do."

"Does he know you are here this morning?"

"No, Mr. August, he does not. I have a job to do and he is a busy man. Your situation is not the only one on our docket today." For the first time since he had uttered a word, Mr. Duggan gave me attitude with more than a modicum of edge. It became clearer what an unadulterated scumbag he was.

"So your boss doesn't know you have shit for brains and are here to extort me? He doesn't know you are a complete douchebag. The only thing you are leaving here with is a few broken bones, a formal complaint to the mayor, and a report to the paper that you are a corrupt dirtbag."

Duggan didn't say anything.

"Cat got your tongue, dirtbag? Or has the watchdog got it?"

I moved toward Duggan intending to pick him up off the ground and throwing him onto the street. As I took my first step forward with a red face and violence pulsing through my veins, ASK ran toward me at full speed and kicked me square in the testicles. I was too incapacitated to say a word and fell unceremoniously to the ground in a ball of misery. Through a haze of pain, I watched and or heard the following:

ASK dropped to my side and said, "I'm really sorry, but if you hit that guy you'd be in jail, and I need notes for tonight's performance. Also, you're much bigger than I am, and that was all I could think of. Sorry."

Dr. Rosenstein knelt next to me and his prescription was, "Breathe. Testicles are very resilient, and I imagine yours are more than most."

Susan Golden approached Duggan and handed him sheet of paper and a pen. "Sign this, you bastard, and sign it now, quickly." Duggan perused it with dispatch and did as he was told.

Gary Golden got chest to chest with Duggan and shoved an eight-by-ten envelope at him. Then he grabbed the front of Duggan's shirt and said in a rather intimidating whisper, "Take this money, you prick, and get lost. Consider it a gift from my grandfather, but don't go thanking him. If I hear you come back to August with anymore bullshit, here is some good advice—don't. You're not even allowed in here if you buy a ticket. You are a lowlife prick. You have until the count of ten, and then I mess you up."

Duggan took the envelope and leaned over a bit to where I was slowly recuperating on the damp ground. "Thank you, Mr. August. May you have the best of luck the rest of your summer."

Gary Golden punted him a good fifteen yards with a stunning kick to the ass. Duggan stumbled a bit but made it back to his car, climbing in and driving off into the misty morning.

Secunda surveyed the situation. He took a draw on his stogie then with a big smile said, "Well, that was interesting. How about we take a brief respite for breakfast and then continue. Would someone help Sammy off the ground and find him a comfortable seat out of the rain?"

"It might help if he sat on a pillow," Elliot suggested. ASK, perhaps out of guilt, said, "I'll get one," and he ran off to find a cushion.

I noticed it was just past seven o'clock. What else could this day bring?

62

Fifteen minutes later I lay on my back under the eave of the theater, protected from what had become a steady, cold summer rain. The company had just witnessed a series of events that was not in the fine print of their employment agreements. Nevertheless, it seemed to pass quickly, and the morning din in the dining room rang with spirited talk of impending rehearsals.

Veronica had brought me some breakfast: orange juice, soft-boiled eggs, and crispy, well-buttered English muffins. She told me I was a hero for my "restraint," lacing the word with sarcasm. "If it wasn't for ASK, there would have been no restraint," I pointed out.

She jumped all over that. "You were an idiot, Sam. You wanted like so many other morons to lead with machismo. You're smarter than that. So actually ASK was the hero. Maybe he should be rewarded with deviant sex."

I was chastened. I should have been smarter. Think first. Get the facts and don't lead with my chin.

Jojo visited the temporary infirmary and told me I had notes and rehearsals in an hour and that after this morning's distractions I had better be at my best. When I asked her to line up a call with my dad at six in the evening, she softened and said, "Sure. I'll tell him to expect to hear from you."

"Oh, and Jojo, could you send a telegram to Mr. Foster, Ellie's dad. I think his first name is Steven. See if he can find some time in his schedule to talk with me. Ten minutes is all I need."

"Sure. And we'll keep that between you and me, right?"

"Yup." That was all there was to say.

Sidney pulled up a folding chair and sat facing backward on it, resting his chin on the back of the chair. He made no effort to stay out of the elements, and rain spotted his shirt.

"College boy," he said, "yous a good solid kid. Yous tough and unafraid, which is both good and bad. Yous can only win so many battles in life. Only so many. Even if yous fucking Jim Lonborg, you lose, particularly on short rest. Take a blow. Decide what is important and fight those fights. Then you win. The ones you pay no attention yous might lose anyway, probably. Yous a winner kid, but only when you figure that part out. Call me if yous need me. And when yous feeling better, stop by for a drink. Oh, and keep being nice to my Veronica sweetie, otherwise yous lose everything. Love ya, kid."

He walked off into the rain like Shane. I wanted to shout, *"Come back, Sid!"* but my balls still hurt. I rested in silence for a bit. The rain pelted the deck and was relaxing in its exactitude. My attitude was all that mattered. I could control that. I was committed to making it work today.

The cops wandered over. They had an air of contrition and stood a few feet away as if to make sure it was okay to approach me. I sat up and grabbed Sid's chair, placing it out of harm's way from the chilly rain. As the senior agent, Officer Warren did the talking. "Sam, we are here to help. What went on here this morning is not what we represent in our department. Trust me. You already have had a day and a half. Now you have to go to work. We'll plug the damn for the day and let you catch up. We'll be back at six and we'll figure out how to win this one, as well as those problems facing Miss Foster."

"Yeah, Sam," added Officer Richardson. "I have done some reading about your guy Capra—actually Ellie read it to me mostly. He said something like, 'In the fight of all great causes, it is at times when we feel lost, that we are closest to finding our way.' I'm here. Feel better and we'll check in later."

Warren added one more thing. "I told your people if Colon calls you again they tell him you're off limits and that he has to go through me first. Hey, you have a good day, kid. Make some music."

Gary Golden walked up the three steps to the deck and handed me a large glass of grapefruit juice. "I understand you don't drink coffee because you wake up wired. True?"

"Yup. The problem for me is not waking up, it's falling asleep. So thanks. This has pulp in it."

"Squeezed it myself," Golden said.

"Wow. I guess the war is over."

Gary dropped to his haunches so I could stay seated and away from the rain. The precipitation seemed to hit him and bounce off the way bullets do off the chest Superman. He captured my gaze, and I have to admit I was confused. Yet I was ready to listen. That much I had learned these past weeks.

"Sam," he said, "I want to be your friend. I didn't want to be a few weeks ago, but now I do. I am badass enemy, but I can be a good guy if I am on your side. I'd like to be on your side and I want you to trust me. I even talked with Veronica about it and we'll straighten things out so this can happen. She told me to talk with you, said she'd sign up for whatever is good for you but that it was your choice. I'm going nowhere. I am a local dick who fights too much and takes some graft and punches around a few schlubs. I like you. I've watched you these past weeks. But no one can make a difference alone. I want to help you."

"Wow," I said, "I thought you were here to beat the shit out of me. Life is full of surprises."

"Yeah, it's true." He offered his hand.

"Lots of questions," I said.

"They'll wait till after rehearsal. By the way, I think Secunda is hysterical. Saw the show three times and paid every time."

"Let's meet at the Full Sail at eleven tonight and see if the new beginning is real."

"Guarantee it is. I'll be early. Thanks."

"You know the Bible teaches grace. Let's hope you're right."

Gary considered this for a second. "I dated a girl named Grace once. Good for the Bible."

After he left I stood up, rearranged my damaged testicles, and rethought the events of the morning. I took a deep breath and walked into the theater for my rehearsal. I was ten minutes early. What to do with the extra time?

My dad always told me that it is the unexpected in a deal that rattles the cage, so here I was with everything I needed to deliver the show except a lack of distraction. What was my choice? Blow up like *Apollo 1* or stand true to my goals?

One day at time. As of this morning, it was the best I had to offer.

63

Sylvia, a distant, much older, cousin of mine worked for the RAF during the London Blitz. She looked at radar screens all day on the lookout for the German Luftwaffe. Every day, ten, twelve, fourteen hours a day. Then she would go home. Every night the city was bombed. Yet people went out to buy food, take an evening walk, or and even see a movie or a show at the Royal Shakespeare Company.

One day a high-ranking RAF officer offered Sylvia two tickets to see John Gielgud play Hamlet at an evening show of the RCS. Thrilled, she got to the theater early to soak up the experience. John Gielgud! She and her friend took their seats, fourth row center. Just then the stage manager stepped in front of the curtain and made an important announcement.

"Mr. Gielgud will not be performing the role of Hamlet this evening." The audience murmured their dismay. "The role of Hamlet will be performed by Mr. Gielgud's understudy, Mr. Laurence Olivier."

Okay, they all thought, *we're here, we've dodged the bombs and the bullets. Let's see if this Larry bloke is any good.* I guess he was, since he would later work often.

Just before the end of the first act, sirens went off; the city was under attack. The stage manager announced that the performance would recommence once the "lights out" was lifted. He hoped everyone was enjoying the show. The bombing ceased, and about fifteen minutes later the performance was completed. Mr. Olivier took the star bow as Hamlet, the first of many times he would play the role.

The next day, my cousin went back to watching radar screens and looking for Germans. Life goes on. It simply has to, otherwise what would we all do to fill our days? Now, I'm not suggesting that the events and distractions of earlier this morning were tantamount to the London Blitz. Of course not. Not even for a moment.

Yet what I was thinking as my rehearsal began and everyone was focused, all in good humor and actually working at a heightened level, was that life does go on, and as long as it does, we should make the most of it. In London, they did this as they tiptoed through the bombings. Here today at PBT, six o'clock would arrive and Colon might reappear. At eleven, I'd meet Gary Golden, my new best friend. Until then I'd work, and on my breaks I would check the radar to see if anyone else was trying to blow up the building.

64

In addition to the minutiae that goes into a rehearsal, today we had two major things to accomplish. One was a "star" issue about Katherine Fitzgerald and her position in the lead role. She was either going to meet the challenge or fall short. It was not a question of ability but psyche, which is always a deep-rooted conundrum. The other was fun, but could lead to tedium if we were not on top of our game. It would require focus and creativity from everyone; we were going to run the scene that ended the first act as many as twenty times so we could set up the first act finale perfectly. With each run, the artists had to bring something new to the scene. If they did, it would be time well spent. If not, then both the scene and rehearsal would be deadly. We chose to work on the end of act 1 first.

Funny Girl is the musical biography of the great Ziegfeld star Fanny Brice. It was a huge hit on Broadway and made Barbara Streisand an international sensation. She won both the Tony and the Oscar for her performance in the lead role. Like all classic musicals, it has some brilliant moments and a few clinkers that I am sure the original creators wish they had the liberty to fix before opening night. Act 1 ends with one of the great musical numbers in Broadway history, "Don't Rain on My Parade." The setup is simple, the execution difficult.

Producer Flo Ziegfeld forbids his star to go and meet the man she loves. She defies him, intent on leaving the show. She books a train ticket to be with her lover. Ziegfeld sets her straight, saying if she blows off her responsibilities, she is through. He throws down the gauntlet and exits the train station, leaving her to make a life choice: the man or the career. When Ziegfeld exits he is followed by his minions, which include press, staff, other actors, and Fanny's best friend, who in our show was played by Ronny Feston.

Moving fourteen people around a stage is not an easy task. Subtlety and nuance are essential. The timing has to work, the visual has to be arresting, and most important each of the fourteen actors has to play something unique to him or her. Each has to have a point of view and personal reaction to the situation. Everything must appear to be happening for the first time.

The scene takes place in the early 1920s at a New York railroad station. The performers are dressed in the more formal clothes of the period. The setting is adorned with all the accouterments of travel that a major star like Fanny Brice would enjoy. Fanny's dilemma and her conflict with Ziegfeld are the heart of the scene, but without the supporting cast the scene will play unbalanced and fall flat.

First I blocked the scene that came before the big confrontation, then the exit. I placed the supporting players to draw the audience's eye to center stage, where the big showdown would occur. It was essential for the characters to be aware that a confrontation was brewing, amping up the energy so when Brice/Kat makes her entrance, the scene is just short of breathless. The stars enter in full conflagration and all eyes are on them.

"Flo, I'll be gone a week. Your follies will survive," she says.

"You are the star of my follies and with that you have a responsibility . . ."

"What about my responsibility to me!"

I stopped the rehearsal.

"Kat, what's left?" I asked "You still have the whole scene to play, and you're screaming at him like a crazy bitch. Be vulnerable. Coax him. Seduce him. Let him know you'll die if you lose this man. Then, when he says no again, get angry and use the anger to infuse the song."

She ran it again and it was better. Then again and better still.

Secunda, who was playing Ziegfeld, had it right from the start. He was royalty and he was powerful, and he didn't give a damn about her or her man or her love. He cared about one thing, selling tickets, and to do that he needed his star to be on stage and not chasing a dream of puppy love.

He listens to her plea, and for an instant there is a glimmer of hope in the audience's heart that he will acquiesce. Then he says, "Damn it Fanny! If you get on that train you'll never work again."

I asked Secunda to pause to show his power. I suggested he lower his voice to practically a whisper and show his strength through an innate knowledge that no one ever says no to Flo Ziegfeld.

He took a moment to allow the note to register. Then, "Damn it Fanny! If you get on that train you'll never work again!" he shouted. He held one, two, three, almost four beats and added in a heated whisper, "Never is a long time, young lady, and I mean what I say."

He exits and everyone follows, leaving Brice alone on stage.

We ran the exit a couple of times and it looked okay. Yet it was void of any color; it was all sort of gray and nondescript. We talked it over. We asked each actor how his or her character felt. Did they side with Ziegfeld or Brice? Did they resent the intrusion into their life? Did they wish they were her or did they wish they were Ziegfeld? Did they have a boyfriend or girlfriend waiting in the next city? Did they fear that this conflict might affect their jobs? And so forth. Make a choice, make it your own, make the scene about many people, make it about every individual on the stage, not just the two leads.

The talk was fun. The scene was energized and each time we ran it, it had more color, more excitement. It has been said that the only people in the theater who don't know what happens in a show are the characters, and that started to ring true in our rehearsal. We ran it over and over. Each time it was better. I was ready to let it be, revisit the scene another time.

I called ten and said we would start with the opening after the break. Ronny Feston raised his hand. After yesterday's histrionics, I wondered what was in store. "What's up, Ronny?" I asked.

"Would everyone mind if we ran this just a couple more times? I'm feeling almost comfortable and if I have another couple of shots I can set it. Everyone?"

It was silly, but I felt so proud of him. I had been hard, perhaps even abusive, yesterday, and yet here was the kid that had blown us away at auditions.

I walked from the house to the stage and put my arms around him, patting his little mop-top head.

"You rock, Ronny Feston." I said. Then turned to the cast and added, "Let's run it again for Mr. Feston and then we'll take ten."

ASK started to clap, slowly at first, then Julie then Cindy then Rush then Trudy. And now the applause came from everyone with whooping and cheering and clapping as if Feston had just sold out the house. It was wonderful to be in the building for those few minutes. We rehearsed the scene three more times and Feston was better with each go round.

During the ten, Mary Holly, our ingenue lead and costume designer, approached me along with JB, Jojo, Duncan, Secunda, Ellie and the good Doctor. She looked both troubled and a bit fearful.

"Sam, we can't build the clothes for 'His Love Makes Me Beautiful.' We don't have time and we don't have the money. Even Josh said we don't have the money."

I turned to Secunda and asked, "Are you not feeling well?" Then I looked back at Mary. "This is the big production number in act 1. How can we do it without production value?"

"I have a thought," said Jojo. We looked at her as if she were E. F. Hutton.

"I think we should do the number in rehearsal clothes. The girls can wear leotards, which are sexy, and the guys can wear simple clothes that will add color. It will also save us tech time. Anyway, the most important bit in the song is the reveal that she's pregnant, and that stays."

I stood up and kissed her on both cheeks. "Problem solved." I said. "Jojo, you got any thoughts on world peace?"

"Later," she said. "Now we have rehearsal."

Later that afternoon, Fitzgerald told me she couldn't rehearse anymore. The penultimate number in the show was a ballad about how losing her man for all practical purposes ended her life, well at least emotionally. Kat had talked for weeks about how she wanted to sing that song and stop the show and give everyone goose bumps. Now, for inexplicable reasons, she couldn't rehearse.

I turned the rehearsal over to Ellie and sat with Elliot to discuss this unexpected situation.

"Kat is pulling diva shit," he said. "She's fine. She sang great during the show last night and this morning at rehearsal. She wants attention. That's it."

I was a bit stunned by his intensity. "She's got to be upset about you moving on with Diana. Attention is maybe what she needs."

"Not from me! Been there, done that. I didn't sign up to play Joe Gillis to Norma Desmond. I'm sorry. We all have real problems, we don't need to make them up. " He stormed away.

I called Jojo over. "Jojo, tell Kat she should take the rest of the afternoon off. Get her some tea and lemon. Have the town doctor come by and check her throat to see if there is any problem. Tell her she has to be ready for tonight. At break, tell everyone we're going to run the scene into the song and Lexie will cover for Kat. Then let's see what happens. Have Elliot rehearse the song with Lexie on the red deck so she is prepared. We'll see who is truly under the weather or who is just putting us on hurricane alert."

"Done," she said.

Thirty minutes before we broke at six for dinner and free play for the company, we set the scene with Lexie ready to fill in for Kat. Lexie Dawson was wrong for the part. Too pretty, too sexy, too perky, but she could sing and she could give you chills when she did. She knew she was a pawn in the game of ego, but it mattered not. She was poised to remind everyone of Wally Pipp and a guy named Gehrig.

Everyone loves this sort of thing. You know, the understudy stepping out of the chorus and setting the world on its ear. The theater was packed. It seemed that everyone had found a moment to take a break just as Lexie was about to sing. And sing she did. Home run. Everybody cheered and whooped it up. Then they cheered some more. Lexie was very moved and gracious. We broke for dinner.

Jojo came up to me within minutes and told me Kat was feeling much better and could do her show tonight and would like to set an early rehearsal in the morning to make up for the time she'd lost today.

I don't believe in homeopathic medicine or Chinese herbs, but after that day I knew that what heals you quickly is competition and the fear of being left behind. Maybe Lexie should be a doctor because she sure knew how to heal the star.

It was almost six. My day was about to begin.

65

Officer Richardson was waiting for me as I left the theater. The rain had picked up and he was seated in his squad car staying dry. Alongside the officer was JB, and they were chatting and smoking. I knocked on the car window and he rolled it down to say hello. JB bid farewell, shook hands with Richardson and said, "It was nice talking with you. Please come by and see the next show. I'll give you the VIP treatment."

I thought cigarette smoke sucked and didn't want to speak in the car, so in spite of the heavy rain I suggested we walk over to the parking lot to chat. The lot was well landscaped except for an area that separated the cars from the back stage of the theater. We'd let the summer grass grow tall and it actually was quite beautiful, like long-stemmed, amber wheat out of some beer commercial. When the sun was setting, or on a day like today when the sky was gray and ominous, it all added up to a special sort of theatricality, suggesting that Mother Nature was the best scenic designer there ever was. As Officer Richardson and I walked into this towering maze, I thought of Cary Grant in *North by Northwest* using such a meadow to escape that crop duster.

"What's up, Scott?" I asked. "Anything new since yesterday? Ellie do anybody since I saw you last?"

"Hey, that's unnecessary," he said. "I thought she was a friend of yours. We are just trying to protect her, that's all."

"Really? When did you start thinking about protecting her, Scott? When it became inconvenient for her to get naked with you? Make some demands on your schedule? Or impose on your time? Maybe she should have been protected from you. Did you ever think of that, hotshot?"

Officer Richardson was more than shocked by my aggressive attitude. In fact, so was I. He needed a smoke to get his wits about him. His crisp uniform wilted in the steady rain. Just like his body.

"Actions have consequences, my man and now you're part of the Ellie situation," I said. "I had a friend in college who used to say you could fuck any girl once and you never had to call her again, but if you fucked her twice you had a responsibility to call and blow her off with some respect. Warped, I know. How many times did you sleep with Ellie?"

"What are you doing?" Richardson asked, clearly flustered. "I like Ellie. I'm worried about her, that's all. That's why I had Chief Warren call you. That's why I am here tonight."

"I'm confused, Scott, I really am. Not looking to get in your face. You say you're worried. Well, I'm terrified. This is not what I signed up for. What do I do, send her to her room without dinner? She is a woman, not a teenager, damn it."

Scott took a long drag and exhaled the weight of the world.

"You'll forgive me, officer, but I think you're blowing smoke here and it's heading up your ass. You're a decent guy, so if you really cared about Ellie, you'd be talking to her. You'd find a way, you'd figure it out. You wouldn't push it on me and go grab a beer. I'm not her father and I didn't fuck her until she became a nuisance. If you don't talk with this girl and be a man about it, then you're an ass. It's that simple. How'd you feel if she was your sister?"

"Ellie is hanging with a bad crowd. That's it. How she got there or what happened between me and her is not important. She doesn't talk to me anymore and she goes out alone without the other girls here. She's been seeing this guy Johnny Colon. Pretends he has more money than he's got. A punk. Small-time loan sharking. Tough guy. Way too old for her, and married. He has been arrested a few times for bar fights and beating up on women. Not connected or anything, just a bully. I tried to talk with her. She won't speak with me, so I thought you were the next-best option. You know, you got a lot of good things going for you and until ten minutes ago I thought you were a pretty good guy. She's your friend and your problem."

"What if she was your sister, Scott? How would you handle this?"

He took a short drag on his smoke and flicked the butt into the tall wet grass. "See ya," he said, "only when I have to."

"Truth is hard sometimes, officer. Make sure you enjoy that beer. It helps you swallow a big lie."

I found that I was so extremely sad that my heart actually hurt. I watched him walk to the squad car and open the door. He took his cap off and shook it so the raindrops wouldn't sit heavy on its brim. He obviously had enough on his mind; he didn't need any more weight to cloud his thoughts. Responsibility was burden enough for one rainy night.

I stood in the tall grass for a long time. I was drenched through to the skin yet my head was still mired with debris. What a fucking day. Capra said, "Everything important in life happens in the rain."

I walked to the office and asked Debbie and Diana to find something else to do. I paged Ellie and said she had a call waiting. She arrived within a couple of minutes. She looked adorable. Her hair was matted from the rain and gave her a sweet, waiflike appearance. She had pretty brown eyes and perfect skin. She immediately noticed the phone was in its cradle and her expression changed from anticipation to concern.

"Nobody called, Ellie, but we need to talk."

She took the chair across the desk from me and sat down cautiously. The rain had caused her T-shirt to cling to her body, and other than the dark frown she wore she was absolutely delicious. I wondered what made people do the things they did. Swim in the ocean on angel dust. Overstep their rights and be verbally abusive. Drink too much and drive. Throw a punch rather than talk like a man. Fuck some girl with a promise of more. All of those sins applied to me, and now I was going to talk with Ellie Foster about her indiscretions? What a hypocrite. The words of every parent played in my ear: "Do as I say, not as I do." But I wasn't her parent. For the time being and with the clock ticking, I was only her friend.

I told her what I had heard. I tried to offer no bias, just concern for her safety if not her reputation, and last for the jeopardy her actions might put the theater and her friends in if something should go wrong.

Her response was immediate. No contemplation or moment to measure a rebuttal. "Fuck you, Sam. You hired me to choreograph the shows here. I'm doing it and I am doing it damn well. You don't know anything about me. When we were together in school that lasted all of what? . . . long enough for you to shower and wash me off before you found some other conquest. Don't give me any self-righteous BS about your concern for me. I'm a big girl. I'll take whatever ride I want on my own time. You had no problem with me riding you back when."

"Ellie . . ." I tried to interject to no avail.

"You have any notes for me, then let me have them now because I have a date after the curtain comes down."

She stared at me with such violent contempt that I found the episode almost more than disturbing. I was in way over my head and at a loss as to what to say or do next. I got up and tried to hug her, which she rejected as if I were a leper.

"Notes?" she demanded.

"No," I said. "You're doing a great job. I'm sorry if I offended you."

She walked out into the rain without another word. I sat back in the desk chair and looked out the window. It was raining so hard I thought I saw a boat with a bunch of animals floating by. Boy oh boy, that Capra was one smart fucker.

It was almost seven when I placed the call to my dad that I had asked Jojo to set up. I tried him at his office where the phone rang and rang with no result. I then called home with the same endgame. I felt young and overwhelmed and in need of a grownup to talk things through.

I remembered how when I was younger my folks were always offering to get me something from the kitchen or help with a chore or homework assignment. Then one day, I asked my dad if he could get me a glass of milk. He replied, "What, are your legs broken? Get it yourself." No malice at all, just the changing of the guard. I was no longer a little kid.

Right now it would be really nice if someone would offer to bring me a glass of milk.

66

Oftentimes we'll go to a play or musical that's packed, and we leave wondering if all those enthusiastic patrons had been lobotomized before curtain. Other times we sit in an empty building and ask, "Why isn't anyone here to see this? Don't they know what they're missing?"

It was like that for me at PBT before Bobby put us in the parade. Before that, as one headline had read, PBT LIGHTS UP PLYMOUTH. Terrific shows. No people. Now we had the opposite problem. Neither rain, nor sleet, nor snow would keep audiences from their dates with the third row on the aisle, and tonight was further proof of Plymouth's growing commitment to our cast and company.

When I was seven I started collecting baseball cards. They were a luxury item to purchase out of my small allowance, so to have any sort of meaningful collection I had to win them from friends in "flipping contests." I practiced and became what might be called a hustler of baseball cards. If it were pool, Paul Newman would have played me in the movies.

I enjoyed the competition, and once the cards were in my possession I would study the player's statistics until I had memorized every one. Every player, every homer, RBI, and stolen base. For instance, Jerry Lumpe hit thirty-four doubles in 1962 while playing for the Kansas City Athletics. There wasn't anything subjective or ephemeral about the back of a baseball card. If a player hit .330, he was good. If he batted .211, he'd be on a bus back to the minors. It was clear and precise, very much the opposite of the theater business, which is nothing but irrational or completely insane.

The rain hadn't let up all day and now as curtain time approached it was almost comical in its intensity. Yet every ticket was sold! SRO made for a rather colorful array of umbrellas held by those waiting in line hoping for a cancellation. And all on a Thursday night. Nothing made sense. We weren't bad when the house was sparse, and we weren't world-beaters now that there was a battle for every last seat, even the one in the corner behind a pole.

There is nothing like the theater. There is no other entertainment medium that can deliver the surprise a live performance on the stage promises. Every night is like a snowflake unique unto itself. Tonight's performance of our fluff thirties silly musical was proof positive. There was a terrific classic tap number in the middle of act 1 in which our character actress Mary Saloshin led the chorus girls in a wild, crazy, joyous ride into insane silliness. Mary was all bones and elbows and made Olive Oyl look like she needed to eat a salad. She owned the number from the downbeat and wore it like a glove. With flourish she built and built it. Unless you were Satan, you couldn't help but smile from start to finish. Tonight the mirth meter was off the charts.

As the number reached its peak, one of the backup dancers, the lovely Carol Duteau, had the misfortune of having her halter top unhook behind her neck; she had to continue in just her dance pants, tap shoes, and a smile. Wow! What a way to steal a scene.

Carol was up there dancing with her luscious breasts, which had graduated from Yale, beautifully bouncing for the entire world to see. It was like a gorgeous train wreck. You *had* to look. You knew you shouldn't but you couldn't help yourself.

Carol kept dancing as if nothing had happened. It made no sense; she should have bolted off stage, but for some inexplicable reason she chose not to. The rest of the girls fed on the energy from her courage and abandon; the audience was in awe of her beauty, her guts, and some unconscious, unmitigated confidence that allowed her to tap on through without missing a beat. She went from role player to superstar—and no doubt about it: she had a sensational, glorious set of boobs.

The number ended and the audience cheered. Then they stood up and roared. The cast broke character and applauded Carol with every fiber of their clothed bodies. There were whistles and hollers and a drum beat from the orchestra, and everyone kept letting Carol Duteau know she was something else . . . and oh those boobies.

Whether she was in shock or denial or liked the attention, she made no effort to cover up and took repeated bow after repeated bow. The spot operators crisscrossed their lights so they resembled klieg beams at an opening night in Hollywood. It appeared the frenzy would never end, and I began to wonder if she would cover up before catching one hell of a chest cold.

Finally, and as further proof that tonight was the perfect evening to attend the show even by boat if necessary, Secunda, who was playing the comic lead Moonface Martin, walked center stage and stood next to Carol. The cheering continued. In the spirit of classic burlesque he made googly eyes at this stunningly beautiful, half-naked girl and placed his head gently against her naked tatas. He rested there for quite awhile—nice work if you can get it—then placed his face directly on target and shook his head vigorously and joyously from side to side. He turned to the audience and held their gaze. What could he possibly say? Or do?

With a slight nod to Groucho he said, "I have been so busy with rehearsals I haven't been keeping abreast of things."

Huge laugh.

"I love this job. And it involves money too. But don't worry, I don't pay them very much!"

More laughter. Lots of it.

He then removed the costume sport jacket he was wearing and draped it over Carol's shoulders. He took her hand and walked her center stage into the hot light of the two balcony spots.

"Ladies and Gentlemen, Miss Carol Duteau."

Carol took a deep bow and smiled from somewhere she had never been before. Wherever her life would lead her, she would never forget this unexpected bit of magic when in the blink of an eye she became the epicenter of this small yet overwhelmingly loving universe.

By the end of the next afternoon, you could find many auto rear windshields freshly painted and shouting throughout town, I LOVE YOU CAROL! WILL YOU MARRY ME? Never had a girl had so many choices, or such a growing number of acolytes. It is true the show must go on and it will, long after we are all gone. I doubt, however, that there will ever be another evening to match that rainy night in the old barn in the town where the Pilgrims had set up shop.

67

As I walked up Garden Road on the way to my eleven o'clock meeting with Gary Golden at the Full Sail, I heard breathless footsteps following me, gaining ground. The rain had finally slowed and the entire beachfront was now cloaked in a dense low-lying fog. You could hear the ocean without seeing it, and the streetlights glowed like old-fashioned gas lamps. The sound of wet footsteps behind me was unnerving. I wasn't sure whether I should stop and face down my pursuer or wait to see if he was headed for a rendezvous with another. In fact, I wondered if perhaps my overall fatigue and apprehension had fabricated this faceless menace.

But I could hear clearly the approaching heels of my pursuer as they pushed down on the pavement. So I quickened my pace and braced myself as the footsteps came within arm's length.

"Sam! Hold up," someone shouted just steps away. "Hey man, wait, slow down." I recognized the voice and slowed to face it. Out of the haze ASK appeared. He had changed out of his costume and was dressed in jeans and a gold PBT T-shirt, but he was still wearing his stage makeup. It made him look ghoulish and frightening in the distorting light.

"Alan, what are you doing? Did you come to kick me in the balls again?"

He reached his arm out to hold me in place while he gulped for air. The long run had taken its toll.

"No, of course not. I didn't want you to go alone, that's all. I came after you because I thought you might need help. You know, backup."

He had his hands resting on his knees and his breathing was decelerating. It appeared he was going to make it.

"Backup?" I asked. "You mean like on a cop show?"

He nodded his assent and saved some air by doing so.

"You know, ASK, with your makeup on and in this light you really look like Howdy Doody." Then I began to laugh from someplace down deep.

ASK laughed as well. "Hey, I'm sorry about this morning. I didn't know what else to do. You okay?"

I took a long time to respond. After all, it had been one crazy night. And although Gary Golden had spoken of his desire to be friends, perhaps it was all a setup.

"Alan, I don't know. How do you think I should be?"

"If I knew, I'd tell you. I thought if I showed up we could figure it out together."

"That would be good. That would be really good."

ASK moved toward me and offered an awkward hug. If anyone were around they'd see a funny snapshot of the diminutive ASK with his arms around the six-foot-four me. After a moment, he said, "I love you, man. You're not alone. I know you think I'm a little imp, but remember dynamite comes in small packages."

"Kaboom," I said. I patted his head, and we continued together to my appointment with Gary Golden.

Gary was seated at a two-top overlooking the deck. ASK took a barstool, ordered a beer, and acted as lookout. We had decided I should talk with Golden alone. I sat across from him and watched while he drank tequila neat with a beer back. I hadn't noticed before, but this was one good-looking guy. He had a strong jaw that emphasized his chiseled features. He had dark, piercing eyes and a smoldering look complimented by a five o'clock shadow. His body was broad at the shoulders and tapered at the waist, like a middleweight boxer who could cast a shadow longer than his reach. He had a disarming model's smile, and carried himself with confidence and élan.

"Spooky out there. I thought I'd run into Basil Rathbone," I joked.

"Don't know him. Does he work with you?"

"No, it was a joke. Rathbone was an actor who played Sherlock Holmes in the movies. It was always foggy in those films."

He smirked a bit. "How the fuck would I know that?"

"Are you going to beat me up?" I asked lightheartedly, to test out the landscape.

"You want me to?" He smiled. "I think you might want a drink instead. Or I could buy you the drink then kick the shit out of you if you'd prefer."

"I'll just go with the drink for starters and take a rain check on the random violence," I replied.

Gary responded with a polite chuckle and motioned to Doobie at the bar for another round of drinks. He waved at ASK and held up a peace sign suggesting that he could relax; no SWAT team was needed at the moment.

We sat silently until the drinks arrived. He asked that the waiter hold a moment while he raised his glass to toast. We both downed the shots of Cuervo. Then Gary signaled the waiter to bring another round.

We sipped our beer and took each other's measure.

"Sorry about the angel dust," he said.

"Yeah, that really sucked."

"Didn't think you'd try to swim to England."

"Wouldn't have smoked it if I had known it was laced with that shit."

"I shouldn't have done it. I'm sorry."

I locked on his eyes and decided he meant it. "I accept. Why'd you do it? Try to fuck me up like that . . ."

He ran by the question and left it unanswered. "You know, I never saw a show until you came to town. Where you learn that stuff? In college?"

"Some of it. Mostly in college I learned that I wanted to try to earn a living at it and find out if I might be good enough to do so. And how to chase girls, of course."

"I don't know anything about it, but you seem pretty good at the whole thing. I mean, you and your group are the talk of the town. As to the girls, you have some lookers working there, so congrats on that as well."

"Thanks. I guess I'm good enough to get everybody's attention. Now what I need to do is learn how to keep it."

I looked over at ASK, who was engrossed in a sports debate with Doobie. It was a bit disconcerting to note that if Gary decided to stomp me to death, ASK would be too involved to notice.

I hesitated a moment but then ventured forth. "I mean no disrespect, but where did you learn to shake people down? And why me?"

"College," he said, smiling.

"What school teaches Extortion 101?"

"It's an extra-credit course." He said this with a grin, and we both laughed. "Boston College. I went to BC for two years and then dropped out."

"Why'd you leave?"

"I got tired of the BS. The football coaches telling me what to do. Same with the professors. The whole being bossed around thing didn't work for me."

He took out a pack of cigarettes and did that thing smoker's do where they smash the pack a few times to tighten the tobacco before they light up. He offered me the first option.

"Don't smoke," I said.

"Mind if I do?"

"Yeah, I kinda do, if you don't mind."

"That's why I asked." He put away his smokes. "Hungry?"

"I'm not looking for any trouble Gary, but what are we doing here? First you fuck me up, then you shake me down, and now you want to buy me a burger. You make a bet with someone on how big a schmuck I might be?"

"You got a hot switch on you," he noted without animus.

"Yup, my Achilles heel. Maybe I should breathe. But everybody's strength is also their weakness."

"Temper's a bad thing. Can get you in a whole lot of trouble, you know. I told you this morning I wanted to be friends."

I drank my beer until the glass was empty. I walked over to the bar and told ASK it was all right, but if he wanted, he should hang around. Then I ordered another two more Cuervos with beers to back 'em and returned to the table with the drinks in hand.

"Okay," I said, "let's drink to new friends and how all that works between us."

"We talk," he said.

I jumped in. "Gary, why'd you do that stuff? Why'd you come at me? Was it sport or real?"

"I dunno. You ever see somebody, strangers mostly, and they just piss you off? They have a nicer car or a better-looking girl . . . Everybody likes 'em. Everything is so easy and you think, 'Why can't that be me?' And since you can't be that person, you fuck with 'em or bring 'em down to your level so that you could feel better?"

In a quiet way I was stunned. I looked long and hard at this guy. He was the grandson of Dr. Barrows, who was wealthy beyond means. He was great looking, clearly smart enough to attend Boston College, and sufficiently talented as an athlete to play football there. He thought my life was easy and I thought he was a misguided tough guy. I took some time with my beer so I could ponder the situation and concluded we were both just two angry young fools. He had done what he did to me and I responded with equal unnecessary vitriol. Perhaps we could be friends, but it was certain we wouldn't be if we judged each other from a distance. We were young men trying to find our way; it was clear we each needed a compass and road map as much as the other.

"So you're human," I finally said. "My dad jokes about how you can never be too thin or too rich because he's neither, but he is still a great person. The Bible says something about envy being 'where jealousy and selfish ambition lead to evil vile practices.'"

He sat there pensively and waved away the waiter who had come with a free round from Doobie. "I thought you were Jewish," he said.

"I am, but it doesn't mean I haven't read some of the Bible. I'm also not Italian but I eat pasta."

"I never met a Jewish guy before. Gotta admit you're no different than me."

"Yeah, I am," I said. "I'm sure my dick is bigger than yours. It's a curse we Jewish guys have to bear."

He laughed long and hard, and then after a beat laughed again as if he'd found something new in what he thought was funny.

"That's a problem for you?" he asked.

"A big one," I answered. "Enormous." And we laughed again.

The fog was lifting, and with the lateness of the hour, the moon had taken full flight. It all seemed so cinematic: as two strangers connected there was light, and in that moment there was magic.

"You know what else the Bible says about envy?" I asked.

"Never read it nor been to church, so I doubt I do." He said that more as confession than as fact, and I found it winning in its openness.

"Well, it says something like 'many people are motivated to find success because they are envious of their neighbors and that such pursuits are meaningless and tantamount to chasing the wind.' You get the drift."

He got up, stretched, and looked out at the ocean. He appeared younger than when we'd first met. He spoke to Doobie across the empty tables, asking for the round of free drinks he'd called off earlier. He then sat back at the table and looked at me for a long while without saying a word. The drinks arrived, and still nothing.

Finally, he said, "What motivates you?"

"Not envy. That's one thing I am sure of. I think I want to make a difference. Make people think about their lives, where they're heading. Try to do the right thing. Make others laugh or escape from a bad day. Hit a homer. Be liked. 'Seek my bliss' like Joseph Campbell said."

"Who's he?"

"A writer, philosopher."

"You're a smart guy. Maybe that's why so many people like you."

"Hey, man, we're all smart about different things. And I am not so certain these days that too many people are liking me. You think my life is easy? That's irony for you. I thought yours was and built you up in my head as an asshole. Right now, my life is getting the better of me. I feel I'm like running a race and trying to finish with a stitch in my side. I'll cross the ribbon, but the chances of getting home first are fading."

He considered this for a moment then said, "You know who I think are the best-looking girls at your place?"

"They're all gorgeous. But everyone has their favorites."

"Ellie and Katherine."

"Everyone thinks Ellie's a beauty, but Kat's a little tough for me."

"How about you?" he asked.

"Slam dunk. Veronica."

"You don't know everything about Veronica."

"I don't know everything about anything."

"You don't know everything about Lizzy Barrows either."

I nodded. "Pay the bill. We'll grab ASK on the way out. I want to introduce you to the best-looking girl at PBT. It would be good for her to meet a nice guy like you. On the way, we can talk about Veronica."

I expected it would take a lot more time to talk about Veronica than our short ride to the Moondog would allow. Unfortunately, I was correct. Gary had known Veronica her whole life, and as he shared some history and I connected the dots, it became unsettling. Tonight I had no time for questions. They would have to wait till another day; some privacy and discretion.

The blue neon sign of the Moondog was blinking uneasily. *Funny*, I thought as we entered the place, *blue and uneasy both match my mood.*

The last time I had visited this local hangout, it ended with Secunda clocking Gary Golden. Tonight I entered with an unexpected ally. The bar was packed. It was the height of the summer season; the people were all pretty available and wanting. There was expectation in the smoky air, and, although festive, the room radiated a certain unsettling heat. The music was charged and there was a whole lot of bump and grind going. It was also hot, sweaty humid, and close. The temperature added a touch of danger and edge to the vibe. Anything could happen.

We pushed our way through the dense crowd and ordered three beers. It was wonderful how many people greeted us. We were almost famous, and even ASK, who was only a secondary player in our shows, was given the VIP treatment. Free drinks and arm candy. For the first time in his life women were throwing themselves at him, but he was unavailable and uninterested.

Gary, ASK, and I talked about sports and girls, and he queried ASK on how it felt to be in a show, wondering where he found the courage to perform in front of strangers and what was the best part of the gig.

"Sharing a dressing room with all the dancers," ASK replied.

Gary's eyes widened. He now wanted to be an actor.

I grabbed us another round and began looking for Ellie, hoping this was one of her stops. It didn't take long to discover her sitting at a table with several people, all strangers but one. I only wished they had remained unknown.

"Gary, Ellie is over at that corner table. Do you know any of the guys she's with?"

On recognition of Ellie's escorts, his mood darkened. "Fuck, she's hanging with Johnny Colon. He's a punk. Shit. Let's just fix this now."

He started pushing his way across the room. We were right behind him, which was a good thing, because it was clear that Colon was not happy with the pending interruption.

"Hey, El," ASK said as if she had been expecting to see him. "Introduce us to your friends. Wow, this is a great place, first time here for me." He thrust out his hand to one of the men at the table. "Hi, I'm Alan. I work with Ellie at the theater."

Ellie seemed both embarrassed and pissed off. She tentatively made introductions to Colon, Jake Strong, and Tim Morgan.

What the fuck is she doing with these guys? I wondered. They were too old for her and looked like they ran guns or dope or were paid to provide muscle.

They obviously knew Gary, and their reaction to meeting us was monosyllabic. I made an effort to bring the energy back to positive with a big show of how nice it was to see Colon again, which was rebuffed by another terse response.

"Been calling you for two days now, August, and not a word back. Don't keep a lot of friends that way."

"Sorry, Johnny. Been crazy. But I was going to reach out tomorrow for sure, or if you like we could talk now."

"I have a date right now, pal, and she's had just enough to drink where she could be a whole lotta fun. Not a good time for me."

The guy was a pig. I felt ashamed for Ellie and frightened by the explosive potential of the situation.

"Ellie, we have an early day tomorrow. Why don't we all finish our drinks and get home by one? We'll go settle up at the bar and come back in a few to get you home all right."

"I'll get her home when I'm good and ready," Colon said. "I helped you out before, August. Don't make me regret it now. I think you guys should blow. There are plenty of girls here for you to take home. I'm in charge of Ellie at night. She only works for you during the day."

Ellie looked stunned. She was silent. She didn't look any of us in the eye. She had clearly had more to drink than was appropriate with this crowd.

"Colon, I think we'll come back in a while and take her home," Gary said. He was firm yet avoided being confrontational.

"You won't be doing shit," Colon replied. "Now get out of my face."

"We're going to leave you guys alone to say good night," ASK said, trying to defuse the tension. "We'll be at the bar, El, whenever you're ready."

Colon had the energy of a wounded animal. He was a forty-year-old gym rat who had put on too much weight, yet still thought he was twenty-five and fit. I would have clocked him, but that would surely have lead to an ugly result. Our collective goal was to get Ellie out of this safely and deal with the fallout tomorrow.

"Hey, twit," Colon said to ASK, "don't ruin my night. In return I won't fuck with yours. See ya." He grabbed Ellie's arm, turned her away from her friends, and pulled her into the corner behind their table into harm's way.

The music that had sounded so festive when we arrived was now the soundtrack of a scary thriller. The rest of the Moondog crowd hadn't noticed the skirmish and continued on with their merriment. I was at a loss as to how to proceed.

Gary leaned in close so I could hear him over the din of the nightclub. "I'll give this ten minutes and then I'm taking Colon outside and you take Ellie home. You stay away from any shit. It will be all right. Just stay out of it."

He pushed me toward the bar. He clearly knew this milieu better than I. Behind us, I could hear Colon and Ellie arguing. Then I heard him slap her and tell her harshly to shut the fuck up. *Stay out of it my ass*, I thought. I turned to go after him, but Gary blocked my way.

Colon was stroking Ellie's hair and comforting her now. "Sorry, babe. Drink your drink and we'll go have some fun."

I was sick to my stomach.

Out of nowhere, she pushed him away and bolted for the front door. Colon took a moment to save face with his cronies and muttered, "Bitch" as he chased after her. He kicked the door wide open and headed after his "date."

Both Gary and I pushed across the room and through the ass-to-ass crowd to follow. I saw that Colon's cohorts were about to pack up and head outside. ASK, proving that dynamite comes in small packages, threw himself fearlessly in their way, and Gary and I moved out through the crowd to the parking lot. It was hot and the air was heavy.

Off to the side, we heard shouting from Colon and a frightened whimper from Ellie. We found them both next to his black Eldorado convertible. He held her hair and was pulling her roughly into the passenger side of the car. I was grateful that Officer Richardson had alerted me to what my friend had gotten herself into. I was unfazed by a potential brawl, but I was afraid of what this guy might do to Ellie.

Gary didn't hesitate. He ran full tilt toward Colon and shouted, "Let her go, you fuck—" He leapt without finishing and kicked Colon squarely in the side of the head. Colon released Ellie to keep his balance and moved toward Gary. Wounded animals are dangerous, and he had a head start. Gary circled around to his right and hit Colon three times to the face with quick left jabs. I felt he could have knocked him out with a good right cross, but that didn't seem part of Gary's agenda.

He backed away after each jab to give Colon a chance to regroup, and then hit him again with a trio of jabs. He then started shouting obscenities and baiting Colon so he'd come looking for more. Gary beat him until about a sixth round when he released his right cross then he grabbed him at the same time so Colon couldn't go down. He slapped him repeatedly across the face, then grabbed his hair and pulled him over to Ellie, who had not moved since Gary took over.

"Apologize to your date, you fucker." Gary demanded. "Now, you prick!" He pulled Colon's head up by his hair so he was looking at Ellie.

Colon looked at Ellie and said in a barely audible voice, "I'm sorry."

"Now ask *us* to make sure she gets home safely," Gary said venomously. Colon had no option but to acquiesce. Gary rabbit-punched him so viciously I was surprised Colon's neck didn't snap. Colon ate dirt and gravel and ceased to move.

ASK, who had watched the whole thing from just outside the entrance, jumped five feet in the air shouting, "Holy fucking shit!" Ellie ran into my arms, and with tears running down her face she allowed me to offer some comfort. Gary knelt down next to Colon and in a calm and scarily serene voice said, "This is the last time you ever see her. Get it, fuckface?" Without giving Colon a chance to answer, Gary kicked him in the groin for good measure, to make sure he understood.

He looked at Ellie and said, "If it's possible, you are better looking crying than when you smile. Give me a minute to wash up and then I'm going to get you a milkshake and then home safe and sound. Milkshakes are the best thing for making a bad situation sweet."

At that moment, the neon sign stopped blinking and all the letters went out except M O O. Maybe Gary was on to something with this milkshake idea. We would just have to wait and see.

"Moo," I said to myself, and then followed with a final word to the unconscious Colon. "You know, you didn't have to have a cow."

68

I began the morning with a call to my dad, filling him in on recent events. Talking them over with him alleviated much of my anxiety; speaking with my father always relaxed me. It was a good place to visit. He told me that he and my mother were going to arrive in two weeks to see the close of *Funny Girl* and stay through the opening of *Company*. They would be bringing my aunt and uncle as well.

Then I shared a problem with him that I couldn't find a solution for, and I was running out of time. Zach Rush was playing the romantic lead in *Funny Girl* and needed to wear a top hat in a particular scene. To our shock and chagrin, Rush's hat size was 8½. He wasn't the Elephant Man; he just had a freakishly large head. Mary was unable to make a hat that big in the shop, and we had scoured Boston.

"You know what they say about guys with big heads?" my dad asked.

"Dunno, big brains?"

"How about guys with big feet?"

"Big dick." I knew that one.

"Nope, big socks," he said and laughed. We had played this routine many times.

"You're an idiot, Dad."

"Sammy, I'll find the kid with the enormous head the top hat and get it shipped to you in time for your tech. Love you, sweetie."

"Love you too, Dad. See you soon."

The hat arrived on Friday morning, and fit perfectly.

I then called Officer Scott Richardson to report on the Ellie situation and thank him for his concerns. I also offered apologies incase I had been disrespectful, but before I could explain, he said he understood that I was in uncharted waters. He suggested that Ellie file a police report to keep it on record. I thanked him again and hung up.

Then I called Mr. Foster's office at Dupont and left a personal request that he call me at any time. After the call, I met Secunda and we headed to the gym for a long workout. We sparred three rounds in which I didn't land a punch. Something had to be done.

We returned to the compound. I showered and set off for the dinning hall to have breakfast. Whatever tensions, resentments, or distance I had felt earlier in the week were nowhere to be found. In fact, the energy on that Friday morning was like the lovefest at Woodstock. Bottle it and you were rich.

Marc Seconds's article was on the front page of the *Patriot Ledger*. It was the buzz of the morning. His reporting was honest as it told of the tensions and problems he had witnessed, yet it also addressed with great appreciation and admiration the talents assembled at PBT. He mentioned several actors by name including Feston. Additionally, he wrote highly of everyone's work ethic and ability to put their squabbles, confrontations, and distractions aside to deliver a better performance the following night than the previous one he had attended. There were numerous photos and mini-interviews with members of the company.

Everyone was ecstatic; they all had the start of a scrapbook. Marc even had kind words for me, saying I was "a young man to be reckoned with" and that I would make my name in the professional theater more quickly than anyone could imagine. He urged his readers to scoop up any remaining tickets because this was a "special group spending time with us during the summer of '76." He never once mentioned how terrific it must have been to play with Carol's now world-famous breasts.

I walked to the theater to begin my day.

69

Funny Girl was our third production and we had all learned much from the previous two. Most shows don't rehearse for a mere nine days and then go before an audience. Yet that is the experience of summer stock. We had done fine with *Cabaret,* when everyone was fresh and on their best behavior. We hit a small speed bump with *Anything Goes* because of fatigue and time lost preparing and performing at the parade. Now we had a formula, a paradigm within which to work, and I felt more confident about what we needed to accomplish before our upcoming day off. It also didn't hurt that we had the wind at our back from the news story this morning, which would certainly help us navigate through the next two days.

There are five primary areas in putting on a show.

The songs. The learning and preparation of all the musical numbers for both the principal performers and the chorus players, whose background vocals are often more complicated because they deal with harmonies and complex choral arrangements. Often the chorus members are also dancing while singing; so for those of us who find it difficult to walk and chew gum at the same time, we can appreciate the challenge.

The production numbers, specifically the choreography. The entire company often performs in the former, and even those who are not great on the beat or with their feet have to find a way through. The dancers need to learn their steps for as many as five or six numbers at PBT, all within days.

The staging and blocking of the show. The entrances and exits, where everyone stands once they are on stage, and how to focus the audience's attention. When the entire company is on stage, the spacing and the placement of actors is important so the visual for the audience is always exciting and a continual surprise. Then there are the small scenes; how, when, and where do the actors cross, sit, stand, turn. As important, how to manipulate even the most subtle movements; the turn of a head or the touch of a shoulder, and more, can influence a scene.

The technical elements. The lighting, the costumes, the scenery, and props all have to be added and become part of the actors' performance. There are times when a performer has ten seconds to change costume, stripping out of one while his or her dresser is putting on the new one. There are set changes that are like a magic act: scenery is flying in from above or being trafficked in from the wings, actors are changing clothes or running to their next entrance, and if something goes awry people get hurt and it all goes downhill from there. These quick changes have to be planned like clockwork; orchestrated and scripted in advance. The lighting designer has to see all of the above days before his tech so he knows what part of the stage needs color or specials or projections to highlight the scenes and dances, and to help cover the myriad set changes so they go unnoticed.

The sound design. The sound designer has to blend the voices in big numbers so the lyrics are heard in balance with the orchestra and the larger number of people in the chorus do not overpower the lead performers. The sound must be natural, enhanced yet still coming from the mouths of the performers not to seem robotic, detached, or inhuman.

At PBT all this and more needed to happen in nine days. That's the fun of it all. That's the challenge. That's the work.

I had set Friday's rehearsal as a work-through. We'd start at the top and plow through with the intention of getting the entire show set by the end of the afternoon. If things were sloppy we'd stop and work on them. If they needed adjustment we'd give notes. So that on Saturday we could run the sucker without stopping; show the designers what it looked like; orchestrate in principal all the technical ins and outs; get the actors set on their marks and actions in the scenes; have the dancers know their steps and hit their "five six seven eights." All the while using the stage as a blank canvas on which to paint an arresting visual, one where the audience was almost forced to look, use their imagination or miss something important in the telling of the story. We had to control the audience's eye, keeping them surprised and eager for more.

If Friday was a workday, Saturday was like being on a roller coaster that only went down. If you screamed no one would hear you or pay attention; they were having their own problems holding on. We were flying without a net, and it was fantastic! By the time Saturday afternoon rolled around, we would have done the impossible, mounting a major musical, and even in its rawest form it played. We would be breathless and exhilarated, wanting to polish and lock in everything we had accomplished that day. We would be like the reader of a great novel who can't wait to finish the page so they can turn to the next one to see what happens before racing to see the next one and the next and the next . . .

Believe it or not, it was a hell of a ride, one where the moment it ends you want to get right back on because you simply can't believe it was that much fun. It's like your first kiss, a walk-off home run, or a buzzer beater for the championship. It's your kid's first word or first step. It's sex for the first time or your wedding night. It's making your first million, connecting with God, or making a child smile. It was my work, and it all started in ten minutes.

I was exhausted just thinking about it, yet itching to begin. I guess I just didn't know where to scratch first. Wherever I chose, it was sure to feel so very delicious.

70

I spent the entire day inside the theater. So much for a job near the beach. It was a good day. Solid work and no off-stage drama, just what was in the script. Most of the stops had to do with music and dance and not within the scene work. It was interesting to watch Ellie work with the dancers, running and rerunning their routines. She would do the steps downstage and as they mirrored her, the numbers came together with confidence and verve. I wondered how she did it, how she held up after the night that had ended just hours ago. We all have demons—and strengths that allow us to overcome them. Ellie was a much more complicated woman than I had ever imagined.

When I finally left the building for our six o'clock dinner break, I saw Gary smoking a cigarette at the redwood table that had become the epicenter of the compound. He was relaxed and waved me a friendly hello, then stood and gave me a macho hug.

"We have to finish our talk about Veronica and Lizzy," he said. "Don't want to leave you hanging or wondering where the story goes."

"Okay," I said with trepidation. "When?"

"I'm taking Ellie out for supper. How about after the show? I'm coming to see it tonight. I already paid for my tickets—fourth time. I'll check in with you at intermission."

"You are a great man, Gary Golden," I said, then moved away so he could greet Ellie as she approached wearing a wide grin of ease and contentment. It said more than words could ever hope to convey. I headed back to my room. Rest was what I needed most, and to achieve it I needed to make sure I had no encounters along the way.

Veronica was sitting on the bed wearing a towel and brushing her freshly washed blond hair. "Hey, big boy," she said. "Got a minute for your honey?"

I answered by turning my hug into a long, lingering kiss. Before it went any further, though, I was fast asleep.

An urgent knock on my door startled me awake as the clock read 7:46 p.m. JB shouted that Mr. Foster was on the phone. I sprinted to the office, picked the phone off the cradle, and pressed the blinking light on line one. "Hello," I said breathlessly.

"Please hold for Mr. Foster," said a flat nondescript female voice.

I held for a full ten minutes before Ellie's father got on. "Bob Foster, here. Who do I have?" His voice was brusque and to the point.

"Sir, this is Sam August. You were kind enough to return my call."

"Right, Sam." He had no idea who I was. He may have vaguely recognized the name from somewhere. "How can I help you, Sam?"

"Well, sir, do you know who I am?"

"Of course," he lied.

"I'm working with your daughter up here on the Cape, and I just wanted to let you know how she was doing and how grateful I am for her work and how proud you—"

He interrupted. "She's my girl, of course she's doing well. I got a letter from her just last week." He sounded as if I was some worthless underling to be placated instead of listened to. He was rich and powerful and his phone rang every sixty seconds. He could write a check for tuition or a house or a hospital wing or . . . As I listened to his bullshit I thanked God he wasn't my father.

Then I interrupted, with enough force to be heard. "Sir, I think you should find the time to come up and see what your daughter is doing here.

It's important, sir." I let that linger for as long as possible, then continued. "You're busy, sir, I know that, yet I can only stress that Ellie has to see you here even for just one night or it will really damage her."

He cut me off as if we were in a negotiation. "Young man, that's a rather inflammatory comment, a bit presumptuous to say the least."

"No, sir, it is not presumptuous. It is profound. I suggest with all respect that you find a way to come up and see your daughter. That's it. That's all."

"Goodbye, son," he said, and the phone went dead.

My face flushed with embarrassment, but it only took a moment for me to realize that it was he who should feel ashamed. Then I had two quick thoughts. One was that part of becoming an adult was having the wisdom to trust when bad behavior was just that and not a reflection on me . . . to learn to trust in my character, my intent, and my decency. The other was an affirmation, a reinterpretation of my dad's comment about never being too rich or too thin. He was wrong. It was better to be surrounded by those who loved you and remembered your name.

It was nearly curtain time, and I raced across the compound to see the evening's performance. Through the grace of God, Bobby Stevens, and Marc Seconds's article there was not an open seat to be had. I stood at the back of the house next to JB's Officer Tommy and his partner, the blue-eyed Cutler, who had almost hauled us away some weeks ago.

"Hey, Sam, I hear we're all going to P-Town on Sunday. Supposed to be hotter than a half-fucked fox in a forest fire."

"Nice image, Tommy," I replied. "I guess I'm the last to know, but it sounds fun."

Cutler chimed in. "So is that dancer going to be naked tonight?"

Schmuck, I said inside my head. With all decorum, I replied, "Walter, it's live theater. You never know."

Then I settled into a corner to take notes. Little did I know as the overture began that Carol's bare breasts of last evening would be considered tame compared to what awaited us tonight.

Heigh-ho the glamorous life.

7 1

The building was buzzing with the energy of great expectation. The sold-out crowd had come ready to have a terrific time. The orchestra played the overture. The music was crisp and snappy. The tunes were hummable and danceable, and they set different expectations and promises as to the fun evening about to begin.

The curtain rose on the first number, which was a silly choral ditty in which all the characters sang about the joy of the Atlantic crossing they were embarking on. The number was contained madness, sort of where the joke holds its breath on the verge of turning blue, then goes *bam* and the show gets shot out of a cannon. Sixteen bars before the lighting of the fuse to an explosive and wild beginning, the door off stage right opened with a loud jolt. There was split focus among the actors as they wanted to remain in the scene but the distraction in the wings was hard to ignore.

We had a streaker! A buck-naked, overweight streaker with a large belly, chunky legs, jiggly hairy ass cheeks, and substantial man-boobs. His back could have used a haircut as well but there was no time for grooming. He ran directly to center stage. Shook a few surprised hands, waved at the stunned audience, and began to make his way to the house-right exit at the back of the auditorium.

Secunda watched him do his shtick at center stage, all the while checking out the gaping jaws of the audience. This guy was no Carol Duteau. As he started to make his way off stage and up the aisle for his escape, Secunda looked into audience with an expression that provoked expectation. He took the streaker's hand and urged him to bow yet again. "Ladies and gentlemen, my mother-in-law," he said.

Then to a cacophony of whistles, catcalls, boos, and applause, the man enjoyed a couple of elaborate bows. He then ran up the aisle naked into the night. Waiting just outside the door was Office Cutler, who had come to see something naked on stage. This was clearly not what he'd had in mind. The streaker burst through the back door and ran right into his arms. The big, sweaty, overweight bowling ball was trapped by a pissed-off cop. As Walter cuffed him and drove away, I felt disappointed for him. He'd gotten a hairy fat-assed guy instead of the cotton candy that was Carol Duteau.

I had no concerns about the streaker incident. There was a terrific story in the whole deal, and I was certain Bobby would put the correct spin on it. A couple of thoughts flashed through my mind, however. One was to wonder how quickly Cutler could book the naked guy and then get home to shower. The other was to consider whether one could truly take pride in his work if every night brought some sort of outrageousness. *Please let tomorrow be just the show*, I thought, *the simply glorious romp of summer stock without surprises or histrionics.* I went back inside to watch the rest of Friday night's perform-ance. It was a really good show even though everyone remained clothed.

Saturday morning, the wind whistled off the water. The sky was an un-spoiled sapphire blue that blanketed the ocean. The whitecaps were angry across the sea. Gusts hit low and forceful off the ocean making it feel more like November than late July. Doors were slammed shut by the force of the wind, and those scurrying about the compound huddled under sweaters or hooded sweatshirts. It was weird, yet it gave great resonance to the adage "things can change as quickly as the wind." I lay in bed next to Veronica and watched her sleep.

Gary had not spoken to me last night. He had brought a gaggle of friends to see the show and, using his newfound clout as a theater good guy, was able to find nooks and crannies where they could sit. We missed each other at in-termission, and postcurtain they all raced out with Ellie for what I hoped was a healthy, happy, and safe evening.

I could only imagine what past he'd share with me about Veronica when we continued our talk. As I looked at her lying next to me radiating peace and calm, I decided I didn't care, that I didn't even want to know. She made me happy. She was a good friend and she was kind and giving. Perhaps I even loved her, if one really knows how to do that at the age of twenty-one. What-ever had happened before I met her was of no concern.

It was early. I had a little time to myself and elected to take a run to the beach. I dressed quietly and left our room without waking her. Once outside, the wind lashed at me like a whip and howled something indecipherable. I ran hard toward the ocean where the blustery voice of nature made it sound like someone was down there crying. I decided I should listen to the sounds of this strange morning. Perhaps they were trying to convey something I needed to hear.

That Saturday morning everyone worked, but it was clear they could feel the seconds pass as the clock moved inexorably toward freedom. No rehearsals or responsibilities. Just thirty-six hours of unbridled joy. When you're twenty-one that adds up to a great many possibilities.

Our rehearsals were stupendous. We rode the roller coaster of excitement I had hoped to achieve when we worked through Friday. It was a glorious, breathtaking ride as things came together, scenes worked, and little bits of business, color, nuisance, and mischief spiced the whole adventure. It went so well that before lunch we added a wrinkle of an idea to rehearsal. It was an exercise, triple time, in which we played a scene sped up beyond any sort of reasonableness. It was productive because we all found things we hadn't played before; when you run stuff at triple time you don't have time to think. As important, it was simply fun and goofy and added a sense of insanity and reverse perspective to hard work and commitment. It was a vacation without responsibility. It was silly, manic, and over the top.

So as we broke for an hour at two in the afternoon, with our last rehearsal set from to go from three to six, I thought of when Veronica had asked how much money I had on our first date and the answer a mere twenty-three dollars. The amount had grown to something worth millions. The efforts and dedication and effervescence everyone in our company had brought to the table each day had earned them a day of nonsense and abandon. It was just hours away and all of us held our breaths until the clock signaled us free.

We ran the triple-time rehearsal to end a perfect morning and then broke for lunch. It went so well and so many ideas worked that I felt I was indeed the next George Abbott. During the break I ventured out into the compound for some air. I thought about this morning and the howling wind urging me to listen. What was it trying to say to me?

72

The answer blew in all too quickly and without finesse. We had finished our rehearsal at six sharp. The quality and accomplishment of the morning had continued, and we ended the day with smiles and a rocket pocket full of energy and good will. Tonight's show looked to blow the roof off the old barn and promised a curtain call under the stars.

I lingered for almost two hours, working through tech issues for the next show with Kasen and Duncan. Duncan was insisting on certain scenic pieces coming up through the stage floor, which, although a charming if not inspired idea, was well beyond the scope of a small summer theater. Such an effect would require a hydraulic lift and substantial rehearsal to make it effective and safe. Kasen insisted we could handle the cueing and Duncan promised he could secure the lift on favor. How could I say no? They both wanted to create something special, so I jumped on board.

I left the building to the sounds of a catfight. Parked in the middle of the compound was the shiny, red Mercedes that belonged to the cat woman herself, Lizzy Barrows. She was standing at the box-office window shouting obscenities at Veronica who manned the fort alongside Diana Cohen. Veronica was returning the volley with equal vigor, throwing haymaker after haymaker. One could easily be convinced that she'd grown up in a truck stop. Everyone on premise was riveted by this display of mutual ill manners and outright contempt. As entertaining as it might have been, particularly in another time or place, it wasn't working for me at all. My heart sank as I thought I needed to deal with one more challenge before I could truly say my day was complete.

JB arrived at the melee, and I stopped to watch rather than enter the fray. If not for the enormous animosity flooding the compound, the sight of these two tall beauties being separated by the diminutive JB would have been comical to watch. The girls shouted at one another, but what they had to say was not important. It was the way they said it that conveyed the power. They looked like a manager and umpire in full dispute. It might have been a bit perverse, but they both looked terrific. I began to find the whole scene some-what titillating.

Suddenly it was over. Veronica ran toward the beach with an angry inten-sity that hung in the air. Lizzy Barrows pushed away JB's offer of a handshake and without a word hopped into her expensive car and left in a fury of dust, spitting gravel, and rage.

It took a few moments for everyone to regain a sense of normalcy, almost as if we had all witnessed a mugging or drive-by. JB watched the car fishtail out of sight and looked at me with a mixture of bemusement and defeat. I walked over to her slowly. She grabbed my arm and wordlessly dragged me into the office and slammed the door.

She was flushed with anger. I stood there waiting as if summoned to the principal's office for some heinous act. She lit a cigarette and smoked it all within one, two, three puffs. Then she lit another and exhaled so severely I feared for my safety.

"Did you sleep with Lizzy Barrows?" she asked finally, practically spitting the question in my face.

"No. No, I did not," I answered honestly but without a clear or unblem-ished conscience.

"Did you come on to her?"

"No, I did not."

She steamed and she smoked. If only we could sell the energy, we'd have been rich.

"JB, what happened?" I asked.

"Why are you such a schmuck? Why do you think first with your penis and not of the consequences? Now we have a real problem."

"What are you talking about?"

"And pretty girls are the worst. They're all about their own shit and noth-ing else. I thought we all came here to work. Why do you only spend time with the beautiful girls?"

"I spend time with you, JB," I said, realizing that "schmuck" was applica-ble as the words left my mouth.

She lit another butt. I was fortunate it wasn't me.

"I like pretty girls because I am a shallow dirtbag," I said. "Now tell me what the fuck is going on. Stop shouting at me and stop giving me the third degree."

She flopped into her desk chair, swirled around, and looked out the window into the compound. It was after eight and I noticed there were no cars in the lot, no one at the box office .

"Joanie, what's going on?" I asked with growing concern.

She continued to stare out the window. Ronnie Feston was now walking across the compound. There were no other people in sight.

"JB?" I implored.

She spun around slowly and stared me down. "Your girlfriend and Mrs. Barrows hate each other. I don't know why, but they do."

"JB, that's not news. You've known that since that first night at the Moondog."

She held up her hand to shut me up. "Because they hate each other, Mrs. Barrows bought all the seats for tonight's performance and came by to inform us, at the eleventh hour, that she would be the only one attending the show. Your girlfriend called her a few unsavory names and then it turned into a full blown "fuck you" fest with a lot of "bitch" thrown in. Veronica actually bit me when I tried to keep them from beating each other to death with their tits. Can't we just have the *drama on the stage*? Do you know how foolish we will look playing in front of her and the few standees who'll be showing up any minute now?"

"Hey, enough! You want to shout? *Well, I can shout much louder than you!!!*"

Although neither of us spoke, the office was far from silent. You could hear our brains working and stomachs churning. I stewed and grew instantly insane. "Fuck me," I shouted. "Fuck me!" I picked up the desk phone and threw it against the wall, where it shattered. I kicked the desk chair opposite JB sending my foot through the slats in the back. My ankle got stuck and I lost my balance and fell to the floor, smashing my right cheekbone against the shelf on the wall, then falling on my assbone awkwardly and landing in a cascade of program inserts, which covered me like large snowflakes. This whole thing sucked.

"Fuck me! Fuck me!" I shouted again as I got up slowly from the floor. My ankle might have been broken, but I was too far gone to notice.

"That's helpful," JB said, her words dripping with malevolence. "Do you have anything else to say other than 'fuck me'?"

I took my time with that one. Slowly and quietly I answered, "How about 'fuck you'? Does that work for you?" I said this with a smile.

JB also smiled, although you had to know her well to realize it was mirth and not a bout of gas. "How would that help?" she asked.

"It couldn't hurt."

"Is your ankle all right?"

"Yes, but it's my ass that really hurts. I fell on my fucking ass, and I scraped my face on this fucking shelf. Who put this shelf here anyway?"

"You did."

"I did? Well, fuck me."

"And we are back to the beginning."

My ankle was throbbing so I sat on the chair I had kicked, but sitting made my ass hurt so I stood up. "JB, it was hard to miss with all the shouting but just so I am clear, what did Lizzy Barrows say?"

"You mean without the obscenities?"

"That would be preferable."

"Nothing."

"Nothing?" I asked with mock incredulousness.

"Mrs. Barrows said that your girlfriend was a cheap whore, that you had offended her numerous times since you arrived in Plymouth, and that she simply wanted to embarrass you in any way she could."

"And you said . . . ?"

"I tried to calm the two insane vixens and mollify Mrs. Barrows. I told her it would be very unfortunate if we played the show to one person. Then she interrupted me to say she had paid for the seats and intended on seeing the show. I asked her if she would like to come on another night when she could enjoy the evening with a full house. She said something rather unpleasant, slapped away my hand, and told me she'd be back for curtain."

JB got up from her desk then sat again. She stood yet again and walked around her chair three times, sort of the way a dog circles the spot where it intends to pee. She lit a cigarette and leaned across her desk with manic in her dark eyes. "Well, Sammy, it's eight-seventeen. Your dice."

I thought for a moment and then sat back down, because my ankle hurt more than my assbone "Fuck me," I said.

JB walked quickly across the small room to the office door and bolted it shut. She turned back to me and said simply, "Okay." Then walked over to the chair and dropped into my lap. She sat with her head on my chest and we both breathed deeply. She smelled like an ashtray and I of fear and inexperience. Neither one of us was any picnic.

"You know 'fuck me' is just an expression," I said. "I say it sometimes when I am at a loss for words or when I find myself in a situation where I'd rather have dental surgery up my ass for a week than face the music."

"You're never at a loss for words."

"You're right. Strip naked now."

At that, we both laughed so slightly that combined it was a mere chuckle.

It was 8:20. I unbolted the door and looked outside. There were six cars in the lot; Barrows's red two-seater was parked in the center of the compound. I was certain she had one of those vanity plates that read I AM ONE GIGANTIC FUCKING ASSHOLE. There were about eight people lingering in front of the box office. The full complement of staff was around. Ironically, the weather was absolutely stupendous, clear skies and just a soft breeze off the water. If Capra was right, and he usually was, rain would follow.

"JB, this is what I want you to do. First, go tell Diana to explain to the people waiting for standing room that we can't help them tonight because we have a private group that bought out the whole house. She should apologize for the inconvenience and offer them free seats for any future performance and then get them off the premises. Have Debbie hold the house closed until I've finished talking with the company. I want the entire company on stage in five minutes sharp. Tell Jojo to round everyone up and keep them quiet—no incessant chatter. Tell them I'll explain everything at the meeting. Make sure everyone is in costume and ready to go. You speak to Mrs. Barrows and explain that we'll be going up a few minutes late. Be nice! If you see Veronica anywhere, tell her I said to go wait on stage with the cast. Do all of this fast. But give me a hug first."

She stood and we hugged one another as if we were both going off to war.

"Are we doing the show?" she asked.

"I haven't figured that one out yet. I don't know how this plays out. We will very shortly, though."

"I guess so," she said and headed for the door.

"JB," I said, "you know you are one beautiful girl."

Without a word, she left the office and ran across the compound to do my bidding. I watched her and took a moment to think about what I intended to say or do. It was the second time in recent days that I had stared out that window while confusion danced in my head. The first time I thought about a glass of milk. Right now, I thought a Drano on the rocks was far more appropriate. As I thought through my potential actions, I remembered an old, familiar but telling story.

A man is walking along the shores of the beach when he stumbles upon an old-looking lamp bottle. He picks up the bottle and rubs some of the sand off it. Out of the blue, a genie appears! The stunned man asks the genie if this means he gets three wishes.

"Three wishes is only a fable," responds the genie. "You only get one wish. So what do you wish for?"

The man does not hesitate. "I want peace in the Middle East," he responds. "See this map? I want these countries to stop fighting with each other and I want all the Arabs to love the Jews and Americans and vice versa."

The genie looks at the map and exclaims, "Hey, guy, be reasonable. These countries have been at war for thousands of years. I'm out of shape after being in a bottle for five hundred years. I don't think it can be done. Make another wish and please be reasonable."

The man thinks for a minute. "Well, I've never been able to get my ex-girlfriend and my new girlfriend to be in the same place at the same time even for a minute without pulling each other's hair out," he says. "It's really embarrassing and I don't know what to do. Couldn't they just get along when they run into each other and not start World War III? That is what I wish for: make it so my ex-girlfriend doesn't make my new girlfriend so unhappy all the time."

The genie lets out a deep sigh and says, "Let me see that friggin' map again . . ."

I saw Veronica enter the side door of the theater, avoiding Lizzy Barrows. She was clearly unhappy and her face showed recent tears. I had to move so, throwing caution to the wind, I left the office and sprinted across the compound to the theater. I entered through the stage-right door and there in glorious chaos, faces creased with concern, disoriented and befuddled, was the entire PBT company. They were clearly wondering what would happen now that Cruella De Vil had appeared and announced her plan to make trouble. Some were in full costume and makeup, others freakishly unfinished. Several wore their wig caps sans hair. A few were partially dressed or in preshow garb.

It was time to speak like Winston Churchill and save us all from falling apart. No one was dying and no one was in jeopardy. We were all simply facing a new mountain to climb. To my surprise I was actually jazzed; I jumped in full throttle. If I was going to be shot down, let it be Midway rather than Pearl Harbor.

"We have a problem," I began. "Perhaps 'problem' is the wrong word. Rather we have a decision to make, a group decision forced upon us. It is not fair or right or just that you've been put in this position. We must choose between art and community. Although I'll feel the ramifications of whatever action you choose to take, good or bad, I'm prepared for those consequences. First and foremost, I choose all of you."

For the moment I had everyone's complete attention.

"The facts are this: several weeks ago a local resident purchased our entire house for tonight. Every seat. In the past thirty minutes, we learned that it had never been her intention to distribute those seats. She purchased them simply to embarrass me by having you all play to a single person."

I was immediately peppered with angry questions.

"Who did such a thing?"

"What an asshole!"

"What did you do to piss this person off?"

"You don't expect us to do the show, do you?"

"One person? Come on, Sam, give her back her money."

"Tell her to go to hell."

There were other comments as well, all of them troubled and angered at the pettiness of the whole thing. Even those who supported playing in front of only one person were fuming, sensing a certain violation of their growing professionalism.

"The person causing all this commotion is Lizzy Barrows aka, 'fucking bitch with a hole in her heart.' But please don't allow me to color your opinion of the woman."

There followed murmurs acknowledging the problem. Comments of dismay blended with a few small chuckles as to my description of our adversary. Then the company's gaze returned to me. Furtive, distracted, and edgy.

"The way I see it is that she sucks, and whatever you choose to do tonight, she'll still suck tomorrow while you are all enjoying a well-deserved day off."

"We should begin our day off right now!"

"I don't think we should play to this freakoid."

"Let her ride her broom somewhere else and fuck with somebody else."

The words came, fast and hard. And all on top of one another. It wasn't clear who said them, yet it was a point of view shared by many.

"I can tell her there is no show this evening because some of you are sick and can't go on. For what it is worth, I think that approach puts us in the pigsty right along with Mrs. Barrows."

There were some head bobs of acquiescence, many more of discontent.

"Or I can tell her to 'eat shit and die,' give her a refund, and explain that we won't be played in this way. I would probably leave out the 'eat shit and die' part, but the intent would be clear."

The responses to this suggestion were filled with concern as to the loss of money, our pride, our dignity. I swelled with relief and gratitude.

Veronica raised her hand to speak. She began awkwardly. "Lizzy Barrows is someone I have known for a long time. We used to be the best of friends. Then, well . . . she took a wrong turn and I guess she got lost. She has done terrible things to people who are close to me. I do know that her behavior is intended to hurt me and not you . . . All of you, my new friends, are the unfortunate conduit for pain inflicted long ago. I wouldn't let her in the building at all. She will never find her way back to some sort of grace or decency. Her wealth has left her without a . . . a moral compass, and although I am trying to understand you all and what is important to you as performers, I'm sorry, but I believe that redemption of any kind for her is hopeless. She's the devil. Please stay away from Lizzy Barrows."

Secunda seemed more agitated than usual. "I don't think we should play tonight."

There followed a chorus of whys.

"To me it's about our community, our family. Barrows is trying to fuck with all of that and we, all of us, must take a stand against anyone endeavoring to damage what we've been building here. We're all part of this community. From the day each of us arrived and signed on, it was to work and expect each other's support. To perform tonight would break the cycle of the respect we've been promised. And Veronica is so upset I'd rather heal her then be noble."

"I'm sorry, Veronica, but this is BS," said Elliot. "Is it about this sick joke being played on us or is it about doing our job? If it's the former, then she's already won. We're all upset and wringing our hands and wasting time."

"I should go talk with her," I suggested.

"To what end?" I was asked in a chorus of escalating frustration.

"Or we could all be Joe DiMaggio."

There were expressions of confusion as if asking, "Joe DiMaggio again?", so I continued.

"Joe DiMaggio once played in a meaningless spring game in Florida. He was Joe DiMaggio. He was the biggest star going. In the bottom of the last inning, he led off with a single. Then he stole second. The Yankees were losing thirteen-to-nothing and he chose to steal second base. He then advanced to third on a ground ball to the right side. So there he is, ninety feet from home with one out and the Yankees down by thirteen runs. Maybe there are three hundred people left in the ballpark. The next batter hits a short fly to the out-field and DiMaggio tags up and runs like the wind and smashes into the catcher as he receives the throw from the right fielder. They both go down in a heap, dust is everywhere, and then the ball is seen rolling away from the collision. The ump calls DiMaggio safe and the Yankees now trail by only twelve runs. They lost the game by that margin."

I still had their attention.

"Stay with me, this is leading somewhere. After the game, all the sportswriters questioned Joe D. on why he had played a meaningless game with such foolish abandon. They said, 'You're Joe DiMaggio! What would have happened if you got hurt and missed the season?'

"'Because I am Joe DiMaggio,' he said, 'there are people in the stands today who came to see me play. Maybe it is the only time they have or will ever see me play. They deserve my best effort. They deserve the real Joe DiMaggio. Because whether there are tens of thousands of people in the stands or a single one, I always have to be me.'

"The sportswriters were chastened and wrote the story having learned something about greatness."

There was silence on the stage. No one looked at one another..

Kopit stepped forward and said, "I am Joe DiMaggio."

Then others followed. Rush. Trudy. Feston. Fitzgerald. The doctor. Carol Duteau and Janet Kessler. All repeated the mantra "I am Joe DiMaggio." And as each person spoke the words, a defiance grew within the company, a defiance and charge that greatness had to be part of their work ethic. It was found in one's heart as well as one's skill. It was the brass ring we were all chasing.

Practically the entire company was now wearing virtual pinstripes. Then Veronica stepped up and joined the ranks. She too was for performing, even if it meant allowing Lizzy Barrows to win her stupid, infantile game.

Secunda walked center stage, turned and faced the group. "I am Spartacus," he declared.

In succession everyone started to repeat Secunda's nonsense. Everyone was now Spartacus. Laughter replaced the tension of minutes ago. We were all Spartacus and we had a show to do.

Jojo quieted everyone and said, "Places in ten. And I am glad to be on this team. I too am Spartacus."

The cast went to finish getting ready. JB shouted to Debbie, "Open the house! Let the crowd in." Then to Veronica, "Open the concession stand." Finally to me she said, "Sammy, I'll find you an empty seat so you can take notes. Oh, and I'll be right out to let Mrs. Barrows know she can take any seat she wants, but with the reminder that there is not a bad one in the whole place."

"One last thing, JB," I said. "Please give this note to Mrs. Barrows."

I quickly scribbled a few words on my notepad and handed it to JB. Without asking, she unfolded the yellow page and read my words.

Dear Mrs. Barrows,

Thank you for attending our performance this evening. We are sorry your friends couldn't join you tonight, but it does not matter to us here at PBT. We will be at our best.

I had signed it Spartacus.

At 8:40, a mere ten minutes later than our usual curtain time, the orchestra hit its downbeat. Lizzy Barrows sat alone, front row center. I knew the show would be terrific, no matter how hard she tried not to like it. Predictably, she was a dead duck from the moment the overture began to play.

One of the lessons I had learned so far during this remarkable summer was that nothing was what it seemed. Maybe down deep people are different from what they show on the surface. Perhaps the rumors and innuendo you hear in passing about a young girl you have fallen for are just that: pure fabrication or all-out exaggeration of the truth. I was past the midpoint of my hundred days, and I sensed that as I accelerated to the finish line, lessons, awareness, and the collapse of a grandiose pedestal awaited me. The simple truths of those who had been part of, even intimately aligned to, my maturation would show their true selves, their true character, their true aspirations.

We did the show and everyone was Joe DiMaggio wearing the armor of Spartacus. They played it for all it was worth. They raced home, knocked over the catcher, and the umpire called them all safe. The crowd would have roared and cheered their effort, but there was only a single fan in attendance. Lizzy Barrows looked like a million dollars. Her hair was lush, her legs were long, and she wore that pink lip gloss that would slay even the strongest of men. She never once laughed or even smiled. She offered no applause. She was a beautiful mannequin. The cast rose above it all and hit the ball deep into the summer night, and it has yet to come down.

At intermission Mrs. Barrows walked to her car, took something out of the trunk, and put it in her handbag. She checked her makeup in the visor mirror. She walked over to the concession stand and bought a rum and coke from Veronica and left a $5 tip. No words were exchanged. I watched closely to make sure Veronica had not sneezed in her drink. The house lights blinked, and Lizzy returned to the same seat she'd held earlier in the evening.

Act 2 played out with the same energy and result as act 1. The show was electric, but it did not generate a single response from our lone attendee. I watched from the back of the theater and truly wondered how fucked up this whole charade had become. It must have taken enormous discipline and resolve to behave in such a manner, and tremendous, unbridled commitment to see the whole thing through to the end of the show.

The show was over and the curtain call began. Suddenly Mrs. Barrows stood up and applauded. Gently at first, as the minor players took their bows, then with growing intensity as the principals made their way on stage. Finally, as the complete ensemble filled the stage and acknowledged the orchestra, Lizzy Barrows was cheering at full voice. It was shocking in its suddenness, and yet it was an emotional release for all of us who had navigated through this unique set of affairs.

The cast was beaming and they all started to applaud in return. Elliot cued the orchestra to play "You're the Top," and in disbelief I watched as the company sang this famous Cole Porter song to our former nemesis. It went on and on and on. Then Lizzy Barrows climbed the three steps onto the stage and asked that the music stop. Elliot, who never missed a cue, did as instructed and the cast stood silently in wait. I stood next to JB in the back of the theater.

Veronica tiptoed in, took my hand, and whispered in my ear, "Great show tonight, honey." I got goose bumps. If someone had asked me to say something right now, I would have come up mute.

Lizzy Barrows spoke. "Thank you all for tonight. You are all truly wonderful. Your performance could have only been given by people who are blessed with lots of generosity. A gift you cannot teach but perhaps I could learn. I came here tonight with a great deal of mad inside me. You made it all seem dumb and left me ashamed. I will come back this summer often and I will bring my friends, so they can experience the joy you have all given me tonight."

LITTLE DID I KNOW

There was not a sound in the building. Nor even a breath of wind or rustle of leaves from outside.

"Mr. Secunda," she continued, "I would like to give you all a gift. I don't sing or dance and all the stores close early here in Plymouth, so please take this gesture of my appreciation to enjoy your collective day off tomorrow. Divide it between yourselves and consider that dinner is on me." She handed Secunda a stack of hundred-dollar bills, shook his hand, kissed a couple of the girls on the cheek, and exited into the house.

The orchestra played another hit song from the show, the famous "I Get a Kick Out of You," and the cast sang along. Secunda passed out hundreds until everyone had received one, and then he gave the rest to the orchestra and crew. Lizzy Barrows drove off the compound honking her horn to the music. As she disappeared into the night, the orchestra faded out.

I didn't get it at all. This woman had come into our house to do damage, to hurt our community. She'd betrayed our trust and then left the hero, showered with song and applause. Was it the money? Were my friends and coworkers so easily bought? Where was their pride?

I wasn't going to forget her intentions, no matter how many hundred-dollar bills she threw my way. To trust her because she now appreciated our talent and ability to create joy? Please just blow me. She was still a black widow. She was still someone who looked to create chaos and woe. I would share my dismay with my friends. I would pay for my own dinner. At least I wouldn't choke on my loss of integrity.

I thought our day off had truly come not a moment too soon. I also noticed that it had been raining. Once again, Mr. Capra was right.

73

We headed east into a new day, the morning haze disappearing under blazing, neon-yellow July sunshine. It was going to be a hot one. Many of us had piled into my blue birthday van while others followed in a cavalcade of auto shows of years past.

Our destination was Provincetown. A small town at the end of the Cape, so close to king's country you could fish in the English Channel with your rod and reel. Provincetown had many stories to share from its varied history. If not for an argument aboard the *Mayflower,* the Pilgrims would have set foot along the shores of P-town and the rock up north would have never found its way into our history books.

The original Pilgrims splintered and many moved onto whaling fortunes and lives of true religious choice. The village that baited the anger and quixotic nature of the ocean had been leveled by myriad hurricanes. Numerous murders from years past to present remain unsolved. Perseverance, courage, guts, and a love of this land with its unending kaleidoscopes of pastel beauty continued to rebirth the small community.

It was home to artists and writers, from the early poets to the great American playwrights Tennessee Williams and Eugene O'Neill. It housed restaurants of eclectic genius in the culinary delights. It nurtured young artists whose work was sold in tiny galleries. It was a town of timeless artisans who toiled in leather and pottery, silver and glass. The fishing community was vibrant and operated as if time had stood still.

Most recently, Provincetown was home to the alternate lifestyles that emerged in the late sixties. Gays and lesbians lived as they wished in P-town, without concern as to the judgments of the cities and towns they left behind. Whether they stayed the summer, a weekend, or a lifetime, it was a small town with no boundaries. It danced all night every night, fueled by the freedoms it offered to all who chose to partake.

We had stopped at Race Point on Cape Cod to play in the largest sandbox imaginable. The dunes were otherworldly. The sands bled into the horizon. Then, just as you gave up hope, looked for an oasis or camel to take you home, the ocean appeared. Just steps away from the last hill, you were back on planet Earth and in desperate need of a swim.

We threw Frisbees and footballs, rolled around like puppies. We abandoned responsibility, carousing like kids during recess. Those of us who had coupled this summer held hands, stole kisses, and cheered our friends as they frolicked with abandon. The undiscovered love affairs, those that had done no more than simmer so far, edged toward boiling point in the morning heat. James had gotten everyone stoned on the drive, and everything seemed new, fresh as wet paint. It felt as if this was all for us. We were privileged, special, touched by some higher being, for mere mortals could not possibly engage in such wonder without divine assistance.

Veronica and I grabbed every moment zealously, almost desperately, as though I was headed overseas to war. I held her hand and heard my friends laugh loud and strong, and the waves took me places I had never been nor imagined.

We found our way to a late breakfast at the seaside Lobster Pot. Seated at long, simply dressed picnic tables that overlooked the Provincetown harbor, we were in a postcard of schooners, deep blues, cloudless skies, and history. We ate eggs Benedict with crab meat, and downed spicy Bloody Marys and fresh longneck clams that had left their sandy homes only minutes before meeting us.

We walked the main hub in town and perused the stores on old Commercial Street. We window-shopped jewelry, leather, crafts, and sex emporiums that made us blush and roused our curiosity at the same time. We stood in front of a place called The Toys of Eros. Its window was filled with male mannequins in leather and strap-on dildos, thousands of colorful beads on strings, and invitations to check their selection of cock rings. A sign offered a discount on edible underwear. Other mannequins wore leather metal-studded collars attached to leashes. There were handcuffs and sex toys whose function I couldn't imagine.

Janet was the most eager to cross the threshold into perversion. I wondered what ASK was thinking. Veronica suggested we go in and I said yes, but my heartbeat quickened as I thought, *Well, let's learn some new positions.* As long as my ass was not involved.

Veronica, ASK, Janet, Kellie, Secunda, and I entered the store. Everyone else went to the nearest bar. Any bravado I might have possessed disappeared when I saw a mannequin with a strap-on dildo fucking another one from behind. "Awkward" was a poor way of describing how I felt. I did notice, however, that I was better looking than either of the mannequin men. Why did I think that important?

The clerk was soft and pasty. He wore black jeans and a black T-shirt from under which his little belly protruded. His belt was studded, and connected to one side was a chain that found its way into his front pocket. He needed a shave or a better attempt at a goatee. He wore an earring in his left ear and had a pin on his shirt that said "ROGER." He greeted us with a big smile and a sincere "Can I help you?"

"What are these blue beads?" I asked with a touch of fear.

Roger was pleased to answer. "They're anal beads."

"And?"

"And what?"

"Well, what do you do with them?"

"You stick them in your anus," Roger replied matter-of-factly.

"Well, of course you do. Where else would you put them, honey?" Veronica said as if someone had suggested you take aspirin for a headache. "We'll take them. What color would you like, sweetie?" I picked red to match the color of my cheeks.

My group was in animated conversation with other salespeople, so I needed to pass the time. "And this?" I asked Roger as I pointed to a circular leather piece somewhat larger than a cigar band.

"That's a cock ring."

I stared blankly.

"You attach it to your erection and pull it tight," he explained.

I winced. "Why would you do that?"

"Because when you come, it's much more exciting. In fact, some people think it makes your penis larger."

"Oops," Veronica said, "my guy here doesn't need that, but we'll take one for our friend over there." She nodded toward ASK.

Roger seemed to look at me in a new light; I was extremely uncomfortable and wanted to leave.

Veronica pointed to a lovely sort of gemstone in a sapphire blue set like a stud for an earring. Roger anticipated her question. "That's a stud for your scrotum."

"I don't have a scrotum," Veronica answered quickly.

"Well, women often use them on their nipples or their labias."

My stomach turned and I wanted to throw up. I no longer found any of this funny.

"Why would anyone stick a stud in their scrotum?" I asked. "Why not stick your cock in the fireplace or light a match and burn your pubic hair off?"

"Well, that would hurt," said Roger.

"But sticking a pin in your scrotum doesn't? Wow, let's have some fun tonight, Veronica. I can stab you in the vagina and you can give me a puncture wound in my testicles."

She giggled at my agitation. I offered a "thank you" to Roger as I left the shop. I wanted to get to the street before I puked. Maybe I was a homophobe or a prude, but anal beads didn't sit right with me. I smiled at the unintentional pun in my head.

Veronica came out a few minutes later carrying an "Eros bag." She opened it and said, "I got you anal beads and a blue cock ring." She thought it clever and amusing. I did not. I wasn't happy. Feeling embarrassed, I walked quickly ahead toward the bar to meet the others.

74

As I raced down the street, I noticed the hundreds of advertisements posted throughout town. They promised drag shows, female impersonators, stunning imitations of Judy and Marilyn. There were ubiquitous, fetching invites to parties. Everything suggested a bacchanal, and as I walked past I wondered who would be the first of my friends to suggest we attend.

The entire day seemed like a precursor to a New Year's Eve bash. The town was festive and friendly. Everyone was coupled, and public displays of affection were the norm. It was odd for me; I was embarrassed and surprised by my reactions to the lesbian and gay couples everywhere. I had always thought lesbian women were big, unattractive, smaller versions of sumo wrestlers. True, P-town had hundreds if not thousands of those women. From the back, you were certain that when they turned around they'd be sporting a penis and a beer belly to boot. But there were many women off the covers of fashion magazines or the centerfolds of *Playboy*. Some of these women were so gorgeous I was considering becoming a lesbian myself.

Then there were the men. Couples who were mismatched: you know, a hunk with a nerd. Sort of Burt Reynolds or James Caan with an Arnold Stang or Don Knotts. There were men who had chosen one another because each was awkward and unattractive, and those who were clones, buffed and shirtless, letting the world know how lucky they were.

After I adjusted, I realized that all these couples, as well as my friends, Veronica, and myself were all connected in their own way, and it didn't really matter with whom. I still gawked a bit much at first, but as the day progressed I felt part of the melting pot and a bit more grown-up. We chatted up other couples. Not all were welcoming at first, yet we managed to make friends quickly, and my attempt to distance myself from this strange and open place evolved into something kinda cool.

Finally, we found our way to the wharf, where we intended to rent a ski boat and wet suits and hum across the midnight-blue waters of Provincetown Harbor. We reserved our time for later in the afternoon and then went off to kill the next ninety minutes.

Across from the wharf was the Provincetown theater, whose long history was jaw dropping to many of us. Plays by O'Neill and Williams had started here, read out loud for the first time on their way to greatness. O'Neill's time in P-town was chronicled in a large exhibit of letters, photos, and hundreds of essays. He was clearly a tortured soul.

Was it necessary to be damaged to be a great artist?

75

By late afternoon our faces were all a bit too sun kissed, our skin raw from the dense, salty water and the hundreds of falls, dives, and inadvertent plunges we had all so happily endured.

Janet suggested we take one last swim at the nude beach about a twenty-minute walk from the wharf. A *nude* beach. A nude *coed* beach. Janet Kessler could sell tickets to see her unencumbered breasts and make millions, yet here she was proposing a group skinny dip to finish our day. Some of us said, "Okay, great idea," while really thinking, *Wow, I get to see Janet's tits or Veronica's ass.*

The nude beach was an amalgamation of many things. None of them sexual, but most of them fun. I found myself checking out the bodies and bouncing boobs of my female cohorts and avoiding the swinging members of my male friends. I was embarrassed to see all the guys naked surrounded by so many strangers, so I looked past it all and marveled at how great Veronica looked without her clothes.

It was all strange; I had spent hundreds of hours in locker rooms with teammates chatting comfortably in the shower. Never gave it a thought. I had seen lots of girls naked, several of whom now pranced like preschoolers along the perfect, white sandy beach. But now it seemed that somewhere in my brain I heard shouts of, *Naked! Everyone is naked! Everyone including you!* Then, as a final sign that this was not for me, I began wondering whether I needed to put sunscreen on my dick, and if so, how awkward would that be as I stroked my penis to avoid a sunburn. After a while, we all took one last swim, which really did feel nice without a suit, and went to the showers to ready for dinner and the bacchanal that lay ahead.

Secunda's parents were married in the summer of 1946. They took a two-week honeymoon on Cape Cod, and when they visited Provincetown they discovered a restaurant called Ciro & Sal's. The place was inconspicuous, sitting in a small alley at the far end of Commercial Street. We decided to dine at this historic, unpretentious establishment.

I strolled slowly behind the others. As we walked I thought about the as-sembled group. We were all playing something this summer, either on stage or through the facade we presented to those around us. Veronica had some-thing I needed to know but chose not to pursue. My friends loved each other from afar but were afraid to make a first move. We all thought of Janet as the sweetest and loveliest of girls, but earlier in the day she'd been buying deviant sex toys and leading a drive to have everyone run around in their birthday suits. I was a neurotic mishmash of insecurities while I led others to believe I was the real deal and on top of my game. At twenty-one, I couldn't sleep through the night without an anvil on my chest. Secunda was so irreverent and direct. Perhaps it was because he had dough and a safety net.

None of us wanted to be real or feel anything. Otherwise, why did we drink so much and smoke weed and cloud our brains? Maybe that's why Roger and his friends stuck their scrotums with pins—no question you would feel that.

76

After a day of adventure and endless ocean games, we were ravenous. We ate as if tomorrow we were headed for war. We had pasta, seafood, fresh mozzarella, an assortment of vegetables with a magnificent garlic sauce that was so good you could bathe in it. We drank jugs of crisp Chianti. We ate steaming garlic bread covered with melted Parmesan cheese. And then there was the foriana, an indescribable taste-bud orgasm. It was a concoction of raisins, pine nuts, parsley, olive oil, red pepper, walnuts, anchovies, and grated cheese. Its aroma was pungent and beckoning as it was poured over steaming, fresh homemade linguini.

It was close to nine o'clock, a spotty moon held high and fast above. The street was packed and each club more crowded than the next. The air was humid and dense. I was pretty certain that before tonight turned to morning we would see some rain. The music and energy was all around, infectious and impossible to ignore. Whatever dark thoughts had hung unspoken quickly disappeared into the laughter and percussive beat of this New England Mardi Gras. Everywhere you looked, people were dancing, manic and in full flight. There was no decorum here, just abandon and a whole lot of grinding. Men and women were shirtless, and the air was thick with the smell of sweat, beer, and sex.

Secunda and Kellie led us into a cramped piano bar. There were transvestites everywhere, tall, statuesque women/men who, other than for their size and formidable shoulders, were true beauties. Their gowns fit them perfectly and their curves were enhanced through the magic of fashion. It was difficult to remember they all wore penises along with their garters and four-inch heels.

Secunda asked the pianist if Kellie could play a tune or two, and his professional reticence disappeared when offered a financial reward. Kellie played fast, loose, and easy, keeping the energy alive and vibrant. People clapped and sang, and the party seemed to take greater flight. Secunda grabbed the mic off the top of the piano, Kellie modulated the beat, and he began to sing a rocked-out version of Sinatra's "I've Got the World on a String." Songs about "sitting on rainbows," "a girl from Monterey," and "falling in love too easily." Anything and everything about being in love.

For everybody was. Secunda could really sing. He was sort of a Jewish white-boy version of Joe Williams, and Kellie really knew how to play. The room was hot. Boys, girls, and those in between rocked and bumped against each other's butts. It was fun. It was real. It was outside my ken of comfort, but I took Veronica and three-four-five-stepped with strangers.

Secunda took it into falsetto and sang to anybody who ever had their hearts go pitter pat or stayed awake thinking of *that* good night kiss. Then he slowed his song down to where he was speaking in a slow rhythm, and everybody joined in for his final lyric. *"I'm in Loooooove."*

The place erupted in applause and cheers. Secunda held his fingers in a V, hunched over, and said, "I am not a crook" in his best Nixon. Pitchers of beer were passed around as everyone took a break and replenished before the next number, the next dance, the next connection. Secunda called Ellie, JB, and Janet to the stage and Kellie began to vamp "Boogie Woogie Bugle Boy." The girls came in on beat and performed the jump-jazz number as a sexy trio that made you forget the Andrew Sisters ever sang that particular tune.

The club began to dance again and, as we found our way outside, the jazz got jumpier and the place seemed to shake with happiness. Maybe you didn't have to stick anal beads up your ass to find true pleasure.

It was misting, just enough to cool us off for the next stop, the famous Crown and Anchor, where the music was so loud you couldn't make yourself heard, the dancing was more a release than an art form, and coupling found a new definition. As we walked up and paid the door charge, there was a clap of thunder and then another. Lighting flashed across the sky. When it began to rain I thought of Capra.

77

I watched the bacchanal inside the Crown & Anchor. The smoke was foglike and made your eyes burn. The music was deafening. I was tired and done for the day. I had to work tomorrow and too much fun was worse than not enough. I felt as if I had eaten five pounds of chocolate and needed some air and, more important, some perspective. I was done with excursions outside the norm for the night, for the rest of the summer, and beyond. I'd do my work, live deeper with my girlfriend, and let those with needs I couldn't understand play that game. I'd pass on the cock rings as well.

I walked as far away from the chaos as the protective awning would allow, sat on an old wrought-iron bench, and watched the rain fill up the sea. I stared into the night for at least a half a hour imaging that Veronica was inside enjoying the manic insanity that was the dance floor of the Crown & Anchor. The air had been cleansed by the rain; my mind as well.

I had started my summer thinking that I didn't want to get lost along the way or fuck up my life before it started. I watched the rain pelt the sand, and it seemed to spell out *You're Okay, Sammy.* Upon closer look, I noticed the words, *So far.*

Veronica came out and sat beside me. She smelled of smoke, and her face was sunburned and flushed from dancing, noise, and circumstance. She surprised me by sitting on the other end of the small bench rather than next to me. Her hair was wild, hanging loose across her face. She sat watching the water, the small waves rolling and lapping the shore. It appeared she was looking for something, hoping for a discovery to leap out of the gentle dark blue.

We sat in silence for a long time. The music pulsed behind us, but with each passing minute seemed to fade away. Soon it was gone. All that remained was Veronica, myself, and a rain-soaked schooner harbor lit by an unmatchable light. Even in darkness, without a moon or stars, Provincetown had a glow about it that no one could explain.

"Are you avoiding me?" she asked.

"Not at all, honey. Aren't you having fun?"

"I am, but I'd have more if you'd come back inside and dance with me."

"I think I'm done with partying tonight. Besides, by the look of you, it appears you have already found lots of folks to dance with you."

"May I ask you a question?"

"Of course."

"What did Gary tell you about me? Why do you suddenly think he's a good guy?"

"That's two questions."

"Okay, may I ask you *two* questions?"

"You already have."

"Well, then answer."

"As to why I think he's a good guy, that's simple. He gave me a sincere apology—or at least I believed it to be sincere. If he chooses to betray me, then I am the fool."

"I thought you were a don't-fuck-with-me kinda guy."

"You misunderstand me, then. I am not a tough guy, I am just the opposite. I'd rather kiss the girl, watch the game, or sing a song than be tough. I'm not afraid of throwing a punch, but it never seems to solve anything, and the misery usually lingers. Life's too dangerous and too small for anything but love."

"What if you're wrong about Gary and he's setting you up for a fall?"

"Then he wins. *What* he wins, I'm not certain. But if I catch him in the

263

act, I'll clock him, and he'll fall down, scrape his knee, and have to buy a new pair of jeans."

"It wouldn't end there, you know. With Barrows, it never does, and you can't ever forget that Barrows is his grandfather."

Again she watched the water. I saw a seagull swoop down out of the night to find a baby sand crab.

"What did Gary tell you about me?" she asked after a long, silent minute.

"Very little. Once he started, I found I didn't care to know, so he stopped."

"Just like that? He stopped?" She asked this with surprise and dismay.

"I'm not a welcoming audience for this tale. When no one is listening, why continue to speak? And I *don't* care. Something bad happened and you were sad. Very sad. But you haven't chosen to tell me what it is, or was. I didn't expect that to happen, but it did. And you're happy now, so all's good."

I got up and walked to the water and absentmindedly kicked small pieces of leftover lunches and dinners into the sea. The seagulls were grateful, but left no tip.

Things stilled again. "I am not what I appear to be," she said.

"You mean you're a transvestite and want to confess? If so, this is the place."

"Would it bother you if I was?"

I thought a long moment. Then I answered, "Yes, Veronica, it would, I don't want to be with a pretty man dressed up like a pretty girl who when she takes her clothes off has a penis. Is that the surprise?"

"No. I don't have penis."

"Good. Feel free to borrow mine whenever the need calls"

She didn't smile or even move. She seemed locked in place and without air.

"What do you think I need to know? I know enough to believe in your goodness and wisdom and big heart. I think you are delicious, and I am blessed every day you chose me and allow me to feel these things. You make me proud. I think of you as a muse, so in much of my young foolishness I worship you."

"What did Gary tell you?"

"*Nothing.* I stopped him because I simply don't care."

"Then you don't need to know?" she asked with frustration in her voice.

The weather, the soft beat from the club behind us, and our positions on the bench all seemed a bit noir for late July. "Only if you need or want to tell me."

I waited a long time for her to speak. "Did you ever kill anyone, Veronica? Steal money? Get banged by numerous sailors during Fleet Week? Cheat on a test? Find a hundred dollars and keep it even when you knew who dropped it? Hit a kid? Hurt a dog? Lie to me? Betray someone?"

With my last two questions I noticed that I'd hit a nerve. Now I was frightened. JB found us right then. Between puffs on her Lucky Strike, she let us know everyone was meeting in forty-five minutes out front to head home. Clearly sensing the tension, she ran off immediately.

When JB was gone, Veronica spoke. "I lied to you and now I can't find a way to erase the lie."

"That's what sucks about lying."

She paused several more seconds before continuing. "Did you know that my brother Eddie used to date Lizzy Barrows and that they had planned to get married?"

"Of course not. You told me she testified against him at trial."

"Did you know that Gary Golden had been Eddie's best friend since the third grade?"

"No, I didn't. Where is the lie in this?"

"It's one of omission," she said softly, "which is just as deceitful."

"Veronica, you don't have to say another word. It doesn't matter to me." I wanted to say something more. Perhaps to say that I loved her, but when that was said I didn't want it cloaked in sadness. "As the Bible says, 'from now on.'" I added.

"Yeah, until you hear shit at a bar or when someone wants to hurt you, and then that sentiment is lost forever."

"Do you really think you are the only one that has darkness in your past? The only person with a burden or doubt or actions you wish you could bury?"

"No, but mine matter, and I need you to hear me so I can feel we are still together and safe."

"Okay, then talk with me. I promise when we stand up together to leave, all will be well."

We sat together on the bench yet she remained as far away as the surface would allow.

"Gary is the grandson of Barrows."

"I know that."

"Gary was Eddie's best friend and Lizzy had been Eddie's girl since when they were in high school."

I listened and nodded slightly.

"The four of us used to spend time at the Barrows estate during the summer. Using the pool and the deck. Running the speedboat. We'd all stay for dinner often. Gary always had money, even if it was just the crumbs Barrows threw his way. But for the three of us, it was all new, and seductive, and hard to turn your back on."

My stomach churned and the anvil was slowly moving into place.

"Barrows would join us by the pool sometimes, have the staff bring drinks. We'd small-talk, it was all fine. He was old and harmless. He talked about trusts he controlled that might help with my education or how he might invest in Eddie or send Lizzy off to Smith College. She'd been fantasizing about it since she was thirteen."

The rain had slowed. It was still steady, but with no wind. As the rain hit the bay water, now smooth as glass, it splintered the quiet calm of the inky sea.

"We believed him. We all did. Even Gary. We asked Gary why his grandfather would be so generous to us, and he told us it was because he was lonely and had more money than he could ever spend. The visits came more often and then invitations, first in Plymouth and then Boston and New York. Eddie wouldn't let Lizzy go on these out-of-town trips and he urged me to turn them down as well. He felt there was an implied expectation, and soon Barrows would call his marker, even though I was only seventeen and it would all lead somewhere very ugly."

We sat a few moments. Veronica was holding back tears and I let her compose herself. I ran inside quickly and found some napkins on the bar near the door.

"I knew Eddie was right, but I didn't care. I liked all the attention, the money. So I ignored the butterflies in my stomach and betrayed myself. Finally he asked, and I traveled to Boston with him. He had meetings that day and he gave me money to shop while I waited for him to finish his appointments. I feigned rejecting the money and said I was there for his company and the dinner that evening, nothing more. He found my protests amusing and played along, convincing me to enjoy myself and spend the money. He expected to see the outfits I was going to buy when we met back at the hotel at five.

"I was so confused. I wasn't stupid, I knew the day was taking me to places I never thought I'd ever face. I wanted to take the bus home, but I was afraid of offending him, and Gary getting angry with Eddie, so I continued on and bought some nice things—real nice, almost a thousand dollars' worth.

"Then I waited back at the hotel. He had arranged a two-bedroom suite where there was a sitting room and two private rooms off to each side. I was there earlier than him, so I mixed him bourbon and I had a glass of wine and put on one of the sundresses I'd bought. He arrived shortly after and was in a wonderful mood. He drank the bourbon and another, and I did the same with my wine. I changed from outfit to outfit and it was all so much fun . . ."

She hesitated. I did nothing to help her over the hump.

"It was fun and . . . until he called in his marker. He told me it was time for us to have sex. I was shocked, even though I had no right to be. Eddie had predicted this would happen, and I knew as well. I just never believed it in my heart. I thought I'd escape the cliché and move on unscathed.

"I was afraid. I felt stupid and embarrassed. I told him I couldn't have sex with him, that it wasn't part of our arrangement. But my protestations rang hollow. I stopped talking and waited to hear what he would say or do. He sat on the sofa in this glorious opulent suite, and I knew then and there that I was a whore. I was a stupid young girl who'd convinced herself that an old, rich man wanted to be with me simply because my conversation was so scintillating. All the while, I did it for *things*. Stuff I never needed.

"He sat a while and then got up with anger creasing his face. He grabbed the last piece of clothing I held in my hands and threw it to the floor. He slapped me across the face and shouted, 'Who do you think you're kidding?' He took money from his wallet and threw it in my face. I should have run away, but I didn't. Instead I slowly picked up the bills from the floor without saying a word. It amounted to nearly three thousand dollars. My mother makes five thousand in a whole year. I poured myself another glass of wine, and without his asking, I gave him another drink. I sat on the sofa across from him holding back tears. I drank my wine in a room filled with silence. It was surreal. I kept thinking if I walked out bad things would happen, even though I knew by staying I would stain my life.

"He spoke as if nothing had happened. He told me about the restaurant where we would have dinner after we went to bed. It was as if I had no choice anymore. Finally, I stood and walked into the bedroom, the bed was a four-poster with a canopy. I removed my clothes and waited for him under the covers. After a while, he came into the room and walked into the dressing area and modestly changed from his suit into an expensive silk robe. Then he got into bed, removed the robe, and lay naked next to me.

"I was crying silently, tears running down my face. He kissed me, and he tasted like age. I didn't really respond, but I also didn't stop him. He was annoyed by my just lying there and insisted I do better. I obeyed, and we had sex. It seemed to last forever, and when he was done, he rolled over and went to sleep. I stayed in the bed because I was too cold to move.

"Finally, I got up and took a hot shower to try to wash it all away. I decided that I could never do this again, no matter the consequences. I got dressed and folded all the clothes I'd bought that day and set the money on top of them. I went into the parlor of the suite and called Gary at home. He answered on the third ring, and I quickly and without emotion told him what had happened. I asked him if he would come and take me home. He spit in my face through the phone line. He was furious and told me I had crossed a line that his grandfather would never allow to be forgotten. He said, 'Finish the deed. Fuck him for a while and then break it off. At least the consequences won't be as severe.' Then he hung up on me.

"I sat in that suite for an hour and didn't move. I had to leave, but I needed some money to get home. I went quietly back into the bedroom and grabbed the money—every single bill. Barrows was sitting up in the bed as if waiting for me to return. I told him how I felt and that I had to remove myself from this situation and that it was over. He barely moved, but he stared me down and made me afraid. Quietly he said, 'Get back in the bed, Veronica. Don't be stupid and throw your life away. We live in a small town and I own it. I can make it very hard on you and your family.' I told him that whatever he did to me could never be worse than what I'd already done to myself. Then I walked out. I was young and stupid, but I knew enough to know that I hadn't heard the last from Barrows."

Veronica was severely damaged, and the healing was not going to begin on the back deck of a club that doubled as a brothel in Provincetown Bay. I swooped her up into my arms and her face found my welcoming shoulder. Height has its advantages. She cried for many minutes. I stroked her hair and whispered that it was all right, that I would make it all right, and that I cared for her more than ever before. "Let's get you home," I said.

I left her there for a brief minute while I found Secunda inside. He was wild, dressed in a gladiator outfit, sword and all. I pressed the key to the van into his free hand and swapped for his Alpha.

"Have fun," I said. "I have to get Veronica home. The party's over."

I put my arm around her shoulder and walked her to the car. We headed back to PBT. She sat next to me looking out the window. The night had cleared, but there were still wisps of low-lying fog that whipped across the road like rabbits dodging our headlights.

Eventually, I broke the quiet. "Veronica, I have done some things that haven't made me proud. You're not alone."

I wasn't sure she heard me or wanted to listen. For now there was nothing more to be said. But I knew that over time there was a great deal more that needed to be heard.

78

We pulled into PBT at just past three with dawn waiting in the wings. The place was alive with light and music. While some of us had gone to the edge for the day, many of our coworkers had stayed home to "knit and play bridge." Simplicity and comfort championed themselves this early morning.

Veronica and I had spoken little on the drive back. We needed a rest from the drama stuck to trivial things when we did say anything. In *Casablanca* Bogart told Bergman that "the lives of three people don't amount to a hill of beans in this crazy world." Veronica and I were a pair. Nevertheless, I more than agreed with him. Tomorrow we'd all go back to work, sing our songs, and put on our shows. Additionally, the next few days would add a bit more spice to our stew. My parents.

I hugged Veronica in the middle of the compound. After several minutes, I sat her at the redwood table and asked that she wait a moment while I checked messages in the office. No one had been arrested and nothing had been set on fire. Then I saw a formal-looking envelope on my work desk. The paper was thick, with black embossed letters in the corner that read DOCTOR ANDERSON BARROWS, PLYMOUTH, MASSACHUSETTS. No street address needed.

My heart stopped. Without opening the envelope, I knew it was bad news, and that whatever was written inside was his map to a rocky road.

79

Dear Mr. August:

It has come to my attention that members of your acting troupe have been involved in illegal and unacceptable behavior. These actions violate the law as well as breach the moral clauses that are contained in and are an essential element of your lease on the Priscilla Beach Theatre as countersigned by The Barrows Foundation.

Therefore, in my position as Chairman and as a Director of the Board of the foundation I inform you of the following:

You and your employee Alan S. Kopit will be charged with aggravated assault and attempted manslaughter on the person of Mr. Johnny Colon, who is an employee of my foundation.

Your employee Ms. Ellie Foster will be charged with soliciting and prostitution in Plymouth County.

Due to my knowledge of these pending allegations, I refer you to Paragraph 8B in the lease referenced above. Once I commence proceedings, these charges will put you in default of your lease and you will have forty-eight hours to vacate the premises or face additional civil and criminal action.

I urge you, in the interest of the storied history of the Priscilla Beach Theatre as well as to preserve your own reputation and those of your coworkers that you vacate as is instructed in the agreement.

Regretfully,
Dr. Anderson Barrows

I read the letter twice to be sure it was real. Afterward, I jammed the demented missive into the envelope and stuck it in my pocket. My brain was racing at breakneck speed and my heart beat through my chest. My face was hot and my breathing spotty.

I ran to the Mustang, intending on paying a visit to Barrows despite its being three in the morning. Veronica shouted to me when she saw me. I turned toward her and she did not have to ask if something was wrong.

"Where are you going? What's happened?" she implored while ineffectually grabbing my shirt in an attempt to calm the beast.

"That fuck," I shouted at her as if she had written the note. "That sick fuck. Here, read this."

Veronica needed only to see the first lines and the signature to know that Barrows was seeking the long-promised revenge he had proffered from a hotel bed years ago. I was behind the wheel now and all that stopped me from heading to the Barrows mansion was Veronica holding the door, knowing that if she let me go, our lives would never be the same.

"Stay here with me," she pleaded. "Nothing good can happen if you go to see him now. It's what he wants. You'll end up with Eddie!"

I pushed her away with all my might. She lost her balance and fell to the ground. I should have stopped there and helped her to her feet, but rage was my master.

She pleaded yet again. "Sam, he's old. He'll be over soon. Please don't go there. Please stay with me!" she screamed as if keening. "This will destroy us . . ."

I didn't hear the rest of what she shouted. I was driving toward Route 3 at close to a hundred miles an hour. The deep, jagged cliffs to my right invited a drop of hundreds of feet to the ocean below. They were shrouded in fog, and if I mishandled a curve on this country highway, I would find my way to hell.

80

I drove the Mustang straight through the security gate of the Barrows compound. I grazed the gatehouse itself, leaving behind the littered debris of the silly white booth meant to keep the estate grounds safe. For the first time there were actually guards at the gate, perhaps due to the late hour, but more likely because Barrows expected a guest tonight in fact looking forward to a visitor. The heavy-set guards looked confused as I raced toward the great house like I was on the Bonneville Salt Flats.

I reached the house and jumped from the car before it reached a full stop. Within seconds I was pounding on the front door. Lights switched on to follow. Instantly the grounds were awash in light from the hundreds of windows now alive and wrestled from slumber. Barrows answered the door, dressed in a silk robe, perhaps the one he wore when he used Veronica years ago. I pushed my way in.

"It's late, young man," he said, eerily calm.

"Late?" I shouted. "It's late for you, you sick fuck. What are going to do, call the cops? Try to hurt me? Well, bring it on."

"Perhaps both," he replied, still calm.

Suddenly I realized his demeanor was too practiced. I heard Veronica saying, "Nothing good can happen if you go to see him now." I shut off my ranting as quickly as an angry gust of wind extinguishes a flame. I took a deep breath. I was a fighter who, although wounded, still had many punches to throw.

We stood face to face. The massive living room was silent but for the ticking of the grandfather clock and the crashing of the waves hundreds of feet below. The huge windows looked out into darkness, acting as mirrors in a spook house. There were six of him and six of me in this face-off.

Again he referenced my youth and suggested that a more wizened man would not have allowed these problems to get the better of him.

"My youth is not the problem here, doctor. It is your envy of youth that will bring you down. You think this letter scares me one bit? Trumped-up, bogus accusations manufactured by or paid for by you, a bitter old man who scars his family's legacy and the very greatness of our nation with your aborted dalliances and flights of perverted fiction. You don't have the courage to step out into the light. You're a sniper who hides in the shadows and hopes to hit his mark. What drives you to do such things? You're a predator who looks to inflict pain on strangers simply because their lives are the future and yours is seen through a splintered rearview mirror."

Barrows appeared to be listening. He was correct in his assessment of youth. My naivete was my Achilles heel. I believed in doing the right thing, but in a street fight there are no rules.

"I didn't like you the first day we met," he said darkly. "And I told you so. You weren't ready to carry the burden of leadership or to understand that passion and charm and biceps wouldn't suffice. You didn't listen. Now you call me names and throw around recriminations. What are you but an insubordinate neophyte?"

"Don't misjudge what you read in my eyes, old man. Disdain is a great motivator. So is revenge. I came to Plymouth to reawaken the ghosts in your theater, to make—"

"I know!" he shouted. "To have it sing again. To tell a joke, to make a difference. You make me sick with your precocious rhetoric. You sound like a prissy faggot."

"What are you going to do to me, Barrows? Break my heart by telling me you fucked my girlfriend when she was seventeen? Tell the world that your strong-arm fucker Colon was assaulted by me and the five-foot-six Alan Kopit? You have played emperor for too long. Your 'subjects' are weary of your antics and ready to pistol-whip you for pleasure. You should be using your gifts and your prestige to do good to carry on the Barrows name that was cherished for three hundred years. Instead, you look like the heavy from some forties noir B movie. The truth about you will be revealed, and all your evil pettiness will cascade over this town. Your scandal will destroy you. I'll fight you with all the power of my youth. Your obituary will end up next to the want ads. The next day, they'll wrap fish with it, and the day after that, it will be garbage."

Suddenly, a siren sounded outside the open door and a swirling neon-blue police light painted the walls, flashing color and consequence throughout the giant room. The two security guards I had nearly run down just minutes ago arrived and unceremoniously began to pull me from the house. The squad car was at the ready waiting just outside the front door. I had to make Barrows listen or all would be lost and the possibility of goodness destroyed. I wrestled myself away from the guards and ran to the far side of the room.

"Dr. Barrows, please listen to me!"

"I have been, August, and you make me ill. Your disrespect, your threats. You are merely an unhappy, petulant boy talking as if you could make me fear you. Ha!"

"I'm sorry, sir, truly sorry. But you must hear me. Just months ago when I came to your home I said you didn't know me, who I was and how hard I would work. That I would restore the glory of your building if you just let me. And I have, doctor. I have. PBT sings again and you can hear it loud and long as it ascends into the night sky to join the stars and the moon and makes the constellations grin. Every night the applause fills the air and people go home with a smile in their heart.

"And, sir, you haven't seen it, you haven't been by to see it's magic. Aren't we meant to do *something* with our lives, to touch people, to make the difficult day seem less long and allow it to end with the hope that tomorrow will be a winner. I don't know why, but there's more to PBT than just the shows we are putting on, people come for more than the singing and dancing. They're coming from all over because we are a community and they want to be part of it. Isn't that what you want?

"Barrows is Plymouth and Plymouth has something in PBT that makes its people happier. The families who frequent your stores and whose children attend your schools and work each day here in this town so it is a place to be proud of, they need to be embraced by you, doctor. They are your people and you must allow them to soar. Don't look to close the theater down. Please. But if you do, before you do, come see what we have done.

"Not only have the ghosts been reawakened, but in doing so the town has a bounce in its step. I see it every night. The audiences stay long after the curtain has fallen and they have their kids meet the players, and they take pictures and ask for autographs, and it makes them joyful. It simply makes them happy.

"I'm not asking this for me. I've learned most of what I need to know about myself this summer. And I need to learn a great deal more. I was wrong to shout at you and act the way I did. But it comes from a deep-rooted passion for what I think is good and necessary. I do respect you, Dr. Barrows, and all you've accomplished. You said to me that young people have a sense of entitlement that makes you wonder where our youth is headed.

"But if you stop us then what can we accomplish? You said that we all want to go to heaven but none of us wants to die. That is not true, sir. It is not true. The fifty young people I've brought here and who work your building will go to heaven, for all good reasons. Plymouth is the ocean and the sunsets and history and you. It is also PBT."

All he said was, "Good night, Mr. August." I continued my plea.

"Dr. Barrows, you were young once and I'm sure you had a dream, something that made you get up each morning and attack your days. It wasn't about money, you had that. I imagine it was about leaving your fingerprint on this planet. That's why your name adorns the buildings that are the lifeblood of Plymouth. You would have fought for that dream just as I'm doing now. Youth is many things, one of which is that it makes memories to last a lifetime. Please remember when you were my age and how every breath was life and death. If you do, you'll join our community and not look to shut it all down. But to be part of it and that, sir, is winning."

"Go home and get some rest, Sam. I am sure you'll need it," was all he had to say.

Then the guards pushed me outside and into the back seat of the police car. The siren wailed once, and the sedan spit gravel and headed toward the front gates.

I thought again of Veronica's sobbing words of warning, and regretted with all my heart that she had turned out to be right.

"So, Sammy, are you hungry?" the driver asked. I leaned forward and saw that it was Officer Tommy at the helm of the squad car. To his right was a familiar and happy face giggling and pulling on a Lucky Strike.

"It's late, but the doughnut shop is still open. What will it be, glazed or chocolate sprinkles?" JB giggled.

8 1

We sat on the beach and watched the sun make its appearance. I thought it ironic how the night sky changed into dawn, surprising you even as you watched it all happen. It made me think of the past hours. One moment I was holding my girlfriend close keeping her safe, the next I was a reckless young fool who had put all I had worked for and all those I loved in jeopardy. Whatever drove Barrows, he had indeed bested me. The impatience of my youth and need for a quick resolve; a knockout punch had left me vulnerable to his sage and calculated need to prove that his age and wisdom were the stronger of the two of us. I had never imagined him a foe, but as the realization came into focus I regretted that he was such a formidable one.

Officer Tommy, JB, and I had headed straight for the beach. Veronica was there waiting, less emotional than when I had left her, yet still shaken and looking wan. We sat watching the tide come in and listened to the calming sound of the waves beating the sand, all rhythmic and in time as if conducted by Poseidon himself.

We had eaten the doughnuts, some sprinkled some glazed. JB smoked and Veronica leaned against me wearing an old woolen blanket to shield her from the predawn chill. I went through what had happened several times, my story evolving from brazen anecdote to one of budding concern; it now found its place as a series of scenarios all ending badly.

Barrows was a prick and his actions were inexplicable, but he owned this town and my heroics had not resolved anything. My heartfelt pleadings of contrition and remorse, and my urgings that he remember his youth had fallen on deaf ears. I was Don Quixote and Barrows my windmill. In fact, as reality set in we all realized it was probably only the beginning, the doctor had led me exactly where he wanted: to the precipice, to the arena where I would be devoured by angry lions unleashed—by him and to my end.

I had not said a word for over an hour. I wanted to, in order to break the mounting tension, but as each new thought formed in my head ready to parry our anxiety, they all seemed soft blurred, not fully formed. To say them out loud would only amp up our worries rather than mitigate them. Finally I jumped up. Pacing the empty beach I said, "I've made a terrible mistake. Watching the sunrise is not going to wash my misstep away with the next wave. It wasn't supposed to be this hard. I need help. Stay here, finish the doughnuts. I'm going to fix this now."

I sprinted from the beach toward the theater. It seemed to startle the morning quiet. The birds, all of whom were cooing gently to greet the day, took sudden flight. The calm that dawn brings was shattered by my energy and sense of purpose. I slowed my pace as I reached the compound. The place was asleep. There was a bright light in the kitchen where Ma and her crew were readying breakfast. On the deck outside the stage door Louis Rosenberg played Mozart on his French horn, easy and entirely for himself as no one was there to listen. The dichotomy between his simple love of music and my burgeoning concerns as to Barrows's next move made me smile at the absurdity life offers when the cards are dealt. I listened quietly for a moment and then walked slowly to the office.

The room was cool and dank; it smelled of the hundreds of cigarettes JB had smoked since the summer began. The ashes caught in my throat as I picked up the phone, took a final deep breath, and dialed. And then I saw the

Barrows long, stretch black-bullet limo pull into the parking lot. I hung up, closed my eyes and prayed.

8 2

I was up by six every day throughout the summer. But I had usually slept the night before, so as this endless day dragged on I was tired. My mind and body needed rest. Yet now as I waited to see who might emerge from the car sitting menacingly alone in the stillness of morning, that option was somewhere down the road in the ether, a false promise far away, far way.

I stood motionless in the cramped office and waited for my fate to unfold. Just three months ago I had partied with my friends and asked them to join me in this journey, one that had become a living, breathing presence as real and flawed and magical as the individuals making it all happen. On that night I had told JB, "I am going to direct the shows. I am going to learn how to be a man. I am going to give everyone who crosses my path a memory to cherish. Then I am moving to New York to direct and produce plays on Broadway and become famous."

Big dreams, I thought. *Their pursuit comes with the risk of crippling disappointment. Swing for the fences with all your might and hope, and perhaps the ball will hit the sweet spot and you'll see the crowd leap to their feet and roar, showering you with light.* I glanced over at the tall amber grass where I had confronted Officer Richardson just days ago. It could have been a field in Ohio or Iowa a million miles away, simple and serene. But it wasn't. It was here and it was just me waiting for the act to end and for the curtain to fall. Whether Barrows emerged alone or with a police escort, I knew I had little left in my quiver with which to fight on.

The passenger door to the stretch opened and Barrows appeared. He looked fresh from the shower, rested and dressed for a yacht club brunch. As wired as I was he was the opposite, calm, confident, and stately. As he took a long, purposeful look around the compound, his eyes rested on the marquee Bobby had so meticulously designed and the SOLD OUT TONIGHT sign trumpeting our recent successes. He watched and listened to Louis Rosenberg play the horn and he strolled a few short steps to the flower garden that surrounded the parking lot.

We had planted that garden when we arrived and it had thrived under the constant care of the PBT minions. Barrows picked off the top of a tall purple cosmos and after a beat flipped the petals into the street. He then turned his attention to the dining hall and the arrival of some of the company's early risers, straining to hear the morning banter of youth as they greeted the day.

Barrows's visage never changed, stoic was his expression, a smile nowhere to be found. He walked across the gravel driveway that was fresh and bright, free of the potholes and decay we had found when we first arrived. He stopped at the redwood table where Trudy and Zach were running lines and drinking steaming hot coffee. Their exchange was friendly, and Barrows shook hands with a slight bow and moved on. He found his way to the box office and stared at the seating chart beside the ticket window. After a long while he walked to the front of the theater and disappeared into the old barn.

I watched this all, alone and silent, in the office. I wanted to scream. I felt nauseous and frightened. None of this made any sense. I half expected to see the theater ablaze and in ruin. I had aged more than a decade by the time he exited the building. His face wore a smile, something I had never seen in the old man. And his eyes his eyes, . . . well, they had light behind them instead of the soulless dark stare I had seen only hours, but seemingly days, earlier.

Ellie Foster was running a dance step on the deck and he stopped to watch her from a distance. She ran the routine several times and then called Janet Kessler over from her breakfast where she sat holding hands with ASK and inquired how it looked. Ellie then taught the step to Janet and they danced it together happily, like puppies rolling through a pile of autumn leaves. They hugged one another when finished. The Cape Cod morning sun cast a halo over their glossy, pretty hair and shone upon their young, flushed faces. They walked over to the redwood table to join their friends.

Kasen walked out from behind the scene shop unshaven, weary, and covered with paint. He asked Barrows if he could help him. Barrows indicated no with a shake of his head, and then Kasen shook his hand and an introduction had been made. They walked over to the breakfast table under the giant maple and Barrows took a seat surrounded by youth. ASK appeared out of nowhere and placed a plate of Ma's breakfast specialties in front of Barrows. Pleased, the doctor took the offered napkin, placed it over his lap and began to eat breakfast!

What'll happen next? I wondered. *Is Barrows going to smoke a joint with James?* Just when you think you know something, you realize you don't.

Elliot was rehearsing certain members of the band behind the red house and more music found its way into the morning. Soon Mary Holly's crisp, bight soprano joined the band; breakfast was now accompanied by talent and lyric and joy, a trifecta you couldn't buy at any price.

Barrows stood and backed away from the group waving friendly goodbyes. He then parked himself in the center of the compound and turned slowly in a circle, taking in the PBT grounds. His focused gaze was steady, as if gathering information. He spotted a small piece of paper that marred the driveway, bent over, picked it up and placed it in his jacket pocket. He noticed a lone flower withering on its stem and broke it off and placed that in his jacket as well. Barrows then turned toward the office window that looked out on the compound and his eyes met mine. He seemed to know I'd been standing there. Time had run out.

I walked toward Barrows and as I closed in he said, "Come with me, Mr. August." He headed back toward his black limo and I followed. "Mr. August, might you join me for a discussion in my car?" he asked. And then he added, "Please."

When I didn't respond he repeated his request, this time making it more of a command.

"Dr. Barrows, after last evening's events I don't think it wise that I meet with you without my counsel in attendance," I replied.

"All right, young man, but counsel is not needed. I heard you last evening. I heard your anger and then your passion. You had valid things to say on both accounts. Your first verse only gave me greater resolve to shut you down. You see, a summer here is much like a long race, a marathon, and I still believe you will run out of air before you reach the finish line."

"Dr. . . ." I began.

"Shut up, August, and listen. I did so last evening and now it is your turn."

"Yes, sir," I replied.

"When you get to be my age you have lived so many lives. I forgot that I was your age once, as it was so long ago. The years have blurred those memories and . . . well, I have come to resent that loss of clarity. You remember every word of our meetings yet so do I.

"My counsel, Miss Golden, told me to 'give you boys want you want'—that you were not responsible for the world turning. She was right. The world will continue spinning until I am gone and long after. So I have chosen to leave you alone and see if you can finish this race you have so eagerly begun.

"I am not an ally, but until you trip up I will no longer be a foe. I have told you that I thought it took more than charm, good looks, and biceps to be a leader *and*, my young friend, it takes much more than words—which you never seem to be short of."

"I am now, sir. Are you letting us continue?" I asked, my voice choking with emotion.

"I am offering an uneasy, tenuous truce. You have done well here. Your friends admire you and they work with all their heart. There is something in you, August, that deserves a chance to swing the bat. Finish the job, or I will make sure you end up on the bench where glib, clever references to Fred Lynn won't save you."

He gave me a letter on the foundation's letterhead that backed up his promise, then got in his black limo without another word or an acknowledgment of goodbye. As he drove away I breathed deeply and held back tears. "And good luck to you as well, Dr. Barrows. You unmitigated son of a bitch," I said. I was grateful of course, but I guess I need the last word.

"The ghosts are singing again, doctor. You've seen it with your own eyes. Don't fuck with the ghosts once they've reawakened." I reread the letter he had given me. Then I folded it and put it in my back pocket

I watched the tail lights of his car disappear down Rocky Hill Road. Looking over at the PBT compound with all its happy and, yes, youthful activity,

I noticed that the entire place was bathed in sunlight. It was 8 a.m., so I walked to the dining hall to get some breakfast.

8 3

We returned to rehearsal promptly at ten that morning. No tardiness, a sense of purpose in the air. The day off had proved valuable. Although short in duration it tossed certain pettiness asunder, and once I was back to work my skirmishes with the town bully, although still rattling inside my, brain did so in a whisper. PBT was reinvigorated for the days ahead.

The company finished its run of *Anything Goes* with panache. Tickets continued to sell. New laughs were discovered and joined the established money moments in the bank of mirth. We rehearsed *Funny Girl* during the day, and sometimes after the curtain had come down we ran a number or two until the clock hit midnight. We did not have a single streaker, naked bouncing breast, or visit from the local extortionist. The police did not summon me for a powwow and no fisticuffs were caused by the women who worked and played under our banner. PBT had settled in the way a good team does during the dog days of August. We played steady and hit in the clutch. We made the big play when necessary and the dead, red punch-outs kept us in every game.

Funny Girl premiered the following Monday. The show was in terrific shape, as were its stars Fitzgerald and Rush. Lizzy Barrows brought thirty people with her to the opening and mingled with members of the cast long after her guests had gone home. I still didn't understand, so the blackness in my heart toward the Barrowses remained my secret.

Veronica had no contact with Lizzy that night, part of our uneasy truce. We were a couple, as entwined in one another's lives as we were when we slept entangled like vines in the jungle. We'd figure out the rest of her story when the time was right.

Johnny Colon had been booked on assault charges for his indiscretions with Ellie Foster.

We ran the table on *Funny Girl*. On its closing weekend we had one expected visiting group, a friendly, loving surprise, and a black limo that arrived with the promise of turmoil and a smoldering simmering scent of trouble.

First the good news. Michael Kasen, who worked tirelessly as our tech director, had his dad visit for the last performance. Mr. Kasen was blown away by what he saw—not just the show itself but the entire gestalt of PBT. Michael's dad was a powerful attorney who represented transport owners in New York City. He was a tough guy, for sure, but underneath really a gentle giant. Late Saturday night, he approached me.

"Freddy Kasen, Michael's dad," he said extending his hand. He had a firm handshake. I'd been taught you could judge a great deal about a person from their handshake.

"Yes, sir, I know that. He looks like you."

"I'm better looking." He laughed and his tough-guy demeanor faded away.

"Of course you are, Mr. Kasen. What was I thinking?"

"Sam, question. Would it be all right with you if I spent the day here working alongside Mike? Help out any way I can?"

Here was a man who had gone toe to toe with the Teamsters, stared down New York City unions, and prevented strikes that would have crippled a city. As a young attorney he had represented Robert Moses, who built Jones Beach and much of the New York City subway system. Mr. Kasen was the real thing, a man of substance and fire, and *he* wanted permission to work in our house.

"It would be an honor, Mr. Kasen," I said with a small, respectful bow. "Let me get you a hammer."

From that moment, Fred Kasen threw himself into everything. He built sets alongside his son. He commented throughout the day that the time he spent with us made him feel young. He flirted with the girls and offered praise to everyone on the premises. He ate breakfast in our dining hall on Sunday morning and even gave a toast to "youth and opportunity and fearlessness." He hugged me when he said goodbye and promised to invest in my first New York venture. Then he shook his son's hand and drove off in his white Lincoln Continental. Mr. Kasen was our lovely surprise.

Mr. Foster, the man in the limo wore a dark suit and a red tie with a matching pocket square. He had a jutting jaw and an almost military manner. He was gruff yet polite with everyone and asked at the box office for the best seat in the house. Informed there were no seats to be had, he got a bit in Diana's face and insisted to talk to someone in charge. I saw the exchange and interceded immediately.

"Mr. Foster, sir, welcome. I'm so glad you made the trip."

He looked at me with a distrustful and professional eye. "You are . . .?"

"Sam August, sir. We spoke about Ellie over the phone. Let me get you a seat and then I'll run and get her."

"So, Sam, you were the pushy young man throwing around words like 'damage.'"

"Sir, I used that word because I thought it was true that she could be hurt and you needed to hear it. I'd also like to believe I was caring and not pushy, but as you know in your work, whatever it takes to get the job done, right, sir?"

"I have to say that this is an impressive place you have here, much more than I would have expected. I guess congratulations are in order for you. Ellie writes that she has really prospered here and that she has enjoyed the dancing and wants to continue with it after the summer."

"Yes, sir. She is a great person and she is so dedicated and so talented. I don't know what we'd do without her."

"Well, you'll have to figure that out, son. I'm taking her home tonight. I'll see your show and then we'll be off."

I countered with a quick jab. "No, that won't be happening." My eyes met his and held their own. "Ellie has a contract with me, and we'd suffer real damages if she breached that agreement. Also, Mr. Foster, I have no tickets to sell you. We're completely sold out and I won't be able to find you that seat I mentioned a minute ago. Sometimes it pays to plan ahead. Sorry, sir. It was nice to meet you. I'll let Ellie know you're here."

As I started to leave and he took my arm and spun me around to face him.

"You listen to me, kid. That contract you're throwing at me is for what, a hundred, two hundred dollars? I'll buy it out for lunch money and this will all go away. I am taking my daughter home tonight. This whole situation is too dangerous for her to get vested in, she has other more important things to do with her life. So let's not play games here, boy."

"My name is Sam, sir. I don't play games, but I do honor my commitments and I expect others to do the same. Ellie has friends here who are counting on her."

"I don't know her friends."

"Perhaps you should. It might help you know your daughter a bit better."

"I'll buy out her contract for five thousand dollars. I am taking her home."

"Neither her contract nor her soul are for sale! Neither am I, sir. Now, if you'd like to see our show, I can accommodate you. But if you're here to cause a problem for me, then I'm respectfully ending this conversation."

He was seething. His power tie and scowl weren't working on me. I had no stock options in his corporate tower, nor was I vying for his approval.

"I'll pass on the show," he said briskly and waved for his driver to come around.

I dashed to the office and grabbed the PA mic. "Ellie Foster, please come to the compound immediately. Your father is here to visit. Your father is in attendance. Please come to the compound ASAP!"

My recklessness had halted Mr. Foster before he climbed into his car and hid behind the tinted glass that shielded him from being human. Ellie appeared and dashed to his side, hugging him tentatively. He softened ever so slightly. Diana, knowing somehow that her girlfriend needed assistance, ran out from the box office waving a ticket as if it carried the winning numbers to the Irish Sweepstakes. She proffered to Mr. Foster and he had no choice but to take it. Unless he was Houdini, it looked like he'd be seeing Ellie's work on stage tonight. After that it would be up to the two of them to figure it all out. I had my parents arriving and needed to prepare. One must, even for the best of invasions.

Mom and Dad arrived minutes before the final performance of *Funny Girl* on Saturday night. It was so good to see them both. My father was a very handsome man in his early fifties who carried himself with great confidence. My mom, Phyllis, was a beauty even as she approached the big five-oh. She had red, curly hair, an easy smile, and a figure and long legs that matched any of the girls working at PBT. My aunt and uncle were with them, and they all beamed as they raced to their seats just in time for the downbeat.

The show went extraordinarily well. It had that special magic closing nights always have, sparked by the company's desire to hold on to something that will never come around again. True, there would be other shows, but it was the last time for this particular one.

I worked throughout the performance and needed to do so after curtain as well. Our next show was *Company* and, as I had feared, the heavy hydraulic scenery Duncan had designed was nearing the clusterfuck stage. We'd have to work through the night to strike the *Funny Girl* set and quickly mount the complicated machinery that was part of the modern design and character of *Company*. Additionally, we had a new light plot that needed a refocus and numerous costume quick changes to cover. Most important, because of the sophistication of and difficulty learning it, we had yet to stage the act 2 opening or rehearse Fitzgerald's big eleventh-hour number. I'd have very little time to visit with my parents, if at all. I truly hoped they'd understand.

I joined everyone outside about twenty minutes after the applause ended. I had been working in the scene shop on the set problems, and as I walked across the compound I was delighted to see my folks chatting animatedly with my friends. They rose to greet me.

"Sammy, oh Sammy, it is so good to see you," my mom said as she hugged me, smelling of Shalimar and gin. She proceeded to kiss me relentlessly, as if I was five and she was putting me to bed. My dad offered a more dignified hug. His scent for as long as I could remember was Canoe, warm and comforting.

"I am so proud of you, Sammy," he said. No praise could have meant more.

I said hello to my aunt Rene, my father's younger sister. Rene was a true beauty and would have been a big-time fashion model if life had dealt her a different hand. Her husband, Morris, was so happy with the evening he pranced like a puppy and shared his delight in a jumble of words. The kindest man I knew, he spoke as if his mouth were filled with marbles. Throughout the years, I'd responded to his energy rather than what he was actually saying because I could never really understand him.

My mother strolled over and began to dance with me as she sang a song from the show. She never could remember a lyric, but she could sing "Dah, dah, dah, dah, dah, dah" with the best of them and make it her own. She was always sweet when she sang, and it reminded me that my mom was once a young girl.

Zach cut in and took over the song and dance, and for a moment I thought my mother was dancing with Clark Gable. I was uncertain whether to enjoy the moment or call for a gurney in anticipation of her passing out.

"Dad, Uncle Morris, we have things to do. We have to strike the set and ready the new one by morning. Pizza and beer are on the way. Come in and grab a hammer. Mom and Aunt Rene can visit with everyone while we work. It should be fun. Then on my break in the morning we can all have breakfast."

"I'm eating here," Morris said. "I'm told the food is very good." Or at least I think that was what he said. "@//%@^&**@ Sammy, %@&*%, hammer, &&#^%, pizza," he said and headed to the theater to go to help out with the strike.

My father stole his bride from our leading man, took her hand in his, and walked her across the compound. Rene stayed behind at the redwood table talking with her new best friend, a tall blond beauty who hung on every word.

84

Every person who worked at PBT was busy inside the building. The mood was festive, but it was not a party. Kasen barked orders and things happened with alacrity and purpose. Scenery flew in from the loft and was rigged and sent away to await its next appearance. James, ASK, and Doobie held positions on top of tall A-frame ladders and turned white-hot Fresnels, Lycos, and beam projectors until their lamp hit the correct spot and Duncan approved their moving on to setting the next instrument. Dr. Rosenstein and

Louis Rosenberg reset the orchestra's amplification and played short riffs from *Company* so that the new sound levels were ready for tomorrow's tech run. Racks of costumes left the stage and new inventions rolled in to take their place, a swoosh of color flying across the crowded stage. Jojo spoke to everyone on headset. Feston and Secunda kept the mood light by improvising a play by play of events and accomplishments as late night turned into early morning.

In the middle of all this Feston says, "Eighty-year-old Jewish guy walks into a confessional at church and says to the priest, 'Fathder, Fathder, I am shutpping a sixteen-year-old girl.' 'That's disgraceful,' says the priest. 'Anyway why are you telling me? You're a Jew and I'm a priest.' 'Why am I telling you?' the old man asks? *I am telling everyone!*"

Secunda: "A hamburger and a French fry walk into a bar, the bartender says 'sorry we don't serve food here.'"

Feston: "A potato walks into a bar and all eyes were on him."

Secunda. "E-flat walks into a bar. Bartender says, 'We don't serve minors.'"

The good doctor hit a "ba-dump-dum" from the orchestra pit.

Feston: "Skunk walks into a bar and says, 'Hey, where did everybody go?'"

Secunda: "A woman and a duck walk into a bar. The bartender says, 'Where did you get the pig?' The woman says, 'That's not a pig, that's a duck.' The bartenders says, 'I was talking to the duck.'"

The work continued despite the insanities. They played dueling bad jokes, matching one another for twenty, twenty-five times, never missing a beat. Finally to institutional relief, Secunda ended it all with, "Thank you, thank you, ladies and gentlemen. We will be here all week. Two shows on Saturday."

Then everyone booed and hissed. There were cries of "get the hook!"

Feston stepped forward and did a dead-on imitation of Secunda's Nixon. Hunched over and with his hands in a V he said, "I am not a crook." The work continued.

I always thought of the set turnover as a melancholy time. Endings are hard, yet without them beginnings never happen. The energy and the busy worker bees reminded me of the Lilliputians all working together to keep Gulliver tied down, or a group of Santa's elves chugging along on the way to Christmas. The scenery often dwarfed the workers and the disparity in size was amusing to watch, easy to enjoy. You could sit quietly in the back of the theater and observe as one environment was replaced by a whole new world, all in minutes like real life in flash-forward photography.

Veronica made her presence known. She was clearly working the room, making sure that at tomorrow's breakfast she'd be one of the specials. Tall blonde over easy. Every few minutes she would take someone's elbow and ask them to take a break from their chores, then bring them into the house to say hello to Herb and Phyllis. Rene and Morris were like supporting characters as each scene developed, and before long act 1 was finished.

The hydraulic was a disaster. It simply did not work. Hydraulics are meant to move things fluidly up and down. Ours was inert. Duncan continued to beat on it the way a doctor insists on endless defib paddles to revive a long-dead patient. No one was angry, just freaked out about our limited options. Duncan had designed a truly imaginative set and Kasen had built it correctly under great duress. But it simply didn't work. And it was essential to the whole design.

Company took place in the upscale environs of a frantic, breathless New York City. The set had to be fluid, continual effortless motion of the high-tech, chrome, and metal buildings that were the essence of "the Apple." We were faced with a tech rehearsal scheduled to start at 10 a.m., with less than five hours to find a solution. The motors on the hydraulic elevator were as dead as being 0 – 2 against Seaver in afternoon shadows. We were going down.

We drank endless cups of coffee; light, sweet, strong joe laced with Jim Beam. The buzz was nice, but the answers were nowhere in the building. Just as we reached the nadir of our despair, James walked in with a big smile on his face. No doubt he was stoned. He was followed by an equally jolly Doobie and a group of six guys I had never met, huge mountain men whose muscles were topped with muscles and whose necks were the circumference of thirty-gallon trashcans. Two of the behemoths carried large workout benches, and the other four barbells of great size. James sent the fellows down under the stage telling them he'd be with them in a moment.

James showed me a simple drawing of two weight benches arranged in a manner whereby they connected to the dysfunctional hydraulic elevator. Placed on the benches were sets of four cylinders that each held several hundred pounds of barbells. Poorly sketched, yet clearly part of the equation were six freakishly large muscled men. James had solved the problem! He intended to replace automation with old-fashioned hard labor. More astonishing was the fact that he'd brought the muscle with him at five in the morning and was stoned to boot. I thought of Charlton Heston rowing that war galleon in *Ben Hur*. If the Romans could rule the world without automation, we at PBT could move scenery the same way. It was genius. It was a miracle. It was why James, even through the haze of marijuana that engulfed him, was the smartest guy I knew.

With great relief I cheerfully exclaimed, "How long will it take to build this thing?" Then I kissed him on both cheeks, we cranked up Sinatra on the stereo, and he sang "The Good Life."

Less than an hour later we found it worked. The elevator rested on a platform attached to the barbells. On cue, the six goons lifted the thing in unison from under the stage and it meshed perfectly with the hole we had cut in the floor. It was smooth and precise, and because of the overwhelming strength of our crew, not a single grunt was heard. Sunday was off to a good start.

8 5

I needed a respite, at least for a little while. I also needed and wanted to see my parents. It was too early to wake them and visit over breakfast, so I decided a short run was the best option.

Veronica was already up and dressed to kill. Her hair was freshly washed and blown dry with a perfect curl to it. Her makeup was subtle and soft, her blue eyes highlighted by shadow simply dazzled. She wore a lavender halter-top that showed off her soft, tanned shoulders and taut, bare midriff. It was incredibly sexy yet decorous at the same time. Only Veronica could pull that parlay off successfully. Her faded blue-denim skirt was tied with a royal-blue satin sash and it too offered enough modesty along with a spectacular glimpse of thigh.

She greeted me with a gorgeous, welcoming smile. "Good morning, sweetheart," she said. "I ran you a hot bath. It will refresh you and get you ready for the day and this evening."

"This evening? What about this evening?"

"You are having dinner with your parents and Rene and Morris."

"I am?"

"Yes, I called Marty Stanhope at the White Cliffs and preordered the whole thing. You'll only have about an hour and a half at break and this way we can all have a relaxing visit."

"A bath?" I asked. "I haven't had a bath since I was six. Anyway, I thought I'd meet them for an early breakfast in about an hour."

She put her arms easily around my shoulders and spoke to me as if I wasn't very bright. "Bad idea, big boy," she said. "Herb and Phyllis left real late last night and need to sleep in. I told them I'd pick them up at eleven and show them the town, take them to the beach and some of the knickknack shops. We'll drive by the Barrows estate and I'll tell the tale of how you jousted with the Black Knight and won." She kissed me. "Then we'll meet you at six-thirty for dinner."

Herb and Phyllis, Rene and Morris. How long had we been married?

"Veronica, my parents don't do well in second position. I'll take a quick run, shower, and at least have coffee with them this morning."

"Honey, no. I explained to them last night that wouldn't happen, particularly with the set problems. They're fine. They really are. Now skip the run and take your bath."

"I am not taking a bath. I am not a bath guy. I will take your advice though and not try to fit too much in this morning. I'll see you at six-thirty." I kissed her long and sweet. She smelled and tasted delicious. I must have smelled like smoke, dust, and burnt coffee. She didn't seem to mind. She kissed me again. I realized it didn't bother me at all that she was stage-managing my life and my parents. "See you later, baby. I gotta run."

I burst out into the compound and found my second wind as I began a leisurely run toward the beach. The weather was perfect, the sky as blue as Veronica's eyes, the sun warm, the air crisp and bright without a touch of humidity. It was a gift to my family from the meteorological gods. Postcard vistas, centerfold girlfriend, busy, productive son. A trifecta for my folks. As I ran along the ocean I smiled, thinking that perhaps twenty-one wasn't so young and that early August in Plymouth, Massachusetts, was a perfect time to embrace the glories of youth.

It turned out to be a blessing that I had not scheduled breakfast with my parents. Jojo had come down personally to find me by the shore. Despite the hydraulics solution, we had other problems that needed remedy. We had actor problems. In fact, the whole production of *Company* had careened off its path and was headed down the bumpy road to oblivion. For the first time this summer, there was a sense of doubt in my collaborators' eyes, and it showed in the carriage and confidence of both Ellie and Elliot.

Jojo called a production meeting so we could identify the problems and make some plan to find solutions. We only had so many hours to work before Monday's opening. I decided we'd dry tech the show with stand-ins. This meant the actors would not be part of setting technical cues. We would use kids, locals, or visiting parents to stand in the places that needed to be lit. We'd mark the spots with glow tape and pray the actors found them when we had a chance to run the show.

We'd do the same thing with sound cues. We chose Secunda to sing all the songs and set all music levels off his voice. Elliot was to rehearse Fitzgerald alone on her number, and she'd sing it with the orchestra for the first time at the dress or first performance if we ran out of time. Finally, Ellie would work in the parking lot—not a great place to stage the act 2 opening—and use a tape as her musical support.

No one would be allowed to show doubt or concern around the actors. The spin on our circumstances would remain positive and confident. This was part of growing as a performer. It should be fun to learn to swim in deep, shark-infested waters against a riptide that could sweep you out to sea and drown you like a rat in the black, icy ocean.

I wanted to place a pistol against my temple. This promised to be a train wreck.

I had one final thought before we began our individual rehearsals. As time allowed, we would rehearse the opening until it was perfect, then the close of act 1 until polished and sure. Then we would grab hold of the act 2 opening, and last the finale. If that's all we could manage, then at least we might fool 'em all with a good start and better finish.

We broke the huddle and went to work. I felt a bit like the guys at the Alamo, or Butch Cassidy and the Sundance Kid, or even Bonnie and Clyde. None of them had a chance in hell of getting out alive. Unfortunately, neither did we.

We took no breaks. We had snacks and lunch brought in while we rehearsed. We rehearsed scenes in and out of light as cues were set and reset throughout the day. Actors worked their scenes as the costume department dressed and undressed them, refitted the clothes, and redressed them again. We didn't have time to stop and do anything with a proper or singular focus. However, as the day wore on, progress was evident.

Ellie got the opening set for act 2, polished the first number in the show, and revisited earlier teachings. The actors ran lines and found little bits of business on their own, while the tech aspects of the show swirled around them and slowly coalesced. The company voted against a dinner break and worked straight through. They were wonderful, committed professionals, and we fed off each other's energy. We talked through scenes because we didn't have time to run them, and you could see the focus and concentration on all the faces as they locked in their beats, their blocking, and their dance steps.

When we finally stopped to breathe and send everyone to bed for rest, it was past midnight. I was sure no one would sleep soon; they'd retrace the day and commit it even deeper to memory. Rehearsals were to begin again at eight. Although it was a glorious, inspiring fifteen hours of work, we had yet to run anything in sequence.

I knew I had missed my dinner with Mom and Dad. I had asked JB to call the White Cliffs and explain. What were my options? A surgeon doesn't leave the patient on the OR table before finishing and sewing him up. I returned to my room, showered, put on a pair of boxers and climbed into bed. Veronica was nowhere to be found and had left no message for me in the office. I was too tired to figure out where she might be, but was positive she was taking care of her summer-in-laws. I'd find out in the morning. I rested my head on the pillow and thought, *God bless the blonde.* A heartbeat later I was asleep.

I awoke at 7 a.m. with Veronica lying next to me in bed. I had been so sound asleep I hadn't noticed she was home. As I threw on my clothes and washed up, she briefed me on yesterday's events. The day had gone swimmingly. It was a lovefest with both my father and uncle, who told her if I didn't marry her, they would. They had stayed at the White Cliffs until early morning dancing, dining, and getting the VIP treatment from everyone who crossed their path.

They all understood I had to work, but pleaded with her to make sure we could visit tonight before curtain. My dad also wanted me to know that his boss, Bill Hockman, and his wife were driving up from New York to see the show. I found that news both surprising and disconcerting. Hockman was a douche. Veronica couldn't stress how important she thought it was that I see my parents that evening. She said my uncle was a dear and my dad a gentleman, and that she figured both my mother and aunt had hollow legs, for it was the only place they could have put all that alcohol.

I kissed her. Thanked her. Told her I missed her face and headed for work.

8 6

Monday was a replica of Sunday. We pecked away at problems, and the musical began to take shape. It found some rhythm, but as of four o'clock we had still not begun a full run-through in costume and makeup, with sound and lights and all our fancy scenery moving in and out. Fitzgerald had still not sung her number for anybody but Elliot in a rehearsal, as each time we got to that moment we said, "And then Kat sings. Now let's move on." I gave the company a much needed thirty-minute break. You can only run so fast or so far before you collapse in a heap. They all needed to breathe.

I sat in the theater. Alone. I had insisted all work stop and even the tech crew step outside and remember there were trees and blue sky in our lives. I waved away anyone who offered to bring me food or drink and I wasn't interested in discussing options. The break ended promptly at 4:30 p.m. The company waited for instructions.

"I want the crew out here in the house with me. I want to run the opening all out, and I want the crew to watch. No scene changes and no costumes. Jojo, I don't want you calling any cues. Elliot, have the orchestra play like a motherfucker." I paused and took in everyone's gaze one set of eyes at a time, then added, "I want everyone to have fun. You guys on the crew don't get to see the shows from the house often, so enjoy. Christmas in August here at PBT."

So they ran the opening. "Again," I said. "This time have fun."

They ran the opening again. It was fun.

"Okay, good," I said. "Jojo, I want to run the number again, this time with just Elliot on the piano. I want the actors and the band in the house, and I want all the scenery to move and the light cues given and the dressers to step out on stage and show us the changes they make throughout. I want you to call the cues on the god mic so everyone can hear them. I want everyone in the house to pay attention. *Close* attention."

They all did what I asked. "Again," I said.

They did it all again. However, this time the faces of the actors and musicians creased with a revelation, an epiphany that they were all part of something bigger than what they each did on the show. They realized that if you took any of the cards off the table the whole thing would tumble.

"Okay, good," I said. "One last thing. Elliot, could you have the orchestra play the exit music. I would like everyone else to just listen. Doctor, please have your guys play their tits off."

They did.

"Okay," I said. "Now, Jojo, set places. We are now going to run it for real. All in, see what we have."

We did, and what we had was really good. The first eight minutes of our show were fucking great. What followed was the unknown, a potential belly flop into nowhere. Wearing my nerves out loud was not the way to lead. I swallowed the bile building inside my stomach.

"Okay," I said. "Zach, will you mind standing center and singing 'Being

Alive,' and would the rest of the company stand out here with me and listen?"

He was fantastic, and I thought, *When you have Gossage to close out the game you usually win it.*

I asked Fitzgerald to do the same with her number, her first time with the orchestra or in front of anybody but Elliot and me in rehearsals. She was tentative. I wished I had stopped with Zach. I needed to draw another ace, but I came up empty. With no other options, I moved on.

"Jojo, is there anything we need to run for safety? Are there any scene changes where someone might get hurt?" She told me there were two, so we ran them each three times. It was almost six-fifteen.

"Jojo, can you have everyone in the company, the crew, and the pit on stage, please? Everyone. No one works. We are all going to talk, if only for a few minutes."

The entire population of PBT found their way to the stage.

Jojo offered me the god mic but it was unnecessary. What I was about to say didn't need any artificial amplification; I knew everyone was going to listen even if I spoke in a whisper.

"Hi guys," I said. "You are all amazing people. You have so much courage. I'm certain if I opened you up I'd find the hearts of lions and the souls of angels. I know many of us came here this summer to experience the work and take on challenges we hadn't faced before. I also know that ASK came to spend time with Janet, and look how that's working out!"

ASK blushed and accepted mock congratulations from his friends. Janet leaned him over her thigh and kissed him on the mouth for at least a full minute then dropped him on the stage floor like a rag doll.

"You see? Miracles do happen. When ASK regains consciousness, you can ask him. We have what we have and what we have is pretty great. I just had you see it for yourselves. But I'd be lying if I said everything else in this show is that ready, that good. So we all stand here, in this moment and wonder . . . and, well, unfortunately we won't have our answer till the band plays the exit music a few hours from now. But that's cool. In fact, I find it all a bit titillating. But then again, I find most things titillating."

I took the measure of the others in this foxhole with me. They looked good, even happy. I continued. "So this is what we're going to do. We're going to remind ourselves that Namath beat the Colts, and that the Mets won the World Series, and that Willis Reed hit those first two shots on one leg and the Knicks beat the Lakers. We're going to think about all the stories we've heard about people coming from out of nowhere and winning the race, getting the job, or saving a life. We're going to play the game, the whole game, all out till the whistle blows. The best news for us is that we can. We're here and we can.

"Hundreds of people would change places with any one of us in a heartbeat, but none of you would let them. The people coming here tonight don't know we ran out of time and never ran the show. The only people who have that information are you. I don't think you should tell anyone, and furthermore I don't think they will ever know. You guys are like a newborn baby. Everybody wants to kiss you because you are so fucking cute. Don't show any fear."

Jojo raised her hand. "We have no curtain call. What are we doing for bows?"

"In a minute," I said. "Two things first. First, when we break, I don't want any of you to think about the show. Take a nap. Take a run or a swim. Have sex. But don't think. Eight o'clock will be here fast enough and you can reenter this orbit in a half hour.

"Second, some of you are aware of this story and some of you aren't, but I think it's worth quickly sharing. In a previous life I was a jock. I wasn't always a theater geek. In fact, I had a full scholarship to play big-time football, but days before I was supposed to leave for school I was in a really bad car accident and couldn't play ball anymore.

"Some guy had fallen asleep at the wheel and hit my car at more than a hundred miles per hour. My car flipped over and went through the divider. It was hit again by a car going the other way and rolled over several times. One of my friends in the car was thrown hundreds of feet from impact, but when the car finally settled it had somehow landed on top of her legs. I was knocked unconscious, but when I woke up I heard her screaming. I was fucked up myself. I had split my head open and was stuck in the windshield bleeding from cuts that took hundreds of stitches to close. I heard her shouting, and somehow I got to where she was, and in one motion, with the one arm that still worked, I picked that car up off of her and tossed it away like Superman."

It was a good story and it was true.

"Then I passed out, of course, and woke up in the hospital. The human mind and body can will us to do practically anything. Adrenaline is a wonderful elixir and a cure-all for when we have no idea what to do next. Tonight, use it. Trust yourselves. Flip that car over. And when the bows are finished, then and only then can you pass out at the hospital. Okay?"

Gravely, everyone tentatively nodded their assent.

"Good. Now, as to the bows, we don't have time to stage them, so this is what we're going to do . . ."

87

I washed up in the scene shop sink and headed outside to meet my parents. I found my father alone, seated on the white bench under the dogwood tree. He was doing that thing where he rubbed his forehead with the middle and index fingers of his right hand. When he did that;, it always meant he was agitated. His expression confirmed it.

"Dad, are you all right?" I asked.

"Yeah, yes, I'm fine," he replied.

"Where's Mom, Aunt Rene, and Uncle Morris?"

"They took the Hockmans out for supper. No one was sure you'd be available and they needed to eat."

"Of course, I understand. It's been quite a day for me. We have time for a beer if you'd like."

"A beer? You were supposed to have dinner with my employer. You know, I just took this position a few months ago."

"You took a job, Dad. It's a job."

"Samuel, we all drove up to see you and you've been too busy to see us."

I always knew when he called me Samuel that the conversation was heading down a dark road. "I was doing my *job,* Dad. I was handling the responsibilities of my *position.*"

"Don't be glib with me."

"I'm sorry. And I'm sorry for not being available. Veronica told me you were all having fun and I shouldn't worry."

"Missing time with your mother and me is one thing. And you have no time? None whatsoever? How would you feel if the situation was reversed?"

"I would like to believe I would understand. You always told me to be busy. 'Go kill the people.' Am I supposed to do that on Bill Hockman's schedule? I didn't know I was working for him as well."

"That's enough. This whole thing is embarrassing for me."

"What whole thing? What are you talking about? You're this upset because I'm busy, because I'm behind schedule. What's that about?"

He did the thing with his fingers on his forehead and then got up from the bench and walked a few steps toward the beach. When he turned around he practically ran at me.

"It's not about being busy or behind schedule. Your mother and I talked you up and this show tonight is going to be a disaster. How could you let that happen?"

I got up as well and went right at it with Dad. He was a large man but I was four inches taller, and due to the slight grade where I stood, I appeared to tower over him. "You think my show is going to be a disaster? How do you know? You been working it, Dad? Been in rehearsal giving notes . . . ?"

"Samuel, you haven't even had a run-through. That's what your girlfriend told us. Bill was very upset that he drove all this way to see what is really just a rehearsal."

"Hey, fuck Bill Hockman. I think he's a dirtbag, and I don't like the way he treats you anyway. Also, my girlfriend has a name. It is Veronica and she has been nothing but nice to you."

Maybe this would just end somehow, the lights would go out or someone would streak naked across the compound.

"Bill's limo drove him up here," I added. "I remember you telling me he doesn't drive himself anywhere since he got so fucking rich."

"I can't let him see something that's bad. It will be embarrassing for both me and your mother. How can I explain it?"

I couldn't believe what I was hearing. "Explain it? You think you have to explain me? Hey, am I only worth showing off or showing up for if I'm

299

winning? You thought the show was pretty good the other night, didn't you? Why don't you and Mom come back when the reviews come in? This way if they're bad you can just stay home."

"We have a lot invested in you this summer. It's unreasonable for you to be so defensive."

"I'm not defensive, I'm angry. What do you have invested? Money? Time. Some fatherly advice? You bought us a hat? Send me the bill. You think I'm not worried about tonight? I'm a goddamn mess. I haven't slept in three days. Veronica—my girlfriend—told me that Rene and Mom were making the bars rich in town last night. Maybe they'll just pass out during the overture and when they wake up we'll tell them what a good time they had."

"Listen, Sam, you want to play in a big casino like this one, then you have to deliver or face the music. You can't have important people come and see shit."

"Whoa. What important people? Bill Hockman? He's important? Not to me he's not. To me he's just a big fat Jewish slob who makes the world anti-Semitic. And don't give me platitudes about casinos and shit. How much does a chip cost up here? What's the ante to play in my life? If you only wanted to see me win, then read the box score before you buy a ticket. Oh, and by the way, your tickets were comped. You're embarrassed? Well, I'm ashamed. You tell me what you'd rather be."

Maybe it was the surprise of the whole confrontation, or my fatigue, or genuine shock that my dad was actually saying these things to me. Whatever the cause, my eyes welled with tears and my lip started to tremble. I began to cry, slowly at first, and then with big sobs that made my shoulders heave and snot run down my nose. I walked quickly behind the theater to the north side and out of sight from the patrons and the entire compound. I cried for a few minutes and then began to compose myself. I wiped my nose on the sleeve of my T-shirt and rubbed my eyes until they were dry.

Rather than return to speak with my dad, I looked down at my clipboard and the dozens of notes I had yet to address. It made me feel worse, and I felt like I needed to punch something or hurt myself. I stared at what until an hour ago had been important insights and I did so for a long while. Now they meant nothing, a big blur like an eye chart held too far away.

I stood for a moment, motionless. I thought about smashing my face against the elm a few feet from where I stood, but I didn't want to hurt the tree. At last, I ran around the side of the building and saw my father drive away.

I went to the box office and told Diana that if the seats in my parents' name weren't picked up by curtain she should sell them to the first people on the waiting list. Then I walked slowly toward the elm. It seemed the right thing to do.

88

I went to my room and changed into more presentable clothes. I told Veronica what had happened, and although she had no suggestions, it was nice to have a sympathetic listener. I checked the box office at 8:15 p.m. Even before I asked, Diana told me my folks had picked up their reservation for six tickets and paid cash; Debbie had seated them in the third row. I peeked in the house and was relieved to see them reading their programs. I felt less anxious.

Veronica and I went to the balcony and stood against the side wall. We could see the stage and much of the audience, so we had the option of watching the crowd or the performance itself. There was a pleasant animated opening night buzz in the house. This was our fourth and penultimate debut. We were like a team on the way to a pennant. We were a hot ticket, and the disparity in audience anticipation between our first opening and now was a real compliment to our hard work.

I was really just a stupid kid. I was trying my best to do something of note, and it had gone well so far. But eventually people booed everyone, even Joe DiMaggio. Skills eroded or expectations failed to be met, the tide turned, and you found yourself swimming against the current. Would we pull a rabbit out of the hat tonight or would the pep talks end up as just talk and nothing more?

Every seat was taken and we had standees downstairs. The house lights went to half and then to black. The show started, and I held my breath. As had happened that afternoon, the first eight minutes dazzled and won the house over like Ann Margaret and Jayne Mansfield visiting the troops in Vietnam. I exhaled and took another long breath, held it to see what would happen next.

Buoyed by the success of the opening, the cast plowed ahead with a fragile confidence. They got early laughs and found their light. The scenery moved and the show played, spinning out like a novel in galley form. There were errors and typos, but the story worked and the author was forgiven. We dropped lines and took errant crosses that made the staging seem skewed. Nevertheless, everything was played with such joy and panache, and a challenge to those watching that said, "Find a reason not to like us, we dare you."

Act 1 flew by. The songs were performed with more verve than the scenes, but as each page turned the company knew they were pulling it off. They gathered momentum and the audience simply ate them up. No one seemed to notice the errors in blocking or the scenery that arrived a beat too late. Some sang sharp or came in on the wrong count, and lyrics were reinvented when someone's mind went blank. It mattered not. We had climbed a mountain, afraid to look down along the way for fear of falling hundreds of feet to our death. As the first act ended, though, we were in the lodge at the top of the hill drinking hot cocoa laced with expensive brandy. Veronica held my hand so tightly through the first sixty minutes that when the curtain came down and she let go, my fingers were numb.

We still had act 2 to play, and there were mines waiting to explode on every line, lyric, or light cue. I stayed hidden out of sight in the balcony throughout the intermission. I stood in the shadows and gripped Veronica's hand till both our circulations stopped.

Act 2 started with a long drive into the rough and a triple bogey. The adrenaline that had carried the first half of the show had waned like a tequila buzz that needed one more shot. Then Fitzgerald sang her song, "Ladies Who Lunch," and this time she found her legs and threw a spiral that landed in someone's outstretched hands for a breathtaking touchdown. Then Rush sang his song, "Being Alive," and there was not much left to say. When you are breathless it is hard to be cogent.

The remaining land mine was the bows, since we had only talked them through, never once rehearsing them. The idea we had discussed was for all the couples in the show who loved the Rush character, as well as the single women in his life, to walk center and say goodbye to him, since he was ready to move on from his shallow and superficial life. I had given each couple and each girlfriend an entrance number to follow to say farewell. We had not timed it to the bow music or had any idea whether it would work.

Well, it did.

The emotion of our day, the fear of failure that weighed heavy on all, found a release in the simple fact that we got through to the end. And the audience was moved and affected and our job was done. It all boiled over as the characters said goodbye to one another and executed a curtain call that in reality had taken the story past the real ending of the script. It was our promise of a better future for the fictional Rush character that we had all spent the last two hours getting to know.

The cast cried as they played out this improvisation. Their emotions ran high, crossing the footlights and entering the consciousness of all in attendance. It was a transference whereby the people in the house imagined, or remembered, a time when they lost someone and life moved in another direction. It was melancholy, and it was moving, and people cried real tears. We had caught lightning in a bottle.

I stood in the balcony, still holding Veronica's hand, and cried for the second time that night. This time the tears were sweet, like melted rock candy. We took the stairs off the balcony and headed into the compound.

Before we left the building, I noticed Ellie Foster dancing playfully with a stranger down near the front of the house. She moved gracefully, almost intimately, with an older gentlemen dressed in crisp jeans, white sneakers, and a yellow, flowery Hawaiian shirt. *Oh no*, I thought, *has she moved on from a good start with Gary to the sordidness of liaisons with men way beyond her age?* And then I realized what was happening. My incredible night had just got better, and my heart danced along with Ellie and her mystery partner—who turned out to be her father, sans his red power tie and aura of discontent. He had his arm around his daughter, joy in his step, and adoration in his eyes for his beautiful little girl.

For so many reasons a celebration was about to take flight outside, and although I had no desire to be the pilot, I certainly wanted a seat on the plane.

89

The great Broadway producer-director George Abbott opened his hit musical *Damn Yankees* on May 5, 1955. The following morning, the reviews hailed it as the Great White Way's next musical sensation. The opening-night party was filled with the joy that rave notices bring, yet it also included a rehearsal call for the next morning at ten sharp. Mr. Abbott felt that although it was a big hit, the show still needed some work.

On Planet PBT *Company* was a smash, but I didn't call a rehearsal the next day. Instead I gave everyone the day off except for notes that were set for six that evening. Last night we had all dodged a bullet. For all practical purposes, though, no one knew it but us. The audience hadn't noticed the mistakes, which was a blessing. On the other side of the pendulum, I learned they often didn't realize when there was magic either. They embraced it all. They came for a good time and we delivered on their needs. They set their bar far below the one we were using to judge our personal accomplishments.

Within that lesson was a profound disappointment for an idealistic young man with artistic aspirations. The next time I was in trouble, the next time the scenery was a clusterfuck, or fatigue had set in, would I work as hard as I had the past few days? Or, with this new life lesson, would I simply say, "Fuck it, it's good enough. No one will know the difference anyway." How sad that would be?

Bill Hockman threw his big, fat, sweaty arm across my shoulder, stuck his big, coarse face in mine, and shouted in his big New York accent, "What a night, my boy! What a show! Now we know who has the real smarts in the August family. Right, Herb? Right Phil?" Then he laughed so loud it made the birds fly away and the waves reverse direction and head back to England. Who did he think he was, Woody Fucking Allen?

I wanted to say, "Fuck you, you fucking fuck. Why don't you take your big, stupid face back to New York and continue to make people dislike Jews?" But I didn't. Instead I said, "Thank you, Mr. Hockman, Mrs. Hockman. I am so glad you enjoyed the show. I know it was a long trip and I appreciate the effort you made in coming."

"It was our pleasure, my boy. See you on Broadway." He smacked me on the back, but before walking into the crowd to find some other schmuck to bore, he barked a crisp order at my dad. "Come on, Herb, introduce us to some of these kids." And then he was gone. The stars reappeared in the night sky and the man in the moon smiled.

I spent a few awkward moments with my family and made plans to meet for a nice brunch the next morning. I made the perfunctory rounds and then bowed out and went to sleep.

Sometimes you eat surf and turf, other times it's franks and beans. They're both good, just different.

90

I arrived early for the breakfast with my family. I had come alone, thinking and feeling that I needed to see Mom and Dad without distraction. My mother had gotten some sun while in town, and she looked flush and healthy. My father had abandoned the rubbing of his forehead and replaced it with a big, open smile. They told me my aunt and uncle would be joining us shortly.

Then, as it had been for as long as I can recall, we didn't talk about the ugliness of yesterday evening. It sat on my chest like the proverbial six-hundred-pound gorilla. Better to pretend you're not sick and die than to deal with pain of getting well. So we danced and we vamped until we became five instead of three. I told anecdotes of my summer's adventures and they told me how terrific the show had been last evening, how proud they were, and how much they'd enjoyed meeting Veronica. We'd had these conversations before. The shows had different titles, the girls had different names, and sometimes the score hadn't always come out in my favor.

I had so much cause to love my parents, and if for no other reason than they were my parents. Recent experiences were going to change our relationship. To grow up, I needed to grow apart for a while: to truly stand on my own, to listen to my heart, to set boundaries. Then, at some point in the very near future, we could become close again, perhaps closer.

As we sat and talked, I felt happy. Our familial love was sort of like a ride on the bumper cars. It was electric and silly. Sometimes it was an open ride with the wind in your face; other times it was a head-on crash with whiplash.

Shortly after one o'clock, I walked them all to their cars to say goodbye. Just before my dad put the car in gear, he grabbed me behind the neck and pulled me close. He hadn't shaved that morning, and his face was scratchy with whiskers. He whispered in my ear with power and fervor, "I would be proud of you if you walked on that stage last night and belly flopped. I was wrong to speak to you the way I did. You're my boy. Sometimes even unconditional love isn't enough. I love you, my son." He pushed me away so he could look me in the eye. His gaze was strong, his eyes filled with passion. "Hey, Sammy. Kill the people."

He drove onto Route 3 south, heading home. It had been nice to hear his apology, and of course I would honor it. But as I climbed into my car, I had a couple of thoughts. Why did he have to whisper? And more important, why did I have to kill anybody? Why wasn't trying my best all day, every day simply enough?

9 1

Five shows in ten weeks. Four down and one to go. We were entering the final turn at a full gallop toward the roses. The atmosphere had changed with our schedule, the weather and the wind. *Company* was the last big show of the summer. We were closing the season with *The Fantasticks*, a piece with a small cast of characters, lesser musical needs, and a spare, simple set.

There was less to build in both shops, and we had scores of actors who no longer needed to rehearse throughout the day. Those not in the last show lived the lives of film stars. They slept in late, strolled along the beach, and swam in the warm, crystal-clear August waters. They took day trips to local sites or, when asked, assisted Kasen or Mary, who now had more workers at their disposal than the Triangle Shirtwaist Factory. The land mines appeared to have all been swept away. The icebergs had melted and it was smooth sailing into port and home.

I had some free time for the first time since my meeting with Barrows in early May. I spent it wisely, mostly with Veronica, simply being two young people in something that was more than "a boy just passing through." I also spent time with my close friends ASK, Elliot, James, and Secunda. The first three had places to go after Labor Day, and Secunda would find a way to fill his days and help build the GNP. We even arranged an afternoon of hooky by giving a rehearsal to Jojo and attending a day game at Fenway. But by the fourth inning, with the Sox hammering the As, we wanted to head back home, all of us suffering severe separation anxiety from the daily tasks that had consumed us these past weeks.

The following Friday, on the evening of our penultimate performance of *Company*, I returned from a long run on the beach. The past few days had morphed gracefully into late summer, bringing with them a hint of its end. You could stumble on crimson-red or pumpkin-orange leaves, putting us all on notice that the long, lingering days, the best of the season, were no longer plentiful, that fall was just hours away. The air held a different scent off the water; the energy of dusk less active, now infused with calm.

I had taken to running barefoot in the wet sand, and as I did my steps would churn up mud against my chest, to the back of my thighs and up onto my neck and face. Until I had time to shower and change, I looked like a young boy who had endured a friendly mud fight with his pals. When I reached the compound I found a little red Mercedes parked and still, front and center. My stomach flipped. I had no need or desire to speak with Lizzy Barrows, especially not when I was covered in sand, mud, and sweat.

She called out to me before I had a chance to disappear. "Mr. August, hello. You'll be happy to know I just bought every seat you had available for the final performance." If this had been my first exchange with this woman, it would have been lovely. However, what she had proffered in the past kept the butterflies darting inside my belly.

"That's lovely, Mrs. Barrows. Will you be having actual people sitting in those seats, or will you be using them to store your sweater and handbag?"

"Sam, that's not very nice. I've been back many times since that night. Can't we forget all this bad stuff? Leave it behind us?" She actually seemed to mean it.

"There is no *we*, Mrs. Barrows. And, no, I can't forget. What you did was wrong. The game your husband tried to play with me and his threat to my friends was also wrong and I have no reason to forgive you."

She stared at me as if I had slapped her. Clearly she didn't hear a lot of "no" on the Barrows estate. "But it all worked out. I've made a lot of friends here. Andy has stayed away. Even he wants to make amends, maybe talk to the press and say good things. Please, can't you and I be friends as well?"

"No," I said. "Just because you drive drunk and get home without killing someone doesn't mean it's an okay thing to do. And just because someone evil says they are not doesn't make it so. No, we aren't friends."

"You've let Gary in. Why not me?"

"You've both been living in shit, doing bad things. I guess I think he's trying to climb out while you're still stirring the pot."

"You don't know that. You don't know about a lot of things in this town . . ."

"I know what I need to know."

"No second chances?"

"Always. Just not for everyone, Mrs. Barrows."

"Sam, why did you sign the note 'Spartacus'? Who was he"?

"Come on, Lizzy, you don't know who Spartacus was? You never saw the movie with Kirk Douglas?"

"No, I was out whoring around," she said with self-effacing irony. I offered no protestation on her personal assessment. I imagined it was true. "Tell me who he was."

I considered whether I should spend the time. It's always better to be kind, particularly when you're winning. So I told her. "Spartacus was a Roman slave, a gladiator. He led a slave army of misfits against the Roman Empire in the Third Servile War. He fought against oppression, privilege, the aristocracy. He was crucified by the legions of Rome."

"That's sad." She looked confused, as if I were speaking a foreign language.

"After the Romans captured his forces, they told the slave army that if Spartacus was identified he would be the only prisoner crucified. Rather than betray their leader, each of the five thousand members of his army stood up and proclaimed, 'I am Spartacus.'"

She had been listening with interest until the last part, when her expression turned sour and dismissive. "That's arrogant," she said. "That's why you signed the note 'Spartacus'?"

"No, I signed it that way because Kirk Douglas and I are the same person. Never seen us in the same place at the same time, have you? Enjoy the rest of your summer, Mrs. Barrows, and give my best to 'Andy.'" I turned and headed toward the house.

"Sam, come by tonight. Anderson's away. We'll have some fun . . ."

I kept walking, opened the door and entered my room. From the window I watched Lizzy Barrows climb into her fancy, red sports car all coiffed, buffed, and so terribly gorgeous. Yet so desperately sad.

"People often get lost on the way to anywhere, let alone to a rendezvous that will change their lives," Lizzy had told me over drinks that first night at the Full Sail. I knew there were many songs that mirrored her life but at that moment, I couldn't think of a single lyric.

I walked into the bathroom to shower and checked myself in the mirror.

I didn't look anything like Kirk Douglas. I was taller, and he had that hole in his chin. I climbed into the tub, turned the water on, and washed off the mud.

9 2

I watched the performance that night. *Company* was my favorite of all, brimming with originality and a great score. Our version had matured into something of substance. True, it had its share of pretensions inspired by youth. At our tender ages, we really didn't understand nor had we lived through the issues that drove the older characters in the play. Nevertheless, we did a fine job. We played it with tremendous commitment; as a result the show provided entertainment and emotional catharsis.

As important, Zach Rush was simply fantastic in the lead role. He was the personification of a leading man: tall, handsome, intelligent, graceful, alert, and generous. And Zach could sing. He made every song his; he owned the lyrics. As I watched him that night, I felt that even after I had grown old and seen dozens of productions of this show, no one would have played the lead as well as Zach.

After the performance, I stood on the deck outside the theater and watched the crowd walk to their cars. I enjoyed doing this. It was tactile. People had come to our house, plunked down their money, and left with a good feeling. There was quality in our product, the best of the American Dream, a cherry on top of the nation's birthday cake.

Jojo approached me. "Sammy, Rush needs to speak with you. He's in his dressing room."

"Okay, Jojo. Thanks." I headed his way without a second thought.

As a lead player, Zach had a private dressing room. It was small but it was his. He had decorated it with mementos of his summer: photos, telegrams, letters from fans, invites from numerous women who had come to see him. Taped to his mirror was a picture of his girlfriend, Paula, a rare equal to Zach in both beauty and grace. On the opposite wall he had posted all his reviews as well as the interview he had done for the *Boston Globe*. That particular piece was framed in expensive dark wood.

The door was open and Rush invited me in. He looked tired and much older than when we had first met in the basement of Tufts University. Zach had carried the season and made it special. His hard work and professionalism had raised the bar for everyone at PBT. He had made us more than a group of kids leaving college behind, and because of him we were better than most.

He asked me to sit. Turning away, he looked into his dressing-table mirror for a long time without saying a word. He had called this meeting; he would speak when he was ready. It began to feel like a really long time to sit in silence; worry crept into my chest.

And then finally, "Sam, I don't know how to say this to you . . . I've been trying to figure a way . . ." He continued to stare into the mirror, speaking to my reflection as if he were hoping I wasn't really present. "I'm leaving tonight. I have to. I love it here. I love you and Secunda, Jojo, Trudy, but I have to leave . . ."

As his words faded out I felt my breath disappear. This was a kick in the groin, a punch to the solar plexus. I looked at my reflection in Zach's mirror and saw the color drain from my face. "Why?" was all I could find to say.

"I got a job."

"You *have* a job."

"This is a union job. I get my equity card. It's what I always wanted."

"You *have* a job."

Zach continued to talk to my reflection. I heard footsteps descending the stairs, and in a moment Secunda appeared at the door, happy and chomping on one of his stinky cigars.

"What's up?" he said, clearly unaware of the situation.

Zach moved his gaze from the mirror to look directly at Secunda. "I have to leave, I'm sorry."

"Zach has another job," I said in a monotone. as if repeating the news a thousand times would make it go away. "He's leaving us to get his union card. It's what he's always wanted."

"When?" asked Secunda.

"In the morning, at six," Zach said. "They're picking me up."

Secunda was immediately in his face. "Who? Who is picking you up, Zach? Are they going to stay long enough to finish fucking us before they take you away?" A switch had been flipped and he was out of control.

Zach sat motionless and let Secunda scream at him. His face flushed bright red. Finally, when Secunda was finished berating him, Zach said, "I have to think about my career, Josh. I came here to start a career. To get seen, to find an agent. This is a Broadway tour with a big star. They're offering me a lot of money. I have to do what's right for me."

"There's only one way to do the right thing, Zach, and that's to do the right thing," I said. "Can't they wait till you're done here?"

Before he could answer, Secunda jumped back in. "I'll . . . we'll . . . pay you ten grand to finish here. They can't be paying you more than ten grand."

"We are not paying Zach ten thousand dollars to finish the job, Josh," I said, now on the edge of fury myself. "We're not doing that. We're not paying Zach-fucking-Rush ten thousand fucking dollars."

Secunda got in my face. "What are we going to do, Sammy? We blow up here if he leaves. Do we cancel the show tomorrow? Close early?" He turned to Zach and pulled back from rant to request. "Zach, will you stay if we pay you the ten grand?"

"It's not about the money, I want to get in the union. This is a big chance for me." Zach seemed to whine as he offered this bullshit defense.

"Josh, we are not paying him to stay," I repeated.

"Then *I'll* pay it to him. I'll find the money."

I leaned toward Zach. "No one will pay you, Zach. You are staying and finishing this job. You are staying and finishing this job. You are staying and . . ." I tried to be firm without a show of anger, but it all began to get the better of me. "You know, Zach, when we gave you this job you told *us* it was a big chance for you. Remember that? Now you found a prettier girl, so you're gonna run off and leave us at the altar? No fucking way."

I wasn't shouting, but there was menace in my tone. The room was airless, a small underground box without windows. You could hear our brains working overtime to find a way. Our hearts beat out loud.

"I can't turn down the money," Zach said after what seemed like minutes. "I can't."

"I'll pay you the money!" Secunda shouted. "Now stop it!"

"You said it wasn't about the money and now it seems that it is," I said. "Is this a holdup? You think this is the last union job you're ever going to be offered? You'll walk into an audition in two weeks and get another job, and then another. You're too good."

"Sammy, its only money." Secunda said. "Its only ten grand."

"Shut up, Josh," I shouted. "I will not let you give Zach any money. He made a deal with us and with everyone upstairs and with everyone who bought tickets to see him in the next show. What about *my* money, Zach? What about the money I lose if you walk? Don't I matter in this equation? You think there are no consequences other than a little guilt? Not so. I'll be there at six tomorrow when they come to pick you up. I'll tell their company manager that you walked out of your contract with us. Maybe it will happen with them as well. I'll run into you down the road. Do the right thing, Zach. Please, for both of us."

He said nothing. He eyes roamed the room, looking at his clippings and invites and telegrams.

Secunda leaned in close to me and said in a harsh, angry whisper. "I'm going to give him the cash. This has all been too good for it to blow up. I can't look people in the face if it blows up. I'll be ashamed. It's only money."

"Zach should be ashamed, Josh. Zach *will* be ashamed! I'll be ashamed if you pay him. Ten thousand dollars is more money than I ever had. My father didn't make ten thousand dollars last fucking year. If he leaves, we figure it out. You can't buy everything." I wasn't shouting but I was close.

"Fuck you, Sammy. I have the money. You see?" He reached into his pocket and pulled out a wad of bills, waving them in my face. Then he turned to Zach. "I have the money!" He took a match from the dressing room table and struck it on the wall. The flame billowed; he lit a C-note with it and used it to fire up his cigar. He was manic.

On his second or third puff, I reached back and clocked Secunda on the side of the head. He lost his balance and stumbled against the wall. He knocked the framed *Boston Globe* interview off its hook and it fell to the floor, smashing into dozens of pieces. He managed to remain standing, but he was stunned and silent. Zach was caught in a hurricane; things were out of control and he could no longer close the door for protection.

I looked around the room. It was broken. It smelled of cigars and fear. "I'll see you both at rehearsal tomorrow," I said. "Do the right thing, boys. Our decisions are the only part of us we can really control."

I walked up the backstage steps and across the stage. I was meeting Veronica at the wharf. It was her father's birthday and I had been invited for cake.

93

I met Veronica and her parents at the piano bar of the Carver Inn. The place was the finest Plymouth had to offer. The hotel sat atop the knoll in all its colonial majesty and peered out into the bay. It had been built decades ago, and as I walked though the paneled hallway I could hear the ghosts of America's past. It was the Ritz for Pilgrims.

I found the Chapmans at a small, round table by the big bay windows in the rear of the bar. They were open to the night and a gentle breeze caressed the room. I greeted Julia, Tom Sr., and Veronica's oldest brother, Tommy. We had all seen each other several times since our first meeting. They remained a handsome, grounded family without pretense.

"Sam, it's so good to see you—and away from the theater, my goodness," Julia said as she gave me a hug.

"So, Sam, summer is winding down. How are things?" Tom Sr. queried.

"They're good. They're very good, sir." I gazed at Veronica as I replied because that made my answer true.

Mrs. Chapman served me a piece of birthday cake. Yellow sponge with chocolate fudge icing and pink-and-white roses. My slice came with half a flower. Tommy Jr. filled my glass with champagne and toasted his father on his birthday.

"This cake is really good," I said. "Sir, what did you wish for when you blew out the candles?"

"Easy. I wished for my son to come home soon and that my daughter meet more quality young men like yourself. You've made a big difference in a great many people's lives here. We'll miss you, Sam."

"I don't think you've seen the last of me. I'd like to believe this is all just a beginning."

Mrs. Chapman raised her glass again. "Well then, that certainly is a lovely present, isn't it, Tommy?"

Before he could answer, Veronica rested her head on my shoulder and said, "Yes, Mom, it is wonderful. I feel like not only is it Dad's birthday, but Christmas as well."

The pianist started playing Cy Coleman's "The Best Is Yet to Come" as if on cue. I looked out into the bay. The moon had risen to its highest of heights. It was a beacon, a beam that could guide you home.

94

I thought about setting the alarm to wake me in the early morning. I decided it wasn't necessary; even if I fell asleep I'd awaken before six without assistance. I dressed and walked across the compound to the dining hall. I made myself a large, hot cup of coffee that I laced with gobs of heavy cream and many sugars. There was a slight chill to the morning and the coffee swept it away.

I walked to the redwood table and took a seat. It was twenty minutes to six. I had read that God never gives you more than you can handle. Therefore, I needed to have faith, a belief in God's promises even though they remained unfulfilled. The grounds were quiet. Still. The sky looked like a cyclorama in a big-budget musical. Nightfall turned to dawn, and the blue it brought was almost unearthly. I sipped my coffee and waited.

I heard a door close in the back of the red house, then footsteps approaching. My heart skipped a beat. Then another. Into view walked Secunda. He was dressed down this early morning. T-shirt and sweats. He also wore a big bruise above his left eye. He walked right past me into the dining room without saying a word. Minutes later, he returned with two cups of coffee. One was black, the other the way I liked it. He sat with me at the table. It was five minutes to six.

We said nothing, and it was painful. The silence, the tension, and what seemed like minutes passing were mere seconds on each check of my watch. We continued on. The sun ticked higher, birdsong greeted the morning. In the distance you could hear the waves lapping the shore. It was now twelve minutes after six.

I heard more footsteps from behind the house, and this time my heart stopped. No one appeared, however, and I figured it was one of the girls returning to her room, strolling down the walk of shame.

It approached 6:30. No ride had come for Zach. I wanted to move, to finally speak with Secunda but was afraid. At 6:42 he got up from the table. "I'll be right back," he said and headed toward the red house and the room where Zach Rush slept. In a few minutes he was back.

He sat across from me. "Zach is in his room. He didn't leave. I woke him. He is not going anywhere."

"Why didn't he say something?"

"He said you told him you would see him at rehearsal and it was understood. He told me he thought you would know that."

"Fuck me."

"Okay," said Secunda. There was no rush in this stilted conversation, only relief. "I didn't give him any money."

"I know that."

"How?"

"Because I have faith. And I believe in you."

Secunda looked at me, surprised. I was quiet. "Okay. That's a good thing." I drank some coffee. He did the same.

"Hey, Josh," I said, "how about I buy you breakfast?"

"Only if it's expensive."

"That's just fine. You just can't eat a lot."

We headed into town to share some eggs Benedict, caviar, and toast bathed in high-end English marmalade. As we drove down Rocky Hill Road, it was good to note that I was breathing again.

9 5

The final year of my high school football career featured the most exciting game ever played in the fifteen-year history of our school. It came at mid-season. We were 5–0 and our opponent was a perennial powerhouse we had never beaten. They stood at 6–0 and were ranked number one in the county. We were ranked a close second.

Considering it was the East Coast and not Texas or Oklahoma, the game was a huge deal. The papers hyped it up all week, as did the local radio. The crowd was practically a sell-out, with nearly five thousand fans in attendance. The game began in inclement football weather; it was a raw, late October afternoon. Whenever the sun tried to make an appearance it was parried, engulfed by dark, ominous clouds that turned into a biting, cold rain before the first half ended. Nevertheless, every play was hard fought, and the crowd— made up of classmates, foes, parents, girlfriends, the local media, forty or so college scouts—was involved big time on every play.

The first time we got the ball, we went three and out and had to punt. I performed the long snaps and had hiked the ball to the punter flawlessly the past three years. This time I failed. The ball soared over the head of our kicker, Billy Kensington, and was recovered in the end zone by our opponents. The game was less than ninety seconds old and we were losing by seven. I was devastated and certain I'd seen some of the college scouts leaving the stands. "Fuck me," I said.

Sports, like life, offers you grace, redemption, and a second chance. On the next series, I intercepted a pass in the flat and ran fifty-three yards for a touchdown. The game was tied at seven.

It stayed that way deep into the third quarter. The rain was coming down heavy now, in slants. As players, we eschewed the elements and just beat each other into the ground time and again, getting up slowly from the freezing turf. With just over fifteen minutes left in the contest, we had to punt again from the shadow of our own goal line, and my heart beat loud and long as I prepared for the long snap. The quarterback called the signals and I hiked it to the punter.

"Motherfucker!" I did it again! Never in three years, and now twice in the same game. More scouts left the stadium, and my teammates were probably wondering if someone had paid me off. Our opponent recovered the ball on the two-yard line, just six feet from our end zone and a potentially humiliating defeat.

Our defense huddled in stunned disbelief. I went insane and shouted at them as if I had lost my mind. "I suck. I am shit. I suck. Sorry. Sorry! Sorry! Fuck me! I really suck! We have to stop them. We have to stop them."

And then we did. We actually did!

We stuffed three runs in a row and I made one of the tackles. Then, on fourth down, Pete Laird sacked their quarterback for a nine-yard loss. It was a classic goal-line stand. For all practical purposes, the game was over. True, there were minutes on the clock and the score was still tied, but we knew we had won.

We blew past them after that. The final score was 28–7. For the record, I never screwed up another long snap again, ever.

96

When Zach Rush had done the right thing and decided to stay, it was in essence our goal-line stand. I knew without a single doubt that we were home, that we had won and nothing was going to dare get in our way. The finish line was just steps away and crossing it would lead us all on to one last celebration. I believed that party would be more profound than raucous.

The remaining days were filled with melancholy, laughter, hugs, and tears. The company played all day and gathered each night in the theater or in the wings. They'd grab a small piece of the house, a spare chair in the orchestra pit, or an open step in the balcony and watch *The Fantasticks*. The little heart-rending show with its simple but ever-so-profound message talked to us every night.

Following the performance, we'd linger on the deck and watch the crowd walk to their cars. Many of us would stay until the taillights of the last customers' cars disappeared into the night. The air had turned chilly and seemed to make us all vulnerable. No one wanted to let go; we needed to hold on to this as if it was all a first love affair. So in pairs or en masse we all stayed up late and held our lovers close, or looked deep into the eyes, the hearts, and the souls of the friends we had made these past hundred days. Many nights we'd stay up until dawn and then walk to the beach to watch the sun come up, knowing it was one less day we had left in heaven.

One night, as Veronica and I watched the cars drive off into the night, we had our arms around one another and I felt I could stay in that place, in that moment, until the day I died.

"Sam, we've made it through the summer. I'm happy again and you made it happen."

"No, sweetheart, *we* made it happen. You are my go-to girl. Trust and courage and your sensational body all played a part in our lives here."

"You look rather fine naked as well."

"Who said you looked good naked? I was just pointing out that you have a rather alluring figure is all. Doesn't do a thing for me."

"Shut up, you big goof."

She said no more, but I could tell her brain was working overtime. And I knew there was something important on the way.

"There's only one part of the story that I still think you should know," she said. "But you never asked."

"Well, then I'm asking now."

"After I left Barrows's hotel, I couldn't go home. I checked into the Parker

House Hotel. After all, I was rich with his money. I stayed there for two days. I never left the room. I watched TV and ordered up. I drank too much. Then I called my brother Eddie and told him what had happened."

As she talked, Johnny Dawst and his family approached us. Johnny owned the local pizza place where we had often gone for late-night snacks. He asked me to sign his program and if he and the family could get a picture. I signed and then we posed. Veronica pressed the flash and I was part of the Dawst family forever.

Veronica jumped back in as they walked away. "I took the bus home. Then I went to meet Eddie at the Moondog. He was there with friends, all the faces I had grown up with, and he called me over to the bar. He hugged me and told me he was sorry, that he'd do something about it and that I wasn't alone."

Veronica walked over to the concession stand and brought back one of those airport bottles of brandy. Was it the story, or the lateness of the season and the hour that made it cold? The brandy helped.

Veronica continued. "I thought that was it. Eddie and I just stood there. We drank too much for sure, but we just stood there with Eddie hugging me for comfort. Then Lizzy came in. She was with a couple of girlfriends and she had been drinking. She saw us at the bar but didn't come over. Eddie called her, but she and her friends went to the other end of the bar. Eddie was upset, so he and I walked over to Lizzy. He asked her what was going on and she didn't even turn around. Then in an instant Eddie and I both saw what she was wearing on her hand. I was sick to my stomach. Eddie grabbed her and spun her around. 'Why are you wearing that ring?' he asked her. He was in her face and shouting. The Moondog got quiet and everyone in the place looked at Eddie."

ASK and Janet called from across the compound and said they were heading to the Full Sail—Doobie was buying—and we should meet them there. I shouted some incomprehensible acquiescence and waited for Veronica to continue. She untangled from me and leaned across the railing of the deck.

"Lizzy looked at him for a really long time and seemed to spit her answer in his face. 'I got married, because when your sister walked out on him, the old man called me to say the faucet was off. No more fancy lifestyle, just more endless, nowhere, blue-collar bullshit. But unlike Veronica the nun, *I took the deal*. I got married this morning to Anderson Barrows. I'm *rich* now and that's what I want. You can't give that to me, Eddie. You can't give that to me.'

"Then she turned her back to my brother. The whole bar was eyeing him. It was so sad. I grabbed Lizzy by the shoulder and made her look at me, asked her how she could do that to Eddie, how she could do that to herself. Lizzy glared at me and waved her wedding ring in my face. 'This is why,' she said. For a million reasons that will take my lifetime to list I slapped her, then grabbed her hair and pulled her to the ground."

Veronica was looking directly into the night. It had gotten late, and the compound was empty now. Her eyes welled with tears, but didn't roll down her face.

"Some stranger at the bar pulled me off of her and threw me away. Eddie hit the guy several times in the face and then smashed a bar stool against his head. He pulled Lizzy off the floor and slapped her so many times you couldn't count. He looked like he was going to hit her, but even in his rage Eddie couldn't do such a thing. He just began screaming at her. The guy he had hit was laid out on the floor and didn't move. The bartender, Joey, leapt across the counter and tackled Eddie, and some of the others held him down. Joey screamed at Lizzy to get out of the place. The craziness stopped, and Eddie started to cry. Forever . . . He cried forever.

"The police came and arrested my brother. Then the EMS arrived and took the guy to the hospital. He was okay, but bruised and had a concussion. He didn't even press charges, but the new Mrs. Barrows did, with lies about Eddie's intent and made-up allusions to his abusive past. She perjured herself in court, and Barrows pulled the puppet strings he had threatened when I left him alone in Boston. That's when Eddie went to jail."

She wiped the tears from her eyes and sighed. I took her hand in mine. "I love you, Veronica." She turned to me slowly, put her arms around me and rested her head on my chest. About a minute later she said, "I love you back."

97

Later that night, with dawn just around the bend, I threw on some shorts and a sweatshirt. I walked to the office, sat at my desk and turned on the small lamp. I noticed it was the only light on in the entire compound and it seemed to work a bit hard to light the room. I found some blank paper and wrote the following:

Dear Mrs. Barrows:

Until tonight, I thought I knew everything I needed to know. It is remarkable how wrong I was. Arrogance, I suppose. Not that I have any answers, no secrets or revelations from me. Yet I do believe that wounds run deep as rivers and that they don't heal without help, a salve of kindness.

So much sadness. So many lost years. And more on the way unless you take the first step. You must lead the way, leave selfish pride to wither and die, replace it with action and truth. Truth stands the test of time. Lies corrode the foundation that we all need to live a decent life. Honesty endures. Help everyone in this maelstrom of pettiness and sorrow find a way home. End this cycle of sadness.

Lizzy, recant. Pull some strings. Make your influence lead to second chances for us all. Think of Eddie. Do the right thing. It is the only part of us we are really able to control.

It would be a start. A beginning to a better life for you. Time is running out.

Sam

I put the letter in a PBT envelope and scribbled *Mrs. Barrows* across the front. Then I walked quietly to my car and drove slowly to the Barrows estate. After sliding the note under the front door I got back in the Mustang and drove home.

When I got back to my room, I slid under the covers with Veronica. I'm fairly sure she never even knew I'd been gone.

98

All endings are also new beginnings. It was suddenly closing night. The company seemed to pace through the day. Everyone anxious about the coming night yet eager for it to begin. The parking lot began to fill around 6 p.m. We greeted our patrons with gratitude and grace. All the faces and personas that had floated in and out this past summer were in attendance. It was not possible for everyone on the premises to find a seat inside, but many were content to stand out on the deck and simply listen to the last performance. Not a lot of words were spoken; feelings were expressed through a hug or a gestures or the gaze into someone's eye. Or, truth be told, the avoidance of eye contact that might lead to tears.

The curtain went up on time, and the small show played beautifully. The applause after each number lingered in the night; we hoped it might hang on a moment longer before it must turn into memory.

Zach sang the last lyric of the summer and the orchestra played the last simple note on harp and piano. The music stayed with us all, even past its time. We could still hear it in the old barn when in reality the wind had swept into the next day, the next summer, another lifetime.

The audience began to applaud, first for the small players in the show, then louder and longer for the principles, and then, as if possessed, they brought it up a notch so the orchestra could take their final bow. The applause turned into cheers and continued loud and long. After the bows had ended and the stage lights gone to black, still the applause continued, becoming rhythmic, as if an encore was needed. We had nothing left in our trunk of magic. Still the cheering would not stop.

The stage came up in a flash and the audience cheered as one, a voice so strong and clear it promised to wipe the slate clean of all the sins or slights or compromises that anyone, anywhere had ever authored. The cast walked to the front of the stage and applauded in return. They waved to the audience and threw kisses. The entire PBT company entered from the wings; even Ma, who had fed everyone all summer, walked on stage and found her light. Elliot had the orchestra play "All You Need Is Love" and everyone cried. They allowed the love in the room to envelop them so they could reach back and find the courage to take on all of life's challenges, all sorrow, and those moments where they would need to ask for forgiveness.

I stood in the back and watched it all. I had nothing left to offer, nothing more to bring to the party. I was happy beyond imagination. The summer flashed through my mind like a montage edited by a master, all of it overwhelming my senses and making me numb.

Then the applause turned to a quiet chant; it took me a long while to realize it was my name that filled the room. I stood still, embarrassed and not in any way knowing what to do. Secunda ran down the aisle, took my hand, and led me toward the stage and my company. I climbed the steps and found myself center. Secunda walked into the wings and returned with a hand mic.

He allowed the cheering to continue for a while, then shouted over the noise, "Sam August, ladies and gentlemen. Mr. PBT!" And then, although I would have thought it impossible, the decibel level rose yet again.

I looked into the faces of our audience. There were tears and crazy, manic, happy smiles. I stood there and said nothing. What could I possibly say?

Then Ronny Feston jumped off the stage and ran to greet a silver-haired man accompanied by a much younger, smartly dressed woman. He grabbed the man's elbow and the hand of the young woman and helped them climb onstage. It was Anderson Barrows and his wife. She stepped to the side and walked slowly into the wings. The doctor held his hands above his head and asked that the crowd quiet. After several minutes, the building stopped shaking—stopped soaring—yet no one resumed their seat. Barrows motioned for Secunda to give him the microphone.

"Ladies and gentlemen, I am Anderson Barrows. My family has owned this property for almost one hundred years." He motioned for me to move next to him as he continued to speak. "This young man came to see me in early May and asked me to trust him to restore its greatness. To wake up the ghosts that lived within these walls. And I did. At first with reticence, but quickly he won me over. Seeing his courage, his willingness to stare down fear, I was practically forced to embrace him in every way I was able."

I knew his truth and I would tell it, but not tonight. I decided that joy should win as summer ended. He paused for effect and to remove something from the pocket of his blue blazer. The audience remained standing. He opened a fragile, old, folded piece of paper.

"I have here, from my personal collection of the Barrows Museum of Plymouth a letter dated 1623. It was sent from London to Plymouth, and the recipient was John Brewster, the young son of the original settler William Brewster. Its author's name has faded, but the words and sentiment remain. It reads, 'Dearest John, may this letter find you well and safe in New Plymouth. May you find true happiness and freedom in your new home. Many years from now, hundreds of years from now, it is my sincerest wish that your vision have changed our world, and those who have traveled across the ocean with you.'"

There was a hush in the building. Anderson Barrows continued. "I give this priceless piece of American history to this remarkable young man. With you as my witness, it is a gift from us all. This letter speaks to him with the same resonance as when it was written over three hundred fifty years ago."

Anderson Barrows gave me the letter and offered a hug to go along with it. It was quiet for a long time. People were waiting for me to say something, but I had used up all my words. Elliot hit a downbeat, and the orchestra played "Try to Remember." They played slowly with grace and ease. The actors began to sing, and for the last time that season our theater was filled with music. Words were superfluous.

Then a final surprise came when Veronica walked up to me hand in hand with Lizzy Barrows. Both were wearing the widest grins possible without their faces breaking. Veronica took my hand and spoke to me with tears in her eyes. "Lizzy called me this morning and asked for grace. She said that all great journeys begin with a single step and asked me to join her at her side. She said I should do it because it was what you wanted. I asked no questions and said yes."

Tears were now running down her face and I saw that Lizzy was following suit.

Veronica walked a few steps off stage and returned with a young man who looked so much like her that it could have been her brother. It could have been her brother! I leapt into the air and quickly hugged Lizzy, whispering in her ear, "You did it! You found grace Lizzy, you found grace! There's hope for you and for us all. God bless you, Lizzy. Be happy."

Then I put my arms around my girlfriend and pressed against her with the entire power of my will, my soul, my being. She was crying and laughing, not knowing which to own; both were joyous and filled the small stage with another level of magic.

"This is my brother Eddie," she said. "Eddie, this is my boyfriend, Sam."

Eddie and I embraced and said at exactly at the same time, "I've heard a lot about you, man. It's good to finally meet you." For good measure I added, "Welcome home, Eddie. Everyone has missed you more than you'll ever know."

When we broke from the embrace, Eddie shook my hand and said, "I haven't seen a show in a long while. I was able to see the second half tonight and it was really something. But I have to ask you, does this happen every night?"

My girlfriend pushed her brother aside and kissed me and I kissed her back. We stayed that way until the din of glory had faded away and all was mercifully calm.

99

PBT was eerily quiet. I sat alone at the redwood table under the enormous maple that now sheltered me from a steady, warm, late-summer rain. I nursed a beer and waited for Veronica to arrive. We had promised one another to spend one night by ourselves now that everyone had left to follow their respective dreams. I welcomed some quiet time with her after the race the summer had been. I was going to shut the theater down, place a soft ghost light on the stage, and let the ghosts sleep until next year.

I wasn't coming back and Veronica was moving on—alone or together remained to be seen. Plymouth had nothing left for me except a lifetime of memories. I had little else to learn here. I had answered the bell a great many times over the past four months. I had shed the cloak of innocence and was the path of becoming a real man. It would happen soon, but not in America's hometown. I still needed some work to become someone I could be proud of, a person of substance, of courage and character. A man in full. I had set a good foundation and was confident in my ability to do better. Life is not a dress rehearsal.

I was struck by how quickly things change. A day earlier the place had been rocking, bursting with the electricity of promise and hope. Tonight it was the last dying ember of a conflagration before it burns to ash. Darkness had set in, when just days ago the light lingered at the end of each evening and night came on slowly. A summer of heat and light was all behind us now. The rain continued, seemingly unsure whether to drift off or regain its strength to wash away the echoes that danced in the sweetly pungent air.

Veronica pulled into the driveway. The rain had decided to stay, and I could see it clearly, fresh and clean in the headlights of her car. She opened the driver's door and led with her long, tan, and truly fabulous legs. Her hair hung easy to her shoulders. I noticed it was blonder than when we first met, lightened by days of summer sun. Her eyes were beacons of blue. She wore no makeup. Veronica was a true and natural beauty. I was lucky, or perhaps even wise, to realize she would remain lovely long after her youth had left, for Veronica was a woman whose soul led the way.

"Hey, big boy," she said with a wink in her tone. "Looking to get lucky?"

"With who?" I asked.

"Well, I have a bottle of wine and nothing to do till morning."

"So I guess you're my best chance."

"I would think so."

She walked over to me and took my hand in hers. "Take your time," she said. "Say goodbye. You've got to have endings before you have beginnings." Then she headed toward the house, swaying as she walked, her feet not seeming to touch the ground.

The rain continued, creating a sense of calm and serenity, of anticipation and palpable expectation. Not just for this night but for the road ahead.

"Don't go in just yet, honey." I said.

She stopped short of the front door and looked back at me. "It's raining pretty hard, you know. Important things happen in the rain. You taught me that."

Then she walked back toward me as the rain came down, soaking us both. Our clothes clung to our bodies like a second skin. She looked into my eyes and then gently wiped the water off my face while tracing my features as if to freeze them in memory for all time.

"This is important," I said. Then I kissed her, and all that I had lived and learned these past months infused that kiss. I was certain there would be more, but this one I would never forget.

I broke our embrace.

The summer was over. I would take with me the lessons learned, the myriad adventures I had encountered and remarkably survived. I had won this first round in the game of life. The rain came down and washed away a part of me I would never get to live again.

I am one lucky bastard, I thought, *and that was one hell of a first act.*